Blood and Sand

Also by Rosemary Sutcliff

LADY IN WAITING
RIDER OF THE WHITE HORSE
SWORD AT SUNSET
THE FLOWERS OF ADONIS

ROSEMARY SUTCLIFF

Blood and Sand

Hodder & Stoughton
LONDON SYDNEY AUCKLAND TORONTO

British Library Cataloguing in Publication Data
Sutcliff, Rosemary
  Blood and Sand.
  I. Title
  823'.914[F]   PR6037.U936

ISBN 0 340 41518 5

Hodder and Stoughton Editorial Office: 47 Bedford Square, London WC1B 3DP.

For Michael Starforth, who gave me the story of Thomas Keith in the first place and has been unstinting with his help and advice ever since.

My grateful thanks also to the friends and strangers to whom I have turned for help and who have responded with book-lists, instructions for mining a city wall, memories of their own days in the desert or with irregular troops on various frontiers. A special thank you to Rosemary Booth for the words of 'The Foster Brother'.

Author's Note

Almost all the characters in *Blood and Sand* are historical and almost everything that happens in the book actually happened, even to that most unlikely ten-against-one Errol Flynn style fight on the turnpike stair. For only one section of Thomas's life have I drawn entirely on my own imagination: the matter of his marriage. There is no record of his ever having had a wife, but then in the case of an orthodox Muslim marriage there most probably would be none. I felt that he deserved a happy marriage, no matter how brief, and so I gave him Anoud with my love.

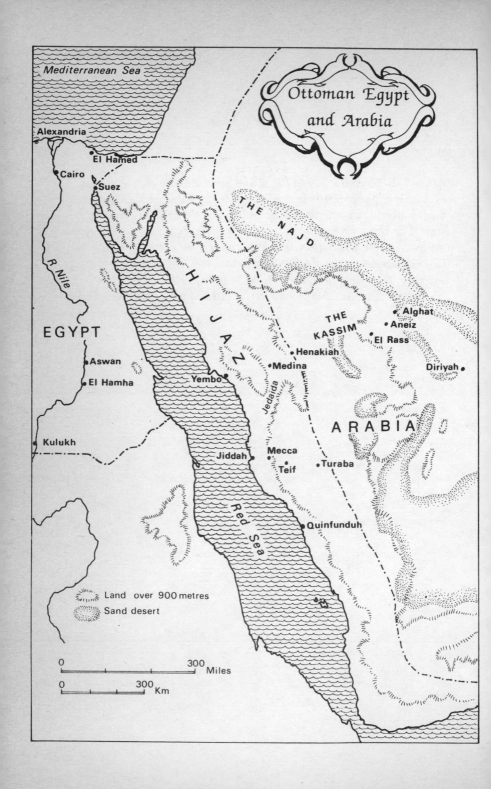

Ottoman Egypt and Arabia

Mediterranean Sea

Alexandria
El Hamed
Cairo
Suez

R. Nile

EGYPT

Aswan
El Hamha

Kulukh

THE NAJD

HIJAZ

THE KASSIM

Alghat
Aneiz
El Rass

Henakiah
Medina

Diriyah

Yembo

Jedaida

ARABIA

Jiddah
Mecca
Teif
Turaba

Quinfunduh

Red Sea

Land over 900 metres
Sand desert

0   300 Miles
0   300 Km

PART ONE

EGYPT

Chapter 1

In the swiftly gathering dusk, the limewashed walls of El Hamed glimmered palely under the fronded darkness of its date palms. From the doorway of the headman's house, now taken over by Colonel MacLeod as the headquarters of his motley command, light spilled out over the once jewel-bright Colours planted in their stands of lashed muskets before the threshold.

Between the low wall of the village and the nearest of the irrigation channels the lights of the camp fires were beginning to strengthen. Camp fires of the 78th Highlanders and beyond them the 35th Foot and De Rolle's Foot beyond again. The night of April 20th, 1807 and away southwards, masked by the tamarisk scrub and the slight lift in the land between, the Turkish forces gathered about their own camp fires, waited also for dawn and the fighting that dawn would bring.

Round one of the fires, just below the village gateway and scarcely clear of the turbaned gravestones of the village dead, the best part of the Highlanders' Grenadier company were gathered. They had eaten their evening meal and fallen to their own affairs and pastimes: here a little clump of heads bent together over a greasy pack of cards, there a man playing dice by himself, left hand against right; a man singing softly for his own ear and no one else's, his gaze on the fire and his hands linked around his updrawn knees, another doing his mending and yet another writing a letter with frowning concentration, leaning forward, the page tipped to catch the flame-light; one deep in conversation with a stray dog, the kind that always hung about an army camp; one who always suffered from religion on the eve of battle, reading his Bible. Most of the others silent or talking together idly as they readied their equipment for the morning. And among these, Donald MacLeod – no relation to his colonel – and Thomas Keith sat companionably together.

Donald, an extremely large fair young man from the island of Lewis who combined the position of company drummer with that of medical orderly in the usual way of such matters, had stripped down his drum and was now reassembling and making it ready for tomorrow's action.

Beside him Thomas Keith, almost as long-limbed but of a much slighter build, was as dark as the other was fair, with an almost Spanish darkness inherited from a Highland fore-mother, though he himself was from Edinburgh; a bony-faced young man with harsh angles at cheek and jaw, a wide mouth that was surprisingly mobile despite the unboyish straightness of the lips; light grey eyes, level-set, and black-fringed with lashes that would have been the envy of any girl.

Just now, with a face of absorbed tenderness, he was cleaning his rifle.

It was one of the new Baker rifles, a marksman's weapon, normally only issued to certain regiments of the Light Brigade, and his possession of it, in place of one of the heavy muskets still issued to the Grenadier companies, testified to his skill as a shot, a skill which he had acquired to some extent even before he had run away to join the army three years ago.

His hands busy with the rod and oily rag, his mind went back over those years to his seventeen-year-old self, to the scene in the parlour over his father's shop on the night that had begun it all. The night his father had told him that, with Grandfather not two months cold in his grave, he had sold Broomrigg.

Almost everything that he had and was, Thomas knew that he owed to his grandfather. Grandfather who at sixteen had been out with *his* father, following Prince Charles Edward Stuart, and had spent upwards of twenty exiled years in the French army, returning pardoned at last to marry the heiress of Broomrigg. Grandfather who out of the gathered skills of those exile years had taught him sword-play and the handling of firearms and better French than the visiting master at Leith Academy could do. Grandfather who had talked Father into apprenticing him to Mr Sempill, the gunsmith, instead of keeping him with his elder brother Jamie at the watchmaking. Grandfather who had taught him to ride on Flambeau.

But Flambeau had gone with the rest. He would never ride the big bay again, feeling the living power between his knees, the demand and response as though he and the horse were one; never feel the thrusting velvet muzzle in the hollow of his apple-bearing hand; never go back to Broomrigg, walking the six miles there and the six miles back on Sundays and holidays that had lit the rest of the week for him.

What had he thought would happen to Broomrigg after Grandfather went out of it to lie beside Grandmother and her kin under the kirkyard yews? He had never truly thought about it. The farm had always been there, the old pear tree by the gable end, the babble of lambs from the February fold. It had seemed that it always would be there, an integral part of life itself.

To his father, the sale had seemed quite a small thing; but to Thomas it had been the end of the world.

It had been in the small sleepless hours of the following night that he had known quite suddenly that he was going for a soldier.

There had been nothing to hold him back; neither his father nor Jamie would be much grieved by his going; there were a couple of schoolfriends he should be sorry not to see again, and Jenny Cochrane the apothecary's niece . . . nothing that would not mend soon enough.

It had been quite easy, for with Bonaparte's "Army of England" massed at Boulogne with their invasion barges ready and the new Alliance with Spain that was to gain him control of the Channel long enough to ship them over, the militia was being called out and new regiments formed the length and breadth of the kingdom, including a new battalion of the 78th Highlanders recruiting at Perth.

He had written two letters that night, one to his father conscientiously trying to explain the unexplainable, the other to Mr Sempill apologising for breaking his indentures, and left them lying where Leezy, the old servant, would find them in the morning. Then, with his scanty savings in his pocket, he had climbed out of the window and set out on the long walk to Perth in the chill summer rain.

He had done well in the 78th, his gunsmith's training standing him in good stead, so that he had gained the position of battalion armourer – not that there had been much competition – even before the regiment had been ordered overseas.

They had had their baptism of fire at Maida in Calabria, as part of a small force landed in southern Italy against French troops already there, the first time that Bonaparte's crack troops had been defeated by British infantry. Then had come Egypt.

Why the Egyptian expedition nobody had seemed very clear, certainly nobody in the rank and file of the 2nd Battalion 78th Highland Regiment, but seemingly it had something to do with the failure of some British bombardment of Constantinople on behalf of the Russians against whom the Turks had closed the Dardanelles. Something also to do with discouraging the French and Ottoman Empires from joining forces; though it seemed to Private Thomas Keith just as unclear why invading one of its territories and mopping up the Viceroy and his troops should discourage the Sultan and his Sublime Porte in Constantinople, in the very heart of that Empire, from joining forces with whoever they chose.

It was not much more than a month since the British had landed and taken Alexandria. Twice since then, the second time only a few days ago, they had tried to storm Rosetta, the gateway to the cornlands of the Delta. Twice they had been driven off with heavy losses by the Turkish and Albanian troops of the Viceroy's army. The second attempt Thomas knew about only by confused hearsay, for ten days ago three companies of the 2nd Battalion, together with five of De Rolle's and the 35th, all as usual under strength, had been detached and sent off four miles further east, with the task of holding the village of El Hamed and the two-mile stretch of reeds and tamarisk-scrub between the Nile and Lake Edko. Eight hundred of them against three times as many of the enemy. But, of course, there were the anti-Turkish Mamelukes camped further upriver; if you counted in their promised cavalry support, that would improve the odds quite a lot. It was a pity the Mamelukes had such a highly coloured reputation for faith-breaking . . .

Thomas returned to sudden awareness of the other men about the fire. Jock Patterson with the usual stray dog, Willie Moffat with the letter he always wrote to his wife and left behind with the baggage train, the fitful interweaving of sounds that made up the voice of the camp and out beyond, in the full darkness that had come down while he was not looking, the lost-soul crying of the jackals.

"Was it a good dream?" asked the soft Highland voice beside him. "I was thinking that if you are to polish that stock much more, the thing would be polished away entirely."

"Good in parts." Thomas grinned and laid aside his oily rag. "Do you mind the night before Maida?"

Donald had got his drum together again and his fingers did not check in their careful adjustment of the pigskin buffs that tightened and tuned the drumskin. "I mind the night before Maida well enough," he said, and then: "The odds were stacked against us that time, too."

The sun was just shaking clear of the shallow lift of land eastwards, and the irrigation ditches which veined the whole countryside were beginning to give back a shining pallor to the growing brightness of the sky; the scene had taken on edge and substance and the shadows of men and bushes lay long-fingered across the land as the British force advanced into action. And for Thomas at least, the queasy coldness in the belly that had been with him through the dark hours and turned the hard tack of the morning issue into sawdust in his mouth, had given way to an odd eager expectancy. He was aware of all things with an etched sharpness that was almost painful: the new light splintering on belt clasp and musket barrel, the heavy flick forward of his kilt against the back of his knees with every step, the company Colours away to his left upreared against the brightening sky above the roll and rattle of Donald's drum and the skirl of the pipes playing "Hielan' Laddie". High overhead the kites quartering the morning emptiness on tilted, motionless wings.

Most of all, from his position on the extreme right flank, the post of most danger and most honour, usually bestowed on the Grenadiers in any battle line, he was aware of empty ground away to the right, stretching towards Lake Edko where surely – surely to God! – the Mameluke cavalry should have come in to their support by now!

Somewhere beyond the low ridge ahead of them there leapt up suddenly the distant challenge of Turkish trumpets, and across the bush-grown crest their own scouts were falling back.

The British ranks were being extended as they advanced in an attempt to avoid being outflanked on that unprotected right, drawing out long and thin like a piece of fraying rope, even before the moment when they saw the lines of Turkish horsemen waiting for them and filling, it seemed, the whole low skyline from east to west. They advanced steadily, holding their fire in stubborn obedience to their orders, though they themselves were coming under fire now from the Albanian infantry.

15

Keep moving. Keep station—

The clarity of that earlier moment was gone, and Thomas's memory of the El Hamed action remained ever after extremely hazy. He had a confused impression of the two battle lines rolling together and the battle shout of the 78th – "Cuidich'n Righ! Cuidich'n Righ!" – and the high Turkish yell seeming to beat together in the swirling clouds of dust and powder-smoke around them; the rattle of their own unleashed musketry at last and the screams of stricken men and horses . . . and then the knowledge that they had ceased to advance, and were surging to and fro over the same ground in all the ugly chaos of close combat.

He never knew how long it lasted or quite how it came to an end, but a time came – it might have been a minute or many hours later – when the British had broken off and were in retreat.

Ever afterwards he was to remember as through that haze of dust and gunsmoke, the Grenadiers pulling back on that exposed right flank, unsupported when they should have been covered by the Mameluke cavalry, contriving somehow to maintain contact with the companies of the 35th on their left, keeping the mass of Turkish horsemen in check. The familiar wicked kick of the rifle against his shoulder. Load-aim-fire, load-aim-fire, load while retiring – kneel – aim – fire . . .

Out of the drifting dustcloud the Albanian infantry were swarming up from the cover of the irrigation dykes to their right and rear, while the jagged turmoil of a moving fight boiled up from their left. They were an island now, cut off and surrounded, men dropping every moment beneath the bitter hail of musket fire. They were making their last stand in the midst of scrubby harvest land and the reapers were closing in . . .

From the crest of an irrigation dyke which the tattered remnant of the Grenadiers had taken and were holding as though it were a fortress, Thomas, still firing steadily through the choking waves of smoke, glimpsed for a few moments the blurred figure of Colonel MacLeod sitting his horse on the crest of the ridge and looking about him as though taking stock of the situation, as though maybe even now looking for some belated sign of the promised Mameluke support. Then a fresh wave of Albanians surged into view and the solitary figure in their path went down.

After that there was only smoking chaos, the smell of blood and filth and burned powder; Willie Moffat falling beside him with half his head shot away, and somewhere in the midst of it all the scream of the pipes still playing "Hielan' Laddie".

And then something that was not so much pain as a sense of enormous shock as though he had been kicked just below the left hip by a mule. He was down on his face in the mess of Willie's blood and brains. He managed to struggle to his elbow and get in one more shot. But the time for shooting was over; his ears were full of the nearing hoof-drum of the Turkish cavalry and all around him men were fixing bayonets. The chaos began to swim and darken as the battle rolled over him.

Chapter 2

Thomas lay on his back on the old camel rug, his arms folded behind his head and stared up at the thatch above him, and considered the situation. He had had plenty of time to consider the situation during the couple of days since he had emerged from the scorching fog of fever resulting from his wound, and there was nothing else to do but watch the spread-fingered, swivel-eyed chameleon on the mud wall, set there to keep down the flies, and the light change from morning to evening, from dancing heat-haze of noon to blue velvet of night, beyond the doorway of the village headman's house, no longer British army headquarters, where he'd been brought when the fighting was over.

There were only eleven survivors of the Grenadier company. Of thirty-six officers and seven hundred and eighty men detached to El Hamed, not one had got away to rejoin the main body of the expeditionary force. He had those facts clear in his mind, having gathered them at one time or another from Donald MacLeod; Donald sullenly grieving for the loss of his drum, but mercifully restored to possession of a few tools of the surgeon's trade, who had got the musket ball out of his thigh and spent agonising hours probing for bone splinters and any threads from his kilt that might have been carried into the wound to infect it and cause gangrene. Donald MacLeod who had then nursed him like a lassie through the wound-fever that had almost inevitably followed.

What he was not clear about – what neither of them was clear about – was why they had been separated from the rest of their kind and left here in the headman's house in El Hamed while the rest were sent back to Cairo as prisoners of war. He knew only that it was by command of Ahmed Agha, the Turkish general in command of El Hamed. The man's face, fleshily handsome, the eyes in it dark and prominent like black grapes, had drifted in and out through the pain and fever-fog of the first days, looking down at him consideringly from under

18

the elaborate folds of gold-fringed turban, speaking to him in good French which he had done his best, gathering his confused and aching wits together, to answer in French as good, though he could not now remember a word of what they had said. The first time seemed to have been on the edge of a dyke with the ugly smells and sounds of a spent battlefield all about them, other times here in the headman's house. Several times, he had come, Donald said.

But why the special interest?

In the first days, he had been past caring; but now an interest in his future was beginning to wake in him, and he cared a good deal. If only the Albanian orderlies had more than three words of French, or he and Donald more than three words of Turkish, or a single word of Albanian, they might have found out.

A shape loomed into the doorway, for the moment blotting out the dazzle of evening light, as Donald ducked his tall head to enter, a smaller shadow at his heels. Donald had spent every moment of the past days that he could spare from Thomas himself, helping among the Albanian wounded in the village, who without him would have lacked all help save for the clumsy butchery of their own barber-surgeons. It was in the course of his work among them that he had picked up Medhet (that seemed to be his name) who had brought himself in with a sabre gash across his ribs, who seemed to be a self-appointed soldier rather than just a hanger-on with the Albanian force, and who could not be a day more than fourteen. Donald had dealt with the flesh wound, and Medhet had promptly shifted his allegiance and attached himself as friend, surgeon's mate and general dog's-body to the big Lewisman.

After helping him to dress Thomas's wound and sitting beside him on watch when the fever was at its height, he had divided his loyalties, or rather spread them wider to include both young men.

Now he set down the bowl of warm water and strips of linen that he had been carrying, and came – a cheerful-seeming callant with a wicked faun's face, naked save for the tattered remains of his kilt-like fustanella and a strip of bandage line across his chest – to squat beside Thomas and give whatever help was called for, including keeping off any flies that were beyond the chameleon's range.

Looking at them, the urchin and the big fair-haired young

man, Thomas realised with a sudden feeling of warmth that they were probably the only living friends he now possessed. Donald was folding back the bandage with intense concentration, easing it away from the wound where it still stuck. His hands were sure and delicate in their work; but his down-bent face looked weary almost past belief, and it was unlike him to have no word to spare while he worked.

"Could ye not have left it until ye came to sleep?" Thomas asked. Donald shared the room in the headman's house and it would at least have saved the special coming in and the going away again.

The big man shook his head. "I'm needing to see it in the daylight. Ye canna judge, by a palm-oil glim."

"It feels better," Thomas said hopefully, "no' so hot."

"It *is* better." Donald was bathing the wound, pressing gently, exploringly. Only a little pus came out now. He took up a small flask of arak from among the tools of his trade. He had always been a believer in the use of whisky to keep a wound clean from infection. And now with no whisky he had discovered the native palm spirit to be just as good, and fortunately the Albanian Muslims and the Egyptians of the Delta seemed not to consider it as alcohol, so it was easily come by. Now he poured a few drops into the wound.

Thomas drew his breath in with a hiss as the spirit bit on the still raw flesh. "Ach, damn you, Donald!"

Donald put the stopper back into the flask and reached for the bandage linen. "Be glad you can be feeling the good fire. I was none so sure at one time the wound was not going to mortify."

But his voice was as leaden as his weary face. Exhaustion, Thomas had seen in him before, this was something else. "What's amiss, then?"

Donald glanced up for a moment, without pause in his careful bandaging: "I lost a man but now – out from between my hands."

Thomas thought: 'A man of the enemy. One of the men that killed Willie Moffat and the rest.' But he did not speak the thought aloud. Maybe when you were striving to save living flesh and it went dead under your hands, it did not seem like that. "Ye'll have done the best that ye could for him," he said, aware that that was barren comfort, too.

"Aye," said Donald, "and until yestere'en I thought that maybe he'd a chance." He finished off the bandage. "He was a bonnie fighter; but now he's food for the jackals, and the heart is sore within me."

"I'm sorry." Thomas reached down to set his hand on the other's wrist as he tied the final knot.

"'Never get involved with your patients.' That's what our surgeon told me once. 'There's no sense in the both of ye bleeding.'"

"Maybe that – the getting involved wi' your patients – is what makes ye a good surgeon."

Donald shook his head. "It's not that, makes me a good surgeon."

"Something does. Something makes you an even better surgeon than you are a drummer, Donal' Finn."

"Aye." Donald agreed seriously, and for a moment they looked at each other, the rest unsaid between them. Then he gathered his gear and drew his legs under him to get up. "I'll be none so ill, if I get the chance." He got wearily to his feet. "Medhet is biding with you – he understands. He'll fetch you some soup by and by. Aye, and see that you sup it."

He turned and ducked out through the doorway; and the urchin, grinning from ear to ear, settled himself to keep the flies at bay with a swishing palm frond, his eyes fixed on Thomas's face like a hound pup, adoring and eager to please.

Almost at once voices sounded outside; the doorway darkened again, and Thomas brought his gaze down from the thatch as another tall figure came stooping in. For an instant he thought that Donald had come back for something, then saw that this was a much older man, darkly saturnine of face, and wearing a white abba loosely flung on over what looked like the uniform of a French army officer.

Thomas had heard of the French gunner colonel seconded to the Egyptian army to assist Muhammed Ali, the Ottoman Viceroy, in building up the new artillery arm of his forces, who had arrived at El Hamed last night to take possession of the three captured British field guns, and hazarded a guess as the man paused by the door.

"Colonel D'Esurier?" He managed a rather sketchy salute.

The Frenchman came forward. "And you I think, are Private Thomas Keith of the 2nd Battalion, 78th Highlanders? I had meant to come earlier but I have been fully occupied with this business of the field guns, and now it is later in the day than I had imagined. If your wound troubles you too greatly or you are too weary to receive visitors . . ."

Thomas was not used to being spoken to after this fashion by senior officers, but it seemed that he had passed beyond the boundaries of his own familiar world, and, therefore, as nothing was familiar nothing could be strange. In any case, here was his chance to find out things that he urgently needed to know. He got a firm hold on his thinking processes, which still seemed not completely under his own control. "Will you be seated; I apologise for the lack of anywhere but the floor."

Colonel D'Esurier folded up like a surprisingly elegant camel on to the mat beside him, Medhet giving back warily, the least possible amount. "I have not spent three years in Egypt, much of the time in the desert, without becoming well used to sitting on the floor."

Thomas waited until he was settled, and then asked him the most urgent of the questions, "Monsieur, what has happened to the rest of us – the prisoners, the wounded? Is all well with them? We heard that they – we – were safe under the protection of Ahmed Agha, but . . ."

"But you do not trust Ahmed Agha? Quite safe, and in Cairo long since." The Frenchman's face flickered into a faint sardonic smile. "You will have heard of British heads carried on Turkish lances, and set up over town gates? – a time-hallowed custom of the Ottoman empire. Let me assure you they were taken only from dead men. The prisoners and wounded are in no danger – save that which besets any wounded man until his wound is healed. Nevertheless, they are not so much safe by reason of the Agha's protection as because the Viceroy wishes to resume friendly relations with Britain as soon as may be, and has ordered all prisoners of war to be well treated, after being taken alive in the first place, and has reinforced the order by proclaiming a bounty of seven Maria Theresa dollars per living man – twenty in the case of officers. If there's one thing the Turks and Albanians understand, it's dollars."

Thomas nodded, his eyes fixed gravely on the other man's face, and asked his second question: "Monsieur, can you tell me why Donald MacLeod and I have been separated from the rest?"

22

"Donald MacLeod? – Ah, the young surgeon?"

Thomas saw no reason to explain that Donald was officially only a medical orderly. "Was that on the Agha's orders? We have been – anxious."

D'Esurier's lips twitched. "Assuredly you do not trust him, do you. You should be flattered; the Agha is hated by his men, he is cruel and greedy and his vices are in a class by themselves; also they call him Ahmed Bonaparte for the good opinion that he has of himself. But he is a superb cavalry general as brave as a lion – and a good judge of men."

"Maybe if I knew for what purpose . . ." began Thomas, his mouth uncomfortably dry.

The twitch at the corner of the Frenchman's mouth broadened into a smile. "I believe you may set your mind at rest on that point: you are both of you much too old for the Agha. No, like most Ottoman generals, Ahmed Agha has his own private guard, and he feels that he has found two worthy acquisitions to its ranks: a skilled surgeon and – if I may say so – an extremely personable young soldier who speaks French, knows how to bear pain like a gentleman, and is the best swordsman and shot in his regiment."

"Who told him that?" Thomas demanded, startled.

"Apparently you did, when he questioned you as to your skills more or less as your surgeon friend was engaged in removing the bullet."

"I must have been more far-gone than I knew."

The colonel looked at him with a seeing eye. Ahmed Agha was not alone in being a good judge of men. "But it is true, I think, yes?"

"Yes," Thomas said.

"So – it is very simple. He bought you both from your Albanian captors – paying an officer's bounty for each of you, and something over, beside."

Thomas struggled up on to his elbow, "But, Sir, he has not the right! We are both prisoners of war!"

"As to the right, Ahmed Bonaparte considers himself above such questions. But in this case I do not think that either of you will suffer by it." Colonel D'Esurier quietly changed the subject. "You speak excellent French, better than I had expected, though the Agha told me that it was as good as his."

Thomas heard the faint sheen of steel in the other's voice, and

23

knew that for the present, at all events, there would be small chance of changing the subject back again.

"My grandfather was out with Charles Edward. After, he was twenty years in exile and served them in the French army. When he came back, he married into a farm close by Edinburgh; and when I was born and old enough – my father was a master watchmaker and silversmith in the city – I used to go out to him at every possible moment. It was he that taught me the language."

"Ah, the Keiths seem to have the wild goose blood in their veins. Are you by any chance related to the famous brothers – the Earl Marshal and Field Marshal Keith who served under Frederick the Great?"

Thomas caught his breath in a crack of laughter. "Only in the sense that every member of a clan may claim kinship with every other. I am not a gentleman even if I can bear pain like one – though I think my grandfather would have claimed to be."

"Mine also." The colonel was amused and thoughtful. "I wonder if I can make the same claim. You have to remember that I joined the revolutionary army; I was a republican until three years ago, when we all became imperialist overnight."

They looked at each other a moment in silence. Then Thomas asked, "In the Imperial army is it the custom for colonels to coming visiting privates?"

"In other words, why have I come? Ahmed Agha felt that, as a student of men, I should perhaps be interested in his new – acquisitions. And your surgeon has no French and I, lamentably, little English. A pity."

The mention of Donald jerked Thomas back to an earlier part of the conversation, and gave him the strength to hold to it for his friend's sake that he had lacked in holding to it for his own. "Monsieur le Colonel, forgive me, because he has no French and therefore cannot ask it for himself, I must return to this matter of our position and ask for him as well as for myself. Since we are prisoners of war, what happens if, when the time comes for the rest of us to be repatriated, we wish to be repatriated also?"

The Frenchman hesitated an instant, then yielded. "I think that Ahmed Agha, if he still wishes to keep you – which is by no means certain, for he is a man who sometimes confuses will with whim – may well try bribery. I do not think that he will seek to

24

keep you by force. That is not altruism; he is no fool, and only a fool would keep a personal physician or an officer of his guard against their wills. It would be risky, do you not think?"

"So we would be free to go?"

"When the time comes, you may not find it easy; but free to go, if you persist, certainly. Meanwhile, my friend, I suggest that you accept the chance that the gods have sent you." He drew his long legs under him and got up, hitching at the loose shoulders of his abba. "I have stayed long enough, and you must rest. But I think that we shall meet again."

When he had gone, Thomas returned to staring up into the reed thatch overhead. "The chance that the gods have sent you . . ." What chance? A new strange life for which he would have to pay by deserting from the old one? Well, he would not have to make that choice yet, not for months, maybe a year; certainly not while he was spread all over this stinking bed. But ever since he had emerged from the fever he had had this sense of another door shutting behind him . . . He had never felt a strong bond with the regiment, though he had kept faith and given them the best that was in him in exchange for his pay. It was Willie Moffat and the rest that he had felt the bond with. Maybe that was how it was with mercenaries. Maybe that was how Grandfather had felt towards his French regiment . . . He was still too weak to think very clearly, and had used up most of what clear-thinking he had while Colonel D'Esurier was here. He was still prone to drift easily from waking into sleeping and back again, across a hazy borderline between the two . . . And Willie Moffat and the rest were dead; all but eleven of the Grenadier company. And it was as though their deaths had cut the bonds of custom and loyalty behind him . . . "The chance that the gods have sent you . . ."

The reed thatch overhead was becoming lost in shadows, and beyond the shadows? His mind had drifted back to the cracks in the ceiling plaster of the old house in Leith – cracks that had formed the map of a Far Country, mighty rivers, and mountain ranges that were damp stains in the daytime, forests where danger, striped and spotted and golden-eyed, stalked the shadows among the trees; and always something on beyond . . .

The light of a palm-oil lamp wheeled across the thatch, and he blinked back into the waking world to find Medhet kneeling beside him, a bowl that gave off a greasy-smelling steam in his hands.

"Effendi – Tho'mas Effendi – soup."

Donald would have taught him that.

Thomas heaved himself further up on the pile of folded rugs that served him for pillows, and took the bowl. It was broth of some kind, herb-smelling and with rice in it, and mercifully fewer gobbets of fat than usual. He gulped it down, scraping out the solids that remained in the bowl with his finger, for he was beginning to be hungry, while the boy sat and watched him worshipfully.

Thomas emptied the bowl and handed it back. Then on a sudden impulse – it was only later that he understood the idea behind it, that if he was going to live in this new world he should be able to communicate with it – he repeated "Soup". Then touched the boy's forehead with the tip of one forefinger saying, "Head".

By the end of that first lesson, he knew the Albanian words, and Medhet the English ones for Head, Heart, Soup and Sword (the last drawn with a finger in the dust beside him).

It was not perhaps a large vocabulary with which to enter a new world, but it was a start.

Chapter 3

A while after moonrise the felucca, the breeze spilled from her sails, poled in to the bank of the great river, into the velvet blackness under the date palms where a group of figures waited for it. The two young men standing on deck, silent among the hushed activity of the sailors, turned to look at each other, seeing only anonymous shapes in the Turkish robes given them in place of the uniform stripped from them as from all the prisoners and the dead after El Hamed. Seeing each other insubstantial in the wind-stirred palm shadows as though they themselves were of the dead.

Somehow they had not expected their parting time to come until they reached Cairo later that night; but presumably Ahmed Bonaparte, wishing to keep his new acquisitions quiet from the Viceroy for the present, had decided that Cairo might be too public. They had parted from Medhet several days ago, leaving him to rejoin his adopted regiment much against his will, since they could not bring him with them. In the month since Colonel D'Esurier's visit, they had learned, all three of them, to communicate reasonably well in a bastard mingling of Albanian, French and Scots-English, with a few words of Arabic thrown in, drawing closer together in the process, and at parting the boy had wept on both their necks, "You are my brothers – my heart will sicken without my brothers . . ."

"Do what you can for Medhet, if you get the chance," Thomas said. "You are more likely than I am to come at the ear of Ahmed Bonaparte, at least in the next few months."

"You know fine that anything I can be doing, that I will," said Donald.

From the shadows on the bank a voice spoke in stumbling French, "The hakim is to come now – by the general's orders."

"The hakim is coming," Thomas returned. He put his hand on the big Lewisman's shoulder, "I'm thinking I'd no' be here tonight if 'twasna for you, Donal'. I've my life to thank you for."

"Aye," Donald MacLeod agreed, with the regal courtesy of his race, "and it is glad I am that it should be so, for I had sooner it was I that saved it for you than another man."

"Effendi – come!" said the voice from the bank with increased urgency. "You must go."

"Aye. I am wishing that we might have followed the same road; but we shall meet again. Meanwhile – the sun and the moon on your path, Thomas Dhu."

"And on yours." Thomas returned the old Highland form of farewell, and wondered with sudden desolation how long it would be before he heard the tongue of his own kind again.

They clapped each other on the shoulder, and Donald MacLeod hitched up the unfamiliar folds of his abba, and setting one foot on the dipping gunwale, sprang ashore. Hands came down to aid him as he scrambled up the bank, and he was lost in the black velvet shadows.

The rais, the captain, gave a high sing-song order and the sailors bent to their poles and sent the felucca out into open water and the fierce white light of the moon.

Thomas spent the night on deck, partly for the sight of Cairo and the vast square-set peaks that he knew were the tombs of dead Pharaohs slipping by on the eastern shore, partly because it was better to be fallen over occasionally by the crew than to suffer the stifling heat and the bed-bugs below in the cabin.

Watching the city slip by in the dark, the glimmer of domes and minarets pale in the moonlight against the hills eastward, he wondered where his fellow prisoners were, if indeed they were still in the capital. Was it well with them? Would Donald have the chance to make any kind of contact with them?

For the while, he longed with a feeling akin to homesickness, to be with them, in whatever evil condition, to know the comfort of his own kind round him, instead of being out here on the breezy river with the white uncaring moon, alone, unless of course one counted the felucca's crew, and the two Albanian troopers who seemed to be his escort, now sleeping peacefully in the stern . . .

All next day they made steadily on upriver, the north wind filling the felucca's tapering sails that were like gulls' wings half-spread to take flight, and most of the crew, taking their ease while they could, lay half-asleep in the narrow shadow of

28

the gunwales, twitching like old dogs; and Thomas, for whom
all things about him were too new and strange for such daytime
sleep, squatted on the rais's own mat, lent him as a sign of
friendliness, on the deck which was also the roof of the cabin,
and watched the life of the great river go by. Filling his eyes and
mind full of the sights and sounds about him, helped to keep
him from thinking too much about sundry other matters. There
was plenty to watch: other traffic on the Nile, speeding upriver
before the light but steady north wind, or coming down again
with furled sails and crews straining at the oars, the slow
mournful rise and fall of their rowing chant coming across the
water. On either side the banks were high, bare and sandy,
waiting for the rising of the waters that would bring another
year of life, and which would start – if he had understood the
rais's explanation, mostly delivered in sign language – any time
now. And life moved along them like a painted frieze wound on
rollers, showing now a plantation of date palms, now the mud
huts of a village set on slightly rising ground to be clear of the
inundation, each with its dovecot and slender white minaret
from which at the time for prayer the muezzin's call would
come out to them across the water, and the crew would rouse
and turn themselves to Mecca and pray, then return to their
work or their sleep. Sometimes there would be a string of
camels, desert-coloured against the desert behind, and the
sound that came across the water would be the beat of their
bells. Sometimes the banks would sink and disappear in tall
wind-swayed reeds. Sometimes wild duck flew over, now and
again there was a crane wading stilt-legged in the shallows and
always, far beyond the east bank, marched the mountains,
blue-fissured in the morning, turning lion-tawny as the day
passed and the sun moved over. What lay beyond them,
Thomas wondered, beyond the long ranges that looked as
though they rimmed the edge of the world? To the west there
was nothing beyond the bank except the sky; he supposed there
was the desert, but out here on the water, so low down, you
could not see.

'If I lived long enough on this river,' he thought, 'I should
come to believe that the world was shaped like a sword-blade
instead of an orange, reaching only from those palm trees in the
west to those mountains in the east, but running on north and
south for ever.' And suddenly gave a little shiver as though

touched by a cat's-paw of breeze off the water, as it came to him that that might be exactly what he was going to do.

He shook his shoulders. 'Och awa'. Dinna' be such a fool, Tam Keith; when the peace is signed, ye've only to demand to go back wi' the other prisoners, and they'll have to let ye; Donal' too. Ye have Colonel D'Esurier's word for it . . . But if it's no' just as easy as that?' whispered a small chill voice at the back of his neck. 'Then – then I'll just have to break out eastward and see what's over those mountains . . .'

Late in the afternoon the felucca rounded a great slow bend in the river, and a short way ahead he saw yet another village; another huddle of mud huts among date palms, presided over by the twin heavenward-pointing fingers of minaret and tall slender dovecot, another irrigation wheel powered by another pair of plodding weary oxen. But on the bank above the landing place a little group of men appeared to be waiting for them, and even at that distance one seemed faintly familiar.

Shouts came across the water. The rais cupped his hands and shouted back. More shouts came from the bank, and at an order from the rais the steersman put over the steering oar and the felucca headed in for the landing place.

Close under the bank, the village was lost to sight. Only the creaking wheel bailing its never-ceasing arc of dripping pots to fling the Nile water into the irrigation channel, and the little group of men on the landing slope. The sailors shed the wind from the sails and, as the felucca settled lightly and with much shouting against the bank, the man who Thomas had been eagerly looking at came down the slope and stepped aboard.

Thomas got to his feet, and all the 78th Highlanders was in his salute. "Sir."

Colonel D'Esurier returned the salute casually. "Ah, at last! I was beginning to be afraid I might have missed you." He spoke to the rais, and the felucca was poled out from the bank. One of the crew brought another mat and cushions from the cabin.

"How does the leg?" he asked, as the two men settled down.

"Better by the day," Thomas told him, "though I am still as lame as a duck."

But he was not going to waste the heaven-sent appearance of the French colonel in general courtesies and polite enquiries as to his health; and plunged straight in with the question he most desperately needed answered: "Sir, what news of the rest of us?"

"The rest of you?"

"The prisoners."

"Still held in barracks in Cairo – around four hundred of them. There would have been rather more, but – the mortality rate among the wounded – the hot climate . . . You understand . . .?"

He spread his hands in a gesture of deprecation that had all France in it.

Thomas was looking at his own hands, hanging loose across his knees. "I understand," he said heavily.

"But I think there will be no more deaths now. Oh they had a bad time on arrival – paraded through the streets to the glory of His Excellency the Viceroy – if I do not tell you, others will – but His Excellency's order that no harm should come to them has been strictly obeyed. Negotiations are already under way with General Frazer for their repatriation when the British evacuate Alexandria. Meanwhile" – a tinge of amusement stole into the Frenchman's voice – "our consul in Cairo has made it his concern to see that they receive a sufficiency of fresh vegetables, to obviate the risk of scurvy."

Thomas missed the tinge of amusement. He had another anxiety more urgent to himself than the first. "Donald was taken ashore last night, somewhere below Cairo . . ."

"I know. It was partly to set your mind at rest on that score that I came – having given my word to Ahmed Agha that I will not speak of your existence or whereabouts to the Viceroy. Really the cloak-and-dagger aspect of this affair might become tedious if it were not also faintly amusing."

"Then you *can* set my mind at rest?" Thomas said bluntly. He did not find anything even remotely amusing in the situation.

"Ah yes, I think so. He is now in Ahmed's household, where for the present he will act as assistant to the general's private physician."

"He will hate that."

"I daresay. But it will be for only a short while. When a suitable time arrives he will enter the general hospital which was founded during the French expedition of nine years ago. A military hospital originally, though now open to all. I assure you he will not be tied full-time to the general's disordered bowels."

31

"Will he be able to make contact with the British wounded?"

"Alas! no. His existence is to be no more advertised than yours, until peace is restored between Egypt and Britain, when the general hopes to come to some – amicable arrangement with your government in the case of your friend and yourself. I told you something of that before; do you remember? Or were you still too dazed with the fever?"

"No, I remember. But I do not think you ever told me that we were to be split up, Donald remaining in Cairo while I was shipped off up the Nile."

"I was not conversant with the general's immediate plans for you myself at that time."

"And now you are? Would you mind passing them on to me; I do have a certain personal interest."

"You are to go up to Aswan to train with the Bedouin cavalry stationed there."

There was a small sharp silence between them, fringed and feathered round by the sounds of the felucca under sail, the pad of bare feet, the slap and whisper of water along her sides. Thomas was thinking hard in the stillness within himself. He had heard things, vaguely, during the past month as he picked up more of the tongue of his captors, of the crazy political and military situation in Egypt; of the constantly changing roles played by Turks and Albanians and Mamelukes – Mamelukes, men of that strange slave-born military breed that seemed to be beyond the understanding of other men, divided among themselves into pro-Turkish, pro-British (the force that had betrayed them at El Hamed had done so under that flag) and pro-Independence factions. He had heard still more vaguely of the newly formed and still forming Bedouin Irregular Cavalry. Something deep within him that had not stirred to the idea of a place in Ahmed Agha's personal bodyguard, nor of a golden bribe, stirred now and lifted to the thought of horses; the living power of Flambeau between his knees, the sense of completeness, the asking flowing down the reins and the response flowing back . . .

But that was not a thing to be spoken of to anyone else. "How far is Aswan?" he asked at last.

The other gave the merest trace of a shrug, "Something over a thousand kilometres."

"A thousand—" Thomas began, and checked. "Like this,

all the way?" he glanced up at the bird-wing sweep of the lateen sails against the depth of blue.

"Except when the wind fails or goes round to the south-west, and the crew has to furl sail and take to the oars," D'Esurier told him. "Then of course progress becomes even slower." He smiled, "It is possible, just, to survive the boredom. Myself, I have made the trip three times. Admittedly, I was able to go ashore, pot-hunting or to explore certain ruins which interested me. Whether you are allowed ashore or not will probably depend on the goodwill, or the carelessness, of your escort."

"And if I am not?"

"I can only suggest that you cultivate a lively interest in the life of the river-bank."

"Crocodiles?" said Thomas, without enthusiasm.

"Crocodiles, or hippo if you like, when you get far enough south. I was thinking rather of the birdlife. I have never known such richness of birdlife even on my own Charente Maritime. Wild geese, teal, snipe, kingfisher and hoopoe when you come in close. Look, even at this moment, the black and white bird over there at the edge of the reeds. That is an ibis – sacred to the ancient Egyptians—"

He felt quickly in the folds of his abba, and brought out a notebook and lead pencil, riffled through in search of a clean page, and began to draw, supporting the notebook on his knee.

Watching the sure quick movements of the pencil point, and the essence of the bird captured in a few deft lines on the paper, Thomas made the surprising discovery that the bitter-faced gunner colonel was a brilliant bird artist. "I wish I could do that," he said.

D'Esurier smiled at his tone, "Have you tried?"

"Yes, at home – around Edinburgh. I have not the gift. I can make and chase the design on the silver lock-plate of a pistol – strapwork and interlacing, even a formalised flower. I can't catch the likeness of something living."

"No?" The Frenchman put the finishing touch to a feathery reed tip, and flicked the page over. "The followers of Muhammed say that only Allah may do that . . . For myself, I find enough pleasure in the exercise of what skill I have to make it unlikely that I shall ever embrace the faith of Islam."

Thomas looked at him in surprise. He had heard, of course, stories of forced conversions of their Christian captives by

Barbary pirates and the like; but the idea that a Christian (were the French still Christians?), at any rate a Western man born and bred in a Christian country, should ever speak so of becoming or not becoming a Muslim was something completely new to him.

Colonel D'Esurier, in the act of putting away his notebook, looked up and caught the young Scot's startled gaze upon him, and quirked his eyebrow. "It happens, my friend, it happens. Have you never heard that Bonaparte himself has always had a great admiration for the Muslim faith – so much so that, realising it to be the only thing which holds Egypt together, during the 'Ninety-eight expedition he set on foot plans for a possible mass conversion of the French forces involved."

Thomas was silent a moment. "No," he said at last. "I hadn't heard that. What happened?"

D'Esurier's lip twisted in sardonic amusement. "The plan fell through. I believe a compromise might have been reached on circumcision, but not on the use of wine."

Thomas gave a crack of laughter, and then, in the light of his Presbyterian upbringing, was shocked at himself for having laughed. In the past few months his education had been progressing rather too fast for comfort.

Silence settled between them for a while, the Frenchman leaning back on his elbows, his narrowed gaze going up to rest lazily on the cross-line of the main spars; the Scot sitting forward with hands linked round updrawn knees, his gaze questing straight ahead, past the high curve of the prow. But when D'Esurier broke the silence, the subject of their talk had not changed. "I must go ashore at the next village. My horse will be waiting for me there. But before I do – " He rummaged under his abba again, and brought out, probably from the same place as his notebook, a thicker volume which glowed crimson and gold in the westering light.

"We had three Arabic-speaking scholars with us on that expedition," he said as if there had been no break in the conversation. "They were part of Bonaparte's private entourage – the general's menagerie, the more irreverent amongst us called it. He set them to making a new French translation of the Koran, of which this is a copy. It has lost something in the translating of course, but it has kept something too. Take it as a gift from a friend, which you may find useful."

34

He held the book out to Thomas, who took it carefully, handling it with a craftsman's respect for the work of another craftsman, but without opening it. "Thank you, Sir, I shall treasure it – a gift from a friend in a land where I am a stranger."

The words sounded stiff and over-formal in his own ears, but the gift had startled him afresh, and he felt awkward, and not quite sure how to handle the situation.

Colonel D'Esurier saw his uncertainty and added, "If you are to serve with and maybe eventually command Muslim troops, you should at least be familiar with the Koran."

Thomas said, "Yes, Sir, I do understand. The Koran is their Holy Book as the Bible is ours."

"And as the Torah is the Holy Book of the Jews and all three in many places identical. We are the People of the Book, we three." The Frenchman's cool measuring gaze met Thomas's. "I wonder, my friend, if you do understand. The Muslim's Faith, the Muslim's Book, affect their daily lives much more closely than Christianity and the Bible affect the life of the western European soldier." (Thomas's mind went back to the 78th Highlanders, and he could well believe it.) "The Spaniards are probably the nearest to Islam in terms of the all-pervasive impact that religion has on their lives – which could be because most of Spain spent a few hundred years in the hands of Muslim conquerors and had to be wrested back for Christianity by their forefathers."

He drew his legs under him and got up, and Thomas realised that, unnoticed while they talked, the felucca had been nearing the bank and now was running in towards the landing slip of the next village.

"Study it, during your trip upriver. God knows you'll have enough time – at least it may provide a change of occupation from studying the wild life of the Nile," the Frenchman said lightly, and turned towards the gunwale as the felucca bumped alongside.

Left to himself, Thomas settled down again, with Colonel D'Esurier's gift in his hands. The book was bound in soft crimson leather, gold-tooled with arabesques whose exquisite intricacy made him itch for an engraving tool, and the silver lock-plates of a pistol under his hand. This was the kind of artistry that he could handle, that he understood as though it were some secret that one was admitted to as to a brotherhood . . . He opened the book.

But the light was too far gone for reading. If he wanted to read he must go down to the bug-infested cabin and call for a lamp to be lit. Well, there was all tomorrow for reading, and the day after; and the week after that . . .

He sat on, the French translation of the Koran open on his knee, while the sky flamed to blazing crimson overhead traced with the long wavering skeins of wild duck flying over, and the river echoed back the colour like bright arterial blood flowing between banks that brimmed with indigo shadow.

From the next village, across the water, came the plaintive wild-bird wail of the muezzin, and the crew of the felucca, for the fifth time that day, betook themselves to prayer . . .

Chapter 4

Within its rough defences of mud-brick and camel-thorn, the fortified camp at the El Hamha oasis away beyond Aswan and the fourth cataract was more like an ordinary Bedouin encampment than any kind of army post. But there, with two squadrons of Arab irregular cavalry and an attached troop of Sudanese camel-men, Captain Zeid ibn Hussein was responsible for the so-called peace of almost a thousand square miles of desert west of the Nile and north of the ill-defined frontier, and for the safety of the caravans coming up from the south.

Into this remote and self-contained world Thomas came ashore from the felucca a month and more after passing through Cairo. He had read the Koran through twice and got a few suras of it that seemed to hold especial potency for him off by heart. He had broken up a fight between his two guards, and added considerably to his store of Albanian and Arabic phrases and his knowledge of the habits of river birds. But he was still a little unsure at times that the whole thing was not some kind of dream.

His position in his strange new world was an odd one. He was a trooper in a Bedouin cavalry regiment, his duties the same as those of any other trooper, but a trooper undergoing officer training and with certain privileges. Bulbul his beautiful chestnut mare was a personal loan from Ahmed Agha himself, and by the Agha's orders he was receiving an hour-long Arabic lesson every day. He shared Zeid's black goat's-hair tent as though he were a fellow officer, sleeping in the western bay, the third bay, beyond the servants' and cooking quarters, where in a household tent the women's quarters would have been.

The daily routine of the camp had opened to let him in, and closed over behind him. And in some ways it seemed to him that the transition was not much more than it would have been for any infantryman changing to any cavalry regiment, and he had been used to the ways of horses and horsemen since he was seven years old. In other ways it seemed strange almost past belief. It took him a while to learn to ride in the Arab manner, with no bit or snaffle, controlling Bulbul only by a rope from her braided woollen headstall in his left hand – all Arab horses carried their heads slightly to the left; and after his first lesson he understood why – beside the usual control of knees and voice and the sharp-cornered stirrups that could be used as spurs in time of need. But from the first lesson the mare herself was a joy to him; the power between his knees, the sense of one-ness, the willing response, all the joy of a woman, he thought; and did not even notice the fact that he was no longer shocked by the thought which would once have shocked him to the core. And once he had mastered, with her help, the art of riding her, the mounted sabre training of the long-shadowed mornings and evenings was a joy to him also.

There was musket practice, shooting at straw targets, the butt of the jezail scorching the cheek, eyes reddened with the dust that veiled the target; mounted musket practice too, chaotic and noisy with shouting and the drum of hooves beside the crack of the discharge, firing from hip or shoulder with no time for steady aim. Picket duty came soon, and then his first desert patrol; five days out, with the water rationed and commissariat consisting of unleavened bread and a handful of dates evening and morning; days when the khamsin blew and the sky was bruise-coloured and the whole world seemed to sweat. And back in camp the relief of shade-trees and water; and the Arabic lessons generally in the evening with Zeid ibn Hussein.

He was thankful that Bonaparte's expedition of nine years before had made Egypt, if not into a French-speaking country, at least into a country in which a fair proportion of people had a few words of French, and some, the young Bedouin captain included, spoke it fluently. At least that meant that there was one other person at El Hamha he could talk to – and a couple more among the troopers with whom he could exchange a few words before he had to fall back on his own floundering attempts at Arabic. Without them he would have been cut off indeed, surrounded by men whose jokes he could not share, whose long stories round the evening fire of dried camel dung he could not follow, whose dark gaze he could not read.

For that reason, for his own sake as well as out of gratitude to Zeid who, he realised, was having to take the hour of the daily lesson out of his own scant off-duty times, he set himself almost fiercely to the task of learning Arabic, forcing himself to talk to the other men and not fear to make a fool of himself. And indeed he made surprising progress.

"Show me your hand," Zeid said to him one evening, and when he held it out, set his own alongside it, the long dark Arab hand whose slender shape made the grip of most Arab swords too narrow for comfort to a Western swordsman.

"You see? We both have it, the long fourth finger."

And when Thomas looked up questioningly, "Do they not say among your people, that the man with a long fourth finger has the gift for other men's tongues?"

The evening meal was over, and the daily lesson, which generally took place over coffee in the captain's tent, was over also. But the long-drawn-out ritual of coffee-making and drinking was still going on. Across the shallow firepit with its low fire of brushwood and dried camel dung, with its array of four brass coffee pots, three hearth-blackened, one brightly polished, but all with their parts to play, the shallow bowl in which the beans had been roasted, the mortar in which they had been pounded and the bag of cardamom seeds, the two looked at each other, cool northern grey into eyes of dark warmth with the sun behind them. "For each tongue I have had – I have – a good teacher," Thomas said.

Zeid took up the coffee pot and leaned forward to pour, for the third time, about a mouthful of the strong black liquid into the small engraved brass cup which the young Scot held, as custom and good manners demanded, between the thumb and forefinger of his right hand. He had been learning other things than the Arabic tongue since coming to El Hamha. "May you have teachers as good when you come to learn Turkish in the service of Ahmed Bonaparte," said Zeid. He poured into his own cup and set the pot down. "It is a sad pity. You will be wasted among the general's pretty boys. Here with the Bedouin cavalry you would not be wasted, but among your own kind. You shoot like a Bedu, a short while longer and you will ride like one also. But I think that you will never have much skill in the intrigues and the jockeying for place and power that goes on in a great man's following."

Thomas thought again of Colonel D'Esurier's promise that Ahmed Agha might try bribery when the time came but would

not actually keep him against his will if he demanded repatriation with the rest of his kind. But he did not say anything, even
to the young Bedouin captain whom he was beginning to look
on as a friend. Maybe the less he said to anyone on the subject,
the better.

"That would mean a change of overlords," he said, partly to
steer the talk away from the danger point, partly out of genuine
interest. "What kind of man is he, the Viceroy?"

Zeid ibn Hussein laughed softly. "Muhammed Ali? How
should I know? I command two troops of his Bedouin Irregular
Horse, I do not walk in his private garden."

Thomas took a sip of the bitter black coffee – not even in the
parlour of an Edinburgh merchant's genteel lady, he had long
since discovered, was the ritual of good manners as complex
and unyielding as in the black tents of the Bedu – "No, but you
must have heard things, formed your own opinion. A good man
or a bad one? I have heard both."

"You are very young, my brother; give it a few more years,
and when you are my age you will have learned of the many
shades that lie between day and night. The Viceroy is of the day
and the night and the dusk-colour that comes between. He is
not of the common run. How else would an Albanian tobacco
merchant turned adventurer come to be Viceroy of Egypt? He
is strong – too strong for the liking of the Sultan and the
Sublime Porte at Istanbul, who, so I have heard it said, are
beginning to regret that ever they recognised him as Viceroy,
two years ago, fearing that he is too strong for them, backed as
he is by Albanian troops. Trouble may come of that one day . . .
It is said that they have tried to stop more Albanians coming in
to his following; but it is said also that His Excellency continues
to smuggle in another shipload every month or so."

His hand went to the coffee pot again, but Thomas gave his
cup the slight sideways shake which indicated that he had had
enough. "It is surprising that the Viceroy rests his strength so
completely on the Albanians. From the little of them that I saw
in the Delta, they seemed brave enough, but half-trained and
very ill disciplined."

"Well observed, O General," said Zeid, with a hint of silken
mockery. "But they are the only infantry in Egypt with any
discipline at all. The Turkish regiments are all cavalry; so are
the Mamelukes – magnificent light cavalry when they happen to

feel like fighting, useless when they do not. And the native farming folk, the fellahin, have been so long barred from carrying weapons by Mameluke tradition, that they have become meek and without mettle, nothing but tillers of the land and growers of pumpkins."

"Tell me about the Mamelukes," Thomas said. "Who are they? What are they? I have heard things here and there, but I do not understand."

"So, I will tell you of the Mamelukes, and you shall understand. Because the fellahin were not fighting men, even from before the rise of Islam, the caliphs of many hundred years ago must needs buy soldiers from other lands. There have always been merchants who handle the trade, buying twelve-year-old boys from the wild horse country away beyond the sea that I believe is called the Caspian. Girls too, at times, for wives and concubines, though the Mamelukes are not above carrying off girls from the Nile villages when the mood takes them. They come of a hardy people, perfect natural riders; and the Mameluke nobles who buy them train them in the use of sword and bow – firearms they consider beneath them – as though they were their own sons, and give them their freedom when they are of an age to bear arms."

"But if they have wives, do they not have sons of their own?"

"Yes, but only those brought in as slaves can rise to high rank among them."

Thomas began to doubt very much if Zeid's explanation was going to make him understand much better than he did before.

Zeid saw his bewilderment and smiled. "It is the custom," he said as though that explained all things. "But in our world a freed slave is still bound by unbreakable ties of loyalty to the man who brought him up. Him, he is prepared to die for, as he is for whoever he takes service with after his old master's death, but he owes no loyalty to the State or to the rest of the army. Only to his own leader. So – as it happens with warriors brought in to fight for a country that chooses not to fight for itself – they grew strong; too strong. Yet it is said – I do not know the truth of it – that in their day they were great princes in the land. I do know that five hundred of them were personal bodyguard to Saladin. Now, they are still strong, but they have taken to fighting one another and so fallen apart into three camps: those who count themselves as friends of the Turks, those who would

41

cast in their lot with the English, those who stand for an Egypt free of all outside rule save their own. If they could join spears they might be great again, instead of only dangerous; but they cannot, knowing one another for faithless dogs. Yet even so, before long I *think*, the Viceroy will send troops against them here in the south, and even over into the Sudan, for the longer they are left to swarm, the greater will the danger of them grow."

"That makes good hearing," Thomas said, looking into the low fire. "You do not need to tell me of their faithlessness. If they had kept faith with us at El Hamed most of my friends would not be still out here – what the kites and jackals have left of them."

"Nay, I had not forgotten." Zeid got up and slung on the heavy bandoleer, and reached down his jezail from where it hung on the nearest tent pole. In a short while he would be making his late rounds of the camp. "Before long, also, I think the Viceroy will seek to raise troops for a first time from among the fellahin; for the present all the native-bred troops that he can count on are our three regiments of Bedouin Irregular Cavalry." He hitched at his sword-belt. "We are raw with our newness, the birth-blood still on our faces. Not much better disciplined than the Albanians as yet, maybe; but unlike the fellahin, the peasants of the green Nile Valley, we of the desert have always been warriors. Now we learn to be soldiers, which is altogether a different and maybe a harder thing."

"The 78th was a new regiment three years ago – all our honours still to win," Thomas said bitterly, thinking of El Hamed.

Zeid sketched a half-mocking gesture of salute, "We be brothers, you and I." He crossed to the open side of the tent, and stood looking out. "It is too dark to see the difference between a white thread and a black," he said, quoting the Prophet's decree as to the proper time for the last prayer of the day; and a few moments later, as though in response to his words, the long-drawn wailing call to prayer reached them from El Hamha village, and he moved out into the darkness freckled with camp fires and shifting shadows. It was allowable to pray alone if need be, but better in company, and Captain Zeid ibn Hussein had gone to share the last prayer of the day with his men.

42

Thomas remained behind in the tent, looking into the sinking fire. He heard the rough-edged musical wailing that was the voice of the camp at prayer, and beyond it the jink of harness from the picket lines and the bubbling snarl of a disturbed camel, and somewhere far off the desolate hair-lifting cry of jackal in the outer night. He was used now to the feeling of being shut out, but familiarity did not seem to make it any easier; rather the other way in fact, as time passed and he drew closer in other ways to the men he lived among. He had thought at first that it was only because they did not speak each other's language; and that, the simple raw need of humankind to communicate with humankind, more than any long fourth finger, had made him quick to pick up the tongue of the men around him. But now that he could obey orders without a pause for frantic translation in his head, now that he could follow the gist of a long-winded campfire story and exchange insults with Ali Zim of the camel train, he still had the sense of being shut out; and had it most strongly when the call to prayer sounded across the camp.

Nobody made the slightest attempt to thrust Islam upon him. Zeid, who beside his language lessons, had taught him Arab table manners and patches of highly coloured Egyptian history, and would discuss with him all things under Heaven from the secrets of horse-breeding to the fancy rhythms of the pestle to be used in coffee grinding and the relative price of whores in Thebes and Aswan, maintained a courteous silence on all matters that had to do with religion, and drew a veil behind his eyes if ever the subject came up.

Yet the Bedouin troopers spoke and presumably thought of Allah and His Prophet constantly, and not in the casually blasphemous spirit of the 78th. They seemed to live in Islam far more consciously than most Scots or English lived in Christianity. He remembered Colonel D'Esurier likening the Muslims to Spanish Catholics. He was an Unbeliever, and that was the real strangeness, the real barrier between them. Not very much of a Believer, even in his own faith, he realised suddenly; maybe the gulf was not between two faiths so much as between the all-pervasiveness of one and the reservations of the other . . .

Long before he left his father's house on that long walk to Perth to enlist, he had known that his God was not his father's God, not the stern Presbyterian God, for ever accusing, for ever having to be begged for forgiveness of Sin, the crushing sin of being mortal man. He did not know who or what his God was; maybe that was something he was going to find out in this strange new life.

Yet what faith he officially had, was the faith of his own people, and to abandon it would be disloyalty. He shifted abruptly, slamming an open palm on his knee. Who was asking him to abandon it?

But he envied the men out there, gathered with their faces towards Mecca through the darkness that was too thick to tell a black thread from a white. He envied them sore.

A few mornings later, Thomas woke with the first green light of dawn glimmering beyond the looped-back tent curtains, to distant shouting and a scattering of shots from the western edge of the camp. Still only half awake, he plunged up from his mattress, and not waiting to pull on his abba over the thobe and loose ankle-clipping drawers in which he had lain down to sleep, caught up the combined bandoleer and sword-belt lying ready to his hand, and flung it on over his shoulder. As he did so, Zeid appeared an instant in the tent opening. "Get some clothes on, and your headcloth, the sun will soon be up. Then down to the horse-lines." And he was gone.

"What's happening?" Thomas called, but got no answer. He reached for his pistol, checked that it was loaded, and thrust it into his waist-shawl, felt frenziedly for his headcloth and camel-cord headband, and dashed out, completing his ready-making as he went. By the time he reached the horse-lines he was wearing headcloth and camel-cords somewhat over one eye, and retying his waist-shawl as he ran, to make his pistol more secure.

Shadows were making for the horse-lines from all quarters. His Sudanese askari, half-naked, was there before him and had finished saddling up. The captain's groom was cutting the grey horse free as Zeid vaulted into the saddle. Thomas set his hands on Bulbul's withers, and next instant was in the saddle also, and feeling for the stirrups and headcord as his man cut the tether. He urged the mare round beside the captain's grey. "What's happening?" he demanded again.

"Raiders driving off most of the Second Squadron's horses. The guards must have been asleep!"

44

Man after man was swinging into the saddle, voices all round them calling down curses on the raiders' heads. Thomas held his mare close to the shadow-paleness of Sara's flank as the captain heeled her into a gallop and headed along the northern perimeter of the camp. It was not the first time that he had seen action since he joined the Bedouin cavalry, for the long patrols had not been uneventful; there had been that brush with tribesmen for possession of a water-hole; there had been the day when they came on a band of Mamelukes raiding one of the frontier villages . . . But it was the first time that he had ridden out beside ibn Hussein in pursuit of raiders; and a sweet fierce joy was on him not quite like any that he had known before.

The drum of horses' hooves was swelling behind them as they swept the plundered lines of the Second Squadron; and men on foot came running, shouting agonised curses and excuses, to point out the distant dust-cloud faintly visible in the first light of dawn and the last light of the sinking moon. A few knelt, jezail at shoulder, still firing at the dust-cloud now far out of range. Abu Salan, the leader of the Second Squadron, came crashing up with a handful of his men mounted on their few remaining horses. The captain cried to him. "We cannot both be out of camp at the same time, that thou knowest, bide in command here till I return." And as the man flung up his hand in acceptance of the order and reined back with a blind and stricken face, headed on at full gallop out into the desert, Thomas half a length behind.

Not much over a mile and the sun-baked dusty plain gave them over to the sand of the desert proper, slowing alike their own speed and the speed of the reivers far ahead. The light was growing, the sky brimming with it like a cup, and the broad track of the raiding party became as clear to follow as a paved road, until at last, cresting a great curved dune, they caught sight through their speeding sandstorms of the quarry they hunted. The blurred torrent of stolen horses flowing up the slope of the next dune far ahead, the mounted raiders, at least twenty of them, in the rear and on the flanks. Distant shouting and shots to urge on the hindmost horses came back to them. There were probably more reivers further forward at the horns of the drive which were already over the skyline.

Following the captain just ahead, Thomas pulled his head-cloth across his face until only his narrowed eyes were left unguarded to the sand, and settled down to ride as he had never ridden before.

The sun was up and beginning to cast their shadows out before them like rippling banners along the slopes of the great dunes. They were gaining on the raiders; there could not be more than four hundred yards between them. The sound of shouting came back to them more strongly on the wind, together with a ragged scatter of shots. But snatching a glance over his shoulder, Thomas realised that, mounted as they were on the two best horses in the squadron, they had far outdistanced the foremost of the troopers following behind. Zeid had done the thing forbidden in all the drill manuals: in a charge never get more than half a length ahead of your men. Well, so far as he, Thomas, knew, the drill manuals did not cover the pursuit of horse-raiders. He laughed and set to work to narrow the gap between himself and Zeid, that the captain should not come up with the enemy without at least one trooper at his shoulder.

Bulbul was the swiftest and most sure-footed mount he had ever ridden; he leaned forward along her neck, sang and shouted to her words of endearment and encouragement in French and Arabic and the broadest of Lowland Scots. "On wi' ye, ma bonnie burd!" And she laid back her ears to catch the love-tones, and leapt forward in response. Inch by inch they were overhauling the grey mare until the bay's head was level with Zeid's knee, and once again Thomas was riding half a length behind.

Suddenly four of the rearguard, who had been riding the last slope with their chins on their shoulders, checked, and wrenched their horses round to charge the leaders of the pursuit before the main body of troopers could come up. Zeid turned in the saddle to see how far his men were behind him, and at last Thomas drew level.

"You take the two on your side, I'll handle the others," Zeid shouted.

"Aywa, Sidi!"

Thomas urged his mare forward again, taking hurried stock of his opponents as they closed at a gallop, the lefthand rider swinging his jezail from his back as he rode. Thomas waited to the last instant, then as the long muzzle came up, dropped him with a pistol shot, seeing with a kind of detached interest,

46

something like a small red flower appear between the man's eyes as he flung up his arms in an odd disjointed way and pitched from the saddle.

He thrust the pistol back into his waist-shawl, and drew his sabre.

With the raider's wild-eyed horse plunging on past him, he wheeled Bulbul in a tight lefthand half-circle across the path of the second man now thundering towards him, then at the last moment swung her back to drive in his attack from the unexpected side. The raider, taken by surprise, his blade already started on the blow that should have taken Thomas's head from his shoulders, had to change direction when it was already too late, and his stroke, with little power or control behind it, flew wide.

Thomas, with a yell as savage as any war-shout of the tribes, delivered a crashing backhand cut as he passed. He felt the jar of it all up his own arm as the blow landed true between the man's neck and shoulder, hurling him from the saddle.

Thomas checked the mare and turned her back on her tracks. After the wind of their going, the heat seemed to settle round him like a swarm of flies. The second rider lay where he had fallen, face down, his blood fountaining crimson into the sand that supped it up.

It was the first time that he had ever killed with a sword; rifle, jezail and pistol were different, there was no actual contact in the killing. With the blade it was as though he had felt the life go out, shared a little in the dying. For that instant they had been linked together, he and the horse thief, in a one-ness, a consummation as potent as that of love-making, before they went their separate ways. And in Thomas's belly there was a strange mingling of sensations; awe and exultation and a kind of angry desolation, above all a strong desire to go away some-where and be sick.

He stooped from the saddle to clean his sword by stabbing it again and again into the sand.

A short way off, Zeid was cleaning his own sword in the same way. Four bodies lay in the sand, and the foremost troopers were coming up in a dun-coloured cloud of their own making.

Thomas rode across to the captain and saluted before sheathing his blade.

Zeid's face lit into his slow silken smile. He leaned across from the saddle and flung his arm round Thomas's shoulders. "Four clean kills," he said. "Now for the rest of the hunting."

The shadows were long again and the western sky kindling with the fires of sunset, when they rode into camp. They had had their hunting. They carried captured weapons, and drove more than forty horses won back from the raiders. They had killed a dozen more men. Only a handful of well-mounted tribesmen each leading a stolen trooper-horse had got clear. A mood of triumph was upon them. And for Thomas there was something else; for no very good reason, a sense of comradeship with the men he rode among, that he had not known before.

"It was a good hunting," Zeid said as they rode in past the quarter-guard. "Of such things are the Brotherhood made. Of such things and others beside."

Before the commander's tent, when, having left their mounts at the horse-lines, they came up through the camp together, they were greeted by the sight of two pairs of horses, certainly not cavalry mounts, tethered there and before each a kind of trophy of swords and daggers, a couple of battered jezails and, in the case of the right-hand pile, a slender bamboo lance tasselled with black ostrich feathers. Evidently the two men whom Zeid had bidden to take the captured horses back to camp from the scene of that first skirmish had brought with them the rest of the spoils of war, and they had been meticulously divided to await the return of their rightful owners.

Thomas's Sudanese orderly stood by the nearest pile, grinning, "Thine, Effendi."

Thomas grinned back. "As thou sayest." He touched each of the mares on the forehead in token of acceptance and ownership, then took up the sword of his second opponent and stood looking at it. It was no Arab weapon, but straight-bladed with a cross hilt; the sword, unless he was very much mistaken, of a European knight. Memory flicked back to the working drawings and illustrated histories of such things which he had pored over in the armourer's shop in Edinburgh, and told him that the quillons suggested French workmanship – thirteenth century. He had heard of Crusader swords lovingly cared for in Arab families, handed on from warrior father to warrior son, but had not thought ever to hold one in his own hands.

48

"So; that is a prize worth the having," said Zeid's voice in his ear.

"Aye," Thomas said softly, almost worshipfully, his gaze not lifting from the great sword in his hands. And then, "Is it permitted that I make a gift of it to Colonel D'Esurier? He would value it as greatly as I." It was good to have something to give, good to be able to express gratitude in tangible form, after having owned nothing but his own soul, and not too sure about that.

"Assuredly it is permitted," Zeid said, "and it would be permitted also, if it seems to you good, that you should make a gift of the other sword to Ahmed Agha."

Thomas looked up in surprise, "The general must have many swords, all of them richer than this one."

"Of a certainty. But nevertheless, as an expression of gratitude, I think it might well have its uses . . ."

"This is all a new world to me," Thomas said after a moment.

"Therefore I offer guidance."

"And I accept it." After all, Thomas supposed, he did owe thanks to the Turkish general, especially in the matter of Bulbul, though he had a feeling that in Zeid's mind the expression of gratitude was very much a means to an end. "As to the horses – " he began, and checked. He had been going to say, "Abu Salan will have more need of them than I, since his squadron is still short of mounts." But he realised suddenly that while his whole attention had been taken up with the Crusader blade, the leader of the Second Squadron had joined them. He caught the look that passed between the two men, and knew that presently there would be a calling to account between them; but not here, in the view and hearing of other men; and sympathy for Abu Salan twinged within him.

"I have no need of them," he said, "and no cavalry camp can have too many remounts."

He saw his askari's disappointed face, and laughed. "Nay, Juba, do I not ride the best horse save one in all the squadron? What should I be wanting with more?" He took up the jezail and tossed it to him; it was better, he knew, than the man's own. "Here, take this to console thee." And he saw the grin split Juba's dark face as he caught it.

"The giving of gifts is a fine Bedouin custom," said Abu Salan unexpectedly, "but you should keep something yourself, for a battle trophy."

Thomas heard the difficult generosity in the other's tone, and responded as best he could with a rueful grin as he stooped and picked up the last weapon in the pile, a long Sudanese knife. "I keep this. A good dirk always comes in useful, and I lost mine along with all else, at El Hamed."

Later, in the commander's tent, the unpleasant things which had to be said between Zeid ibn Hussein and the leader of his Second Squadron safely said and done with in decent privacy, Thomas came in from his duties and found Zeid squatting beside the hearth and the place full of the scents of coffee and cardamom seeds. "Coffee, but I think we will forgo the lesson for tonight, I doubt if the wits are very clear in your head or mine. And other lessons you have studied today in any case."

Thomas sat down, stretching himself wearily. "The importance of giving gifts to the right people?"

"Is that never done among your own folk? One sword was given from the heart, let that content you . . . I was thinking, also, that you have begun to make a friend of Abu Salan, whose friendship is well worth the having, when you might very easily have made an enemy." Zeid tipped coffee from one to another of the waiting pots, and checked, looking up in the act of setting out the two little brass cups, as though coming to a sudden decision.

"Did you hear what they were saying down at the horse-lines?"

"I heard something, but I am not sure that I understand," Thomas said guardedly.

"They were saying that you were of the stuff of the Warriors of the Prophet, and a sad thing it was that you should be an Unbeliever and therefore damned."

Chapter 5

"No one will seek to persuade you," Zeid had said over the coffee pot a few evenings later. "In certain parts of Arabia, it would be another matter. Here in Egypt, no. Yet we should be glad, all of us who wish you well, if you should feel the call to embrace Islam."

The wall of silence which had existed between them on that one subject until the day of the raid, seemed since then to have dissolved away.

"Also there is this," he had added, playing with the ears of the brindled saluki bitch who was seldom far from his heels. "You were marked on your forehead at birth to be a soldier and I think to lead other soldiers. Allah gave you the gift, and no man should deny the gift that Allah has bestowed upon him. If you were a Muslim there would be no rank in the Egyptian army closed to you by reason of your foreign birth. As a Christian, you may rise to command two squadrons of irregular horse and a desert outpost; no further."

"That might be far enough," Thomas had said, and left the matter lying there.

It was after that that he took to the desert, walking and riding by himself in his off-duty times, thinking long thoughts, and for the first time in his life, looking into his own soul. He wished that Zeid had not said that about his army prospects. It confused everything, because to change one's faith for the ambitions of this life would surely be as bad as to change it from fear of death.

The thought went round and round in his head as though the choice was one that he was actually going to have to make – which was daft, because of course it could not be more than a few months before the British prisoners were repatriated and his time with the Egyptian army came to an end, and he would be away back to his own ('And how far will you rise, what glory are you like to win with the 2nd Battalion, 78th Highlanders?' said a small ugly voice within him.)

On an evening that seemed no different from any other, he had begged off from the customary Arabic lesson, and Zeid, taking one look at his face, had let him go. He was just back from a three-day patrol, and weary to his bones also. Thomas had gone off on foot – the men who saw him go glancing at one another with a light touch to the forehead, for to men born and bred to the great emptiness of the desert, this passion for solitary exercise was beyond comprehension – without any clear idea of where he was heading; but his feet took him as though of their own accord to a place to which they had taken him many times before, and which was the right and seemingly appointed place for that particular evening.

A great sand bowl, where the shifting of a crescent-shaped dune had laid bare a gigantic sandstone hand, its forefinger longer than the height of a man. Just the hand and its own shadow in the emptiness, and nothing more.

Egypt was so full of vast ruins, broken statues ten times the size of a man, half lost, half found in the drifting sands, that there was nothing strange about it, though it had given Thomas a shock of awe the first time he came upon it. It had grown familiar since then, and he sat down as one might sit down beside a friend; aware as he always was in that place, of contact with other times, other men, other faiths. A good place to think.

He settled his back against the huge kind hand, his own hands round his updrawn knees.

With the fort and the oasis village out of sight beyond the dunes, he might have been alone in the world, companioned only by that potent shape of worked stone. A hawk must have used it as a perch since last he was there, and slashed its signature of black and white mutes across the gigantic tawny forefinger, but now nothing moved save a winged speck circling high overhead. The emptiness of the place poured into him like water into the body of a man parched with thirst.

Was there really so much difference between his own faith and that of Zeid? So much of the religion he saw practised about him seemed familiar to his Presbyterian upbringing: the simplicity and lack of ceremonial, the exclusion of graven images, the concept that no priesthood should come between a man and his God. Any Muslim of good character, he had learned, could lead the prayers in the Mosque, though in practice it was generally a teacher, a man who had taken it up for his life's work.

Again, as many times before, Thomas took out and looked at the samenesses. Again his mind went back to the Koran, lying in his quarters back at the camp, to the 18th Sura describing the coming to Miriam of the Angel Gabriel:

"I am the messenger of your Lord, and have come to give you a holy sign."

"How shall I bear a child? I who am a virgin untouched by any man?"

"Such is the will of your Lord," he replied. "That is no difficult thing for Him. He shall be a sign to Mankind saith the Lord, and a blessing from Oneself. This our decree."

But before that came the 5th Sura: "Then Allah shall say, 'Jesus, son of Miriam, did ever you say to Mankind "Worship me and my Mother and Gods beside Allah?"'

'Glory be to you,' he will answer. 'How could I say that to which I have no right?'"

Had Jesus ever actually said that he was the Son of God? Thomas was not sure, despite those Sunday afternoons in the back bedroom of the house in White Lion Wynd. He knew that Jesus had said he was the son of Man . . .

Yet it was the differences rather than the samenesses, after all, that had been calling to him and more strongly during these days with Zeid ibn Hussein among the men of the Bedouin cavalry, calling him away from Christianity with its doctrine of sin and redemption through sorrow; its concept of being doomed to play everlastingly the part of the accused, with God for one's judge, angry or gentle, but still one's judge, through all eternity, burdened for ever with guilt in a sin-blasted world, for ever having to protest not innocence but repentance, with salvation or damnation hanging in the balance. In Islam, it seemed, a man could look forward in trust, if he had lived his earthly life worthily, to starting again in a new life somewhat like it, but immeasurably better. "Savouring the beauty of his days", the days given to him by Allah the All Merciful, in whose hand he could rest without having to endlessly justify himself.

And yet not a soft faith, a faith edged and tempered as a sword blade, giving a certain pride, demanding a certain purity.

Again he was reined back to old ties, old loyalties. Again he wished Zeid had not pointed out the advantages of conversion

53

to a career soldier. He might have known that far from encouraging him to change his faith, it would make it harder. He checked between one breath and the next. But of course Zeid had known perfectly well, and what had ease of choice to do with changing one's faith? He had touched on a far worse temptation on the evening of the raid: ". . . of such things are the Brotherhood made. Of such things and others beside . . ."

Thomas looked at his own hand spread-fingered on the sun-purged stone of the great hand beside him, and cursed himself for a fool. 'What am I tearing myself to pieces for? Over and over again, and all without need. When I am repatriated it will be over and done with, and presently I shall look back and all this will be like a dream.'

All this?

The joy of Bulbul that was sharper and sweeter even than the joy of Flambeau had been; mounted sabre practice in the cool of the morning; the scent of the desert after a heavy dew. Dark mobile faces around the evening fires, and voices telling stories of which as yet he could understand one word in three. Arabic lessons with Zeid over the endless cups of coffee. The comradeship, hamstrung still by the lack of a fully shared tongue, but which was not quite like any comradeship that ever he would know again. The voice of the muezzin five times a day, calling to prayer . . .

And permeating it all, lacing it into one, the desert itself. He had learned long ago, during boyhood talks with the seamen down at Leith docks, something of the hold the sea had over the men who lived by it, no easy affection, a personal and demanding relationship entering heart and mind and soul. You could love the sea or hate it, often both at the same time; but once it had laid hold of you, you were seldom free of it again. Something in that great emptiness, the power beyond the power of man, the aloneness that was perhaps an aloneness with God, was in the desert too. Was that what bound him to the men of the Bedouin Horse, as seamen are bound together?

He lifted his gaze from his own hand on the sun-baked stone, and looked about him, suddenly more acutely aware of his surroundings then ever he had been before. It was drawing on to sunset, the sky that had been deeply and fiercely blue, heavy with its weight of colour, when he sat down, fading to harebell in the east, beginning to glow with the reflection of far-off fires beyond the march of the great dunes westward. A little wind was rising as it often did towards sunset, raising a faint veil of blown sand along the surface of the ground, raising too from the blown particles the sound, only just within the compass of human hearing, that was the song of the dunes. The sun clung for a last moment to the wave-lift western skyline, and the shadows, dark bloomed as grapes, spilled over and came flowing down the slopes, though in the east the mountains still caught the light and stood up gold and tawny against that dim harebell sky. High overhead the hawk hung bivvering, his wing-tips touched with fire. And for one moment that seemed to be held in the heart of time, while not in itself having anything to do with time at all, Thomas felt the one-ness of the sunset and the singing dunes, the hawk and himself and the great quiet hand that cupped all things in the circle of its own quietude.

In that moment the ceaseless painful attempt to get things straight in his heart and head fell away. And in the sudden stillness within himself, not into his mind but into some more inward part of himself came a sense of enlightenment.

He had been trying and trying, bruising himself with the effort to think rationally about changing Gods, but there was only one God, his own and Zeid's and the God behind the beast-headed gods of the men who had carved the great calm hand against which he rested. "Ours is the one true God," men said and they were right. All men were right. Only one God, though men gave Him different names and attributes and prayed to him in different words with different forms of worship. But always the same God, and the names and the prayers and the forms of worship were man-made.

For a while, he never knew afterwards whether it was three heartbeats or an hour, for it was still outside normal time, the sense of one-ness, the certainty of a Truth behind all truth remained with him. Then a sound, beautiful in itself, but belonging to the world of men broke the circle of perfection. The soft beat of camel bells, a dark brown sound with a bloom to it in the evening stillness. He found he was on his feet, though he did not remember having risen. And the sun was gone; and along the crest of the long dune, against the lines of the sunset that now were staining the sky to the zenith, the dark shapes of the laden camels were strung out; one of the great caravans coming up from the south, pressing forward to reach the caravanserai at the oasis before darkness came upon them.

It was time he was getting back to duty.

When Thomas arrived back in camp he found signs of a new arrival, tired mounts being unsaddled and led off to the horse-lines, a handful of weary Turkish troopers standing about. And when he asked a passing trooper of his own squadron the who and wherefore of the newcomers, the man told him they were the escort of an army messenger who had just ridden in from Aswan.

There was no reason in the world why the arrival of a messenger from Aswan should have anything to do with him or his affairs, and yet, making his way up through the camp, Thomas, not yet quite returned to normality from the state of heightened awareness that had come upon him in the desert, felt a faint stirring within himself, a sense of impending changes.

In the shadowed entrance to the headquarters tent, Zeid stood talking with a Turkish officer. Thomas skirted them widely and went on to his own quarters. The lamp had been lit, and on his bed-rug lay a flat packet. He picked it up and held it to the light, seeing that it was addressed to him in a small meticulous hand. Presumably it was something that the messenger had brought. But who did he know in Aswan? He drew the small dagger from his bandoleer sheath, and cut the scarlet thread and folded back the rustling paper. He was holding a book much the same size as his copy of the Koran, and with the same kind of delicate gilded tracery on its black leather cover. He opened it at the title page and saw that it also was in French.

> "Ali ibn abu Talib
> The True Caliph
> The Commander of the Faithful
> The Sword of Allah"

he read, and guessed that it was from Colonel D'Esurier even before he turned his attention to the folded sheet of paper that had fluttered free as he opened the book:

"I rejoice that we shall shortly be meeting again at El Jizzan, where I am at present superintending the mounting of guns on both the river and the desert side of the defences." Normally that would have pulled Thomas up with a jerk, but he seemed to have brought a great quiet with him out of the desert that evening; and it was with him still, and he merely registered the statement and read on: "But since I have always found reading, together with my pencil, to be a great lightener of the way on a journey, I send you another French translation, commissioned at the same time as the Koran, which you have already (and which I imagine, unless you have come by some other reading matter, you are able to recite almost off by heart!), hoping that the life of Ali ibn Talib, the Prophet's son-in-law, may give interest to the noon-tide halts." Thomas smiled within himself at the French colonel's idea of travelling. In his own experience, when on the move, the noon-tide halts tended to be spent on picket duty or coping with various emergencies, or with one's headcloth pulled across one's face to keep out the sand, trying to catch up on the sleep one had lost the night before, when a jackal crying too near the camp had stampeded the camels. He read on. It was a pleasantly discursive letter; not the letter, somehow, that he would have expected from the somewhat sardonic Frenchman. All was going well with Donald MacLeod – that made good reading at all events – plague had appeared in the Delta as always at that time of the year; and between these two items, almost in passing, came the news that the peace negotiations between the British and Egyptian governments were almost completed, and the repatriation of British prisoners about to begin.

The quiet which Thomas had brought with him out of the desert did not disappear, but it changed its nature, became like the pause and long-drawn breath before action. The answer to the slight mystery of the gift and letter sent so near to the time when it seemed he and D'Esurier would be meeting again anyway clicked smoothly into place. They might not have much chance of speaking privately together, and wishing to give him the repatriation news as far in advance as possible, the colonel had taken this way of doing it. A letter sent for that one especial purpose, possibly to be opened and read by the wrong person, might be unwise, might take on too much importance altogether. But a gift, with a letter enclosed, giving the same news in passing, among other items, would seem very much less worthy of attention.

He laid the book back on his sleeping-rug, and stowed the letter in the folds of his waist-shawl. Outside it was too dark to tell a white thread from a black one; and the high wild-bird note of the call to prayer was wailing across the camp.

Thomas remained leaning against the tent pole until the praying was over and life moved forward again, then straightened himself, slung on his sabre, and went back to duty.

Far into that night, when late rounds were over, and the Turkish officer had departed to his own quarters, Thomas and his captain still faced each other across the sinking embers of the coffee hearth.

"So – I am thinking that in one way or another way, your time with the Bedouin Horse is drawing to a close," Zeid said, leaning back against the camel saddle behind him and looking with narrowed eyes into the flame of the lamp.

"Why?" Thomas demanded, startled.

"See now – Ibrahim Pasha, the Viceroy's elder son, is at this fine new fort at El Jizzan on a survey of the economic resources of Upper Egypt, which the Mameluke factions between them have torn to rags. It seems unlikely, he being but nineteen (a year younger than you, I think?), but if his reputation rings true, he is well up to the task. What it is to have an old head on young shoulders! And I am ordered to leave Abu Salan in command here – Allah the All Merciful grant I shall find we still have horses left when I return – and ride north almost to Aswan to report to him on the state of the frontier. There is nothing strange in that, but I am bidden to bring the Scotsman, Thomas Keith, with me as an officer of my escort. And that, Thomas, I can only think means that your time in seclusion is nearly over."

Thomas was silent a long moment. The saluki stretched and sighed, her head on her master's thigh. It was an hour and more since he had first heard the orders from El Jizzan which dovetailed so neatly with Colonel D'Esurier's message. He wondered why he need no longer be kept secret from the Viceroy; maybe denying him his right to demand his repatriation with the rest had turned out to be too risky? He realised that in all probability he would never know.

All he did know was that his choosing, which had seemed to

be an indefinite distance into the future, was here. He wondered if he should speak to Zeid now, even before the setting out, as to his natural desire to join the other British prisoners.

He drew a long breath to do so, and heard himself saying, as though it were the thing he had known all his life that he would say in this place and at this time, "Whether I return with you again to El Hamha, or whether I am sent elsewhere, I shall not forget these months with the Bedouin cavalry, nor yet the things that are for the making of the Brotherhood. And whether it be here or in another place, I shall be seeking a religious teacher."

Zeid's fingers checked in fondling the old bitch's tasselled ears. "A religious teacher?"

"So-o." Zeid's fingers returned to their fondling, but his gaze held and returned Thomas's. "I hoped that might be the way of it – one time or another time. My heart is glad within me."

Chapter 6

At dusk four days later, they rode into El Jizzan and after seeing
the horses fed and watered and the men of the escort safely
bestowed, Thomas made his way up to the room in the officers'
block, which he and Zeid were to share. The room was empty,
Zeid having gone off to visit friends. The lamp had been lit,
and shone down from its niche in the wall on to their few
belongings, which had been brought in and stacked on the two
rug-covered mattresses which, together with a tall water jug
and a spare camel-saddle, were the room's only furniture. A
small room that might have been a monk's cell save that there
was no crucifix on the limewashed wall. Bare thatch overhead,
the small high-set window beyond which the dark was opaque
as velvet. The centre of the floor had evidently been swept in
their honour, but the sand-wreaths in the corners lay untouched.
Sand seemed normal in a black goat-hair tent, but in the corners
of a brick-built room it had an alien look. To Thomas, used for
six months and more to the cluttered spaciousness of the long
Bedu tent, one whole side looped back to the open air and the
life of the camp going on beyond it, the small square room
seemed airless and shut away.

Also he was gritty from head to foot, longing to wash off the
sand of the three days' ride. That would have to wait, he
supposed, the jug in the corner was clearly only for drinking.
Well at least he could get into a cleaner shirt. He took a gurgling
pull at the water jug, and turned to get his saddle bag from the
pile of belongings on the rug. As he did so a step sounded in the
arcaded court outside, the door which he had left half-open
behind him creaked on its hinges, and he spun round, his hand
instinctively moving towards the pistol in his waist-shawl, to
find Colonel D'Esurier standing in the doorway.

"Private Keith," said the Frenchman, looking him up and
down with a kind of detached interest spiced with amusement.
"You begin already to carry the look of the desert about you."

"I have only just come up from seeing to the men and

60

horses," Thomas said apologetically. "No time to shake the sand out of myself or put on a clean shirt."

"Ah, I was not speaking of the sand," D'Esurier swung the door lightly behind him and came further into the room. He set his hands on Thomas's shoulders and embraced him on both cheeks. Thomas returned the embrace warmly. They had met only twice, they came of different worlds, and though gratitude had told him on the evening of the horse raid to whom he wished to give the Crusader sword, he had not known until that moment that he counted the French colonel not only as some kind of sponsor in a strange new world, but as a friend.

Now they were holding each other at arm's length, smiling a little.

"They have been good, I think, these months in the desert?" D'Esurier said.

"Not at first. But after a while, yes, they have been good."

D'Esurier glanced down at the two books lying in the tumbled folds of Thomas's clean shirt, one black, one crimson, the delicate gilded arabesques glinting in the light of the palm-oil lamp. "You received my packet, I see."

"And your letter. It was good to get so much news of the outside world."

"I thought it might be," D'Esurier said quietly. "You have come to a decision? At least considered a course of action?"

"I have." Thomas hesitated. He knew that the thing must be told at once, but he was suddenly unsure as to how the Frenchman, despite his gifts, might take it. He nerved himself and said levelly, "I have to thank you also for the life of Ali ibn abu Talib. I read most of it four nights ago. That was the evening the Aswan messenger who brought it arrived, and I had told Zeid ibn Hussein that I wished to take instruction in the faith of Islam. I could not sleep for a long time that night, and it made good reading."

The colonel's brows quirked upwards: "So – farewell the streets of Edinburgh. That was quick decision-making."

"I think I had already made the decision, though I did not know it before." Thomas hesitated. "Yet it was not easy in the making."

"That I can believe. And for that, do you know, I envy you, my friend."

"Envy me?"

61

The colonel laughed a little harshly. "Because for me it would be easy. At your age I was an atheist; now, having grown less sure with age, I suppose that I am an agnostic. I say simply that I do not know. I have no faith to change . . . But now let us talk of other things. You have seen action, I hear, since our last meeting."

Thomas remembered two things, and the first of them was his manners. His guest was still standing.

A few moments later, with D'Esurier seated on one of the mattresses, a camel-saddle at his back, he turned to the second thing, distentangling two long, narrow bundles wrapped in linen from the baggage pile. "Captain Zeid ibn Hussein will have told you that – But of course you cannot serve long on the frontier without meeting Bedouin raiders or the Mamelukes. There was one day tribesmen raided our horse-lines at dawn. We went after them, and he and I – having the best horses – caught up with their rearguard ahead of the rest of our troop. It was warmish work for a while." He pivoted on his haunches, and leaning forward, laid the longer of the two bundled objects in the Frenchman's hands.

"One of the things I have learned during these past months is that it is discourteous to express thanks for a gift. The correct thing, if one desires to express gratitude, is a gift in return. This I had from one of the men I killed."

He sat watching, his arms across his knees, as D'Esurier turned back the oiled linen. A little sand spilled out from between the folds, and the sword lay bare in its new master's hands. He looked down at it a moment in silence, then drew the blade from its modern sheath with a breath of pleasure, and watched the lamplight play up and down the long straight steel. "Sa ha! This is a gift indeed!"

"A Crusader sword?" Thomas suggested. "We had drawings in the workshop – I thought thirteenth century, maybe French?"

Colonel D'Esurier was still examining the sword, his dark face alight with pleasure. "I believe you are right," he said after a short while. "We in the West have learned to think that Saracen blades were always curved and Crusader blades alone were straight. As a matter of fact there are thirteenth-century illustrated manuscripts in the citadel library in Cairo showing both Mameluke and Berber askaris carrying long straight

62

weapons." They looked at each other across the glinting blade, the French gunnery officer and the Scottish armourer's apprentice, linked by shared interest and expertise.

"It is in the quillons that the true difference lies," said D'Esurier. "The quillons which in a Saracen sword do no more than form shoulders to the blade, but projected further, as in this, give the European medieval hilt the semblance of a cross."

He slid the blade back into its sheath. It ran like oiled silk. "I learned the bare outlines of the fight from Captain Hussein while you were down at the horse-lines, and I shall not ask you for the more detailed story: doubtless I shall learn it in due course, but not, I think, from you, for I doubt if you have much skill in singing your own praises . . . At the risk of discourtesy, I thank you, Thomas, for your gift."

Thomas leaned to touch the second bundle. "This is the other man's sabre. I should like to send it to Ahmed Agha. Zeid said that would be permissible – if you agree?"

"Perfectly permissible. Ahmed Agha will no doubt appreciate the gesture – especially as I doubt if he receives many gifts save those made with the purchase of instant favours in view. But I did not think that you felt so much gratitude towards our Ahmed Bonaparte."

"Not before my months at El Hamha, no," Thomas said simply.

D'Esurier smiled, dandling the Crusader's sword in his hands. "Ibrahim Pasha is sending a courier back to Cairo tomorrow, after he has heard Captain Hussein's report; if you like, I can send the sabre with him, under cover, I think, of a letter from me . . . Alternatively, you may prefer to keep it among your baggage until we reach Cairo ourselves and you can present them personally."

Thomas heard all the sounds of the camp very clearly, but seemingly at a great distance. Within the narrow room it was so quiet that if the air had moved he would have heard the sand-wreaths stirring in the corners. "One way or another way," Zeid had said, "I think your time with the Bedouin Horse is almost over."

"I am to go back to Cairo with you?" he said, as though it were quite a small matter.

"Yes. I have two more forts to visit on the way back, but we should be there in five or six weeks."

"What has changed?" Thomas asked, much as he had asked it of Captain Zeid ibn Hussein. "Have the Viceroy's orders concerning prisoners changed, that I no longer need to be kept a dark secret?"

D'Esurier shrugged. "I think not. But Ahmed Agha fought well for him in the Delta, and he owes him something in gratitude. Also the Mamelukes are increasingly a threat and he cannot afford to alienate any of his anti-Mameluke generals. My guess is that the Agha chose his moment with care, reminded Muhammed Ali – oh very delicately – of these things, and contrived to come to a friendly understanding with him."

"But I should still be sent back with the other prisoners if I were to stand on my rights?" Thomas did not care for the feelings of being a parcel in the hands of other men.

"Ah yes. But now it seems that question does not arise."

"No. I was forgetting that for the moment."

"Shall you miss your own army? Shall you miss Scotland? Your father?"

"I suppose I must write to my father."

"I wonder which will grieve him the more, to believe, as he does now, that you were killed at El Hamed, or to know that you have taken service with the Ottoman Empire and that you have changed your Faith? If you tell him the one thing, you must tell him the whole."

Thomas was silent a long moment, staring at his own hands linked about his knees. Then he looked up. "I will not write," he said.

Farewell the streets of Edinburgh, indeed.

Next morning, seated on fine rugs from the viceregal baggage train, in the audience chamber of the headquarters building, Captain Zeid ibn Hussein made his report to Ibrahim Pasha, the Viceroy's elder son. He gave account of the frontier tribes, their strength in men, horses and camels, and of the strength and location of the frequently hostile Mameluke forces. He gave it as his careful opinion that the desert tribes would not ally themselves with the Mamelukes as a long-term thing, but that they might do it short-term if there was a clear material advantage to be gained. The only hope of keeping the Southern Province stable and relatively peaceful lay in dealing with the Mamelukes once and for all, and policing the province thereafter with men such as the Bedouin cavalry: men who knew the desert and the ways of the desert. Also in appointing a competent governor responsible directly to the Viceroy. All these things ibn Hussein believed strongly, and he laid them clearly before the Viceroy's son, simply as a man who knew what he was talking about, to another who needed the same knowledge. And the short thick-set young pasha listened to him, clear, surprisingly blue eyes fixed on his face, occasionally putting in some probing question, for the most part silent. Not yet twenty, he was already showing promise of the brilliant administrator he was to become, and clearly he had learned the useful lesson that other men may be worth listening to.

A little to one side, Colonel D'Esurier, who had been invited to be present, leant forward, occasionally asked a question of his own, generally relative to the fortification of some Mameluke-held strong point, but for the most part also remained silent.

He saw a growing respect in the pasha's intent blue gaze, and could read well enough what was going on behind it. The report probably told him not much more than he expected to hear, after the very thorough advance findings he must have sought – for he was meticulously thorough – before he came south; but knowing the Arab love of words and the twists and by-ways and embroidered ramification of words, he must have expected to spend days in drawing it out, sifting what was useful from what was not, and making his own evaluation. From Captain Zeid ibn Hussein, who in this one thing at least was not typical of his race, he was getting the kind of report, concise and well reasoned, that Bonaparte might have expected from one of his junior officers. Colonel D'Esurier's guess was that the Arab captain would not live out his days in command of a mud fort on the edge of nowhere.

When the report was finished and the clerk taking it down had gathered up his writing materials and departed, the pasha clapped his hands for coffee and sherbet, and for the present turned the conversation to other things.

"Now, what of this new acquisition of Ahmed Agha's? You have him with you?"

"I have him with me as ordered, as lieutenant of my escort," Zeid said; there was regret in his tone. "The colonel tells me that he is to return with him to Cairo."

"You sound as though you did not like the plan."

Zeid spread his hands. "Not greatly. He should remain with us. He is not of the right stuff for the general's bodyguard."

"Not enough of the courtier?"

"I think he might do none so ill at that, if he set his mind to it. He is one who keeps his eyes open and learns by what he sees. But I think it will be a waste."

D'Esurier nodded. "He would not be wasted, you think, in the Egyptian army?"

"He would rise high, I think. And now that he is of the True Faith—"

The pasha leaned forward. "Ah? He has embraced Islam?"

"Not yet, Excellency, but he has told me that he wishes to take instruction."

Ibrahim Pasha fingered his fair beard; a curiously old man's gesture. "I will not ask whether that is from conviction or from good sense. It will have been pointed out to him that the prospects in the Muslim army are better for a Muslim officer?"

"I pointed it out to him myself," Zeid said simply. "It held him back for many days."

"One would expect more sense from a Lowland Scot," D'Esurier murmured. "They are reputed to be as hard-headed as my own people."

Ibrahim Pasha looked from one to the other, and his face broke into a grin that made him look for the moment no more than his nineteen years. "It seems he has two staunch friends in this new world of his. Presently I must meet this hard-headed Scot of yours, who is too good for Ahmed Agha's bodyguard. Meanwhile—" He took up the slender brass coffee pot.

At about the same time that morning, out on the practice ground with its fringe of dusty shade-trees, Thomas and the rest of the escort were at mounted sabre practice with the garrison cavalry.

Mounted practice over, and Bulbul led away to the horse-lines by one of the askaris, Thomas, having no other call on his time for the moment, while Zeid was away, had started a bout of sabre play with Othman al Malik, the best swordsman among the escort after himself, while a lounging cluster of their fellows looked on. The sun was rising higher, the thin shade under the tamarisk and acacia trees growing short. It was still early in the year, but so far south, the heat was already fierce, the beaten earth of the practice ground beginning to dance on the sight like a midge cloud. Both Thomas and his opponent had flung off their abbas and tucked back their headcloths into the black camelhair head-cords to let the air get to their necks and ears. But Thomas could feel the sun stinging on his shoulders through the rough cotton of his shirt, and the sweat crawling like insects down the valleys of his body.

Then in the concentration of the swordplay he forgot everything else.

The bout did not last long, in the growing heat, but it was quick and fierce while it lasted. Finally Othman, whose strokes had for some moments been growing less sure, stumbled to avoid a particularly dangerous thrust, slipped in the fine dry dust and landed on one knee.

Thomas, his own breath coming quickly and the sun-whitened world pulsing a little on his sight, lowered his blade and half leant on it, thereby signifying to his gasping opponent with a swordsman's courtesy that he also had had enough. The man grinned, wiping the sweat from his face with the back of his forearm; and as he did so, Thomas saw his gaze go out and up across his shoulder to something, someone, beyond.

"Bravo! That was a bout well played," said a voice behind him in the same instant. A young voice, warmly vital, rough at the edges in the way of a boy's voice that has broken not so long ago into a man's, and speaking French with an appalling Albanian accent.

And turning quickly, Thomas found himself looking up past the neck and shoulder of a raking chestnut mare into the face of her rider. He was probably not more than a couple of years older than Medhet, a short thick-set stripling, lion-coloured as to skin and eyes and the tawny hair that showed in front of his left ear, where the gold-fringed swathings of his turban had been pushed somewhat rakishly askew. Everything about him seemed to be worn at a rakish angle, as though he had flung everything on in a hurry, to be off about something exciting, and he sat his fidgeting chestnut with casual ease, faintly askew in the saddle.

Something in the boy's own aspect, and the way the crowd had parted without protest to yield him and his half-dozen companions a ringside view, something in the aspect, midway between cronies and bodyguard, of the half-dozen, told Thomas instantly that he was looking at Tussun, the Viceroy's younger son. He had heard that the boy had come up with his brother Ibrahim Pasha, eager to see for himself the desert outposts and the men of his father's new Bedouin regiments.

"You are the Scottish soldier they told me about," said Tussun Bey.

"I am, Sir." Thomas was not sure of the correct show of deference. In the end he made a grave inclination of the head, then brought his gaze up again to the boy's vivid and imperious face.

"They said you were the best swordsman in Upper Egypt. Teach me that thrust in tierce."

"Gladly, if you wish it, Sir."

"Now." Tussun was just about to swing down from the high silver-worked saddle.

Thomas shook his head, smiling. "Not now. It is too far into the heat of the day, and I am overweary to do full justice to my sword or yours. This evening, if you wish."

"I wish it now." The boy's chin jutted a little, but he had checked his movement to dismount.

"We shall both do better in the cool of the evening," Thomas said.

"Do you know who I am?"

"No," said Thomas, truthfully, "but I think that you are Tussun Bey."

They remained looking at each other, the heat-filled silence spreading out from them like the ripples when a fish jumps in a pool. There was a certain half-pleasurable apprehension among the onlookers waiting to see what would happen next. Thomas gathered that the Viceroy's second son was not used to not getting his own way on all occasions, and wondered for an instant if he might be landing himself in serious trouble, but wondered it only somewhere at the back of his mind; the rest of his awareness was entirely taken up with the boy on the chestnut mare, who seemed to focus the sunlight in his own being.

For a long moment still, they remained unmoving, hot tawny gaze and cool grey meeting and locked, while the frown gathered between the princeling's amber brows. Then suddenly it was gone, and his face lit with a smile that could charm the heart out of any woman.

"It shall be as you say, Thomas Effendi. This evening you

will teach me the thrust in tierce, and tomorrow morning I will show you how to fly a falcon."

The companion sitting his horse closest on Tussun's right, straightened a little in his saddle. A man maybe in his early twenties wearing Mameluke dress – Tussun was renowned for his unorthodox choice of friends – and with the blue eyes and fair skin of his kind. Now those eyes which had been lazy in the sunshine were narrowed and attentive, flicking from the Scots mercenary to the Viceroy's son and back again.

But neither Tussun nor Thomas were aware of him, nor, for the moment, of the rest of the watching crowd, nor of the shade-trees nor the sun overhead, having other and stranger things to think about.

They were sprawled side by side on the embankment wringing the Nile water out of their hair and drying off in the sun that dappled through the broad-leaved fig branches overhead before pulling on their clothes again.

The fencing lesson had duly taken place last evening, the lesson in falconry this morning and the memory was still present and vivid with Thomas of the moment when the borrowed salukis had flushed the heron from the reeds, and she had leapt upwards in swift spiral flight and he and Tussun had both loosed their falcons after her in the same instant. Thomas had flown a saker before now, during his time at El Hamed, but chiefly at desert hare, never before at heron, and he remembered, with all the potent clarity of a first time, the quarry climbing desperately the blue circles of the upper air, striving for the needful height to use the dagger bill that was her only weapon, and behind her the falcons with deadly power and purpose mounting steadily on her trail. He could hear again the thin chime of the hawk bells as they climbed, see again through eyes narrowed into the sun-glare, the chase sweeping up and up into height beyond height of burning blue, until at last Tussun's falcon overtopped the quarry and stooped, avoiding the despairing dagger-thrust of her beak, and made his kill. A puff of feathers drifting out of the sky, as hunter and hunted dropped together into the reeds and hounds and men closed in . . .

The lesson over and the day's heat growing fierce, they had left the rest of the hawking party to their own devices in the shade of a thicket of young sycamores, and strolled upriver until they had come upon a half-dead fig tree growing with its feet almost in the shimmering fringes of the inundation. Away beyond, on the usual patch of slightly higher ground, a dilapidated village rose above the usual smoke-coloured drift of irises among its leaning gravestones. No sound to break the noonday save for the braying somewhere of a tethered donkey and the deep hum of insects that might have been the voice of the heat itself.

Tussun, lying now with his still damp hair clinging about his neck, seemed half asleep. For Thomas, sitting with hands linked round updrawn knees, and watching the movements of a small water bird among the reeds, the passing hour seemed something not to be wasted in even half-sleep. Presently, all too soon, the day would be over and there might not be another like it in all his life. Tomorrow he was leaving with Colonel D'Esurier on the slow journey, broken by pauses to inspect gun emplacements, down river to Cairo. Tussun and his brother would remain here a few days longer, but travelling without the constant halts would be in Cairo well ahead of them. Tussun and he might meet again there, but in the city everything would be different.

He was aware of an abrupt movement beside him and when he looked round the boy had come up to his elbow and was looking with concerned interest at the entry scar of the musket ball just below his, Thomas's, hip. It would fade and turn silvery by and by, but now it was still purplish and had the indefinable look of being tight and sore.

"That was at El Hamed?" Tussun said.

"Yes."

"Ssss," the boy sucked in his breath between his teeth. "It must have been a sharp hurt in its time."

"Sharp enough," Thomas agreed. "But I had a good surgeon. In a year it will be small enough – almost – to cover with the ball of my thumb."

Tussun put out a slim brown hand, and with the unselfconscious ease of old friendship, set his own thumb lightly over the puckered and livid place. "In a year, maybe," he said judicially, "assuredly there is a way to go yet." And then: "Who was he, this good surgeon? A Turk? Not one of our Albanian army leeches, I think."

"A friend of mine, from the same regiment and captured at the same time. Donald MacLeod."

"Another Scot?"

"Another Scot."

"What became of him?"

"Ahmed Agha bought him as well as me from our Albanian captors. Donald for his skill as a surgeon, me because he thought I would make a suitable addition to his personal bodyguard." Thomas heard his own voice speaking light and level as though of something that did not matter. It did matter. He wanted desperately to leave the words unsaid, but something deep within him insisted that there must be complete honesty, no glossing over, between himself and Tussun. "I am told that he paid a captain's ransom for each of us," he added for good measure.

There was a stillness except for the braying of the donkey. Then Tussun said: "Allah the All Merciful works in strange ways to bring about His will."

"His will?"

"Do you not see, Thomas? Clearly it is the will of Allah that we two should be friends, and how else could we have come together?"

Thomas knew a sudden sense of added shine to a day that was already more shining then any he had known before, though he had a feeling that Tussun's line of thought would not stand too close examination.

"You are thinking maybe that my friendship is costly, that you have lost many friends at El Hamed," the boy said quickly and gravely, the harsh edges of his voice adding to the note of regret.

"Those friends I would have lost in any case," Thomas said. "Thanks to the Mameluke cavalry."

"Ah, those who broke their faith with you. That is why you do not like the look of Aziz?"

"Aziz?"

"My Mameluke companion of yesterday."

Thomas laughed, and the mood of the moment which had strayed for a little into the shadows, came up into the light and air once more. "I thought it was rather that Aziz Bey did not like the look of me."

"Oh that – Aziz is always jealous of my friends. He would like to be the only friend I have!"

In a while he sat up regretfully and reached for his scattered garments. "It begins to be time we were getting back to the rest."

They pulled on their clothes in companionable silence, having already reached the stage at which two people can be together without always needing to talk to each other, and Thomas, the first to have finished, sat watching while Tussun, whose turban took longer to arrange than his own headcloth, settled the elaborate folds.

Then as Thomas drew his legs under him to rise, the Viceroy's son, one hand on the lowest branch of the fig tree, reached down the other, laughing. "Hup! My brother!" he said in the tones of one encouraging a horse at a jump. And the next instant they stood side by side on the broad crest of the embankment.

They strolled off in the general direction in which they had left the rest of the hawking party, and they were still hand-in-hand.

Thomas was a little startled at the outset, but he had lived six months and more among men who habitually walked hand-in-hand with their closest friends, though he had never done so himself before, and after that first momentary surprise, it seemed to him the most natural thing in the world.

When they came out through the thicket of young sycamores in the lee of which they had left the hawking party, he did expect that they would part hands, but Tussun showed no signs of doing so, and to withdraw his own hand would be to deny his friend and the thing between them.

They walked forward with hands still linked into the midst of the party, under the interested gaze of half a dozen pairs of eyes, under the hot, jealous, angry stare of Aziz Bey of the Mameluke Guard.

Chapter 7

Thomas stood in the midst of his new quarters, and looked about him, appreciative, but somewhat puzzled.

He had expected, once he was in Cairo, to find himself quartered with the Agha's bodyguard; or if that, at such an early stage, was setting his sights too high, then in barracks somewhere in the city, or even left to share Colonel D'Esurier's quarters for the night. Instead, he had been taken over by a most uncommunicative officer of some Albanian regiment or other and brought here, to these two rooms above what looked as though it had once been an armoury, followed by a porter carrying his worldly possessions in a pair of saddle bags. A grey-bearded army servant had unpacked for him, provided water for washing, and the inevitable strong black coffee, a tall swan-necked vase of over-sweet sherbet and a dish of dates; and salaaming deeply, abandoned him to his own devices.

And what was to happen next, he had not the remotest idea.

He felt all at once rather like a lost dog. The past few weeks all the way down from Aswan, he had had the French colonel's company; now, alone in these impersonal rooms that were sodden with age and yet did not feel as though they had ever been lived in by any man before him, he felt again, suddenly and sharply, the lack of Zeid ibn Hussein, and the loss of Bulbul, left behind at El Jizzan to be absorbed into the southern cavalry. He told himself firmly that he would very probably meet Zeid again sometime; and in the loss of the mare he was only suffering what every cavalryman suffered time and again; that at any rate he was now in the same city as Donald MacLeod; and that at some time, somebody, presumably Ahmed Agha or the captain of his bodyguard, or *somebody*, would send for him.

Meanwhile he might as well get to know his quarters.

Stone walled and stone floored, the chambers might, except for their spaciousness, have been monastic or prison cells, but the heavy door that opened on to the head of the circular stair was carved with traceries as perfect in their way as the gilded arabesques on the cover of his Koran, and it seemed that somebody had been at pains to make the place habitable, and even given it here and there an unexpected flash of beauty like the flash of colour on a jay's wing. In the inner room soft rugs of wool and camel hair were spread on the sleeping mattress, and here in the outer chamber cushions and piled rugs made the customary divan along two sides and a zither with a delicately fretted rose lay among the divan cushions; while already for his especial benefit a low table had been set in the centre of the room, and pulled up square to it was a heavy oak chair with, of all things, a mermaid carved on its back, which might perhaps have come from the captain's cabin of some merchant ship. His two books had been carefully set out in the exact centre of the table by the grey-bearded one, who clearly felt that to be a place of suitable dignity for the Koran and its companion. On one wall a silken carpet of Ispahan, golden as evening sunlight, softened the austerity of the raw stone, and on another, opposite the window, hung of all surprising things, a Scottish broadsword, its silver basket-hilt lined with reddish velvet.

Thomas had seen it on first entering the room, but in the pressure of other things had scarcely taken in what it was. Now he crossed to it, took it down and carried it to the window, with a feeling of recognising suddenly a familiar face, touching suddenly a friend's hand.

The window faced north over the crowding housetops towards the citadel on its high spur of rock, but the backwash of the evening sunlight showed him clearly every detail of the weapon in his hands. It had seen hard service; the black leather of the scabbard was scratched and scuffed, the velvet lining the basket hilt still showed its original crimson where the silver had protected it, but elsewhere was faded to the colour of spent rose petals or spilled wine. In one place close to the quillons there was a darker stain. Thomas drew it from its scabbard and stood watching the evening light spill like water up and down the blade. He made an experimental pass or two, and felt lovingly how the perfect balance brought the heavy blade up again almost of its own accord into his hand. Something was engraved close below the hilt. He turned it again to the evening light, and read on one side the name of an Edinburgh swordsmith, not Mr Sempill, and on the other, the name Colin MacKenzie.

Major Colin MacKenzie of his own regiment, killed at Rosetta three weeks before the fight at El Hamed. He remembered for a moment the grey-green eyes and sandy hair and big-boned humorous face of the man who had carried that sword into action. He had not thought of him for close on a year, but now, for a passing wing-beat of time, felt again the pull of his own kind, of his roots behind him, caught again the swirl of the pipes as the line went forward, and wondered what he was doing here.

Eager footsteps sounded on the circular stair, the turnpike, as he already called it in his own mind – and as he swung round the door crashed back and Tussun Bey appeared in the dark opening.

Tussun as usual blazing with life until the air about him seemed to crackle with it. "Tho'mas. Oh it is so good that you are here!" He strode into the room happily kicking the door to behind him. "The sword is good?"

Thomas tossed aside the scabbard and laid the naked sword on the table beside the Koran. "Salaam aleikum", he should have said, but he forgot the proper greeting in sudden delight. "The sword is good," he said, and next instant, half laughing, was staggering under the vehemence of Tussun's embrace. A few moments later, the laughing and exclaiming done, they stood back and looked at each other, each with his hands still on the other's shoulders.

"Is it well with you? Have they treated you well here? Have you all that you need?" the boy was demanding.

"All is well with me. But I shall be glad to know what happens next. Have you any idea when Ahmed Agha is likely to send for me?"

"Ahmed Agha will not send for you at all!" Tussun's face lit with triumph. "I have *talked* with Ahmed Agha, and you are no man of his any more!"

There was a small sharp silence, and then, "Meaning that I am yours now, Tussun Bey?" Thomas said slowly.

The backwash of the sunset was still flowing into the room, but it seemed to him that the gold was fallen from the air like shining dust. He had been right in thinking that everything would be different in the city.

"I trust my price was not too high?" he added. "All men say that the Agha parts with nothing except for gold or power." He dropped his hands lightly away from the other's shoulders.

"I did not mean to tell you that," Tussun said. "The gold was nothing – I have plenty, my father is generous to his sons . . . Ah Thomas, do not look like that, so dark and far off – I thought you would be glad as I am!"

"Forgive me, Sir. It takes a while to grow used to a change of owners. Doubtless I shall feel proper gratitude later."

Thomas watched the life and eagerness drain out of the boy's face. 'He doesn't understand,' he thought. 'Oh God, he doesn't understand. If it could have been Zeid . . .' He turned away and stared blindly out of the narrow window at the saffron fringes of the sunset flying from the great dome of the citadel mosque. He was not at all sure that he understood himself. He had not felt like this about being bought by Ahmed Agha, how was it so different now?

"It was not you I bought, Tho'mas, it was your freedom – freedom for a friend," said the young voice, now painfully level behind him. "I wanted you to help me train the two regiments my father has given me to command. You said yourself there was no proper training in the Turkish cavalry." Then with a burst of misery, "But if it *had* been you I bought, would you not rather be mine than his?"

Thomas drew in his breath quickly, like a man in sudden pain, and let it go again with great care. "I expect so," he said dully.

Tussun's voice went on, stumbling a little now in its vehemence over the French tongue which, though he spoke it fluently, was not his own. "Have you forgotten the morning we went hawking from El Jizzan and I taught you how to fly at heron? It was good, that morning. I thought you would be as glad to be with me as I was to be with you – I would have chosen quarters for you close to my own, but I thought these above the old armoury would give you more freedom and told my people to make them comfortable."

"Your orders have been well carried out," Thomas said. "Was it you who thought of the zither?"

"No, that will have been Ali, my chamber-page, who can play the birds out of the reed beds, and thinks that all men must find the same pleasure in what pleases him. The sword was my idea. I thought that it would please you, a fine sword of your own people; but perhaps you will take it as an insult, because

76

it was taken from one of your people killed in battle. I do not think that I know what pleases you any more."

Thomas thought, 'After all, what are we at loggerheads about? The boy doesn't understand; and if the thing had been the other way over, would I not have paid in good Maria Theresa dollars to get him free of Ahmed Agha? Be angry with the circumstances; don't take it out on the boy, you fool.'

"The sword is good," he said. "Did I not say so?"

He turned from the window, smiling a little. "But among my people we believe that you must never give to a friend a sharp-edged gift without exacting payment – a pin or a farthing – otherwise it will cut the friendship; and you see the wisdom of that belief?" He thrust his hand into the folds of his waist-shawl and pulled out a slim leather pouch. He had received a trooper's pay in the past months, and had generally contrived to keep something in reserve. He brought out the smallest coin it contained, a Turkish sequin.

He saw the anger and hurt go out of the boy's face as he caught the tiny coin and tossed it up, a spinning fleck of gold in the reflected light of the sunset, then catching it, stowed it somewhere in his own waist-shawl.

At El Hamha the Bedouin cavalry had lived in its own solitude, with seldom any news of the outside world. But here in Cairo it was a different matter; news from the outside world seemed to blow in on every wind from the Delta.

Sometimes it brought Thomas a stab of homesickness for his own world, his own kind, but for the most part it seemed to come from a great distance or another life. His days, now that he was official training officer to Tussun's two regiments, were fuller than they had ever been before. For not only did he have the task of trying to instil into the wild Turkish cavalry some idea of discipline and co-ordination and the skills of their trade, but finding that most of their weaponry was in a shocking state, he had to deal with that also, frequently with his own hands, when it was something that the regimental armourers could not handle, even under his instructions. At such times he remembered with gratitude his old master in the shop in Leith Wynd.

Daily, also, he was taking instruction in the Islamic faith from a much respected teacher produced for him by Colonel D'Esurier; a little old man brown and wrinkled and only dimly discernible under an enormous turban, the green turban of a Haji, for he had made the pilgrimage to Mecca and Medina in his youth, long before the holy cities fell to the fanatical Wahabis and the pilgrimages ceased.

And as the weeks went by and the heat mounted, he was becoming more and more familiar with Cairo itself, the city whose life formed a shifting and glinting, shadowed and furtive tapestry into which his days were woven; coming to know it from the citadel to the narrow twisting alleyways of the old city further west, where it was not wise to go alone; through the crooked canyons of the bazaars, smelling of amber and incense, spices and camel dung and things nameless and infinitely worse, and the throat-catching metallic smitch of the copper-smiths; where awnings rigged between rooftops four and five storeys overhead kept out the sun and air. From the oasis and Greek ruins of Heliopolis across the river to the desert beyond the pyramids of Giza and Helwan, where he and Tussun rode hawking from time to time. He knew the barracks, of course, the great Kasr el Nil that had housed the first Mameluke regiments when the world was young. He knew the official houses that fringed the wide spaces of the maidans; and the plunging and snarling chaos of the camel market; and the harlots' quarters down by the Nile bank, where the windows were as discreetly fretted as anywhere else in the city, but the girls sat shamelessly unveiled in the doorways, touting for custom with hennaed palms and soft sing-song voices. Tussun at seventeen had told him which houses he could go to without fear of the pox. He knew the cool arcades of the hospital where he had been told that Donald MacLeod might be found, but Donald was not there, having been swept off into the Delta only a few days before, in the service of Ahmed Agha, whose man he still was. Ah well, there would come other times.

He had been presented to the Viceroy, and spoken to graciously yet again about his very tenuous kinship with Frederick the Great's two brothers, and done his best to satisfy Muhammed Ali's shrewd cross-examination on the battle training of the British infantry of the line, without giving away anything that should not be given away to a foreign power and one that had lately been an enemy.

He had been received into the Faith of Islam, at a ceremony which, together with the celebrations afterwards, had been enjoyed by Tussun and the rest of those present, including several of his fellow officers, considerably more than by Thomas himself. He had gone to it proudly and reverently, as a boy to his rite of passage; but beside the pain of the ritual operation, had found it humiliating, as a grown man, to undergo circumcision beneath the gaze of other men. A thing very far removed from the moment of spiritual awareness in the desert that had been his true moment of conversion, his Light on the road to Damascus. And after, there had been three days of fever and a penis so inflamed and swollen that to sit a horse or even walk had been misery for several more.

But that was in the past, and he was Ibrahim now, Ibrahim Effendi, by way of courtesy, never to be called Thomas again save by Tussun and Zeid, Medhet and Colonel D'Esurier, and one other into whose face he had not yet looked.

On an evening in late April, more than a year since he had been taken prisoner, a still evening with the mirage shimmering over the practice maidan, so that the trees on the far side of it seemed to be standing above their own reflections in water, Thomas returned to the blessed coolness of his own quarters to find Tussun, who as owner of the old armoury had his own key, sprawled on the divan picking dry skin from between his toes with deep concentration, his crimson Turkish slippers lying in opposite corners of the room.

Almost, Thomas said, "Oh most disgusting of urchins, is it needful that you do that in my quarters?" But he remembered in what manner those chambers had come to be his quarters, and the memory checked him. Often it was like that. On the surface all was as it had been before that first evening in Cairo. But that small painful scene had left scars, and there was a shadow of constraint between them, at least on Thomas's side, that had not been there before.

So now he merely stood and looked at the boy, straight brows raised a little, and waited to be told what had brought him there. He had not long to wait. Tussun looked up and grinned. "My mother is holding yet another of her receptions this evening, and I am the bearer of her invitation to it – Come."

Thomas was tired from a long day in the saddle, trying to instil into Tussun's cavalry the rudiments of a controlled charge; in which he was not helped by the fact that, natural horseman though he was, and trained now in Arab ways of

79

riding and horse-management, his years in the British army had been served in a foot regiment. Also he was out at elbows with life for certain reasons of his own, and in no mood to go to a reception, especially at a moment's notice. He played for time:

"The Vicereine does me too much honour, but I am in no state for a lady's salon."

"I can see that – and smell it," Tussun agreed. "Your orderly has warm water in your sleeping quarters, and your feast-day clothes laid out. And it will take your mind off whatever it needs taking off. Go now and get clean and beautiful. I'll wait."

"Your mother cannot even know that I exist. This is all your idea, isn't it."

"No it is not! Oh I have spoken of you to her, but it is entirely her wish that you should attend this reception." Tussun grinned. "My mother always likes to meet my friends, in case they are undesirable."

Thomas checked in the act of slipping his bandoleer over his head. "What does she do if they are undesirable?"

"Nothing really, except to point it out to me. She tries to remember that I am a grown man and free to choose my companions. But at least she feels that she is forewarned." Tussun wagged his head on his seventeen-year-old shoulders, as though he were a greybearded philosopher, but his eyes were dancing slits. "Women . . . One must keep them happy. Hurry now, or we shall be late."

Chapter 8

Ever afterwards the Vicereine's reception stuck in Thomas's memory as having been held, somewhat uncomfortably, at the meeting point of two worlds. The chamber that formed its setting belonged to one world: a beautiful room where the interplay of lamplight and shadows made a fantasy of Moorish arches and slender columns and the delicate intricacy of window frets and the Damascus silken coverings of the cushion-piled divans around the walls; while the gilded curlicues of the French tables and occasional chairs, all acanthus scrolls and sphinxes, and the fragile bird-and-flower enamelled coffee china came from another world entirely. And everywhere Thomas, standing with Tussun just within the entrance, was aware of an uncomfortable clash between the two.

"Presents from the Ottoman ambassador in Paris," Tussun whispered with delight. "Are they not horrible? The letters say that they are identical with the furniture in the Empress's apartment at Malmaison; could this be true?"

Thomas shook his head. He had never been in the Empress's apartments at Malmaison, but he found it hard to believe that there could be such ornate confections of ormolu and black onyx anywhere else in the world.

The room was already crowded, with Turks, Albanians and a few Mameluke officers and senior Egyptian officials, seated on the damask-cushioned divans, while on a chaise longue set on a low dais at the far end of the chamber the Vicereine reclined with her ladies about her, bright as a cluster of tropical birds.

The evening's entertainment trickled by against a background of conversation kept artificially low and monotonous. The delicate china cups were replenished again and again by tall Nubian slaves, looking somewhat out of keeping with the peaceful occasion by reason of the great curved scimitars they wore. And every now and then someone among the guests would be summoned by a cat-footed official to approach the dais and speak for a few minutes with the Vicereine before, at a

81

delicate movement of the head which probably, Thomas thought, went with a gracious smile behind her yashmak, he bowed and retreated to his place on one of the divans, while someone else took his place before the Vicereine.

In due course Thomas's turn came, and Tussun swept him off to be presented. He found himself bowing a little stiffly before the graceful, indolent figure on the dais, careful not to come too close. ("Remember not to try to kiss her hand," Tussun had said. "Our women are not curtain-hidden like the wives of the desert sheikhs, but it is not permitted that any man not their husband or close relatives should actually touch them.")

"My Mother," Tussun was saying, "allow that I present to you Ibrahim, my friend and the training officer to my regiments."

The Vicereine wore only the half yashmak, leaving bare the upper part of her face and Thomas met the remarkably level gaze of a pair of eyes that were lion-tawny like her son's. The gaze was disconcerting, it was so long since he had seen a woman who looked at him openly in that way; but the voice behind the thin silken veil was sweet and warmly throaty. "I am so glad to receive you, Ibrahim Effendi. I have heard so much of you from my son."

"Madame, I am deeply honoured," Thomas said.

"My son tells me that you are from Scotland."

"Yes, Madame, from Edinburgh."

"I have read of your beautiful and most unfortunate Queen, Marie Stuart, La Reine d'Ecosse did they not call her? And of your gallant Prince Charles Edouard, who defeated two English armies more than fifty years ago."

"Before he himself was defeated in the end," Thomas said. "My grandfather was out with – fought for – the Prince, and spent twenty years in exile in France after the defeat, forfeiting his own small family estate." He noticed as he said it, with a wry inner amusement, that he was doing his best to assure the Lady Amina that he was a suitable friend for her son; and saw her eyes narrow in answering amusement, as though she perfectly understood this. They spoke together for a few moments more, Thomas becoming more and more aware as each moment passed, of the girl seated on a cushion at her feet. He guessed that she must be Tussun's sister, the Lady Nayli; but he had not

82

been presented to her, and so judged that it might be bad manners to look at her direct. Yet he was aware through every fibre of his being that she was looking at him, much as he had known sometimes in the desert that he was being watched by something or someone just out of sight.

"This must be such a strange world to you," the Vicereine was saying. "May I hope that your life will be happy here among us. We shall look forward to talking with you again, and to hearing more about your Scotland – my own land is a mountain country too."

Thomas bowed again, and turned away. As he did so his quickly passing glance was caught and held for an instant by the girl Nayli. He had an impression of black eyes, long-lashed and beautiful, under a forehead of milky velvet, and wings of smooth black hair springing from under a seed pearl embroidered cap. Only for an instant their sight-lines locked, then she lowered kohl-painted lids, and he was free and walking back with Tussun to the place he had left.

But afterwards, looking back on his first taste of Egyptian polite society, it was not the Lady Nayli's eyes he chiefly remembered, but the hot blue gaze of Aziz Bey, whom he had found watching him too often for comfort ever since their first meeting at El Jizzan.

"What did you think of my sister Nayli?" Tussun asked as, the reception over, they made their way across the palace forecourt.

"I took care scarcely to look at her," Thomas said, watching the moths fluttering in the pool of light from a doorway lantern. "You did not present me to her, and I thought maybe it would be ill manners – against the custom."

"She watched you," Tussun said. "But then Nayli never did care for good manners, or for the custom, or much else, except doing what best pleases her. Ah well, you will get a chance to look at her in a little while. I am to take you to supper, so it's not worth your while to go back to your own quarters; you had best come back to mine for now."

"This also is your doing, isn't it," Thomas said, as they turned in through the arched doorway under the lantern. "And I have no wish to be thrust upon the Lady Amina for your whim." His tone made the words sound less harsh than they might otherwise have done.

"No such thing! It was arranged from the first that I was to bring you to supper after the reception if she approved of you. And she does, so I am. Besides, there'll be an old friend of yours there."

"Colonel D'Esurier?"

"Not this time. Too busy with his guns for the Sudan expedition. Oh Tho'mas, I wish—"

Thomas checked a moment at the foot of the stair. "Not Donald MacLeod?"

"Still in the Delta, so far as I know." Clearly Tussun cared very little for the whereabouts of the other Scot, "No, your Captain Zeid ibn Hussein."

"Zeid! What is he doing here?"

Tussun shrugged. "Ask my father. They seem to have been together, my brother Ibrahim also, most of the day."

An hour later Thomas and Zeid came face to face before the threshold of the Vicereine's private apartments, and embraced joyfully then stood back at arm's length to gladden their eyes with the sight of each other.

"Zeid! I did not know that you were in Cairo until Tussun Bey told me one hour ago! How is it with the Bedouin Horse?"

"It is well with the Bedouin Horse. And with you? They tell me that the thing is done, and by the Grace of Allah you are of the Faith."

"I am of the Faith, yes."

"And how are you named?"

"I am called Ibrahim, and I begin to grow used to it, but it is strange to lose one's own name."

"To the few of us who were your friends in the time before, I think that you will always be Tho'mas," Zeid said.

Each with a hand still on the other's shoulder, the two of them followed Tussun past the guards on the doorway.

The supper party was a very small one. Apart from the Vicereine and her daughter and younger son, only Thomas and Zeid and a burly dark-faced man with a sabre scar slashing through one eyebrow who was captain of the Vicereine's Albanian bodyguard; and the night being warm and humid, cushions and low tables had been carried out into the inner court of the old harem, which the Viceroy's ladies had taken for their private apartments, though they were in no way restricted to them, as women of earlier times had been. Small lamps hanging among the branches of rose and laurel and oleander shed a soft light that stirred a little with every movement of the air, and gave to the scene a faint magic which it would not have possessed within doors.

Slaves brought basins and ewers of rosewater for them to rinse their hands, then brass trays of kebabs and vine-wrapped dolmas and sweet saffron-flavoured mutton, surrounding the soft brown mounds of rice.

Thomas, making small neat balls of rice with his right hand only, sent grateful thoughts across the table to Zeid ibn Hussein doing the same on the far side, who had taught him the table manners of his new world during those months in the desert.

He was still taking care not to look at the Lady Nayli with too much attention, but it seemed that it was permitted now to glance at her, and answer her when she spoke without looking away, for both the other guests as well as Tussun were including her easily in the conversation round the table, and little by little he began to do the same. Both ladies had laid aside their veils altogether, the Vicereine to reveal a strong face, full-blown rather than fleshy, broad boned and clear eyed, with a warmly generous mouth. The face of a woman who would rule her household so skilfully, the iron hand hidden in its velvet glove, that they would seldom realise that they were being ruled at all. Thomas remembered that she was reputedly the person who, of all those surrounding him, had the most influence over the Viceroy.

The first thing he noticed about Nayli with her face unveiled was how young she was. At the reception, with only her kohl-painted eyes to judge by, he had thought her older than himself. Now she looked to be little older than Tussun, a girl with a charming wilful face, an unformed childish mouth that showed little white teeth, almost like milk teeth when she laughed; and too much eyepaint on her lids.

The meal had ended with dates and dried figs and honeyed pastries, the coffee and the violet sherbet went round again; and when the men returned from the evening call to prayer, the little group in the lantern light melted into new shapes, leaning back for greater ease of digestion or forward in the eagerness of talk.

An argument which, so far as Thomas could make out, seemed to have something to do with the Turkish occupation of

85

Yannina had broken out between the four Albanians. It had been conducted in French at first, like the rest of the conversation at the supper table; but as it grew more fiery it slipped more and more into their native tongue. Thomas and Zeid, feeling that they had no part to play in what seemed to be rapidly becoming a kind of enjoyable family quarrel, seized their chance and drew back a little, settling themselves under a pomegranate bush to talk more quietly of their own affairs. News of the desert and the city were exchanged, and inevitably before long the talk turned to the Sudan expedition, plans for which were now definitely taking shape.

"Your report has borne fruit, then," Thomas said.

"Mine and a good few more."

"It will give you your chance." There was raw envy in Thomas's voice for the unguarded moment.

"That is as Allah wills." Zeid played gently with the amber-studded hilt of his dagger in the way he had when there was neither hawk nor saluki to caress. "Your chance also."

"Oh no, not mine. I heard two days since – the Viceroy, as you will know, is taking a personal interest in the choice of all officers for the expedition, and it seems that I am to continue here as training officer for the new enlistment."

"I wondered what the sorrow was," Zeid said.

"Does it show so clearly?"

"Only to those who know you well. My friend, there will be need of good training officers."

"It is a task for older men than I."

"And it matters so deeply?"

"Yes," Thomas said.

He was watching the four figures in the full glow of the lamplight, one in particular: Tussun, leaning forward into the heart of the light, bright eyed, flushed and fiery with argument, his hands flashing in expression of his thoughts.

Tussun was to go with the expedition; he and his two regiments, under the overall command of Ibrahim Pasha. Tussun looking at this moment younger than his not quite seventeen years, wearing his youth like a kind of bloom upon him; the sideways fall of the lantern light throwing up the strong vein at the side of his neck, where life and youth could so easily be spilled out.

"Remember he is older than he looks at this moment," said

Zeid's voice at half breath beside him. "Old enough to be fathering sons; and has seen weapons used in anger before now."

Thomas looked round to meet his friend's faintly quizzical gaze.

"Oh I know, he can look after himself well enough."

"But not so well as you could look after him? Thomas, my friend, your presence in the Sudan will not turn aside a tribesman's bullet, nor will your absence let it fly more truly to its mark. All that is as Allah wills."

"Blessed be the name of Allah, the All Merciful." Thomas turned the conversation, which had strayed a little too near the quick for comfort. "It is not that alone. You will be going. All the men I have worked with. I shall be mewed up here, training new recruits not to drop their musket stocks on their toes. What chance is that?"

"There'll still be need for good training officers. Let the glory wait for another day."

Thomas was staring safely down at his own hands now, not really listening. "I have been wondering whether it might serve any purpose if I were to make a personal application to the Viceroy."

"None at all, I should think," Zeid said, "but there could be no harm in trying. Tomorrow's audience after the war council would be as good a time as any."

"My brother says he does not think that you can play the zither," said a girl's voice above him, and Thomas looked up to see the Lady Nayli standing over him, and got hurriedly to his feet. "Is that true?"

"I fear that it is true."

"Then can you sing? We have worn the argument threadbare and now we are in the mood for a little music-making."

"Truly – I have no skill—" Thomas protested.

"Everyone can sing if they try," the Lady Nayli informed him, laughing. "Come back out of those unsociable shadows and sing for us now."

"Nayli, do not tease him!" the Vicereine added her warm throaty voice to her daughter's clear high one. "But truly – one of your own Scottish songs? Will you not try for our pleasure? You are among friends, and I can promise that you will not find us an over-critical audience."

"Madame – if it is a command—"

"It is a request."

And therefore the more difficult to refuse without appearing churlish. Thomas found himself drawn back into the central group, trying desperately to think which song out of the Edinburgh streets and parlours of his boyhood would please the Viceroy's ladies. It had to be one that he could manage without making more of a fool of himself than need be.

Oddly, it was Nayli's words that gave him the answer. "Come back out of these unsociable shadows."

Come back – Come back . . .

"I will try," he said. "This is a song that was made by a lady – Lady Nairne – for Prince Charles Edward, though indeed he was dead long since when she made it. It tells him how much his own folk long for him, and asks him to come back."

He cleared his throat selfconsciously, sat up straight on his cushion, and began, shakily at first, but steadying and relaxing as he went:

> Bonnie Charlie's now awa',
> Safely o'er the friendly main;
> Many a heart will break in twa'
> If he ne're comes back again.

He had in fact a pleasant enough voice, young and true, though without much range, and with the faintly rough edges of his Lowland Scottish heritage. Also he was discovering, as he was to rediscover often enough, that though he had given himself fully to his new world, embraced another faith and other loves, he was not proofed against homesickness, now and then, for the world that he had left behind him. And that, though he was quite unaware of it, was giving an ache to his voice that suited the song well.

> . . . Will ye no' come back again?
> Will ye no' come back again?
> Better lo'ed ye canna be
> Will ye no' come back again?

Silence closed over the last lingering note; and in the silence the faint sounds of Cairo by night that he had been unaware of until now, came drifting over the flat roof tops into the court of the old harem, where the lanterns hung among their bushes of oleander and jasmine. A seashell murmur made up of feet and voices and hooves and threads of other music, pricked by the bark of a scavenging dog, hoot of an owl from the trees around the maidan, challenge and reply of sentries somewhere at a gate; and infinitely small and sad and far off, on the very edge of hearing, the cry of a hunting jackal that was the very voice of the desert itself.

"Sing again!" Nayli demanded imperiously, her face flushed in the lantern light. "I like your Scottish song. Sing another!"

"To a guest and a singer of songs, it is better to ask than to demand," said the Vicereine, and to Thomas, "You do yourself an injustice, Ibrahim Effendi, when you say that you have not the gift of singing. Will you sing for us again?"

Tussun said nothing, but his eyes met Thomas's asking also, but not able to ask easily and in words because of that faint unacknowledged barrier that was still between them. And it was for Tussun, a kind of reaching out across the barrier that would still be there when the song was over, that Thomas sang again. A much older and rougher song than the first, and one that he had known as long as he could remember.

"I will sing you 'The Foster Brother'," he said. A second time he explained the words, somewhat hesitantly, for his French, learned from his grandfather and the Leith Academy French master and among the Viceroy's troops, seemed to him suddenly to be somewhat inadequate for the translating of songs. And the translation was for the Vicereine and her daughter, but the song was for Tussun alone:

> Alas, Alas, quo' bold Robert,
> For we were brithers bred,

he sang, having as usual a little trouble with the top notes.

> And sucked we at the ae breast,
> And lay in the ae bed.

> Wild callants were we baith,
> Chasing the red deer herd;
> Each weel kenn'd the ither's hert
> Nor needed never a word.

89

Twa' gallants braw were we,
Tae lo'e ae bonnie May,
Oh, woe betide yon fauce fair face,
Wha' tell'd ye ill o' me.

Wha twined me frae my brither dear,
Closer tae me than kin.
Oh, I would ride through flood an' fire
Tae stand by thee again . . .

Oh, I wad ride the wide world ower,
A thousand leagues and three,
Tae see my brither's face once mair,
And ken he trusted me.

But when the song was ended and he drew his gaze back from
the dark shadows under the oleander bushes, he found himself
meeting the brilliant gaze of the Lady Nayli that seemed to have
been waiting for him all the while. The Vicereine's gentle
praises were in his ears, but for the moment he saw only her
daughter's sloe-dark eyes lifted to his with something in them
that brought the blood surging up from his neck to the roots of
his hair, as though, despite his translation, she had maybe been
hearing other words to the old haunting tune than those he had
actually been singing.

Chapter 9

Thomas took great care with his appearance on the day of the Viceroy's levée, settling the folds of his tawny camelhair abba again and again across his shoulders and fiddling with the gold-fringed muslin folds of his turban-scarf, until the grey-bearded one, who could have done it all much better without interference, clucked like an impatient mother hen.

There was a large proportion of high-ranking army officers in the Viceroy's State majlis, following the morning council. Turkish and Albanian, a few narrow-eyed and wind-burned desert faces, a handful of Mamelukes. (Nothing, Thomas thought, could show more clearly the deep divisions in that strange breed than the men of the Turkish faction, the court faction still keeping up their splendid fighting-cock presence here in Cairo, while the war council made its plans for the expedition against their own kind in the south.) The young Scot, checking with ibn Hussein to slip off his shoes in the sunken area by the entrance, knew most of them by sight, best of all Aziz Bey, staring at him from among a knot of young Mamelukes near the door. He scarcely bothered to return the stare; he was growing used to being watched by Aziz Bey and anyhow he had other things in the forefront of his mind at the moment. He went on with the Bedouin captain to a seat on one of the divans further up the chamber.

The levée was as slow and pompous as such occasions generally were, and he waited with hard-held patience for the best part of an hour. He must not show undue haste, yet to wait too long might be to miss his chance . . . Without turning his head he whispered to Zeid at his shoulder: "Now?"

"Now," the other whispered back. "May Allah smile upon you."

Thomas caught the eye of one of the officials, and when the man came over, gave him his name and rank, and asked him to crave that His Excellency would grant him a few moments' audience.

He saw the message given, the glance flick his way, the faint brusque inclination of the head. The official returned to summon him. Then he was on one knee before the dais, looking up into the brigand-bold face bent slightly towards him. His heart hammering in the base of his throat, he waited for permission to speak.

"You have a favour that you wish to ask of me, Ibrahim Effendi?"

"Excellency."

"Speak then."

"Sir, I understand that I am to remain in Cairo as a training officer during the Sudan expedition. I beg you to have the order rescinded and allow me to formally volunteer for the campaign." He had spoken not loudly, but very clearly, taking pains that every word of his careful French could be heard by those assembled in the Viceroy's majlis, for he had an instinct that this was a thing that must be done very much in public.

It was heard well enough by one of the Mameluke officers sitting just within the door; and even before the Viceroy could answer, Aziz Bey was on his feet. "Excellency, I protest!"

The frown-line deepened between Muhammed Ali's thick brows. "Aziz Bey, you forget your manners!"

"No, Excellency, I remember that I am a true follower of the Prophet, as are the men of all Your Excellency's regiments. We need no apostate Christian in our ranks, nor do we need a British deserter to show us the way of loyalty and faith keeping, a coward to show us the way of courage!"

Righteous indignation blazed in his face. But Thomas, not looking round, caught the ugly note of triumph, of jealousy that thought it had found a way of evening the score. He had thought something like this might happen; almost, he was prepared for it, and he braced himself as in the moment before a fight. His eyes never left the Viceroy's face, but his head snapped up on tensed neck, and he cried out the traditional Arabic phrase:

"I ask for judgment, Oh Lord!"

He felt rather than heard the stir of alerted interest in the crowded majlis. "In the name of Allah the All Compassionate I ask Your Excellency's leave to answer to these charges in my own defence."

The Viceroy pulled gently at his beard; no special interest

showed in his face, but no hostility either. "You may stand up. It is easier to speak on one's feet than on one's knees."

"I thank Your Excellency."

In the act of rising to his feet, Thomas made a quick decision. He could not speak Turkish well enough for the purpose, and in any case, the Turkish officers, like the Mamelukes, would inevitably side with Aziz Bey. If he spoke in French, that would make it easy for the Viceroy, but Muhammed Ali had his extremely competent Arabic interpreter beside him, and the men whose goodwill he, Thomas, felt that he could depend on were the men of the desert.

Standing like a lance before the Viceroy, he began to speak in slow, but reasonably correct Arabic:

"Excellency, Aziz Bey has named me apostate. I was bred a Christian; I have studied the Koran and walked among the Faithful, and my heart has told me that the way of Allah is the way for me. Is that so wrong? When has Islam ever rejected sincere converts?"

Again came the stir and the indrawn breath behind him.

"Excellency, Aziz Bey has called me a British deserter." He checked, though the pause was barely perceptible, save to those who knew him well. This bit needed care. "British I am, by birth; for the rest, I was wounded and taken prisoner; I have come to know and love the men among whom I have served this past year. I can say no more than this: that I come of a race many of whom follow the wandering ways of the wild goose that take us far from our own land; that many of us sell our swords honourably to other lands of our choice, and, having made the sale, keep our side of the bargain to the death. Aziz Bey has called me a coward; if I were so, would I be volunteering now for the campaign in the south, when I could be sitting safely here in Cairo?"

The interpreter, his lips scarcely moving, translated the words almost as they were spoken.

Thomas heard his enemy begin a furious interruption, quelled by other men near him and drawing no flicker of response from the Viceroy, and pressed on:

"Excellency, Aziz Bey has spat upon my honour three times, and among my own hills it is the custom that a man may defend his honour with his sword. I demand that right now."

Behind him this time there was absolute silence. The Viceroy

93

blinked; it was a long time since anyone had demanded of Muhammed Ali, Viceroy of Egypt. Thomas's gaze never swerved from his face, and it seemed to him that he could follow something of what was going on behind it. If he allowed the duel and his Scottish training officer was killed, that would be little loss, though doubtless his young son would grieve for a while. If on the other hand Aziz Bey were to die, that would remove one of the Mamelukes, who was like enough spying on him for the Sultan; and in any case the Ottoman government could scarcely lay the blame at his door, since Aziz had blatantly invited the challenge before all men. If neither should be killed (Thomas was aware that in Egypt, as in Britain, such affairs of honour were supposed to be ended by first blood, though they were frequently fatal all the same), then neither good nor harm would come of it, so far as he was concerned.

He saw the Viceroy come to his decision.

"To each man the care of his own honour," said Muhammed Ali. "The thing is between you and Aziz Bey."

Thomas bowed. "I thank Your Excellency." For the first time he turned from the Viceroy and looked full at his enemy, and for an instant before it was shut away behind a mask of mere disdain, met a blaze of hate such as he had never seen in any man's face before.

He walked across to the Mameluke officer, who rose to meet him as he came. For a few moments it looked crazily as though the fight was going to begin then and there, with as little ceremony as though two hunting leopards had been loosed in the Viceroy's majlis.

Then Thomas said in his best French: "Aziz Bey, you have named me by evil names, Apostate, Deserter, Coward, and for that I will have satisfaction," and lacking a glove to do the thing in proper form, he flicked the back of his hand lightly, insultingly across the other's face.

An odd expression flickered into the hot blue eyes that widened a little while the dark colour flooded into his cheeks: the hate that had shown before for that unguarded moment, but also a gleam of satisfaction. Thomas recognised it, knowing that Aziz was as set upon this duel as he was himself, knowing also that the young Mameluke was accounted one of the best swordsmen in the Viceroy's army.

He felt – he was not at all sure how he felt; but he knew that the thing was destined between them; had been destined since the moment their eyes first met on the dusty parade ground at El Jizzan.

Two hours before sunset of the following day, the maidan within the citadel was crowded, save for an enclosure marked off with silken ropes at the western end, where cushions had been set for the Viceroy's sons and a few senior officers. The crowd were making wagers. Thomas, used to the idea that an affair of honour was fought out in the quiet of early morning with no witnesses but the seconds and a surgeon, had not realised that he and Aziz Bey would be the centre of something very like a prize fight or a popular hanging. He wondered what Colonel D'Esurier would have thought of it if he had not been in the Delta overseeing the shipment of guns from Alexandria.

The sky behind the citadel mosque was translucent crystal, and the shadow of the great dome lay all across the maidan though there was still an hour or more of good fighting light left. Thomas, standing stripped to the waist, with Zeid and a knot of Arab and Albanian friends and supporters, felt the faint stirring of the cooler evening air on his skin, saw the umber and indigo mass of the mosque bulked against the singing western sky, the delicate veining of a plane leaf near at hand, caught the first charcoal smoke of evening cooking fires, mingling with the smell of hot humanity and sun-baked dust, all with the familiar sharp-edged awareness of the last moments before battle.

"Now remember what I have told you," Zeid, who had made the arrangements on his behalf, murmured beside him.

Thomas nodded. He remembered what Zeid had told him; all the good advice of the past twenty-four hours. If Colonel D'Esurier had been there, there would have been twice as much, probably much of it contradictory.

Tussun's advice there had been to contend with as well. Tussun, excited but wildly anxious, had demanded to be the one to act as his second, to make all the arrangements with the Mameluke officer acting for Aziz Bey. "Don't be a fool!" Thomas had told him. "You're the Viceroy's son, you can't get tangled up in this kind of thing." And Tussun had been forced to accept his refusal. But he would have liked to have had the boy standing here beside him, all the same, instead of just now coming into the roped enclosure with his elder brother and the rest of the viceregal party.

His gaze went that way for an instant, then returned to the far side of the maidan, where Aziz would be waiting somewhere among his own supporters. He felt the hilt of the broadsword in his hand, and his thoughts went for a moment to its last owner, fourteen months dead at Rosetta. He was glad that Aziz Bey, having of course, the right of choice in the matter, had chosen sabres. He was well enough trained in the use of both rapier and sabre; but he was happiest with the sabre, and with the superbly balanced blade that had been Colin MacKenzie's he was happiest of all.

There was a slight stir at the far side of the maidan, where the Mameluke and Turkish officers were gathered at the forefront of the crowd, and Aziz Bey, stripped also to baggy red breeches, tucked into the tops of leather boots, stepped out into the open space.

"Now," Zeid murmured.

Thomas stepped forward in almost the same instant, and walked out towards the centre. He turned first towards the little group in their roped-off space before the mosque, and, bringing up his sword, gave the Viceroy's sons the British General Salute. For an instant his gaze and Tussun's met. Then he turned away to exchange the fencer's salute in formal courtesy with Aziz Bey. He gave an appraising glance to the magnificent gold-hilted Turkish sabre the other carried. It was less curved and slightly longer than the one Thomas had seen him use in practice bouts. He must have heard from his second, of course, that he, Thomas had chosen to fight with his Scottish broadsword. Then he turned his whole awareness to the Mameluke's eyes. "Always watch the eyes," his grandfather had drummed into him. "Be aware of the sword hand, but always watch the eyes."

They engaged cautiously in conventional sabre style, getting the feel of each other, testing for strength and skill and speed of reaction. Thomas knew himself to be lacking in the other's strength and experience, but he thought his footwork was better and his responses more swift. He had just about reached that conclusion when Aziz broke into a series of swift feints and cuts to the arm and neck that demonstrated his skills all too clearly. Thomas managed to evade the sudden attack by giving ground, but giving ground was not going to bring him victorious out of this fight, nor – odd the things one thought of when it was really no time to be thinking them – would it do him credit in the eyes of the boy watching him from the roped-off enclosure.

He parried a dangerous cut to his right shoulder, and delivered a stop-thrust that just reached his opponent's breast without breaking the skin. He heard the quickly indrawn breath of the watching crowd above the pad of his own feet, and having brought Aziz to a momentary halt, he stood his ground before the next attack, using the old saltire defence learned from his grandfather in the Broomrigg stableyard. For maybe two or three minutes the unfamiliar swordplay slowed the Mameluke down; then he set himself to batter down Thomas's guard by sheer superiority of physical strength.

Thomas felt the jar of the strokes through his wrist and all up his arm; and then, just too slow to avoid a lunge in tierce, felt something like the fiery sting of a hornet on his left shoulder, and heard again the voice of the crowd like the breaking of a little choppy sea on a pebble shore.

Next instant his sword was bonded, the blade caught and locked by his enemy's just below the hilt. A straining instant more and it would go spinning. He was wrenched round and inward, his face only a few inches from that of Aziz Bey.

He had known well enough that Aziz hated and was jealous of him, that was what this was all about. But never before, even in the Viceroy's majlis yesterday, had he seen such a focused hatred as he saw now in the snarling face so near his own. It seemed to beat upon him, biting into his very soul. If he had known it in his mind before, he knew now suddenly to his heart's core that whatever the normal outcome of duelling in the modern world, Aziz meant to kill him. And trapped and struggling as he was, in the next few seconds he would probably do it.

Well, the thought flashed clear into his mind, if that was to be the way of it, he would soon know if he had done ill to change his faith.

The breath was strangling in his breast, blood pounding in heart and head as he fought to break the lock on his sword. 'Dear God help me! Receive me by whichever road . . .'

It was at that instant that Aziz Bey made a fatal mistake. Sensing the nearness of the Scotsman's breaking point and his own approaching moment of victory, he used his own superior strength to force him back and down, giving room for the final stroke, and in the triumphant contempt of the moment, spat full in his face.

The warm loathsome trickle on his cheek did for Thomas what nothing else could have done, rousing in him a red rage that ran through his body, carrying with it new strength that he had not known he possessed. With a supreme effort he broke the lock on his sword, and sprang back with it still in his hand, then leapt in again to the attack.

The smell of blood had come into the back of his nose and a faint scarlet mist seemed to hang before his eyes. But behind it, his brain was working cold and quick. His grandfather's training was in his very blood, and whereas, a little before, he had tried to use the saltire defence, he swung over now to the saltire attack, shedding French and Turkish swordplay and wielding the broadsword as his forebears had done at Killie-crankie and Preston Pans.

Aziz, who had thought himself already the victor, gave ground before the flashing fury that he had aroused and the alien form of attack, and then gave ground again. Thomas drove him back to the palace wall, the onlookers scattering to give them wide passage, without giving him the chance for a single riposte. Under the wall he drove a slashing cut to the forehead, locked the blade of the Mameluke's sabre under his own hilt – his turn now – and disarmed him with a grinding twist. Aziz's sword flew up in a half circle and came to ground ten or twelve feet away.

A sound that was almost a moan broke from the onlookers. The Mamelukes who a short while before had seen their man as already the winner, seeing him now as already dead; the Arabs and Albanians who had given up hope of their man, seeing him suddenly as the victor.

Thomas raised his sword to strike down his enemy. But the red mist was clearing, and he could not do it; not with the man standing there before him, unarmed, breast and flanks heaving like his own. He lowered the blade and stepped back, gesturing to the other to pick up his fallen sabre. Again he heard the gasp of the crowd. What a fool they must think him; some of them, not quite all. But watching the Mameluke stoop for his blade and turn back with it, feeling the first renewed kiss of blade on blade, he knew better than they did, better maybe than the man into whose eyes he was looking, that the fight was already over.

Aziz fought fiercely as ever, but his strategy and his rhythm were both beginning to desert him. At first he managed to thrust forward away from the wall, but with the next attack Thomas had him giving ground again, and yet again. He was almost back to the wall once more when Thomas, his own heart pounding and the sweat running into his eyes, found the clear opening that he needed, and took it. He feinted to the left cheek and drew the Mameluke's guard up, then lunged in under it, with all his strength for the throat, catching the desperate parry on his basket hilt.

He felt the blade strike home, saw the man's eyes widen in a sudden horrified stare above the red fountain that had opened in his throat. He dropped his sabre to claw at the place where his life was pumping out of him, and with a wet choking sound crumpled backwards to the ground.

Thomas stood where he was for a few moments, his flanks heaving, his heart drumming against his rib cage, the open space of the maidan and the roaring crowd pulsing on his sight. It was over, and he was alive and had the victory, and there was no sense of triumph in him, only a curious spent peace. He stopped and cleaned the stains from his sword in the soft dust, then drawing himself wearily to his full height saluted first the Viceroy's sons, and then, the sense of ritual strong within him, the sprawling body of the dead man at his feet, and turned to rejoin Zeid and his Arab friends who swung forward to greet and embrace him as though, he thought, with a twist of inner laughter, he had scored a goal at Shinty.

"Allah be praised!" Zeid was saying, "Allah be praised!"

It seemed that his God had not rejected him.

That evening, having washed off the dust and sweat of battle, had his shoulder dressed and put on a clean thobe Thomas supped with the Viceroy's sons in the private apartments of the elder.

Tussun's quarters were a wild and flamboyant mixture of luxury and squalor, fine weapons and cheap-jack Western artefacts, a hawk on its stand in the corner that had splashed black and white mutes down the wall and across the cushions of the divan, a highly inefficient mechanical coffee grinder standing on an exquisite inlaid cedarwood chest, a general state of chaos that survived all the attempts of his servants to maintain some sort of order. Ibrahim Pasha's apartments, in complete contrast, were sparsely furnished and full of cool empty space, in which the eyes could rest. No more furniture than was strictly necessary, scarcely anything for ornament, but what there was, beautiful. It was typical of the pasha in that it seemed the room of a man much older than his not quite twenty years.

After the stresses of the day, Thomas was glad of the space and quiet about him, and the company of Ibrahim Pasha, whom he liked and respected, as well as that of Tussun, which could light up the very air about him, but was never restful. He had not really wanted to eat, he had not before killed a man ritually and in personal anger, and the sick taste of it was with him yet, and he was glad when the meal was over. Now the communal pipe on its brass tray had been brought in, and they lounged at ease, in quiet fellowship, passing the beautiful amber mouthpiece from one to another.

"My friend," the pasha was saying, "whether or not you will be allowed to volunteer for the Sudan campaign, none but Allah and my father know. But you have proved today to all who were watching on the maidan, and I make no doubt from behind the palace window frets, that you are a fighting man of the kind that men make songs about."

"Did I not tell you?" said Tussun. His cheeks were flushed and his eyes shining. "Also, did I not give him his sword, for the love that I bear him?"

Ibrahim passed over the mouthpiece of the hookah to Thomas, who took it, looking with pleasure at the enamelled silverwork that zoned it round.

"Assuredly, you told. And I am thinking that tonight, if it is given to Major MacKenzie to know of this evening's work, he will be well enough satisfied with the hands into which his sword has fallen."

Thomas said quietly "I should like to believe that that was so."

He drew in a long breath, his eyes half closed, feeling the calming benison of the tobacco smoke filling his whole being.

Outside in the fountain court there sounded suddenly the ragged tramp of marching feet and a quick exchange of voices, and as the three men turned towards it, a knock came at the door.

Ibrahim Pasha called out the command to enter; a sentry opened the door and an officer of the Viceroy's guard appeared on the threshold, and checked there a moment as though not quite sure of his next move.

"You bring me some message from my father?" said Ibrahim Pasha. "Well come in and deliver it, man."

The officer advanced to the edge of the lamplight; and behind him, Thomas saw a group of soldiers drawn up, and felt a twisting uneasiness in his belly.

"My Lords," the man said, "the Viceroy your father commands your attendance upon him instantly."

"Why?" demanded Tussun bluntly.

The officer swallowed slowly staring straight in front of him. "One of the Sultan's ministers arrived this evening from Istanbul."

"And it is because of that, this so urgent command?" Tussun's gaze went past him through the open doorway, and he ignored his elder brother's warning hand on his wrist. "Do you normally bring half the Palace Guard to escort us to our father when he summons?"

"The escort is not for you, Tussun Bey, it is for Ibrahim Effendi – to the guardhouse. He is under arrest for killing an officer of the Ottoman army."

Chapter 10

"If you must continually choose yourself unworthy friends, you must not be surprised if your friendships are short-lived and come to a sorry ending."

"Ibrahim is *not* an unworthy friend, he is the best friend any man ever had! – you are cruel – Oh my father, I beg you—"

"You have begged enough. Get up," said the Viceroy icily. "Stop behaving like a hysterical woman and go to your quarters."

Tussun had lost his temper more completely than he had ever dared to do with his father before, until, several minutes of storming having made no dent in the Viceroy's decision, he had panicked, and flung himself at his father's feet to beg for Thomas's life.

Muhammed Ali withdrew his feet slightly. He disliked lack of control. "Take him away," he said to his elder son, rather as though he were speaking of an ill-behaved puppy.

Ibrahim Pasha stooped and hauled his weeping brother to his feet, and with a not unkindly arm round the sobbing and still pleading boy, got him out of the private chamber and pushed him into the arms of Captain Zeid ibn Hussein waiting in the audience hall beyond.

"Take him back to my quarters and keep him there," he said "I'll come . . ."

Then he turned back into the private chamber and stood in silence before his father.

The Viceroy seemed to feel his silence as accusation. He signalled to the two confidential members of his bodyguard who had been standing unobtrusively in a window recess; and when they were gone, said wearily, "Do not talk to me of justice and injustice."

"I have said no word," Ibrahim Pasha retorted.

"And sit down! Why should I speak with a son who stands before me like a cypress tree, giving me a pain in the back of the neck."

Ibrahim Pasha sat down on the cushion at his father's feet, but continued to look like a cypress tree none the less.

"Justice is a luxury, a matter for private life. It must give way to such considerations as the safety of the State. I cannot afford to offend the Sultan or his Sublime Porte at this time. Maybe in three or four years I shall be strong enough, but not yet."

"Three or four years will be somewhat late for Ibrahim Bey, my Father."

"One man! Have I not this instant bidden you not to speak to me of justice? You must know, even if Tussun does not, that I have not signed the death warrant simply because an influential minister such as this Abbas Pasha has demanded it – on legally correct grounds, mark you. By the very fact of the demand being made there can be no doubt that Aziz was, as we always suspected, one of the Sultan's agents at this court; and for that very reason, I cannot afford to pardon his killer, however glad I may be that he is dead." He spread his big blunt hands. "It is unfortunate for Ibrahim Bey that Abbas Pasha arrived immediately after the duel – another week or two and we might have sent him back to Aswan for a while until the whole thing blew over."

Then, as Ibrahim remained silent, "You of all men should understand the pressures on a ruler set beneath a stronger ruler. It is not yet two years since you, my elder son, were still held hostage for my good behaviour, in Istanbul. Do you think that was a happy thing for me? I had no choice then; I have no choice now, though by the compassion of Allah there shall come a time when the Sultan shall beg favours of me!"

Ibrahim Pasha moved a little on his cushions, drawing a quick breath. "My father, I will not speak of justice, but there are two further aspects of this sorry business that, with respect, I would beg leave to submit to you."

"If you must." The Viceroy stirred fretfully. "Very well, but do not waste my time."

"In the first place, then, to make good your hold on an eventually free Egypt, you must, as you have explained to me before now, destroy the Mamelukes, and without further aid from the Sultan, but also without openly breaking with him until after the thing is done and Egypt brought back to some kind of economic prosperity. And you cannot accomplish this without the help of the Egyptians themselves. Forgive me, Sir:

you became Viceroy with the support of the Ulama of Cairo; and you will need this support, and the support of the people, and especially the new Bedouin cavalry regiments, when it comes to freeing us of the Mamelukes and then, Insh' Allah, of the Sultan and his Sublime Porte. Over the past few months Ibrahim Bey has made himself a liked and honoured place among Bedouin and Egyptian troops and officers alike. Last evening's fight will have added to his popularity; and to sacrifice him – as it will appear to them – merely to please a Turkish minister, will raise some feeling against you, and what is worse, it will be interpreted as weakness. That could be dangerous."

"There are times," said Muhammed Ali, looking with exasperation at the thick-set young man before him, whom he could not love as he loved his beautiful and infuriating younger son, "when I wish that Tussun possessed a quarter of your understanding of political issues . . . But as for the part which the Egyptians and Arabs will play in possible future events, yes, we shall need their support, but I think that you overestimate their ability and our need of them. We shall rule Egypt when the time comes, through senior officers and administrators drawn from among the most suitable of our own Albanians and from the many Turks who will undoubtedly side with us against the Ottoman rule, which even *they* can hear beginning to creak like an irrigation wheel. The Egyptians will provide useful junior officers and civil servants. The Bedouin cavalry will be useful for a while, I grant you. What is your second point?"

Ibrahim bowed his head in acknowledgment that there was no more to be said on the first point; he had enough sense to know, as Tussun never knew it, when to abandon an argument or at least shift his ground. "My Father, despite what has passed between you and my brother a while since, Ibrahim Bey is the best friend Tussun has ever had. He has become a very good influence – the boy has steadied quite noticeably in the past few months. If you intend, as I think you do, to make Tussun an army commander in a few years' time, Ibrahim Bey could develop into the ideal chief of staff for him."

"A Scottish armourer's apprentice, a deserter from the British army, who has a knack with weapons and horses?"

"He is more than a swordsman and a horseman, he is highly intelligent and developing an interest beyond the day-to-day in military affairs – I have talked with him from time to time –

104

enough to know that. Also he is a man whom other men will follow; I have watched him at practice and wished that I had his élan. Above all, Tussun listens to him as he will listen to no one else."

Muhammed Ali tugged at his splendid moustache in silence a few moments. But in the end, regretfully, he shook his head. "I believe that you are right. If it were possible to spare the Scotsman's life, I would do so. As it is, the mistiming of events leaves me no choice. I have given my word to Abbas that the execution shall take place tomorrow morning. I have signed the warrant and I cannot go back on it, lest I give the Sultan the chance I know he would be glad of to call my stewardship to account." He shifted abruptly:

"It is finished. Go after your brother, and keep him from any act of folly."

Ibrahim recognised defeat.

He got up, bowed to his father, and left the room.

He headed back for his own quarters, entered by a postern door, and rooting out ibn Salik who had been his personal body servant since he was a child, gave him certain orders concerning wine for his brother and the captain who would be waiting in his majlis – Praise be to Allah the All Merciful, the Viceroy's household were not overstrict in obeying the dictates of the Koran with regard to alcohol. Wine was better than coffee at cloaking the taste of what was put into it, and Tussun would probably drink it where he would have refused coffee.

Then he went to the old harem, to his mother's apartments, and when she had sent her women away, gave her a detailed account of what had happened, and all that had passed between him and his father.

She already knew about the death sentence. Ibrahim Pasha had never ceased to marvel at the speed with which everything that happened throughout the court, throughout the whole of Cairo, was known in his mother's apartments. But she listened to him with quiet attention, only the slim line between the brows betraying that she felt any anxiety. When he had done, she asked, "What of Tussun?"

"In my quarters with Zeid ibn Hussein, by now deeply and safely asleep. Zeid too, I fear. I could not spare the time for elaborate plans to make sure that one got drugged wine and the other not."

She bent her head in agreement. "That was well done; we can do without a rescue attempt. I think, though, I am glad it is you and not I who will have to make your peace with both of them later." There was even a trace of amusement in her voice. "And so now, having failed with my Lord your father, you are come to me."

"I have heard – who has not? – that you are the only person who has any influence on him, my Mother."

"I doubt if my influence is strong enough for this," said the Vicereine. "But I think it is just possible that I may have certain powers of persuasion over our guest from Istanbul."

"But, Mother, you do not even know him!"

"No, but I know something about him – I have good friends who from time to time make me little presents for use at just such times as this." She smiled softly and warmly into her son's surprised face. "It may be enough, it may not. I make no promises, but I will try. You will visit Tho'mas? I think that he should not be left to think that Tussun has abandoned him."

"I am going to the guardhouse as soon as I leave you, my Mother."

"So, that is well. Tell him that he has friends; tell him that we are trying to save him. But tell him also that if we fail, we shall not easily forget him."

As soon as her son was gone the Lady Amina called for her most trusted among the harem eunuchs and sent him to fetch Captain Ballatar. Then she went to her little gilded escritoire, and wrote a short note. She was sanding and sealing it when the captain arrived.

"Do you know in which apartments Abbas Pasha has been housed?" she asked.

The man's dark, scarred face showed surprise, and a certain hastily suppressed curiosity. "Yes, Lady, His Excellency is lodged in the Shirkup rooms in the north-west wing."

"Then will you give him my compliments; say how much I regret disturbing him at this late hour, but that I should be grateful if he will do me the honour of paying me a short visit – without delay. If he makes excuses or seems unwilling, then give him this note. If not, then keep it close and return it to me later."

Captain Ballatar's battered countenance showed surprise

106

quite clearly this time, and concern; he was an old and trusted friend.

The Vicereine laughed softly. "Do not worry, my friend; if I am playing with fire, it is not the kind you fear, and I know how to handle it." She gave the scented billet into his hand. "And, Captain, on the way, double the guards in the corridors, and bid your men be at their most alert and salute the minister most punctiliously. Also, when you have escorted him here, remain on guard yourself outside the door, and let him know that you do so. He may be here some time."

Captain Ballatar saluted, and went off to carry out his orders.

As soon as he was gone, and the door safely shut behind him, the Lady Amina went into her bedchamber, locking the door behind her. She opened a great blackwood chest standing in an alcove, and lifted out and unlocked a box of ancient and curiously fretted ironwork lined with fragrant sandalwood. She thrust aside handfuls of gold and silver, coral and turquoise and amber – the jewellery she least often wore, but which yet did not merit a place in her husband's treasury. Underneath it all she withdrew an almost invisible pin and, lifting out the false bottom over a shallow hiding place, went quickly but carefully through several packets of letters and documents within; found the one she wanted and withdrew one sheet, then returned all the rest to their hiding place, piled turquoise and amber and milky moonstones back over all, and returned the jewel box to the blackwood chest. Then she returned to her private salon to await her visitor.

Thomas sat on the edge of the trestle bed in the narrow guardhouse cell. It was late, but he had no desire to lie down. He was so tired, with a kind of stunned exhaustion, that if he lay down he might even fall asleep, and it seemed a waste to spend the last night of one's life in sleeping.

He could still not really understand what had happened, could not quite believe that it had happened at all. The face-change had come about with such nightmare suddenness. He had gone out to fight his duel with Aziz Bey with the full permission of the Viceroy, and he could have sworn, the support of his sons and the whole Egyptian and Arab section of the Court, and afterwards he had gained the distinct impression that he himself had been the only person of his acquaintance to

107

find that the killing of the Mameluke interfered with his supper. And now, here he sat in the guardhouse cell, condemned without trial to die in the morning for the death of an officer of the Imperial Ottoman forces – and dead already, it seemed, to the men he had called his friends: Zeid – Tussun . . .

He shook his shoulders, what could Zeid or Tussun, even Ibrahim Pasha, do against the decree of the Viceroy? But he might have been allowed visitors – one visitor. Och, but what good would that do? Did he really want the boy here, tearing his own heart out with sorrow: making the parting harder for both of them. Better for them both, like this.

His mind did not go back to his boyhood, even to Broomrigg among the low, green Border Hills. It did not seem strange that nobody in Edinburgh would ever know what had happened to him. That was all part of another world. There was an old tune running in his head:

> Oh, I will ride the wide world o'er,
> A thousand leagues an' three,

But even that belonged to his present world, because of the night he had sung it under the pomegranate shadows in the Vicereine's courtyard.

> Tae see my brither's face aince more,
> An' ken he trusted me.

He watched the frantic fluttering of a moth whirling its own dark shadow about and about the smoky flame of the small palm-oil lamp in its niche. He saw the exact colour of the sky, deep green beyond the bars of the high narrow window, and one star like an infinitely small white flower adrift in it. He heard the tramp of the sentry outside.

If he could avoid thinking about yesterday, all the yesterdays, surely he could keep from thinking about tomorrow.

The moth blundered into the lamp flame and fell singed and sodden in the oil, so that the light burned steady again. The pale star moved from the space between the second and third bars to the space between the third and fourth. The sentry's feet passed and re-passed.

Then other feet came hollow-sounding along the corridor and halted outside the door. He heard the rattle of bolts being slid back, and as he turned to face it the door swung open. For an instant he thought that it was Tussun, but the shadow against the wall sconce outside was thicker than Tussun's. Ibrahim Pasha entered and the door clanged to behind him.

Thomas got up, but the visitor gestured to him to sit down again, and himself took his seat on the rough wooden stool below the window.

For a long moment the two looked at each other in silence, even the Viceroy's son a little at a loss to know how to begin; Thomas wondering why with Ibrahim Pasha he always felt himself in the presence of a man his father's age.

"I come to bring you certain messages from my mother," the pasha said at last. "But first I must explain to you why it is I who come, and not my brother."

"No explanation is necessary," Thomas said stiffly.

"Ah, but we both know that it is. And the explanation is simple enough. I have had him drugged. In all probability Zeid also, who I have ordered to keep him close in my quarters, and who will no doubt have shared the wine I had sent for them. Tussun has already called down our father's wrath upon himself for the forcefulness of his pleas and protests on your behalf; and left at liberty he might very well try to break you out of here by force, which would end in your instant death and probably the deaths of several other men beside. I am sorry that, to prevent that, I have had to take a course which has also prevented him from coming to you now."

"Maybe it is a well," Thomas said. "Better without leave-takings."

There was a small pause. Then Ibrahim Pasha said, "It is only right that I should tell you, though I cannot imagine that you will find much comfort in it, that the Viceroy himself regrets the action which events have forced on him. If an important Ottoman minister had not by ill-chance arrived within a few hours of Aziz's death, and demanded the full rigours of the law, there would have been no question of anything but the lightest and most nominal of penalties in your case."

"It is as Allah wills," Thomas said.

"The Beneficent, the Most Merciful. The message from my

mother is that you are not without friends who will continue their efforts to save you. That you should not lose heart, but that I should not buoy you up with false hope."

"It is good to know that I have friends. Will you thank the Lady Amina, and tell her that I thought I had the Viceroy's permission; and that in any case I did not set out to kill Aziz, until it became obvious that he meant to kill me." Thomas could not keep a trace of bitterness out of his voice.

"Under Egyptian law such duels are to the first blood only, not to the death. For a duel to the death a different sanction is required. We should have made that clear to you." Ibrahim Pasha gave a faint hitch to his shoulders, a hint of a rueful smile. "Though what good that could have done is not clear, seeing that Aziz Bey did indeed set out to kill you."

Thomas found himself returning the smile. "Did I not say it is the will of Allah?" He hesitated and his voice tightened in his throat. "There is a question I should like to ask, Excellency."

"Ask then."

"How will the execution be carried out?"

"By a quick and clean method," Ibrahim Pasha said quickly. "The headsman's sword. The executioner here in the citadel prides himself he never needs more than one stroke."

"In my own country, only the great ones of the earth used to be honoured with beheading," Thomas said, looking at his hands lying across his knee. "For lesser men it was – it is – a hanging matter. I am glad that I shall not dance my life out on the end of a hangman's rope."

"Remember there is still hope, though admittedly a slim one," said the pasha. He got up, Thomas instantly, if wearily, following suit. "I shall visit you again at dawn; but in the meantime is there anything that I can have done for you? Some wine perhaps?"

Thomas shook his head. "Not that, I thank you, Sir. But if I may ask a favour – Two who I value as friends are with General Ahmed Bonaparte in the Delta, an army surgeon, Donald MacLeod, and a young Albanian soldier, Medhet by name, who has the makings of a fine officer. If ever you can do so, will you befriend them for my sake?"

"That I can promise. Ahmed Agha shall know that their well-being is of great concern to me; and they shall be taken into the Viceroy's service as soon as the opportunity arises. Also they shall know that you thought of them at this hour. But is there nothing now for you yourself?"

Almost to Thomas's surprise his new faith remained strong with him at that moment. "If a soldier could fetch my Koran from my quarters, I should be very grateful, Sir."

Their eyes met, and Thomas, who had long since realised that the Viceroy's elder son was a just man, but despite his friendly aspect a cold one who made few real friends, saw with surprise the sympathy and regret, almost the warmth, in the other man's gaze. "You shall have your Koran with you in a few minutes. But try to get an hour or two of sleep if you can. All things are easier to face if one has had even a little sleep."

He crossed to the door and gave a single sharp rap on it with the hilt of his dagger. As it opened, he said, "My mother bids me tell you that if we fail, we shall none of us easily forget you."

"My thanks to the Lady Amina," Thomas said. "If we are allowed to carry memory with us, I shall remember also."

Ibrahim Pasha checked a last moment in the doorway. "The Peace of Allah the All Merciful be with you, my friend."

"And with you, Ibrahim Pasha."

Chapter 11

At almost the same time as Ibrahim Pasha was leaving the guardhouse, the Vicereine, with only one of her women in attendance, was greeting her visitor with a charming show of pleasure, thanking him for yielding to her whim by coming to visit her at such short notice, ordering coffee and sweetmeats to be brought.

Settled over coffee and a dish of plump dates and rose-flavoured lokoums she began to ask after mutual friends in Istanbul.

Abbas Pasha, a man built on much the same lines as the silken cushions on which he sat, responded with light and easy chat, but there was an abstracted look about him, as though he was perhaps scuttling about his own mind in search of the real reason behind the summons, as though he had perhaps noticed the large number of well-armed soldiers on duty in the chambers and corridors through which he had passed, and was remembering the number of ministers like himself who had met with unfortunate accidents in Cairo over the past years. Certainly he was aware of Captain Ballatar posted immediately outside the door. And the Vicereine, refilling the coffee cups, read his face with interest.

She was less accustomed to the tortuous and convoluted diplomacy of the Ottoman ruling circles than was Abbas Pasha, but she was a woman, which gave her a certain advantage in any case, and a clever one, and perfectly able to keep the Turkish minister talking all night if she wished, leading him around in graceful circles without ever coming to the point. On this occasion, however, she had no desire to keep up polite conversation longer than the customs of courtesy demanded.

Leaning back against rose- and saffron-coloured cushions, nibbling lightly as a butterfly at a sticky sweetmeat, as though she had indeed all night to spare, she led the conversation to a common acquaintance in Parga, who had died the previous year.

Finally she had reached the starting point for the actual business of the evening. "Such a sad loss to his friends," she said on a note of gentle regret, signalling to the woman sitting unobtrusively in the shadows to come forward again and pour yet more coffee. "Do you remember, I wonder, the letter which you wrote from his house to another friend of mine, Ali Pasha Tepedelenhi" – a soft purr of amusement – "the Lion of Yannina I think they call him, in the summer of ten years ago?"

Abbas Pasha slopped a trickle of coffee over the rim of his cup, and glanced warningly at the woman in the shadows.

The Vicereine sounded faintly amused. "Do not be uneasy. Ayesha is both deaf and dumb. She can repeat nothing of what passes between us."

"Over the years I have had occasion to write to Ali Pasha many times, usually on behalf of the Sultan," Abbas said smoothly. "But I cannot say that I recall any particular letter from Parga in that year. He had fallen out with His Majesty and the Sublime Porte over the pacification of Sula and I scarcely think I would have sent him any letter at that time except on the Sultan's orders."

"This was certainly not written on the Sultan's orders," the Lady Amina said in a velvet voice. "I fear that your memory is not so good as once it was, Abbas Pasha, but alas, that comes to all of us, and it was a long time ago." She slipped a hand behind the silken cushions against which she leaned, brought out a single sheet of paper and held it towards him. "But you will not have forgotten your own handwriting."

The minister looked at the open sheet, and the olive of his face turned slightly green.

"Look at it closely," the soft voice insisted. "I am sure that there was no harm in it, none whatever; but such letters – unguarded – are so easily misunderstood, and, at that particular time, it might be misconstrued as being – almost seditious, would you not agree?"

The minister looked; and the greenish tinge deepened in his cheeks; his eyes bulged slightly, and he looked as though he might be going to be sick. "That page is neither signed nor dated nor addressed," he said at last.

"Not this page, no, but the first page is addressed and dated, the last page is signed. And my dear Minister, I have them all."

113

"I have heard it said of late years that the Lion of Yannina is a treacherous dog," said the minister as though to himself.

"Who has not? But one hates to speak ill of old friends – indeed, we are very distant kinsfolk, he and I." The Vicereine sighed. "It has been such a responsibility all these years since it came into my possession. I have so often wondered what I should do with it; and now – I would be so glad, Excellency, to return it to you."

Abbas Pasha muttered the word "forgery" but without conviction.

"Oh no, it is no forgery. On the other hand there is no copy, so far as I know, and with the original safely back in your hands, even if I were to possess a copy, it could be safely discounted as a forgery."

The Vicereine's tones had become brisker, more business-like.

The green tinge faded a little from the pasha's face, as the smell of a slow and ugly death grew fainter. Supposing that he could pay whatever the price was for getting that accursed letter back unseen by the Sultan . . . "I shall be most glad to receive back this letter, harmless though it is, from Your Highness," he managed a slightly wan smile. "Perhaps there is some way in which I can show my most sincere gratitude?"

"For myself, Excellency, nothing is required but the knowledge that I and all my family have in yourself a friend in the Imperial Divan. However there is one small matter in which you can do a service to the Sultan whom we both serve."

"On my friendship and influence so long as I remain a minister, you and His Highness can always depend. But what is the service which I can perform for the Sultan?"

"Oh, the merest trifle." The Vicereine's hand fluttered a little, and the page of the letter with it. "Owing to a misunderstanding – did I not say before, how easily misunder-standings can arise? – a misunderstanding resulting from the problems of Turkish-French-Arabic interpreting, a young soldier of great promise, British by birth and now a devout convert to Islam, whose only wish is to serve in the armies of the Ottoman Empire, has been condemned to death in the morning."

"The man who killed Aziz Bey?" the minister said, his eyes clinging to his own handwriting on the page the Vicereine held.

"Yes. He was not given properly to understand that the duel was to first blood only, and not to the death. Even so, he did not intend the killing. But you know how it is – an affair of honour – young men fighting in hot blood – a tragic mischance. You could of course not possibly know of the circumstance, and so very rightly you requested this young man's death. My son Ibrahim, whom I believe you know from his time in Istanbul, has put it to his father already that the death of so promising a young officer will be a loss to the Ottoman forces and therefore to the Sultan himself, but the Viceroy my husband has given you his word and signed the order, and feels that he cannot in honour rescind it. In deference to Your Excellency he has refused even to speak of the matter further."

The page of the letter flickered a shade nearer. Abbas Pasha, with a gracious inclination, put out one hand and received it, contriving to appear almost unaware of what he did. "As you say, Highness, I was not aware of the full circumstances behind this unfortunate affair. As a merciful man, I shall be delighted to relieve the Viceroy from his promise, and indeed to request him to rescind the execution order. As to the other pages of this letter . . ?"

"They are quite safe, in a place where it is not very convenient to reach them at this hour of night. They shall be with you before noon tomorrow; meanwhile you will wish to write a note to the Viceroy, relieving him from his promise and advising clemency. I am most grateful to Your Excellency for your understanding attitude. Will it be convenient if Captain Ballatar waits upon you in an hour to receive your letter?"

The minister got up, bowing deeply. The interview it seemed was over, and relief shone from him: "In less. In half an hour, Highness, the letter shall be ready."

Now that he could draw breath and spare a thought for his own danger he wondered what the Vicereine's real interest in the young man was. Maybe he was her lover. If so there might be capital to be made out of that one day.

Thomas must have slept after all, for suddenly the grey first light of dawn was seeping through the barred window to mingle with the last dregs of smoky lamplight in the room. The Koran lay open on the dirty mattress beside him, and someone was rattling back the bolts on the door.

His first thought was that they had come for him already, and something clutched like an ice-cold fist at his belly. But almost in the same instant he remembered that he had asked to be awakened early, in plenty of time to make his morning prayer.

But the man who entered past the guard carried a tray which he set down on the stool. "By the order of my Master Ibrahim Pasha," the man said. "My master bids me tell you that in an hour, after you have prayed and eaten, he will be with you."

There was a lamp on the tray also. Thomas smelled coffee, and sitting up saw small crusty loaves and a bowl of golden-dripping honeycomb, and wondered if the Egyptians were in the habit of giving their condemned men a good breakfast before their execution, or whether this bore some message of hope. But it was from Ibrahim Pasha so it was probably just a kindly gesture, with no other significance either way. It would be easier if he knew. Easier even in the matter of prayer. It was not easy to pray if one did not know if the prayer was to be that of a man going to die and asking, amongst other things, courage to die in such a way as would not shame either himself or his friends, or the prayer of a man giving thanks for a reprieve. Not that he imagined there was much likelihood of that.

A few moments later he heard the long-drawn call of morning prayer from the minaret of the citadel mosque. He got up and turned himself as well as he could judge in the direction of Mecca and made the ordinary first prayer of the day. That would serve in either case, and Allah the All Compassionate would know how to receive it.

Allah is greater than all else,
Glory and praise to thee O Allah. Blessed is Thy name. Exalted is thy Majesty. Praise be to Allah, the Lord of the Worlds, the Merciful, the Compassionate, the Master of the Day of Judgment. Guide us all into the path of the Blessed. . . . Verily my prayers and my worship, my life and my death are unto Allah, the Lord of the worlds . . .

When he had finished praying, he drank some coffee, by now tepid and bitter, and then forced himself to eat a little of the bread, lest men should say afterwards that his belly had been too full of fear to allow food as well.

He had just finished when footsteps again came along the corridor, the door was opened and Ibrahim Pasha came in.

Thomas, who had got to his feet at the sound of the bolts being shot back, stood looking into his face for what seemed a long time, though he realised later that it could have lasted no longer than a heartbeat, trying to read what lay behind the blunt, clever face, the light blue eyes that were such a startling contrast to the dark skin.

Then the pasha moved forward from the shadows of the doorway into the light that was beginning to filter down through the barred window. Behind him the door remained open.

"I am ready," Thomas said.

The Viceroy's elder son gave his rare smile. "There is no immediate hurry; you may walk out of here when you wish."

"When I wish?"

"You are a free man, Ibrahim Bey. My father rescinded the death warrant half an hour ago, Abbas Pasha having most generously released him from his promise."

Thomas acted quite naturally according to the custom of his new world. He dropped to his knees and bending forward, laid his forehead for an instant on the other man's feet. "My lifelong thanks be to you Ibrahim Pasha, and to my Lord your father. I shall be allowed to thank him in person?"

"Assuredly. Also I think it would be polite to do as much for Abbas Pasha, though I doubt if many thanks are due in his direction, your chief gratitude, I believe, is due to my mother." He stooped and made the small token gesture of assistance to rise, a hand lightly under Thomas's elbow as he rose to his feet again.

"The Lady Amina?" Thomas was puzzled. How could the Lady Amina have swayed the thing one way or the other?

Ibrahim Pasha shrugged very slightly, and answered the unspoken bewilderment. "Who, except possibly Abbas Pasha can say? The ways of women are their own – I know only that she was occupied on your behalf last midnight . . . Come now, this is not the most pleasant of places for conversation, and you will doubtless wish to return to your own quarters to wash and change before life goes on again."

Thomas gathered up his Koran and followed him out of the cell, the guards falling back to let him pass, and down the dark tunnel-like corridor towards the open air and the living world at the far end. The clear morning light dazzled him, and the smell of dust and wood-smoke and the song of the birds in the shade-trees of the maidan fell on his senses like a shout.

Did Lazarus feel like this? he wondered, and did not even notice that he was mingling his faiths again.

Figures came towards him – he towards them – and foremost among them, travelling at a wavering run, Tussun with outspread arms, looking as though he had spent the grandfather and grandmother of all nights on the town.

What in Allah's name had been in that wine?

Chapter 12

With the inundation sunk away, and the Nile Valley hazed with the first young shoots of flax and barley pricking through the steaming black earth, the time was almost come to launch the Sudan expedition. But first there was another matter to be dealt with: the matter of Tussun's marriage.

Ibrahim Pasha had been married almost two years before, immediately on his return from his hostage years in Istanbul, to the daughter of one of the Viceroy's Albanian allies. But he had no son as yet to continue the proud new line; and in any case, Egyptian support also needed taking care of. So now, before Tussun went off to his first war, Muhammed Ali was marrying his younger son to a daughter of Sheikh Michal ibn Ishak, leader of one of the oldest and most powerful Cairene families.

Tussun, who had of course never seen his bride, was not especially interested, but quite willing, indeed rather pleased. Now that he was seventeen he felt that a wife was something he should have; a mark of manhood. And his mother and his sister Nayli had both assured him that the girl was not ugly and did not have evil-smelling breath. So plans went ahead, with much haggling over dowries and drawing up of legal documents between the fathers of the bride and groom, and much visiting in closed carriages between the harems of both families.

And eventually the appointed day arrived, and the evening of the appointed day.

Earlier, in the majlis of the sheikh's house in the Fatamid quarter, the wedding ceremony had taken place – if ceremony it could be called, Thomas, present among the bridegroom's friends, had thought; Muslim though he now was, there were still things about his adopted faith that he found strange and alien. And a wedding which consisted in the imam asking, first, the groom and then the bride's father in the presence of a few witnesses if they agreed to the marriage, and in which the bride herself did not take part at all (though he gathered that she was probably somewhere close by, where she could hear what went on) was one of them.

"When I come back from the south," Tussun had said the night before, "I shall set the women to finding a wife for you, Tho'mas, so that our sons may grow up together and be brothers also."

Thomas had laughed. "It is a good thought, but truth to tell I am not sure that I relish the thought of tying myself to a girl I have never seen before the wedding night."

"Ah but it is not like that at all. The women will describe her to you; and when you pull off her clothes on the wedding night, you may find her as beautiful as – as a full moon reflected on still water among lotus flowers. And if not—"

"Aye, if not? How if the women's descriptions are more kind than accurate, and she has a face like the back end of a camel?"

"Then you can always divorce her, after a decent interval, so long as you make the proper provision for her. Or if you do not care to actually put her away, you can take another wife and hope for better fortune the second time."

"I think," Thomas had said, "that I had better leave all that until I am an agha with an agha's well-lined saddle bags."

Now, having survived the day of non-stop feasting, Tussun's friends and supporters had escorted him to the garden pavilion where his bride, smuggled out by a side door from her father's house, awaited him. The young men strolled in shifting groups, or lounged on spread rugs and cushions, drank coffee and sherbet and ate yet more sticky sweetmeats, tossing the usual unseemly jests to and fro while they waited with him for the dusk to deepen into the dark, and the time for him to go in to his marriage night.

Thomas, standing with one shoulder propped against a slender column of the arcaded court, felt himself an onlooker, detached from all the rest. He had overeaten and the rich food sat like lead in his belly, adding to his sense of vague desolation. He wished he did not feel so cut off . . . If Zeid were here, or Colonel D'Esurier, or Donald . . . But Colonel D'Esurier, after a few days in Cairo last week, was back in Suez; something to do with naval gunmountings; and likely to remain there. Zeid had already gone south with a fresh body of cavalry, ahead of the main body of the expeditionary force; and Donald was still in Alexandria, though he would be going south also with the medical team before long. He wrote sometimes. His last letter had contained news of Sir John Moore's death at Corunna and Wellesley's return to the command, and had given Thomas, as news from the outer world always did, a pang of homesickness for the old life and the old regiment which did nothing to cheer him up now. Maybe, he thought, searching for a gleam of light in the surrounding gloom, they would be able to meet when he passed through Cairo. It would be good to see Donald again after this long while, and maybe hear news of Medhet – maybe even see Medhet himself again in the by-going, if, as seemed likely, his regiment was among those ordered south. The gloom which had lightened for a moment, descended on Thomas again. They were all going south, or at any rate would be far out of Cairo; Tussun as soon as the three days and nights of his wedding should be over; leaving him behind. And that was the hard aching core of his dark mood, that, after all, the Viceroy had refused his application to go with the Sudan expeditionary force.

Tussun would be gone with his two regiments, and he, Thomas, would be still tethered here in Cairo, not only powerless to turn aside the spear thrust or stop the bullet that threatened him (he remembered the Vicereine's supper party, and wry amusement winced within him at his own foolishness), but denied the chance to gain military experience, the chance to achieve honour and excellence and certain shining goals that he found mattered to him surprisingly deeply, even now that he was rising twenty-two and might expect to have outgrown such boy's dreams.

"Good training officers are not without their worth," Zeid had said; while Colonel D'Esurier had consoled him, "If it's a war you're wanting to blood your sabre, I do not think you will have so very long to wait." And when pressed for further details he had laughed his creaking inner laugh. "My dear young friend, I am the Viceroy's gunnery adviser, not one of his ministers. But only consider. The Wahabis – followers of Saud ibn Saud, who have spread across most of western Arabia since they poured out from Diriyah and the mountains of the interior a dozen years ago, and whose version of the Faith stands in much the same relationship to the rest of Islam as the followers of Calvin to the rest of Christianity; whose method, moreover, of spreading that version is by fire and sword – cannot, one

121

assumes, be left indefinitely in possession of the Holy Cities and the trade and pilgrim routes. The Viceroy has been building troop transports and armed escort vessels at Suez, rumour has it, by order of the Sultan sitting uneasy on his throne in Istanbul. Put these facts together, and make of them what you will . . ."

Thomas had duly put them together, but whatever he made of them for the future, gained little comfort from them for the present time.

His sense of being shut off from the scene around him, in which he had no part, produced the odd effect of making him more acutely aware of his surroundings than he would other-wise have been, as he propped up his column and looked moodily on. It was a scene half sharp-edged in torchlight, half lost in shifting shadows. The torches burned full-circle round the garden-court, the resin scent of them mingling with the perfume of white-starred jasmine and hyacinth and damask roses, just coming into flower; their flames, teased by the light wind off the Nile, picking out and losing and finding again the laughing wine-flushed faces of the young men, who, knowing that there would be nothing stronger than sherbet to drink in the house of an orthodox Cairene sheikh, had made their own arrangements beforehand; snapping a response of coloured fire from a turban jewel on the gold hilt of a dagger, a gold-fringed cummerbund, an embroidered sleeve, silk that rippled crimson and emerald and saffron. And above the coloured shift and shimmer, the night moths danced like the notes of the flutes and zither the musicians were playing in the shadows.

And overhead also the sudden dark remoteness of shade-trees in the main garden beyond the wall, standing aloof as himself from the vivid scene; and among their twisted bran-ches, as he looked up at them with a sense of kinship, a stealthy client-life of their own, dark among dark, climbing shadows that moved and paused and moved again, the cats of Cairo about their usual night-time business.

One of the prowling shadows, on a lower branch than the rest, checked for an instant into velvet stillness, and seemed to meet his gaze, eyes catching the farthest fringe of the torchlight to become faint green lamps among the leaves. He wondered if that was what had been giving him for some moments past the sensation of being watched. But it did not seem likely that any of the slinking shadows living their own self-contained lives among the night-time roof tops and the branches of planes and oleanders would feel enough interest in the torchlight scene in Sheikh Michal ibn Ishak's garden court, to spare it a passing glance, let alone to single out one human among all the rest for watching. And when the twin green lamps had turned away, and the shadow was lost among shadow branches, the sense of being watched still remained with him.

And remained so strongly that he found himself looking among the faces of his fellow guests, though it was just as unlikely that any of them would be watching him. In fact, one was. Out of the midst of the few Mamelukes standing as they always seemed to do in any company, in a close-knit and flamboyant group of their own, the harsh high-nosed face of Sulieman ibn Mansoor of the Mameluke Guard was turned towards him, the eyes half closed as though he watched from behind a veil. Thomas had met that veiled hostile glance more than once since the evening of the duel; he supposed it was not surprising, for the man had been a friend of Aziz. What he found more disturbing was the presence behind him of the gigantic Nubian, his freedman. Mubarak, who was reputed to be the strongest man in Cairo, well able to break another man's neck with his bare hands, yet he moved as soft-footed as a cat, and reeked like a whore of rose-oil and musk that seemed, coming from him, to be the very breath of all uncleanness. It seemed to Thomas that he could catch the smell now across the crowded court and seeping through the scents of the flowers and hot torch-resin, and his stomach turned a little as always with acute distaste. The best thing to do was simply to shut one's mind to him and assume that he was not there. Thomas assumed accordingly, and giving his full attention to ibn Mansoor, gave him back stare for stare, until after a few moments the Mameluke turned his gaze elsewhere.

Yet still the sense of being watched remained with him.

It was the sensation that he had known before from time to time in the desert, never knowing who or what it was that watched him; the sensation he had known most strongly of all in the Vicereine's salon, when the eyes upon him, waiting for him, had been the long-lidded dark eyes of the Lady Nayli; filled with a kind of hungry speculation.

Something – it was as though the passing memory had

renewed that momentary link – drew his gaze up to the nearest of the shuttered windows in the high house wall to his left, and for an instant he had a sense of unseen eyes meeting his own. There was a flicker of movement behind the delicate window tracery; and he thought he heard a breath of women's laughter above the voices and the music of flutes and zithers in the garden.

He turned his attention firmly back to the torchlit scene around him, his gaze seeking out and coming to rest on the flushed and laughing face of Tussun, his turban at an even more rakish angle than usual, his eyes bright in the leaping torch-light. It was near the time for him to go in to his bride, and the bawdy jests were flying thick and fast; though lacking, by Muslim custom, all reference to the bride's past and reputation, they seemed to Thomas to lack also something of the richness and variety that he remembered from other weddings he had attended, especially during his days with the 78th.

By and by it came to him that he could not stand here indefinitely glooming at his friend's wedding like a jealous lover. He pushed off from the column against which he was still leaning, and shouldered his way forward into the thick of the central group around the bridegroom.

As he did so an eldritch shrieking tore the night apart; a sound rising hideous above the cheerful uproar, which would have raised the hair on the back of his neck, if he had not known it for what it was: the demon lovesong of a pair of mating cats somewhere on the roof top. There was a burst of laughter, followed by a listening pause, as the sounds of hideous ecstasy rose to the stars.

"There you are!" someone cried out thickly. "Greatly are you favoured, Oh Tussun, on your wedding night, the very friends of Eblis have come to show you how the thing is done!"

And looking about for the jester, Thomas saw that it was Mustapha Bey, commander of one of the Albanian infantry regiments, and, according to Tussun, one day in all likelihood to be husband to the Lady Nayli, if long drawn family negotiations did not break down on the question of the dowry. Easy enough to pick him out; a big man built like a bull and as magnificently moustached almost as the Viceroy himself and considerably older than most of those around him, who stood now hands on hips and head tipped back to bellow with

124

laughter at his own sally in a way which Thomas could not feel it merited.

"I *know* how it is done!" Tussun was saying, half angry, half laughing also. He was not drunk, at least not as drunk as Thomas had known him before now, but he was certainly not as sober as strict observance of Islamic law should have kept him. He swung round on Thomas, appealing from one friend to another in a way that showed him not completely sure of himself. "The Daughters of Delight at the House of the Two Pigeons can testify to that, eh, Tho'mas, my brother? Allah be praised, we can show them – you and I—"

Thomas tried to steady him up, without letting his own Presbyterian roots show too clearly. "Allah be praised indeed," he agreed wholeheartedly, but his eyes were straight and warning as they met his friend's, "yet remember that this is a different matter from the House of the Two Pigeons, Oh friend of my heart – this is for the making of sons."

The sense of watching eyes and listening ears was still with him; and the moment he had said it, he wished it unsaid. It was hard to see what possible harm could come of the words, whoever overheard them. Yet the hair stirred a little on the back of his neck, and he wished them unspoken.

Chapter 13

The days that followed were dreich ones for Thomas left solitary in Cairo. Occasionally, when he had an hour to spare, he would have his horse out and ride in the desert, but the desert seemed to hide its face from him. He had not much taste for dancing girls, except in Tussun's company, and had no wish to catch the pox. Even his falcon was deep in moult. There was nothing to do but work, and he worked like a demon to make sure that if he himself might not go south, the relief troops when they went up to join Ibrahim Pasha should be as well trained as mortal training officer could make them.

On an evening upward of a month after Tussun's wedding he was walking back from the Kasr el Nil barracks where he had been sweating his guts out all day over a bunch of new recruits who had no idea how to use their weapons. But his mind had gone back several days to the meeting with Donald that he had hoped for; a hurried meeting snatched on Donald's part from sorting out and repacking the medical supplies whose late arrival had kept him hanging about in Alexandria. Half an hour maybe, after the year and more since they had last seen each other, spent sitting on the steps of the French Hospital's inner court, with a handful of dates between them to take the place of an evening meal that neither of them had had time for.

They had shared the dates meticulously between them, looking at each other and taking pleasure in the sight, exchanged the surface news of the time since their parting, but at least in the beginning, feeling themselves too like strangers to risk anything at a deeper level, for the year between had wrought changes in them both.

"So here you are in a fair way to becoming a famous surgeon," Thomas had said at last, his tongue falling of its own accord into the familiar lowland Scots.

And the Lewis man replied in the more stately tongue of the Highlands and Islands: "Aye, it may be so, one day . . . it may be so . . . And here are you, training officer to the Viceroy, no less."

"An' stuck here in Cairo like a stranded fish, wi' the drums beating an' the pipes skirling away to the south," said Thomas with a fine mixture of metaphor. "In that you have the better fortune of us two."

"Do not be thinking, Thomas Dhu, that I do not know how I come to be a man of Ibrahim Pasha's under the Viceroy."

So Ibrahim Pasha had told him . . .

And now he, Donald, had told something else. "The friends that Allah bestows on him," he had said; and with the significance of the word hanging in the air between them, they looked at each other in silence, one-time Catholic, and one-time Presbyterian. Thomas had heard through Colonel D'Esurier of his friend's conversion to Islam not long after his own. But in their interchanged letters, and through this evening until now, the thing had remained an area of silence between them, of questions that could not be asked for fear of trespass. Now it seemed that the silence was dissolved. No question asked, yet the answer might be given freely, in friendship.

Thomas said, "Zeid ibn Hussein said to me once in the early days, that a Christian might serve in the armies of the Ottoman Empire, at least in some countries – here in Egypt – but that he wouldna' rise to the higher ranks. And at the time I was wishing that he hadna' thrust that knowledge upon me, for it made me afeart that if I chose Islam, it might be for the wrong reason. So for a while an' a while I was torn this way an' that. But in the end I had no choice to make after all, for it came to me – 'twas one evening when I had gone out alone into the desert – that there is but the one God, and tis only the names men give Him an' the roads they take to reach Him that are different." He checked for a moment, wondering if he was talking complete nonsense, and indecently self-exposing nonsense at that. But he had gone too far to break off now. "There was a moment of One-ness. One-ness in a'things . . . I lost it afterward. But the memory was enough."

Donald was watching a small iridescent beetle. He watched it until it disappeared down a crack at the side of the steps before he looked up. "Then it is I that must envy you. For me there was no moment of One-ness; only the knowledge that I had it within me to be a healer beyond the common run, but not

127

in my own world, nor even as a Christian here in Cairo. So I made the choice for that reason, and that reason only."

"I think that Allah the All Compassionate might well find the reason good enough," Thomas said gently.

The moment passed, and he took one of the three remaining dates and asked for news of Medhet.

Medhet, it seemed, was doing well, with already a lieutenancy in one of the Viceroy's newly formed Albanian regiments, but had been sent off with a detachment for guard duty in the Port Suez shipyards and so would also be missing the campaign in the south.

"So I have a companion in misfortune," Thomas had said. "That willna' please the laddie."

"It is in my mind that there will be another war for both of you in a while an' a while," Donald had returned, much as Colonel D'Esurier had done, but with a rueful kindness in place of the dry and detached amusement with which the Frenchman had offered his consolation.

And they had eaten the last of the dates and a few moments later had gone out together to answer the muezzin's nasal call to prayer.

Thomas, on his way back now from the Kasr el Nil, stepped aside to make way for a camel with a vast swaying load of clover that all but blocked the narrow street and, as he did so, a small voice sounded at his elbow.

"Effendi, the Lady my mistress is at the old palace of Fatamid. The time lies heavy on her hands and she begs that you will visit her there an hour after evening prayer tonight and sing her more of your Scottish songs."

He turned, just in time to see a boy, one of the softly rounded, sharp-eyed boys gelded for service in the women's quarters, melt like a shadow into the shifting crowd, and walked the rest of the way back to the armoury deep in thought, and no more aware of the crowds in the streets than if they also had been shadows.

The Viceroy had several residences, both official and private, scattered throughout the city and its suburbs, and the ladies of his household often betook themselves to one or another of the crumbling garden-set palaces to escape the imprisoning splendours of the citadel. So there was nothing unlikely in the Lady Nayli – the message could be from no one else – being in the

Palace of Fatamid. Certainly there was nothing unlikely in her being bored there. But there was something very odd indeed about the secret summons, and as always in anything that had to do with the Viceroy's daughter there was a faint sense of danger to quicken the pulse. Also there seemed to be the whisper of warmth and human contact in his own need . . .

Even so, he would probably have sent his desolated excuses if it had not been for the thing that happened next.

For Donald's news of Medhet had been out of date and when, still deep in thought, he rounded the corner where the street began to run uphill towards the citadel, and turned in through the narrow deep-set entrance to the old armoury, his orderly was waiting for him comfortably camped out at the head of the turnpike stair, with news that he had a visitor.

It was a moment before Thomas recognised the tall stripling in Albanian uniform standing with the evening light behind him, for Medhet had shot skywards in the past months, but there could be no mistaking the urchin's grin that split his face in two as he flung himself open-armed across the room.

"Tho'mas! – Ibrahim Bey!"

"Thomas will do well enough," Thomas said, laughing and holding him off like an over-exuberant puppy. "Eh, Medhet, it is good to see you! But what are you doing here. I heard you were guarding the Suez shipyards single-handed!"

Medhet wriggled with delight. "I and a few more, until a few days since. But now – nay, I do not know how or why, nor do I care – we are ordered south to rejoin the regiment and our place in Suez is taken by a Turkish detachment."

"And so you came to visit me in the passing," Thomas said, "and truly my heart is full fain to see you again after this long while!"

Medhet sobered. "It is good to see you also, Tho'mas, but – it is not for that alone that I am come. It is to ask of you a great thing."

Thomas would have asked if it could not wait until after supper, but clearly the matter was too urgent for any waiting. "Ask then," he said.

"It is that you apply for me – that I may transfer from my regiment to serve under you."

Thomas felt uncomfortably jolted beneath the ribs. "There are few things in this world that would seem to me more good,"

129

he said. "Allah knows it and maybe there will be another time. But if you come to serve under me now, you will altogether miss this Sudanese campaign, and I do not think that is what you have in mind."

He saw the boy's eager face cloud with bewilderment and forced himself to clarify the situation without delay. "Have you not heard that I am remaining here in Cairo as training officer to the new intake?"

"I heard," Medhet said. "But I did not – I do not believe."

"Believe," Thomas told him. "It is true."

"But I do not understand – you do not wish this to be the way of it?"

"I do not wish this to be the way of it, no."

"Then if you tell them—"

Thomas, his hands on the boy's shoulders, shook him gently. "Listen, if you were to go to your commanding officer and say: 'I do not like the orders that you have given me. I wish to do this and I do not wish to do that' – how much difference do you suppose it would make to the orders you have been given?"

"But that is different. I – I am nothing, the least among all the officers in the Egyptian army. But you are a great man—"

"Even generals cannot write their own orders," Thomas told him. "You are not a child, you *are* an officer in the Egyptian army. You must understand these things . . ."

He felt something – a flame of eager hopefulness – die out of Medhet under his hands; saw the bitter disappointment in the boy's eyes and realised that it was not only for a shining plan that had come to nothing, but for the loss of a hero who had failed to live up to his herohood.

Medhet drew back from under the hands on his shoulder. "I will learn, maybe, to understand. I must go now, Ibrahim Bey."

"Supper will be almost ready," Thomas said. "Stay and eat with me."

The other shook his head. "I must go and eat with my fellows."

"So be it, then. May Allah the All Merciful spread his cloak about you."

"And about you," Medhet said in a tight, dry voice and turned to the door.

It had all come and passed and ended so quickly that, for a

long moment after the boy was gone, none of it seemed quite real. But the sensation of bruising and loss that it left behind was real enough. And so was the change that it brought about in his plans for the evening.

"The young one does not stay to eat?" said his orderly who had witnessed the joyful moment of reunion, reappearing in the inner doorway.

"The young one does not stay to eat," Thomas agreed.

"So, then I pour the hot water."

Thomas stripped off and scrubbed himself free of the day's sweat-caked dust, got into fresh garments and ate his solitary evening meal while the last gold faded from the window embrasure and the smoky light of the lamps in the wall niches began to bite.

When the evening call to prayer sounded across the city, he went downstairs and crossed the narrow street to the nearby mosque according to his usual custom. Prayers over, he returned to his quarters and sat for a while, turning over in his mind familiar Scottish airs that might please the Lady Nayli, whistling a snatch of this tune and that and gazing with narrowed eyes into the flame of the small lamp on the table. Then, flinging on over his decent clothes the anonymity of the old brown burnous that he had bought secondhand for rough wear, departed again for the town, heading for the Fatamid quarter and leaving his orderly to look after him with an old man's amusement at the ways of the young, but also with a trace of anxiety.

A lopsided melon-coloured moon was rising as he passed out through the narrow courtyard door and dropped downhill into the city which was touched by its soft, gauzy light as by a kind of enchantment. But as it swam higher the enchantment faded and the light grew colder and more sharp-edged, until by the time he reached the Fatamid quarter the narrow ways had become black canyons below the blank white moon-fire of the upper storeys far overhead, and the daytime bustle of the streets had changed to a furtive flitting. Only the smells, Thomas thought, remained much the same.

He had, not surprisingly, a strong suspicion that the Viceroy's daughter probably had something in mind for her evening's entertainment that went well beyond listening to Scottish ballads, but he deliberately closed his mind to that

131

thought, because if he allowed himself to think it, he would be all kinds of fool as well as a faithless friend, to be answering the summons at all. A courteously worded note of excuse, accompanying a small charming gift – a singing bird in a cage, maybe – costing more than he could afford, of course, should have been his answer. It would have been if he had not been so bored himself, so lonely, so bitterly out at elbows with life; if he could have forgotten the rueful sympathy in Donald's kindly gaze and the worse thing, the unbearably worse thing, in Medhet's eyes.

Thomas narrowly avoided falling over a sleeping beggar curled up in a doorway, and began to be growingly aware of the light pressure of the Somali dagger thrust into the silken folds of his waist-shawl. There was always the possibility, of course, that the summons had not come from the Lady Nayli at all, but was a trap of some sort. He had enemies, he knew, particularly among the Mameluke officers who had not forgiven him the death of Aziz Bey, so he walked in the middle of the narrow way, keeping a quick eye open for shadows, and kept that cool awareness of the small dagger in his waist-shawl.

After the teeming heat of the city, the Fatamid quarter seemed a place where Cairo relaxed and drew breath. Old and magnificent mosques and tombs and palaces crumbling into picturesque dilapidation under a kindly moon that concealed every hint of their daytime squalor, sudden open spaces fringed with shade-trees, shadows of cypress and oleander on white walls, a flittering of bats from an unseen garden; faint and far off the sounds and smells of the great river.

Thomas rounded the corner of the wall enclosing the old Fatamid palace, and saw the long street face of the building, sugar-white under the moon, windowless throughout its whole length, unmarked save for a small deepset doorway a third of the way along, and the shadows of a couple of cypress trees. He made towards the door, wondering what he was supposed to do when he reached it, and prepared to beat on the timbers and shout for admittance in the usual way and enter as publicly as though with a fanfare of trumpets. But before he reached it a small postern door opened in the shadow of one of the cypresses and a woman's voice whispered: "This way, Effendi – come – "

And a hand plucked at the folds of his burnous.

Then he was standing in pitch darkness with the door closed behind him and his hand going instinctively for his dagger. But the next instant a heavy curtain was lifted back and again the voice said: "Come," and he ducked through into the light of a lamp burning in a wall niche in some kind of side chamber that had no obvious reason unless it was a store room. The woman, muffled in the usual black folds, took down the lamp and flapped ahead of him like some great dark moth, and he followed through room after room only half seen in passing, then out again into the moonlight of an arcaded garden-court where lamplight made dim spangled patterns through fretted windows high overhead and on the far side an arched passage let them through into the main garden, the paradise of the old palace.

More faint lamplight gleamed through branches of pomegranate and oleander, reflected back by long narrow strips of water. The woman moved ahead with that heavy moth-like motion and Thomas, following, found himself on the threshold of one of the charming small pleasure-houses that hid themselves in many of the great gardens of Cairo.

The woman checked, saying something softly, and a girl's voice answered small but clear on a note of authority and they went in. As they did so, another dark shape rose and melted into the further shadows.

Several lamps, fragile-seeming as flowers, hung from the ceiling, and the moonlight filtering through panels of airy tracery on the walls filled the little pavilion with a soft confusion of gold and silver, light and shadow in fantastic filigree. The coffee hearth was lit and glowing before the pile of cushions on which the Lady Nayli reclined, playing delicately with the ears of the little grey cat who sat beside her.

She looked up as he entered and smiled. "Ibrahim Effendi, it is kind that you come to ease this sad ennui of mine."

Thomas murmured something about being honoured and folded up on to the spread of cushions she indicated on the guest's side of the coffee hearth. It was the first time he had seen her completely unveiled since the night of the Vicereine's supper party, though he had thought of her more often than he cared to admit, and he was licensed to look at her now more freely than he had been that night. And looking it struck him that her chin was very like the little cat's; proud and small and delicate, sweetly poised above her slender neck, and rather startlingly predatory. Out of his schooldays two lines from

133

Love's Labour's Lost flickered into his mind: "A whitely wanton with a velvet brow, and two pitch balls set in her face for eyes." Even as a boy he had sensed something of the raw desire that lay behind the bitter description . . . But the warning half-memory was gone again almost before he was aware of it, and he turned himself to the promise of the evening.

The Lady Nayli clapped her hands. "Fahama, bring the sherbet and sweetmeats."

The usual three coffee pots were ranged beside the little hearth on which the ancient and fire-blackened fourth bubbled gently giving forth its fragrance of coffee and cardamon to mingle with the sweetness of jasmine and some heavier nameless perfume that seemed to float upon the air like oil on water. And while the woman from the shadows brought out little sugar cakes and sherbet, and poured rose water over Thomas's hands as he held them out to receive it, the Lady Nayli attended to the coffee-making ritual herself, pouring the bitter brew from one pot to another, leaving it a few moments in each for the grounds to settle, until it reached the long-necked pot from which she poured it into the small handleless cup which she passed to Thomas.

He wondered why she chose to perform at any rate the final part of the ritual herself. At her mother's functions – at least any that he had attended – the coffee was made elsewhere and brought in on a tray, much as it would have been in the West, though it was the usual thick, pungent Turkish brew. Maybe it was so that he should see her hands in action and notice how pretty they were with the delicate henna designs on palms and fingertips. He supposed girls were much the same all the world over. But whatever the reason, this was the way in which he had grown used to receiving his coffee during those first days at El Hamha – though in the desert the hands tending the coffee pots would never have been a woman's – and the familiar ritual relaxed the strangeness of the situation and made him feel more at ease.

"You see how I wait upon you myself," said the Lady Nayli. "That is because I am so grateful to you for coming to ease my loneliness. I have not been well – oh, nothing serious" – she touched a hand to her throat – "and the hakima ordered me down here for a few days, for the space and quiet of this place and the gardens. You can have no conception how close-pent one can feel in the harem apartments up at the citadel. But nothing happens here. It is so lonely, so *boring* – Oh, the terrible ennui!"

"If I can help to lift it a little, I am happy," Thomas said, taking a sip of the scalding coffee.

The Lady Nayli sipped her sherbet. "I thought that with all your friends gone south, maybe you would be bored and lonely also."

She gave him a wavering smile, and he realised afresh what a child she was, and because she had sensed his loneliness his heart warmed towards her and he smiled back.

What *was* that scent that hung so heavy on the air, like violet oil but something more than violet oil? Whatever it was, as she leaned to pour more coffee into his cup, he realised that it came from her loosened hair, which swung forward like curtains of black silk on either side of her face. Thomas's pulse began to quicken. Too much of it might make a man's senses start to swim, he thought, and drew back very slightly on the cushions.

"I was bored and lonely also," he agreed.

"And eager to be away in the south, getting yourself killed like a hero? Oh, you men! – and never a thought to spare for the grief that you leave behind you."

He laughed a little harshly. "I do not imagine that I should leave much grief behind me. But, in fact, the question does not arise. By the order of His Excellency, your father, I am chained up here in Cairo as a training officer for the duration of the campaign."

"My father must have a great opinion of you," said the Lady Nayli softly. "Any soldier would serve to send south under my brother Ibrahim, but he trusts you with this much greater matter." She began to nibble at an almond sweetmeat. "Two days since, as I was driven here, I saw many men on horses with their swords flashing in the sun, making swirling patterns of themselves on the Great Maidan."

"Mounted sabre practice," Thomas said.

"That is part of the training?"

For a while they talked about his work, she questioning like an eager child, he answering the questions as best he could. She knew so little and yet it seemed to him that she had a mind, alert and eager for knowledge, that was wasted in the curtained world of the women's quarters. But it seemed at last that she

135

grew weary of the subject, for abruptly she changed it. "Oh, it is too bad of me to tease you with all these questions." She shook back her hair and began to feed crumbs of honeyed almond to the little cat. "Do you remember the evening of my mother's supper party and how you sang to us then? I have not forgotten, so now I shall tease you for another song."

"I am delighted that you should wish it," Thomas said formally, "and I am at your command. Which song shall it be?"

"Oh not one that I have heard before. A new song – new to me."

Thomas reviewed the songs he had been going over in his mind earlier that evening. Not a love song, he decided, though he would have dearly liked to sing a love song to the Lady Nayli. And out of the past, beyond even the second of those he had sung at the Vicereine's supper party, an old, old ballad came to his mind. "This is about a lord of my own people who was slain by treachery and never more came home to his castle and his lady waiting there," and gazing into the small glowing heart of the fire, he began to sing, quietly, almost as though he were singing to himself:

> Ye Highlands and ye Lowlands,
> Oh, where hae ye been?
> They hae slain the Earl o' Murray
> And laid him on the green.
>
> He was a braw gallant
> And he played at the ba',
> And the bonnie Earl a' Murray
> Was the flower among them a'.
>
> Oh long will his Lady
> Look frae the Castle down,
> Ere she sees the Earl o' Murray
> Come sounding through the town . . .

The last brooding notes of the old lament sank away into silence.

"They are sad, the songs of your country," said the Lady Nayli after the silence had endured a few moments. "The words I do not understand and the music is strange to me, but I feel the

136

sadness here in my heart. Maybe that is because my people also are a hill people, though I have never seen my own hills. Can you be homesick for what you have never known?"

Thomas shook his head. He did not know.

"You have known your hills," said the Lady Nayli with a hint of envy after a few more moments, looking up from caressing the little grey cat. "Tell me of them."

And Thomas began to tell, at first a little selfconsciously, simply out of a wish to please her and taking care with his French. But little by little his memory and his tongue loosened, and he told her about Broomrigg, the sheep on the hills and the horses in the stables, the brown burn coming down from the moors, where you could fish for salmon-char in the pools under the birken trees, and his French grew less careful and the odd Scots word slipped in. And all the while the Lady Nayli listened with her dark eyes on his face; and all the while, as though drawn unconscious of herself by his talk, she crept little by little nearer and nearer round the edge of the coffee hearth where the embers burned red and low, turning almost to the red glow of peat on the wide hearth of Broomrigg . . .

Thomas woke to the fact that she was much too close and he was leaning towards her. He drew back, shaking his head a little as though to shake some kind of bemusement out of it. "But I am boring you with all this talk of my country . . . Lady, shall I find you another song?"

She laughed and moved closer yet. "In a little while. Oh Ibrahim Effendi, I am not bored, yet it is pleasant to do other things beside listen to sad songs." And laughing still, she turned and broke a spray from the jasmine in a tall blue jar beside her, drew it across her lips, then reached to tuck it into the folds of his turban-scarf.

The gesture was charming, and for a Muslim woman completely shameless, shameless as the looseness of her gauzy rose-and-saffron dish-dasha which he suddenly realised was open and ungirdled over her silver-worked trousers. A couple of light experimental tugs and she would be naked. Young as she was, it seemed that the Lady Nayli knew as much of the old skills as did any of the Daughters of Delight. He wondered fleetingly if the serving women were watching from the shadows, and then forgot them.

The light silken sleeve had fallen back from her upraised

137

arm, leaving it bare to the shoulder, to the soft hollow between armpit and breast that was perilously near his face. He saw the nest of fine dark hairs. The warm smell of sweat and woman's flesh was suddenly in his throat, more potent than the scent of amber and violet oil, a dark scent that stirred him to the utmost depths. He felt an urgent need to bury his face in the warm sweetness of her flesh, as though he might find there some kind of homecoming. Her hand fell lightly away, brushing his cheek in passing, and she leaned back, the diaphanous folds of her skirt falling in between her slightly parted thighs.

His head was swirling a little. The sense of quickening between his own thighs became hot and fluid, spreading through his loins and belly. His breath shortened and he was shudderingly aware of his manhood gathering itself and rising in thrusting desire. Other needs crying within him too, for refuge, for a one-ness that would drive out the cold desolation left by the look in Medhet's eyes.

The Lady Nayli wreathed herself over against him much as the little grey cat might have done, leaning lightly across his knee, her face turned up to his, mouth a little open like her thighs and with the same suggestion of invitation. He bent towards it.

As he did so, she laughed, a small laugh, cool and charming as a chime of glass bells, and twisted aside and sat up, scooping the cat back on to her lap.

He knew that it was not a rebuff, merely a prolonging of the game of skill that she was playing. He wondered how many other men she had played it with, drawing them on as far as the idle fancy took her, then twisting away, tantalising them with half promises, not denied at the last moment but only deferred, withdrawn a little like a marsh light. Even with his own body still taut with the physical need she had aroused in him, even through the wild, sweet singing in his blood, he recognised exactly what she was doing, and, drawing a slightly shaken breath, he straightened and pulled back himself.

The low embers of the coffee hearth were safely between them again.

"I should like to learn one of your songs," said the Lady Nayli as though the last few minutes had been nothing but a dream, forgotten on waking. "Will you teach me?"

"It will be my pleasure," Thomas said with formal courtesy,

taking care again with his French, taking care also to keep his voice from shaking. Someone should warn her that this particular game of skill was dangerous. "Give me a moment to think of one that may please you."

She laughed again, shaking her head. "There is no need that you should think. You shall teach me the one my brother likes so much. The one I am for ever hearing him whistling and singing under his breath. Teach it to me so that I may sing it also – the song about the foster brother."

How bright her eyes were as they met his; how dark behind the brightness, dark enough to drown in . . .

"The song about the foster brother."

There was a cold stillness in Thomas's belly. Suddenly, and for the first time, he fully understood the cool and ruthless detachment of the girl's interest in people, in what went on within them, in what made them bleed, in the extent of her own power over them. He understood that this was the test of her power over *him*. After he had yielded, she would give him the promised delight, full measure and without stint. The Lady Nayli, he knew instinctively, was one to keep her side of a bargain, spoken or unspoken – but only after he had yielded; forsworn another love, broken faith with certain matters deep within himself.

So the Viceroy's daughter, a faint confident curve on her lips, waited for her power to do its work. But this time, maybe for the first time in her career as a manipulator of human beings, she had miscalculated. The demand which should have completed his thraldom had acted instead like cold water dashed in the face of a sleeper.

"You know the one. Teach it to me," demanded the Lady Nayli with pretty imperativeness.

"I regret – that song is not for sale," Thomas said.

The moment he had said it he wondered if he might just possibly have signed his own death warrant thereby. But he could not wish it unsaid, even so. He waited for something to show behind the girl's eyes, but she seemed not to have noticed the insult. She said only with light mockery: "So solemn, for so small a matter? But no, then, I will not tease you." She reached for the brass pot. "I will make you fresh coffee. This has grown cold."

Thomas shook his head, drawing his legs under him. "You

are very kind, but sadly I must be on my way. I am on early duty tomorrow and I have an arms list to check before I sleep. May I thank you for a most delightful evening."

"It is sad that it must end so soon." She called behind her into the shadows: "Fahama." And when the dark shape reappeared: "Ibrahim Effendi is leaving. Take him back to the street."

When the door in the shadow of the cypress tree closed behind him, Thomas pulled the spray of scented jasmine flowers from his turban and flicked it into the open gutter.

He made his way back to the citadel feeling sick.

And left to herself in the pretty garden-house, the Lady Nayli caught a moth, one of the dark velvet moths that blundered about the lamps, held it for a few moments beating like a pulse in her cupped hands, then pulled it wing from wing and fed it to the little grey cat.

Chapter 14

Three nights later, by an odd contradictory quirk in the Pattern of Things, the Lady Nayli was in fact delaying the attempt on Thomas's life already being lovingly planned in another quarter.

She was entertaining Sulieman ibn Mansoor of the Mameluke Guard at the time.

Sulieman, like many Muslims not of Arab blood, was as fond of wine as any Christian; and when he came to visit her, the Lady Nayli entertained him with wine as well as other pleasures. And being relaxed with all these pleasures, in the late hours of the particular night, he opened his mouth rather too wide, to dwell lovingly on his plans, aided by some chosen friends and followers, to avenge Aziz Bey in a highly colourful manner, which was to leave Ibrahim Bey hacked to butcher's meat with his own broadsword. Vengeance for a friend was a meritorious act, he pointed out, his face between the Lady Nayli's little lemon-shaped breasts.

Over the top of his head the Lady Nayli smiled into the middle distance, her hands not ceasing from their gentle probing movements into the back of his neck, where the hard tightness of an old scar gave her a certain pleasure. She had been toying with the same kind of idea for three days, with no really fixed intention of doing anything about it, but thinking how pleasant it would be all the same if the opportunity were to arise without too much trouble to herself.

"And when will you do this thing?" she asked, conversationally.

"Flower of my delight, I hold the thing in my hands to do it when I choose. Quite soon, I think—". He caught his breath as the henna-tipped fingers suddenly bit too deep, and she gentled again instantly.

If Tussun could be brought into this, how satisfying it would be. There had never been much love lost between brother and sister, and she was quite aware that it was Tussun who had kept

141

the Scotsman from her three nights ago. So her malice spread out accordingly, to include him in her plans. Yes, it would be pleasant, interesting as well, to do him any harm, cause him any sorrow that came, as it were, conveniently to hand. Also, Sulieman, though stupid, was a more exciting lover than some others she had known, and she quite genuinely did not wish to lose him to the headsman's sword just yet, as she most certainly would do if she left him to handle the thing on his own.

"Oh my Beloved and my Lord," she said, "do not be over swift. If you slay the man now, suspicion will fall instantly upon you, who were Aziz's friends. Wait, but a while, until the southern campaign is over and Tussun my brother returns, and it may be that you will even be able to work upon him to give the order himself."

Sulieman tipped back his head to look at her incredulously. "That is surely a dream, oh Flower of Joy. All men know how close to each other are your brother and this Scottish adventurer."

"That very closeness may well make it all the easier to do what you have it in your heart to do," the Lady Nayli told him patiently. How stupid men could be. "Now listen: Certain windows of the garden pavilion in the house of Sheikh ibn Ishak look down into the fountain court, and anyone watching through them such a thing as the gathering of the bridegroom and his friends at a wedding feast may hear as well as see what goes on below . . ."

In his quarters above the armoury, Thomas sat at the table, absorbed in cleaning his double-barrelled pistol. Over the winter months he had begun collecting a few weapons, mostly in bad repair and needing his skill as an armourer to set them right, for the pleasure that the gunsmith's apprentice in him derived from the process.

The remains of his evening meal were on the table, left there by Abdul, who had set the meal and then gone off duty early, to join a nephew's wedding feast. On the table also, in their usual places, the fine goldwork of the embossed covers catching the light of the candles in the three-branched brass candlestick, his Koran and the French translation of the Life of Ali ibn Talib. Presently, before he slept, he would read one or other of them for a while. He had tried once already that evening, but his mind would not concentrate on the written word, and he had turned to the skill of his hands instead, to hold his attention steady.

The Sudan campaign had been brought to a successful conclusion with winter's end, and earlier that evening Tussun, riding two days ahead of his brother and the main Egyptian force, had arrived back in Cairo. From the musket range out beyond the Kasr el Nil, Thomas had seen the dust-cloud of his arrival rising beyond the shade-trees on the river road; and almost, when he came off duty, he had gone up to the citadel palace to join him. Almost, but not quite. Probably Tussun would have to report to his father before he did anything else, after that he should go to his wife, or maybe his own family would absorb him for the rest of the evening. In any case, when he wanted Thomas he would send for him, or come looking himself. The old faint constraint that had lain like a shadow across his relationship with the Viceroy's younger son ever since that first evening in Cairo was with him now; and he had turned away from the first warm impulse, and come back to his own quarters to eat a solitary meal and spend the evening cleaning his weapons and waiting in case the summons or Tussun himself should come.

Had he but known it, Tussun, having had a bath and made his report to his father, having no desire to go anywhere near his wife, especially as she had not had enough consideration to become pregnant after all his wedding night prowess, was in his own quarters with Sulieman ibn Mansoor and a handful of Mameluke friends and supporters, being made sufficiently drunk by them under the pretext of washing the dust of the long ride out of his throat, and carefully pitched up into a state of hurt resentment against his friend Ibrahim Bey.

Ibn Feisal had planted the first dart at exactly the right stage of the festivities, by expressing surprise and concern that Ibrahim Bey was not of their company.

"One would have expected so close a friend to be the first to greet you on your return."

Tussun, who had expected the same thing, but would have gone to Thomas's quarters himself if he had not been waylaid by his present bunch of boon companions, glowered into his wine cup and said nothing.

Rashid took the amber mouthpiece of the hookah from

143

between his lips and passed it to his left-hand neighbour, his eyes half closed as the smoke fronded upward. "Something must have detained him. Allah the All Compassionate grant that he is not ill."

The boy looked up quickly, anxiety for his friend reaching for a moment through the haze of wine. "I'll send—"

Sulieman ibn Mansoor leaned over to refill his cup. "No, no, be easy on that score – did I not see him with my own eyes after supper in the mess, laughing with that young lieutenant of the camel corps, on his way back to his quarters."

Tussun drained the wine in his cup. His face was flushing darkly and his eyes, no longer focusing very clearly, taking on a look of angry bewilderment. He said something thickly about not caring if Thomas laughed with all the camel boys in Cairo.

Someone reached towards the long-necked jug to fill his cup yet again, but Sulieman made a tiny gesture, staying him; it would not do if the boy fell asleep without having reached the needed state of bloodthirstiness first.

"It is possible, of course," a fourth man put in smoothly, "that he is ashamed to face you, after the evil thing that he has said concerning your honour."

There was a moment's charged silence. They were all watching Tussun's face. No one noticed (no one had troubled to notice his presence all along) as Tussun's small personal page raised a suddenly alerted head from where he had been huddled half asleep in the shadows.

Tussun seemed to get his words together with difficulty: "Tho'mas has been speaking ill of me? *Tho'mas?*"

The four exchanged glances and shifted uneasily. The silence dragged on. It was broken by Tussun shouting thickly. "What has he said? Tell me? You *shall* tell me!"

Ibn Feisal said gravely, turning to Sulieman as to the leader of the party, "My brother, I think that too much has been said for the matter to be left now, hanging like an unravelled sleeve. You must tell Tussun Bey all that we had hoped in our concern for his happiness, to leave untold."

And Sulieman, with a great show of unwillingness, but taking up in sad acceptance the task laid upon him, turned to face the drunk and angry and suddenly frightened boy, bending his head over his joined hands in a gesture of humble obeisance, "Remember then, my Lord, that it was for your happiness that we would have remained silent, and it is for your honour that we speak now. The Scotsman who you have befriended has always made a mock of you behind your back. Aye, and not only behind your back, but to your face as well. Do you not remember how, even at your wedding feast, when the mating cats cried out among the branches of the shade-trees of your father-in-law's garden, he laughed and said that the very fiends of Eblis had come to show you how the thing was done?"

For a moment there was a doubtful expression on Tussun's face, as though, far back through the fumes of wine, memory was trying to tell him that it had not been Thomas who had uttered that jibe. Sulieman saw the look and hurried on. "And when you assured him that you knew how it was done – you who are the heart's delight of half the Houses of Joy in Cairo – did he not say to you that this was different, this was for the making of sons – as though all that had gone before had been but love-play and maybe evil practices?"

"Or as though you needed to be reminded of your duties as the Viceroy's son," put in ibn Feisal.

Rashid slipped in his own sting, in the guise of consolation. "When there is a son in your house, Allah the All Compassionate grant it soon, he will no longer be able to put it about that you are no true man, and be forced to eat his words like so much dung."

"He said *that*?" Tussun was staggering to his feet, steadying himself with a hand on the wall niche beside him. His hand encountered the slender vase of late roses that stood there, and he snatched it up and flung it at the opposite wall where it just missed the crouching page and smashed into a ruin of shards and water and mangled flowers. "I'll kill him! – I'll—"

The whole scene dissolved into chaos, through which the four men surrounding the raging Tussun continued with their deadly baiting. At the end, the boy in the shadows slipped off unseen, and made his way out by the side door much used for the night-time comings and goings of Tussun's household and companions. The guards, used to such comings and goings, let him through, and he set off, half sobbing as he ran, into the teeming city night.

Thomas laid aside the ramrod and oily rag, and squinted down first the left and then the right barrels of the pistol he had been

145

working on for an hour or more. Not a speck of rust or used powder marred the inside of either as the light of the candles struck up the prism-bright tubes. He snapped the breech shut and laid the pistol down on the table before him.

Almost as he did so, a small sharp fleck of sound came from the direction of the window. He turned his head towards it, alert and listening, and a few moments later it came again; the sound of a thrown pebble against the window shutter. Not Tussun, he had the other key, and if he had lost it would have come thundering on the armoury door and probably shouting. There was something furtive about this signal, secrecy, possibly danger . . .

Thomas got up, blew out the candles and crossed to the window just as a third pebble struck against the shutter and rattled down the ancient carving. He slipped back the bolt and eased the shutter open an inch or so, sighting one-eyed through the narrow space.

The lop-sided moon was high in a glimmering sky, and looking down, he saw a small figure sitting astride the curtain wall that enclosed the armoury from the narrow street. The pale blur of a face was turned up toward his, and even before the whisper came he recognised Tussun's young page.

It was a hoarse whisper of desperate urgency. "Ibrahim Bey—"

"Ali! What's amiss?"

"Ibrahim Bey. I come to warn you – Sulieman ibn Mansoor – Khalid ibn Feisal and their friends – they are your enemies—"

Thomas opened the shutter a little wider. "You tell me what I know already. Why this haste in the night?"

"They have made my master drunk and told him evil and untrue things that have blackened his mind towards you."

"What things?"

"Does it matter? They have spoken poison – it has to do with his marriage night. They have told him you are spreading it abroad that he cannot beget a son. That among other things, and all the while giving him more wine, and – and you know what he is like when there is too much wine in him. He has given Sulieman his own key to the armoury and bidden him to take ten men and come here to kill you for your treachery."

Thomas simply did not believe it at first. Even remembering Tussun's marriage night and the sense that he had had of eyes

146

and ears beyond the window frets, he did not believe it. "You have half heard something and got it wrong," he said. "Or it was a jest. Your master and I are friends and brothers; and even drunk—"

"No jest." The boy was almost weeping in his desperate urgency. "He bade them bring him your head for proof that it was done. Oh Ibrahim Bey – it is because he loves you. You must run away quickly and hide until his wrath is passed and he remembers how much he loves you . . ."

And suddenly Thomas did believe. With a cold sick certainty, he believed. He heard his own voice asking with surprising calm, "How long before they come?"

"In about an hour – after the midnight guard-change."

"They take their time."

"They hope to catch you sleeping."

"Ten men to kill one sleeping. They pay me a compliment worth the having," Thomas said.

"Hurry! Oh hurry!"

"There is plenty of time – and for you, go back to your master's quarters, and pretend later that you have slept in some corner and know nothing of all this."

"I can help you. I know the dark places of the city—"

"I make no doubt of it." Thomas said levelly, "And so do I, away with you now, back to Tussun's quarters. The mantle of Allah cover you from harm."

"But—"

"Go!"

There was an instant's complete stillness, and then Ali swung his leg back across the wall and dropped from sight into the blackness of the street.

The first thing Thomas did when he was gone was to go down the turnpike stair and check that the small deep-set door at the foot of it was indeed locked. The men coming out of the night had the second key – his mind shied away from thinking who had given it to them – so it would not even delay their entrance; but he knew that lock, it was beginning to be in need of oiling – he had been meaning to oil it himself, but by the mercy of Allah he had neglected it in the pressure of other matters – it would give him warning of their arrival.

He closed and securely rebarred the shutters, then turning back to the table in darkness that was like black velvet against

147

his eyes, felt for and found the tinder box among the clutter of weapons and oily rags, and relit the candles. Then he began to prime and load the double-barrelled pistol. What he chiefly felt that moment was grief more than anything else; and a kind of numbness, as though he had taken a crack on the head which made it hard to think. To make ready his firearms was something that his hands could do with meticulous care and accuracy without any help from his head at all.

"You know what he's like when there is too much wine in him," Ali had said. "It is because he loves you," Ali had said.

He loaded and made ready his pair of French duelling pistols and long vicious-looking horse pistol, and laid them to hand on the table. So much for the firearms. His British rifle hung above his bed in the sleeping chambers, but it would be useless on the turnpike. He picked up his beloved broadsword with the faded crimson velvet lining the basket hilt. Earlier that evening he had been burnishing and oiling the blade, but he unsheathed it now, reading again the name of its dead first owner, seeing the light of the candles run like water along the silken steel. He felt the familiar balance, the way the hilt settled like a sentient thing into his hand and became as it were a part of himself. He had not thought, when Tussun gave it him, that he would use it to fight for his life against men sent to kill him by Tussun himself.

Slow anger began to rise within him, mingling with the grief, not driving it out. Oh yes, he realised that the thing was not of Tussun's making in the first place. It was the skilled work of other men goading him in all his weakest places, until they got from him the order that would save their necks after the thing they planned was done. He remembered again that sense of someone watching, listening, behind the window fret, and wondered if the Lady Nayli also was taking a hand. "You know what he is like when there is too much wine in him" . . . "It is because he loves you". He knew all that, but deep down within him something denied his reasoned understandings. "Brother of mine, if the thing were the other way over, however drunk I was, whatever poison they poured into me, I would have trusted you – *I would have trusted you!*" Whatever the bond between them, for himself he would have called it friendship, Tussun had called it love; maybe it was the same thing; Tussun had broken faith with it, and him.

He laid the great broadsword down naked on the table,

positioning it with care so that his hand could find it instantly in the dark.

It was at that instant that he realised exactly what he was doing. That having been given an hour's warning, plenty of time to run for it and hide in some dark corner of the city until Tussun's rage had cooled, as it certainly would once he was sober, even fling himself on the Vicereine's mercy to save him a second time, he was calmly preparing to stay and fight for his life against odds of ten to one.

And he was not even at all sure why, except that his gorge rose at the thought of the two alternatives.

He closed the chamber door to a two-inch gap. Sulieman and his pack would probably have a lantern, but from the circular stair in anything but full daylight it would look to be shut.

He stuck the double-barrelled pistol and the duelling pair together with the straight bladed Somali knife into his tightly bound waist-shawl, wry and inappropriate laughter suddenly twinging in him at the thought of the fairground sideshow figure he must cut, bristling with such a ludicrous assortment of weapons. He cleared the oily rags and other armourer's clutter from the table and thrust all into the farthest corner of the room along with his crimson leather slippers. If it came to fighting on the stairs he would do better barefoot. Lastly he took down from the wall his cavalry sabre, shorter and lighter, with its curved Damascus blade which might be better for use in the narrow space of doorway or stairhead than the great broadsword.

Then he knelt and turned himself as well as he could judge towards Mecca, and prayed, first according to the custom of the Muslim faith, and then – his teacher had assured him in the early days of his instruction, that it was permissible – in the words, familiar since his earliest childhood, of the Lord's Prayer.

> Our Father which art in Heaven,
> Hallowed be Thy name.
> Thy Kingdom come, Thy will be done . . .

Thy will be done – The Will of Allah – Into thy hands, oh Lord . . ."

He got up, and for the second time doused the candles. Then

he sat himself down beside the narrow crack of the door, his back against the wall, his eyes wide open into the pitch dark, to wait. Presently, as his eyes grew used to the darkness, he began to make out a faint line of grey light at one edge of the window shutter. He heard the faint seashell whisper of the blood in his own ears, felt the beat of his own heart, a little quicker than usual, but not much. From time to time he moved, careful not to grow stiff.

He had no idea how long a time he waited, before it came, faintly up the stairway, too faintly to have wakened him if he had been unwarned and asleep, the sound of a key being turned in an ill-oiled lock.

Chapter 15

Thomas got up, taking the light sabre between his teeth – more and more the fairground raree-show – and drew the double-barrelled pistol from his cummerbund, cocking it in the instant that he did so.

For a few quickened heartbeats of time the silence settled again, seeming to press on his ears as the darkness pressed on his eyes; then, as he strained to pierce it, came the faintest creak of a heavy door being stealthily urged back; another pause, and then a whisper of sound too faint to be called footsteps. And sighting one-eyed through the door crack Thomas saw the darkness lessen before a dim fore-wash of light spreading up from below along the outer curve of the staircase well. He had guessed that they would bring a shielded lantern for silence on the stairs and light to work by if the chambers were in darkness.

The light was growing, fingering its way further round the curve of the stairwell. Still no footsteps, they must be coming up for him barefooted as he was himself. Only the faintest brush and sensation of movement that had no form nor shape to it. A few moments later a shielded lantern came suddenly into view, and the arm holding it high, then the head belonging to the arm, and the bulk of shoulders climbing towards him. Thomas waited a breath of time longer, while a second head came into view, and the glint of lantern light on a knife blade, before he fired the first barrel. In the narrow space the roar of the discharge was deafening. A dark splash flowered suddenly on the wall-curve behind the second head. Before the man had time to fall, and while the roar of the first shot still seemed expanding inside his own head, Thomas aimed for the place under the leader's raised lantern arm, and let him have it through the heart.

The two men crashed backwards together; the stairwell was plunged in reeking darkness as the lantern went down. There was a third shot – probably the leader had been carrying a pistol ready cocked – and a dull slithering sound of falling bodies, a grunt and a startled curse.

Two down, and, if Ali's tally had been accurate, eight to go, said something within Thomas, quite calmly. He threw the empty weapon sideways on to the divan cushions to the right of the door, took the sabre in his right hand, drew the Somali knife with his left, and waited with jumping pulse for what was coming next. For what seemed a very long time nothing happened at all.

They should have rushed him instantly; but thinking to take him by surprise, they had been taken by surprise themselves and they had two bodies to stumble over on the now unlit stair; and maybe Sulieman, finding him awake and ready, was now wondering whether he was alone in the armoury chambers, and if not, how many were with him.

Silently, he swung the door wide, and took up his waiting stance a good sabre-stroke's distance back from the doorway, feet well apart, breathing quietly and deeply. The formless, stealthy sounds of movement began again. And faintly, through the reek of blood and burned powder from the stairwell, another scent reached him; the heavy mingled sweetness of rose oil and musk. Mubarak! Probably Sulieman had brought his giant freed slave in case the door needed breaking down. But be that as it might, Mubarak was coming up at him through the pitch dark. For a moment nausea twisted in his belly, and it was all he could do to keep down the rising panic. The scent was growing stronger, cloying the back of his throat. No sound. At any time the man, for all his size, moved silently as a cat. A sense of nightmare came with him, and partly to quell it and to bring some vestige of reality, Thomas made himself consider how the creature might be armed. Probably only with a knife or his short heavy dagger, possibly only with the strength of his naked hands. Mubarak could kill a man with his hands once he came to grips with him; and that seemed the most horrifying possibility of all.

The scent seemed to be coming at Thomas in waves. No sight nor sound, but a sense of movement, dark within dark, told him that the horror was in the doorway, right before him, stooping to enter under the lintel that was too low for him, hands reaching out ahead . . .

He caught the faint animal sound of the other's breathing and

152

with all his strength he launched a backhand cut at the place where he judged the great bull throat to be.

Two distinct impacts jarred his wrist, one following almost instantaneously upon the other, maybe the first caused by the blade's meeting with an upflung arm, certainly the second was its meeting with the Nubian's neck, though with something of the force spent. He heard a guttural choke, but Mubarak did not go down; he was staggering forward, his silence gone from him. His knife rang on the floor as it fell from what must have been an almost severed hand and next instant Thomas felt the sabre clutched by the blade and wrenched from his grasp.

That left the Somali knife in his left hand. He took a half step forward and drove it in and up under the unseen rib cage, then sprang back.

To his horror he realised that with two, maybe three killer wounds on him the man was still coming on. He heard the slurred stumbling of the bare feet, the breath bubbling and rasping. The reek of blood and rose oil seemed all about him. For one hideous moment his imagination showed him the gigantic Nubian plunging forward with no head on his shoulders, or worse, a head hanging sideways from a neck three parts hacked through, enormous hand outstretched for his throat; dead but not able to fall . . .

He was back to the table now; he side stepped clear of the corner, and his hand found the waiting hilt of his broadsword.

The stumbling footsteps and bubbling, retching breaths were the only sounds in the world. He spared no thought for the men below on the stair who must surely rush him at any moment – he could not afford to unfocus his whole awareness from the immediate horror before him – but at the feel of the familiar sword hilt in his hand the sense of nightmare was leaving him, giving place to something else, something that came of his highland grandmother, the surge of fiery confidence, the smell of blood in the back of his nose, the faint red mist of battle. He brought the heavy weapon up over his shoulder, then crashing down in a savage cut aimed at the place where that terrible breathing told him that Mubarak's head must be. He felt the blow land true, splitting the other's thick skull. He dropped then like a poled ox, and the agonised attempt at breathing stopped on a kind of snore.

Thomas stood an instant leaning against the table, trying to steady his own sobbing breath. The men on the stair must have heard that floundering fall. Feeling for Mubarak's body with his foot, he moved back to the doorway, thrusting the juicy knife back into his waist-shawl as he did so and laying his sword beside the threshold. Then, imitating Mubarak's deep guttural tones as well as he could, he called, "Come, it is done!"

There was an answering shout, and light flickered again on the curved stairwell; they must have managed to rekindle the lantern. All to the good, that would give him shooting-light for a couple more of his assailants. He slipped into the doorway, the first of his duelling pistols ready, as they came surging up. There was a moment's check while they negotiated the two bodies, then they came jostling their way up, one man ahead of the lantern, his shadow leaping black on the curve of the wall. Thomas dropped him in his tracks, slammed the pistol back into his cummerbund and with its fellow, shot the man behind the lantern bearer as his head came round the stone newel. Five down and five to go, said something in the back of his head, coolly keeping the tally. The broadsword was in his hand again and springing forward to the stairhead he cut down the man with the lantern before he had a chance to use his own sabre. Again the stairway was plunged into darkness. Well, his fire-power was finished and he had no further use for shooting light. From below him in the darkness came sounds of chaos, as of men stumbling over one another, men on the edge of flight. Someone was shouting to them to stand; he thought it was Sulieman, but the authority in the voice had an edge of desperation.

Time to go over to the offensive.

Sword in hand, Thomas took to the stairs, climbing over fallen bodies and feeling for fallen weapons with his feet, which found also the slipperiness of blood and filth on every step. The turnpike was a shambles. At the last turn of the stair he checked. He was still hidden in the blackness of the stairwell, but below him was a trace of milky light, and he could make out figures silhouetted against the doorway and the moonwashed courtyard beyond. The man nearest to the doorway, standing actually on the fringe of the moonlight, had something that looked very like a musket in his hand. Allah: What a bobbery pack Sulieman had collected against him! He must be dealt with first. Thomas drew the Somali knife once more. He was no knife-thrower, but it was not a kill he was after, not in the first instance. He swung the blade-tip between finger and thumb and threw left-handed. The knife arched, spinning over the heads of the men below, and caught its target, only a glancing blow on the cheekbone, but enough to serve the purpose. The man jerked, and the musket – Thomas, who knew the habits of the Mamelukes, if they could be persuaded to use firearms at all, had counted on it being already cocked – went off, the ball burying itself harmlessly in the woodwork overhead.

He hurled himself down the last curve of the stair upon the huddle of men below. The musketeer, seeing him coming, flung up the empty and still smoking gun in a desperate attempt to shield his head. Thomas changed his cut from left to right, and slashed in under his guard. Seven down and three to go, said the thing that was keeping tally in the back of his head.

But from the remaining dark blot of men, two had in that moment sprung back and were gone through the doorway in full flight. One remained, standing his ground and blocking the doorway. The moon flickered on the blade of his sword and the backwash of moonlight on the side of his face showed Thomas that he was not Sulieman, who must have been one of the two who had fled, but ibn Ishak, a fellow officer, standing now to cover his retreat, a better friend that he deserved, Thomas thought, manoeuvring for a better position.

He had never crossed blades even on the training ground with this particular man, but he knew that he was by reputation a fine swordsman though not such a one as Aziz had been, and furthermore he must be comparatively fresh.

Thomas realised that the thing might still go against him after all. But, in fact, the fight went his way almost from the start and once he had forced his opponent on to the defensive, was soon over.

Once the Mameluke's blade sliced through his sleeve and he felt the warm trickle of blood from a shallow gash just below his shoulder. The end came when ibn Ishak stumbled over the body of the dead musketeer; for an instant before he could recover himself his guard flew wide, and in that instant Thomas thrust home. The Mameluke officer staggered back with wide-flung arms, and dropped without a sound.

Thomas looked about him for the next comer, then remembered that there were no more to come.

The moonlight showed the old armoury chamber still and empty of all life except his own and for the moment he did not feel too sure about that. He turned to the musketeer lying grotesquely sprawled in the backwash of the moon, and checked that he was dead indeed, then heaved his body clear of the door, urged it shut and relocked it. He did not think that the two who had fled into the night would be coming back; but better to make sure. Black darkness instantly swallowed the scene. He remained a few moments gasping for breath and leaning against the doorpost until the darkness stopped swimming round him, then groped his way like a blind man up the fouled and corpse-clotted stair back to his own chamber, stumbling over Mubarak's body as he entered. He found the tinder box and relit the candles with hands that, now the danger was spent, had begun to shake like a sick old man's. His room stank of blood and ordure mingled with rose oil and musk, but it was not until he had the candlelight by which to see the hacked and mutilated body of the huge Nubian grinning up at him with his head half split in two, that the wave of cold nausea came upon him and he vomited his heart up to add to the general mess of his quarters that in the last few minutes – it could be no more – had become an obscene and stinking slaughterhouse.

Afterwards he washed his face and hands and rinsed his mouth out with cold water from the jug in his sleeping chamber, and with the same water did his best to bathe the wound in his upper arm and staunch the bleeding. He tore a strip from one of his sheets and lashed it tightly about his arm, knotting it off with the help of his teeth. He pulled on a pair of soft leather boots and flung on the old rough burnous over his hideously blotched and dabbled garments. He had no desire to walk through the moonlit streets looking like some spectre of war and massacre. He wiped the great broadsword hurriedly free of blood – a proper cleaning must wait – slammed it back into its sheath and belted it on. Two of the would-be murderers were still at large, and he had no time to spare for reloading his pistols. Then he made his way down the clotted mess of the turnpike stair and out into the clean coolness of the moon-washed night, heading for the citadel.

The guards on the main gate stopped him in the nature of things, but they knew him well, though he did look a bit strange – maybe spent a night on the town and got into a fight, as one of them remarked to a comrade afterwards – and on his explanation that he had urgent business with Tussun Bey, let him through without trouble, shrugging between themselves at the hours kept by princelings and their boon companions.

The guard on Tussun's private apartments seemed in two minds; clearly they had an idea that something was wrong, but were not at all sure what, and in their moment of uncertainty, Thomas walked straight through them, brushing them as it were from his path with the spreading of his burnous.

Reaction from the night's work had begun to set in, he had lost a fair amount of blood, and a faintly dreamlike sensation was coming over him. In the dream he saw various familiar faces, for Tussun's household seemed to be still up and wakeful; concerned and startled faces of people half trying to stand in his way. It seemed to him that the whole night had gone through and it must be the edge of dawn, but he realised suddenly that it was probably no more than two in the morning, a time at which he and Tussun had often enough been abroad together.

He turned to the main door through which he could hear muffled and extremely painful sounds of grief. "Tussun Bey?" he asked one of the faces.

"In his sleeping chamber – not to be disturbed—"

Thomas thrust the door wide and stood on the threshold.

The lamp in its niche cast faint arabesques of light over the chamber, over the grey-bearded figure of Tussun's orderly and personal bodyguard standing just within, over Ali huddled against the divan on which Tussun lay face down with his head in his arms, sobbing his heart out.

All the way from the shambles of the armoury, Thomas had known quite clearly what he was going to say when he came into Tussun's presence: "What in the name of Shaitan do you mean by setting that pack of cut-throats on to me?" But now, standing in the doorway, he was suddenly too tired, the flaming rage that would have flung the words in his friend's face sunk within him to a grey ash of weariness.

Standing in the doorway, he said, "Tussun."

The boy on the bed seemed too deep-sunk in his grief to hear and the desperate gasping sobs went on unabated.

"Tussun," Thomas said again, and this time the voice speaking his name seemed to reach him in his depths. The sobbing ceased on a choking breath, and Tussun's whole body went rigid.

There was a long moment's silence. The old orderly moved aside, as though realising that no defence was needed against the tall man whose clothes showed bloodstained where his hurriedly flung-on burnous had fallen open. Ali scuttled aside from the bed into his usual shadows.

"Tussun," Thomas said a third time. "It is me."

Slowly the rigid figure shuddered into movement, rolled over and came to one elbow, revealing a face blotched like a child's with weeping, but haggard and tormented as a grown man's who had just killed his brother. He was not even very drunk any more; probably the shock of realisation had sobered him.

There was incredulity on the young face, and for an instant stark fear. "Tho'mas!" It was a shaking whisper. "You're – you are not dead?"

And Thomas realised that for that moment Tussun had half thought that he was looking at a bloodstained and avenging ghost. But even so he had made no attempt to thrust him away. Somewhere deep in the fog of his own torn and weary emotions the Scotsman was glad of that . . .

"I am not dead," he agreed.

"But Sulieman—"

"Nor Sulieman. He and one other escaped, out of the ten who came against me."

Tussun was slowly swinging his legs over the edge of the low divan, and getting to his feet.

"Why in Allah's name did you send him and his cut-throats against me in the night?" Thomas asked, but not in the voice in which he had heard it in his mind, all the way from the armoury.

"They said—" Sulieman said, "that you—"

"I—" Thomas began. He had been going to say, "I know what Sulieman said", but a faint movement drew his gaze aside for an instant to meet the terrified and beseeching stare of the page Ali. "I can guess what Sulieman said. Could you not have trusted me? Not even long enough to ask me the truth of his story?"

"It is not true?"

"Of course it's no' true ye daft callant!" Thomas relapsed into the speech of his own people: then, hearing himself,

158

translated. "It is not true. On the sacred name of Allah the All Compassionate, I swear it."

"I will kill Sulieman," Tussun said between shut teeth, and rubbed his face and nose with the back of his hand.

"I doubt if he is still to be found in Cairo."

"I am sorry! Tho'mas, I am so sorry—"

There was a startled silence from the onlookers. Tussun had never been known to apologise to anybody for anything before.

"So am I."

"Forgive me – you *shall* forgive me!" It started as a plea and ended as a kind of desperate demand.

That sounded more like Tussun.

He started forward, arms held out. Thomas was not aware of taking a great stride himself in the same instant. He only knew that they had come together in the middle of the room, that they had their arms round each other. "Brother – my brother—"

Staring over the top of the other's tousled russet head that was butting hot and damp into the hollow of his shoulder, Thomas was suddenly understanding his real reason for staying to fight his crazy Border Ballad battle; that if he survived, by the very enormity of the thing Tussun had done, all debts and inequalities must be cancelled; the small unhappy constraint that he had felt like a shadow between them ever since Tussun had bought him from Ahmed Agha all washed away. If he lived, the slate would be wiped clean, and if he died, it would no longer matter.

And he lived! No debt unsettled save the debt of gratitude that he acknowledged, unexpected and deep within himself, to Sulieman and even maybe to the Lady Nayli.

Across the chamber his eyes rested with quietness on the beautiful wall-hung carpet behind the divan, on the Tree of Life which filled the centre panel, on the birds in its branches, and every bird singing . . .

"Did you really kill eight men?" Tussun asked suddenly.

"Unless they were all shamming very dead when I left." Thomas would have liked to feel triumph, but could feel none, now that the thing was over; all through his life, killing would be at times an ugly necessity to him, never a cause for triumph when once the red mist of the moment was gone.

The boy thrust him back, a hand on his shoulders, to look up at him from arm's length, his flushed face suddenly alight.

"That must have been a fight for heroes! I wish that I had shared it with you!"

Thomas began to laugh, and found it difficult to stop laughing even when the room began to swim, and he found that he had reopened the wound and was bleeding like a stuck pig all over the beautiful tiled floor.

In the fountain court of the women's apartments where the splash and whisper of falling water confused sound and made it hard for any listener more than a few paces off to overhear what passed between them, the Vicereine and her daughter sat together over their embroidery the following evening.

"And so you see," the Vicereine was saying, bending over a piece of delicate gold threadwork that had occupied her whenever she wished to be seen engaged in embroidery for the past six months, "the time has come when we must begin to think of making ready for your wedding."

The Lady Nayli checked her needle in the silken Koran cover that was her own task, and sat up straighter on her cushions with the air of one tensing to the hint of possible danger. "To Mustafa Bey?"

"Who else have we been talking about?" her mother asked patiently.

"I do not wish to marry Mustafa Bey. He's dull – he's like an ox."

"Of course," agreed her mother. "But since when has that been a good reason for not marrying the husband of your parents' choice?"

"My father would not force me—" the girl began.

"Your father has always been softer with you than with his sons. Because he knew that you did not wish the marriage he has let the negotiations drag their feet in the hope that you would learn wisdom and come to like it better. Because of that" – the Vicereine set another stitch and stroked it into place with a careful forefinger – "and because he does not know, or has deliberately turned from knowing, certain things concerning you which are only too well known to me."

Nayli stared at her mother with dilating eyes. "What things? I do not know what you mean."

"Do you not? Oh, but it is too pleasant an evening to mar with the discussion of ugly details." The older woman let the gauzy needlework sink into her lap and turned the full focus of her brilliant gaze upon her daughter for the first time. "It is enough that you should understand this: that you will marry Mustafa Bey and be a faithful and, if Allah wills it, fruitful wife to him, remembering to your heart's core that if any harm comes to him – *or to Ibrahim Effendi* – then it is you who will pay the death-price, as happens when a woman of our Faith dishonours her family and has father and brothers to make the family honour clean again."

"No harm came to Ibrahim Effendi—" the girl began, and checked, hearing what she had said.

There was a long silence filled with the silken whisper of the fountains.

"No harm in the world, thanks to his own powers as a fighting man," said the Vicereine. "No thanks to those who sought the harm, or those who planned it."

"You have no proof," said the Lady Nayli, white to the lips so that the paint stood out livid on her face, but still fighting.

"I daresay I could find it. But it is a more ordinary dishonour that I had in mind. I do not think that Sulieman has been your only lover."

The words were softly spoken but the cut of them was like a whiplash, and the girl's head went back as though she felt the sting.

"Even if Sulieman was – what you say – he escaped, did he not? He is clean away by now, my Mother."

"It would still be easy enough to lay hands on certain other gentlemen of your acquaintance."

"If you knew all this, why did you not—"

"Your father would not wish to lose the means of forming a useful marriage alliance."

Again the silence. This time the Lady Nayli broke it.

"How you hate me," she said through lips that she scarcely seemed able to move.

"No. I do most devoutly wish that I had never borne you, but that is another thing." The Vicereine took up her embroidery again. "So we will make plans for your marriage. The harem will be delighted; they have been wanting a wedding to give them an excuse for new pretty clothes for a long time." She even smiled.

And seeing the smile, the Lady Nayli knew that she was

defeated. She, too, took up her embroidery again and spoke with her head bent over it. "Mustafa Bey and Ibrahim Effendi are both soldiers. How if the harm comes to them that way?" She must at least get her position clear.

"Death in battle, I will accept," said her mother. "For the rest, I can only advise that you take good care of your husband's health and that you pray to Allah five times a day for the safety of Ibrahim Effendi." She began to fold up her work. "There is much to do in the house where a wedding is soon to take place and it is time that we were going within doors."

But her daughter seemed not to hear her; seemed not to be aware of the slow, crimson drops weeping on to the Koran cover from the wound in her hand where she had clenched it on her needle and held it closed. She was face-to-face with retribution, staring with wide eyes at the horrifying prospect of lifelong fidelity and enforced childbearing without chance of escape, to the ox-like Mustafa Bey.

Chapter 16

Colonel D'Esurier had been right in the conclusions he had drawn nearly three years before from the transport and escort ships being made ready at Port Suez. The preparations were complete now and, on the orders of the Sultan and his Sublime Porte, Muhammed Ali was launching an expeditionary force against the Wahabis for the freeing of Mecca and the Muslim Holy Land.

But there were other matters to be attended to first and the Viceroy duly attended to them, including the Cairo Mamelukes . . .

On an evening thick and breathless with the heat of late summer less than a month before the expedition was due to sail, the light of a hundred lamps mingled with the music of lute and zither, spilled out from the many windows of the viceregal reception chambers into the high-walled palace gardens. The banquet for the Cairo Mamelukes was drawing to a close.

A very splendid banquet for the purpose of ushering in better relations between the Ottoman party and that freebooting, soldier-slave fraternity. The Viceroy had sent out the courteous summons to the Mameluke lords and their followers, and throughout the length and breadth of the city and its surroundings the Mameluke lords and their followers had responded.

They had come mounted on their most mettlesome horses and brave in the fighting-cock splendour of their finest attire. They had feasted in the company of the Viceroy himself, with his senior officers and certain other honoured guests such as Colonel D'Esurier, and watched the best troupe of dancing-girls in Cairo perform the Bee Dance which left the wild-eyed dancers by the end virtually naked save for their jewellery and their outflung maenad hair. Even the interminable coffee had come to an end, and the Negro slaves had brought in the perfumes and the smoking incense burners which signalled the end of the entertainment, and one after another the guests were touching hands and foreheads with the heavy fragrance of jasmine and tuberose, holding out the loose folds of their mantles to receive the scented smoke of frankincense and sandalwood. They were taking courteous and deeply formal leave of their host and passing out into the night, into the torchlit courtyard where the palace grooms had their horses waiting for them.

When Colonel D'Esurier also would have taken his leave, Muhammed Ali stayed him, drawing him aside, and a few moments later they were standing in one of the windows, the Viceroy expressing, not for the first time, his regret that on the very eve of the Arabian expedition, his French gunnery adviser was being recalled, giving place to a successor as yet unknown. But even as he spoke he had the air of a man whose mind was not entirely on what he said; the air of a man who was waiting for something.

He had not long to wait.

As the departing guests crossed the maidan, the smother of horses' hooves and men's voices raised in talk and laughter which had been blanketed by the buildings in between broke free and came clear to the window where the two men stood. The sound of retreating festivity endured for a short while, then grew hollow between the flanking walls as the Mameluke party poured into the broad processional way that curved down to the gates.

A few moments more and the sharp rattle of musket fire reached the two in the window and the night was torn apart and made hideous by the desperate shouting of men under sudden attack and the screams of stricken horses.

"My God – what—" began D'Esurier, and before the unruffled calm of his companion, checked on the words and on the instinctive movement that would have sent his hand for his pistol had he been armed.

Almost as quickly as it had flared, the tumult was dying, dead, only one voice raved on, one last musket shot cracked out and the voice was silent.

"Pity about the horses," said the Viceroy of Egypt.

Colonel D'Esurier said nothing at all.

Shortly after, a low quick mutter of voices sounded outside and the captain of the citadel guard entered and crossed to stand before Muhammed Ali in the window. "Excellency, the thing is done," he reported.

"All dead?" the Viceroy enquired.

The captain fidgeted a moment with his ceremonial dagger. "One forced his horse over the low place where they are rebuilding the wall. It's a twenty-foot drop there – the horse broke its back but the rider got away. I have men out hunting him now."

"If they catch him, so much the better. If not, there is little harm," said the Viceroy magnanimously. "No support to be called upon; no secret to be betrayed since the matter will be public property throughout Cairo by dawn in any case, and I think small grief felt in any quarter."

And when the man, obviously much relieved as to the safety of his own neck, had departed, he said musingly, half to himself, half to the Frenchman beside him: "I wonder what possessed them, every one of them in Cairo, to accept my invitation."

"Over-confidence, perhaps," said D'Esurier in a voice that sounded dry in his throat. "A monumental self-confidence that could not conceive of any cause for fear; pride that would not permit of refusal, no matter how strong the smell of danger."

"Or simply trust in the laws of hospitality," said Mohammed Ali. "Oh, my friend, I am not apologising. I am a realist. I have known for a long time that the task of ridding Egypt of the wolf pack must be completed before half the regular forces are shipped off to Arabia, leaving the country wide open to their power-hunger. Tonight's work was not pretty, but it was work that must needs be done."

"Not pretty," D'Esurier agreed. "But I fully understand the need . . . Excellency, need you have made me a part of it by inviting me to this evening's entertainment?"

There was a shadow of a smile under the Viceroy's luxuriant moustache and the strong brows lifted a little. "I believe so. You are returning to France as soon as your successor arrives, and we would not have you carry too harsh a report of us back to your Emperor."

The Frenchman's lean, sardonic face echoed the smile for an instant in perfect understanding. "Which, being however slightly implicated . . . Of course, Excellency, that was foolish of me."

He drew himself together in a small, formal bow. "Now that

the purpose of my presence here is served, may I have Your Excellency's leave to withdraw?"

In the narrow chamber whose windows peered for ever down into the dust-dark crown of one of the hospital shade-trees, the two young Scots had been discussing the forthcoming campaign over the inevitable tiny brass cups of coffee.

"And so I am thinking that the content is in you, this time," Donald was saying.

"Because there's a new campaign?"

The big Lewis man smiled. "Not so much because there's a new campaign as because this time you go with the expeditionary force."

"Aye – my turn to follow the drums and yours to bide behind," Thomas said. "Are ye sore for that?"

"Ach no. I have had enough of the drums. Now, and for a long while past, I am Osman al Hakim."

"You were glad enough to be going, the last time, even so."

"I was wanting the experience. For a surgeon, it is good to be on campaign now and then – that way he will be gaining knowledge and practice in the mending of broken bodies. But for now it is the skills of the physician that I need to practise; such skills as are best gained here in this great hospital that the French left behind them."

"This is all ye've ever really wanted, is it no'?" Thomas said. "An' you the drummer tae a Grenadier company."

"It is not so easy to qualify and make one's way as a surgeon or physician without the price of one's apprenticeship in one's pouch," Donald said simply. "A drummer at least combines it with being a medical orderly. I was a laddie when I joined, with a laddie's high hopefulness in me."

They had spent several evenings together in the weeks since Thomas and Zeid ibn Hussein had returned with the Bedouin cavalry from more than a year of service in the south under Ibrahim Pasha, now Governor of the new Southern Province. A few of those evenings they had spent in one of the riverside gardens where the cool came up off the water after the scarifying heat of the July and August days. More often, as this evening, when Donald was on call and must be at hand and easily found, up here in his own small chamber in the hospital. Quiet evenings of long companionable silences, of setting the

166

world to rights, of exchanged "shop", of occasional heated arguments, and leisurely talk that ranged out into the future or peaceably backwards over days in the windswept islands of the Outer Hebrides or the green hills of the Border Country.

But after this one, there would be no more such evenings, for the time being anyway. Not until after the Arabian campaign was over and the Holy Cities free.

"And it came," Thomas said. "To both of us the chance came."

Donald looked into the bottom of his empty coffee cup for a long moment, then set it down with a small careful clink. "Chance – or the Will of Allah," he said simply.

And Thomas wondered, not for the first time, whether having made the choice, Donald was not more comfortably at home in his new faith than he was himself.

Hurried footsteps came scuffing along the corridor, and there was a scratching at the door which stood ajar for the passage of air between it and the window. "Osman Effendi, it is the man with the lung-bleeding. Come."

"I come," Donald said, and got up from the bench where they had been sitting beneath the window, picking up the metal box that was always with him. "Wait for me," he said to Thomas. "There is still coffee in the pot. I'll be back when I can."

Thomas heard the low quick voices in question and answer, and the two sets of footsteps dwindling into silence, or rather, into the faint multitudinous sounds of the great hospital; a voice raised somewhere and cut off by a slamming door, distant footsteps that came and went, the chink of metal receptacles, the slap and swish of a floor being swabbed down, all with the faintly cavernous note that came of huge wards and long empty corridors. From below in the hospital garden came a snatch of laughter and voices raised in dispute where the gardeners were at the evening watering, the cool hush of water finger-sprayed from the great jars and the scent of earth wet and refreshed after the day's thirst. He leant his head back on the base of the window, relishing the first cool stirring of the evening air, and let his weary gaze drift free about the room.

It was more like a prison cell even than his own, and lacking in most comfort and all ornament. No golden carpet of Ispahan to give beauty to the roughly limewashed walls; only a coarse blanket on the sleeping mattress, a brass lamp of extreme ugliness and the medical books stacked in the wall niches, mostly shabby and battered from the handling of many previous owners, to stand for comfort and beauty and the things of the mind or spirit. But it was a good place for straightening out one's tangled ideas – gathering up loose ends before moving on to the next thing. There was a serenity about it that was lacking from his own quarters above the old armoury, in which he still seemed to catch the whiff of musk and rose-oil from time to time.

Musk and rose-oil . . .

Leaning against the window ledge with the scents of the wet garden whispering up to him and the shadows gathering in the corners of the room, his mind wandered back over two and half years to the night when he had fought for his life on the turnpike stair. Years in which, in the outside world, Talavera and Torres Vedras had been fought, and Sir Arthur Wellesley, now become the Duke of Wellington, had caused Bonaparte to describe the Peninsula campaign as a running sore. Thomas of course knew of that but it seemed far off and just now his mind was running on his own affairs. There had been no keeping the attempt on his life hushed up, not with ten men to be accounted for, eight bodies to be cleared away, and old Abdul returning from his nephew's wedding feast in the midst of the clearing-up process and rousing half Cairo under the somewhat confused impression that the men carrying it out had murdered his master. Not that Tussun had shown the slightest desire to have it hushed up, seeming, indeed, embarrassingly set on proclaiming the story to the greater glory of Ibrahim Bey, his friend and brother. Above in the quiet room, Thomas smiled a little at the memory of the boy Tussun had been, and wondered, not for the first time, what had passed between him and his father, between him and his elder brother returning next day with the main body of troops from the Sudan. Tussun had emerged from the latter interview, by all accounts, ashen-faced and for once in his life speechless. Nothing had ever connected the Lady Nayli with what had happened, but Thomas, with nothing but an instinctive feeling to go on, had remained convinced that somehow, in some way, she had formed a part of the pattern; and indeed for a while he had slept with his long Somali knife under his pillow, and taken care to eat only from the communal dishes in the mess hall; but it seemed that she was too indolent to try again, or had grown bored with that particular ploy. And soon after she had been married off to Mustapha Bey – now commander of the Albanian regiments with the expeditionary force – and maybe that had given her something else to think about.

Soon after, for Thomas also, there had come other things to think about, with the end of his time as a training officer, and promotion to his first command. He had wished at the time that he knew how much of that was due to his gifts as a soldier, and how much to his friendship with the Viceroy's younger son; but promotion in the British army depended too often on another man's death, or purchase-power or the fact that one's father knew the right general, for it to worry him very deeply. He had received his promotion gladly, since it meant a posting south, back to the desert and the frontiers again, and the command of a Bedouin cavalry regiment.

That had been a good year, and heralded in by an event, small in itself but great to him, that was worthy of it. For a few days before he left Cairo for the south, he had returned to his quarters late into the evening, to find Medhet waiting for him exactly as he had done on the eve of the Sudan expedition.

Abdul had already lit the candles in the three-branched candlestick, and they had stood and looked at each other by their light. They had seen each other more than once since that other time; but always in the distance, always in the by-going. And Thomas had known that it must be left that way, until, in the Pattern of Things, the time came round, if ever it did . . .

Now it seemed that the time was here.

"Ibrahim Agha . . . " the boy began, and seemed not to know how to go on.

"Medhet," Thomas said, and waited.

"The last time I came to you with a request, I was but a boy—"

"And now there are grey hairs in your beard?"

The other shook his head. "Do not laugh at me. Nay, but I grow older and wiser. Also I have spoken – more than once – with Donald al Hakim, and from him also I have learned a little from time to time. And now" – he had been very grave, but suddenly the beginning of the old wicked grin was there – "now it has been told me that Ibrahim Agha goes south in three days,

169

and I come to make the same request again, being weary of cities."

"So, and what makes you think that I can pluck a man from another regiment to follow at my heel with greater ease now than I could that first time?"

"It has been told to me that Ibrahim Agha is a great man and lord of a cavalry regiment. To such a one, ways are open that are still closed to a training officer with no command of his own."

"That has the sound of impudence," Thomas told him, aware with relief that he would never again be, to this valiant urchin, something beyond the sum of normal men. That was gone, and in its place he sensed a better-rooted and more durable relationship that would be less taxing to live with. "I will do what I can," he said.

"Then it is sure. And in three days I ride south with Ibrahim Agha."

Thomas smiled, "Tho'mas will still serve when we are alone together as we are now."

And in three days he had ridden south to join his new regiment, with Medhet for his personal aide.

A few weeks since, he had returned to a Cairo still reeling with half stunned, half triumphant shock, from the final fall of the Mamelukes, who had been in some sort its masters for six hundred years.

The work had been begun of course by the Sudan campaign, and continued in numberless provincial skirmishes since, but the heart and strongpoint of the freebooting slave-soldier aristocracy had remained in Cairo itself. Remained, that is, until a few weeks ago.

Thomas had contrived not to be physically sick when he heard about it, but even now the taste of black vomit still rose in the back of his throat at the memory. He wished he could have talked about it with Colonel D'Esurier. The French gunnery colonel's unemotional and objective view might have helped him clear the confusion in his own head. But D'Esurier had returned to France some weeks previously; and his place among Muhammed Ali's advisers was taken by another man.

Surprisingly, Zeid ibn Hussein, albeit with a dry disdainful look to his mouth, as though he had bitten on a leaf of the bitter aloes, had also taken a realist point of view. "You have not had six hundred years in which to practise hating the Mamelukes," he had said.

"Neither has His Excellency the Viceroy," Thomas had pointed out.

"We must assume that His Excellency acts not out of his own desire, but to meet the needs of Egypt. The thing was necessary, Tho'mas, ugly but necessary. If you feel so strongly about it – even remembering their treachery at El Hamed, also that they tried to murder you – give thanks to Allah the All Compassionate that you were out of the way when it happened, and, like me, can show your hands clean without having been ordered to foul them."

That had pulled Thomas up with a jolt. Zeid had an uncomfortable gift for presenting one with choices, even choices that one had not in fact had to make. He was indeed thankful that he had not been ordered to play any part in that final hideous massacre. Sometimes, as here in this austere little chamber of Donald's, which also had a way of bringing one face to face with such questions, he wondered what he would have done if he *had* been involved. He wished he could be sure that he would have had the courage to fling down his sword. Even with the memory of friends and comrades betrayed and rotting at El Hamed, he wished it. But he was not sure; and sitting here in the fading light with the faint evening airs stirring in the branches of the shade-trees outside the window, he accepted for the first time the fact that he never would be.

He was Ibrahim Agha, commander of two regiments of proud desert cavalry, and Tussun's chief of staff in the forthcoming campaign; but he would carry always with him that small ugly doubt, like an old wound that aches when the wind is in the east.

Tussun also had travelled a long way in those two and a half years; Tussun, appointed commander of his father's expedition against the Wahabis, and created Pasha of Jiddah for the occasion. He had two sons of his own now, and had lost his boyhood somewhere in the Mameluke troubles. Too many of his boyhood friends had been drawn from their swashbuckling ranks, so that for him the troubles had had something of the especial cruelty of civil war that divides father from son, brother from brother, friend from friend . . .

The room was sinking away in the dusk. Below in the

hospital garden the voices fell silent, as the gardeners finished the evening watering, left the great jars dripping by the cistern and went home. From time to time footsteps came and went along the corridor. A rim of apricot light began to show round the edge of the part-open door from some lamp kept burning at the near-by stairhead through the hours of darkness.

Presently the door was pushed wide, and Donald's tall shape appeared, bulking darkly against the apricot glow. "Och now, here's a dismal way to be sitting in the dark," he said.

"I didn't notice."

The big Lewis man crossed to the table, and producing his tinderbox from the folds of his waist-shawl, set to lighting the lamp.

Thomas watched the flame flare and steady, and Donald's face and the careful hands tending the small laurel-leaf of light take form and substance as the shadows drew back. "Is all well?" he asked.

Donald's gaze, startlingly blue in the upward lamplight, came up to meet his, with a clear cool look of content in it. "Aye, all is well – for this while, anyway."

For Donald at least, the choice had been a good one, and the way ahead lay clear.

Thomas drew his legs under him to get up, "I am glad."

"Need you go yet? Bide a while longer, and Selim shall bring us more coffee."

Thomas shook his head and finished getting up. "I must get back. We ride at dawn."

He had a sudden acute awareness of the small lamplit cell as being a threshold place; behind him the chapter of his life that had begun at El Hamed, the new chapter waiting for him tomorrow, when the Arab cavalry rode out for Port Suez. At the same moment it came to him that this night might very possibly be the last time that he would see Osman al Hakim, who had once been Donald MacLeod of the 78th.

"The Sun and the Moon on your path," he said, using the old Highland form of valediction.

"And on yours," Donald answered. "And on you, Thomas Dhu."

In the doorway Thomas checked and half turned, looking back over his shoulder. There was something more, small and almost overlooked, that must be said now lest there be no other time. "Thank you for Medhet."

172

PART TWO

ARABIA

Chapter 17

The ancient caravan road from the north rose and dipped with the undulations of the land, through a world that extended no further in any direction than the nearest rocky outcrop of scimitar-curved dune crest, and each ridge and dune crest so like the last that you seemed to carry your own narrow world with you as you went. The early autumn rains had conjured the first wash of green over the desert here and there, but the thin grey scrub of aromatic things, the occasional twisted terebinth tree among the rocks, looked as though life would never reach out a finger to them again.

It had been much the same, except in the few oases, all the long thirty-three days' march from Port Suez. But for Thomas, riding at the head of his Bedouin cavalry, it had a more familiar feel to it than Cairo had ever done. Coming as he had, straight from the world of his Highland regiment to the world of an Arab frontier post, with virtually no contact with the Turkish world of his captors between, the desert had taken him over and become the home of his spirit in the way that the great city and the life that was lived there had never done. Not that he did not hate the desert at times, for all that, as seamen know what it is to hate the sea.

The rain had been too little and too many days ago to leave any trace now on the track, and the dusty sand rose in clouds from the horses' hooves, so that as he looked back the weary columns blurred away into the smoke of it that altogether hid the baggage train and artillery camels bringing up the rear. His throat was dry and his eyes bleared, and he felt gritty from head to foot. But it would be worse for Zeid, riding with the rearguard in the rolling dust of the regiments ahead.

Three years of shipbuilding had seemed an inconceivable delay, and as its purpose became known, the army had fretted with impatience, Thomas with the rest, Tussun most of all. But now he could see that the building period had not been wasted. Other work had been going forward at the same time, work of

175

diplomacy and logistics, that had had no outward showing at the time; the labours of nameless men wearing the faces of merchants and caravan masters out beyond the frontiers of their own world. So the way had been made ready for the coming of the expeditionary force. Wells had been cleared out, the forts along the way properly garrisoned and provided with full grain stores and magazines; and respect if not friendship gained from the local tribesmen, who had not, until that time, experienced fort commanders who paid for the camels they commandeered. And so the whole march had been accomplished without a shot fired in anger.

The track began to rise, and up ahead of them a flurry of shouting broke out from the advance guard. Thomas's thoughts snapped back to the immediate time and place, and he straightened in the saddle. This must be the end of the journey.

A few minutes later he crested the ridge, and saw before him through the dust of the advance guard the white walls of Yembo among its cock-hackled palm trees, surrounded by something that looked more like a vast Bedouin encampment than the base camp of the Egyptian army, and overlooking the fleet of troop transports at anchor in the harbour.

They knew already from the report of their scouts that the Viceroy's infantry force had arrived by sea ten days ago, and the small garrison – not Wahabis but troops set there by the Grand Shariff of Mecca, who was himself only an extremely half-hearted ally of Saud ibn Saud the Tiger of Arabia – had put up the merest token resistance, for appearance's sake, before surrendering. The townspeople, for the most part traders from all the ends of the earth, with no special allegiance to either side, had warmly welcomed the expeditionary force, reported the scouts, reckoning to grow fat on its coming.

Ahead of him, Thomas saw the commander-in-chief, who had ridden forward with the advance guard to catch the first sight of the port, turn in the saddle, waving wildly and setting his horse dancing with his own excitement. He flung up his arm in response, and reined his mare aside from the weary column.

"Ride back to ibn Hussein, and tell him Yembo is in sight," he ordered Medhet who had followed him. "Like the wind!"

And the boy wrenched his horse round in a smother of dust, and with a shrill cry was gone, full gallop. Thomas wheeled his own mare, heeled her into a hand-canter, and rode back down the ragged column at a less headlong pace, calling the news as he went, together with orders to his men to straighten themselves up.

"Awake, my brothers, my children! Yembo waits over the next rise, to see how the Arab cavalry ends a desert march, in column of three, riding straight in the saddle! Wake, and do not cause your mothers to weep for shame that ever they bore you!"

Here and there, hands were flung up in acknowledgment; he saw standards that had been sagging all ways brought back to the perpendicular, weary men straightening in their saddles, pulling their garments to rights, urging their tired mounts back from the straggle they had become into some semblance of a cavalry column, and his heart swelled within him for pride of them, because they were his, and also for exasperation at their slowness.

So at last the regiments, in something raggedly resembling columns of three, their sick lying across the baggage camels, but their heads up, their horses gathered to a trot to the liquid throbbing of the kettledrums, their pennants lifting lightly out on the wind of their going, headed down the last slope into Yembo.

Something over a fortnight later the whole expeditionary force was still there, and in the commander's tent a council of war was sitting.

Tussun had much more luxurious lodgings in the town house of the local shariff, but it had seemed better that the matters they had to discuss should be dealt with in his long black tent in the midst of the encampment, where there would be less risk of the wrong ears overhearing what was said.

Thomas, who had spent the greater part of the day, as he had spent the greater part of every day since their arrival, keeping his troops in proper shape to ride out again when the order came – as by the Mercy of Allah it must surely come *sometime!* – leaned back on an elbow against the camel saddle behind him, and studied the faces of the men gathered about the coffee hearth, some almost strange to him, some long familiar. He saw the faces of the two infantry aghas, that of Salah the Albanian with his hot blue eyes and mouth drawn tight with impatience, the olive-skinned Turkish features of Umar schooled into better control. He saw Zeid ibn Hussein, his cheeks a little more hollow, his eyes a little narrower than they had been at El

177

Hamed, his long fingers playing in the old delicate way with the ears of the saluki who had followed him in. For a moment the narrowed eyes met Thomas's with a flicker of sympathy for his impatience with the slowness of the proceedings.

Thomas's promotion to overall command of the cavalry, Arab, Turkish and Albanian, while Zeid who had been his captain and his tutor was set to command a single cavalry regiment under him, might well have strained the old friendship between them. It had not done so, and Thomas gave the credit for that where it was due. His gaze drifted on to Tussun Pasha, their commander-in-chief and the youngest and least experienced of them all, his turban tipped as rakishly as ever over one ear, but his face harsher and less joyful than it had used to be. Tussun's lion-tawny eyes, with a frown bitten deep between them, were fixed just now on the papers which a short while before had been passing from hand to hand and now lay beside the coffee hearth in their midst.

In the silence Thomas heard the passing steps of the sentries outside, and beyond them the sounds of the camp waking to the evening. On the closed back of the tent shadows passed, black against the reddish glow of the sunset seeping through the tent cloth; from the looped back front a little chill air came in – the nights were beginning to be cold – bringing the scent of burning camel-dung from the evening cooking fires. The saluki sat up and scratched, long and luxuriously.

Tussun's first act on arriving at Yembo had been to send word to the Grand Shariff at Mecca, to inform him that a powerful force of his allies was now in the Holy Land to free it from the grinding and tyrannical yoke of the Wahabis, and to remind him of the promise which it seemed (despite the token resistance of the Yembo garrison) he had made, to call out the tribes and his own Mecca and Jiddah troops to support it. But it seemed that the situation in the Hijaz, the Holy Land, was not at all what certain of the Viceroy's contacts had given him to believe, their reports being based more on what they thought he would wish to hear than on the actual facts.

The answer to Tussun's letter had returned yesterday, and was one of the papers now lying beside the coffee hearth. Thomas had taken and read it when it was passed round the council circle; but in truth he had first read it yesterday within a few minutes of its arrival at Tussun's quarters; the only one who had done so; the only one who had witnessed the young commander's fury.

The Grand Shariff Ghalid, addressing him as a brother, expressed warm friendship, and the utmost satisfaction at the arrival of the expeditionary force, but explained in terms of sweet reasonableness that he dared not declare war on the Wahabis, nor withdraw any troops from his garrisons at Mecca and Jiddah until Tussun Pasha had had at least one success against the Wahabis in battle. If he were to do so, Ghalid pointed out, the Wahabis would immediately reoccupy Mecca and the southern Hijaz, which would leave Tussun himself disastrously isolated.

"We have two thousand cavalry and more than twice as many infantry – What if we go for Mecca or Jiddah in spite of him?" Tussun had just demanded of the council, as he had demanded it of Thomas the day before; and had received from ibn Hussein the same answer as he had already received from Thomas: "Sir, if you do that thing, the Grand Shariff and his forces will fall back into his late alliance with the Wahabis, and you will indeed be left isolated in enemy territory."

It was that that had caused the silence.

Tussun broke it with an abrupt change of position, shifting his weight from one ham to the other, and flinging an arm over the camel saddle behind him. "You are right of course, Zeid ibn Hussein, it is a bad habit you have. Fortunately it seems that at least the thing faces both ways." He flung up a hand in a summoning gesture, and a tall desert Arab caked with journey dust stepped forward from the shadows where he had been standing among the scouts and junior officers.

"Tho'mas," said Tussun, whose own Arabic was somewhat scanty, "bid this man repeat to our brothers of the council what he has already told me earlier this day."

Thomas passed on the order, and the man bent his head for an instant over his joined hands in token of acquiescence. "Sir, I come to you in the name of the merchant Zeid Muhammed el Marouki my master, he that has long been friend to His Most Honoured Highness the Viceroy your Father. I bring you word that the Grand Shariff is in truth no more eager to ally himself openly with the Wahabis" – the man spat precisely into the glowing embers of the coffee hearth – "than with the armies of Egypt. He has replied to a summons from the Prince Saud ibn

179

Saud their leader, that he can make no move openly to help the Wahabis" – again the exhibition of precision spitting – "at this time, lest the Egyptian soldiers should seize Jiddah and Egyptian ships blockade the town."

"How do you know this?"

"The clerk who took down the letter is a man of ours."

"So," Tussun said, "it seems clear that the Shariff and his followers will remain neutral until they see the outcome of the first battle."

"In the words of my birth-people," Thomas said, "he is sitting on the fence."

He used the term for a tribal boundary; and a breath of mingled anger and amusement ruffled through the men in the commander's tent.

But the Grand Shariff's letter was not the only one lying beside the coffee hearth. Tussun's second act on arrival had been to send out a call to arms in the name of the Sultan to the sheikhs of the Beni Jehaine and the Beni Harb, the two great tribes whose territories lay between Yembo and Medina, most of whom had promised the Viceroy's emissaries over the past two years (in exchange for considerable gifts of Maria Theresa dollars) to give their aid and support to the Egyptian forces when they came. The Viceroy, though by no means of a trusting disposition, had been inclined to believe that at any rate some branches of the two tribes would honour their bargain and come in to earn their purchase money. And over the past few days, by messenger speaking word-of-mouth or by clerk-written letter, their response, the justification or otherwise of the Viceroy's belief, had been coming in.

Tussun, acting on private advice from both Thomas and Zeid ibn Hussein, had waited until it seemed that there was nothing more to wait for, and then called the war council.

Only one of the Beni Harb sheikhs had sent a reply in any form, and that a very non-committal one, pleading his nearness to the Wahabi borders and sickness among his camels; but the sheikhs of the Beni Jehaine, it seemed, were made of sterner stuff; several of them had combined to send inviting Tussun Pasha to meet them in Council at Yembo el Nakhl, a day's march inland from Yembo Port, and promising the support of most of the tribe.

When all had been laid before the council a great deal of talk followed. Thomas wondered, not for the first time, if he should ever get used to the sheer amount of words, convolutions and arabesques of words, high-pitched discussion, with long pauses for the hookah or more coffee, long and flowery compliments and devout calls upon Allah or his Prophet, that his adopted world appeared to need in order to get anything decided.

It seemed to him that there was very little to discuss. They could not remain where they were, holed up in Yembo, much longer. That would look like irresolution, even fear of the Wahabis, and would be the surest way of losing their potential allies. They could not advance on Mecca or Jiddah without, as he had warned Tussun, throwing the Grand Shariff back into alliance with the enemy. Their remaining option was to march on Medina, the only city of the Hijaz with a large Wahabi garrison. It was not, he had gathered, the normal policy of Saud ibn Saud to establish garrisons of his own men in his conquered and vassal cities, but rather to leave the task to their sheikhs; but he had made an exception in the case of Medina, partly because of the strategic importance of its position across the caravan routes, and partly because it seemed the citizens were particularly stubborn in their attempts to follow their own old forbidden ways, even to the lavish decorations of the Prophet's tomb.

To take Medina, the second of the Holy Cities, would harm or enrage no one but the Wahabis, and would bring over the warrior tribes throughout the Hijaz. Looking further ahead, it would either provide a forward base for an attack on Najd, or provoke ibn Saud into risking a pitched battle with the Egyptian army at a time and place not of his own choosing.

He listened, putting in a word of his own from time to time, until at last, many words and many little brass cups of coffee later, the war council had reached much the same conclusion.

"So, then," Tussun finally wound the matter up, "it is agreed that we shall march on Medina; and since the road runs through Beni Jehaine country, we shall first accept the invitation of the sheikhs, which will give us a chance to scout out the land at the same time. It is agreed also that Ibrahim Agha shall accompany me with part of the cavalry, to make an impression, whilst the foot and the rest of the cavalry remain here waiting further orders."

"For better or worse, then," Thomas thought, "we are on our way."

Chapter 18

Some days later, Thomas was sitting in much the same position in the commander's tent, playing a rather more active part in another council. But the view spread beyond the tent opening was not the walls of Yembo Port and the transports at anchor in the harbour under the ancient guns, but the feathery date palms about Yembo el Nakhl, the melon fields, and the white huddle of the oasis village about the upward-pointing finger of its minaret; and opposite to where he sat beside Tussun, on the guest's side of the coffee hearth, sat the Beni Jehaine sheikhs, headed by Sheikh Muhammed their leader and spokesman. They were all clad in magnificent abbas of scarlet silk, and nursed fine new gold-mounted swords.

The Viceroy's son with his backing of Arab cavalry had ridden in the night before, to be courteously welcomed and royally if barbarously feasted. But Tussun had decided that the ceremonial gifts should be made at the start of the council rather than at the arrival feast, putting it to his officers that there would be friendly feeling and to spare at the feasting, and it was in the clear light of morning, when the hard talking started, that extra warmth and friendliness might well be needed.

The commander was certainly gaining in wisdom, Thomas thought.

The gifts had been chosen in Cairo, with tact in the case of the swords, which were of the Arab and not the Turkish pattern; with something much more in the case of the ceremonial abbas, for since the Wahabis had strictly forbidden the wearing of silk or any kind of gold ornamentation, public acceptance of these must signify public repudiation of the Wahabi ruling. It had been a calculated gamble, and the gift ceremony had provided a sharply interesting few minutes. But neither Sheikh Muhammed nor his brethren had made any show of hesitation in accepting the silken robes and instantly putting them on over their camel-hair abbas.

But the crowning glory of the gift ceremony (el Marouki's

scouts had reported well and in detail) was the extra gift for Sheikh Muhammed himself of a pair of gold-rimmed spectacles. The old man had accepted them with delight, sending for his own copy of the Koran that he might put them instantly to the test. "I see! I see! This is most wonderful! Allah is good!" he had exclaimed, and now sat peering out through them from among the folds of his headcloth like some large-eyed small desert creature peering out from its hole.

Thomas wondered whether he would sleep in them, and felt a glow of sympathetic warmth towards him. It must be sad to grow old and not be able to read one's Koran, nor see clearly the evening light on the desert, or the faces of friend or enemy.

But the cardamom-scented coffee was making its first round, the return gift-making was over; a superb pair of salukis for Tussun, which would doubtless gravitate to Zeid, weapons, embroidered saddles; for himself a very fine silver watch, Edinburgh-made as were most of the best watches of the day, though the maker's name on it was not his father's. It was stopped, and he did not try to wind it up, having a feeling that there was probably sand in the movement. Well, he would be able to deal with that later. The talking was at last about to start.

Tussun, with the air of a grey-bearded elder, began it by announcing his plan of marching on Medina and by Allah's Grace freeing the second Holy City from its oppressors.

The Beni Jehaine sheikhs greeted the plan warmly, bending their heads in agreement.

"That indeed makes sweet hearing," said one.

"By the beard of the Prophet, a true warrior's plan," said another.

"Surely Allah the All Powerful will aid you in so pious a venture!"

But the question of the moment was whether the Beni Jehaine would, Thomas thought.

There followed five hours of gruelling discussion, while he lent every atom of ability he possessed to the task of helping Tussun bring the sheikhs down out of the clouds of pious platitudes to actual details of the resistance likely to be met with, the best routes, the maintenance of supplies, and, above all, the help and support to be expected from the Beni Jehaine themselves.

Maps made by the cartographers of Alexandria were compared with maps drawn in the sand by two of the sheikhs, and found to be virtually useless, because the distances were marked in kilometres, whereas the Bedouin had no measure of distance other than the camel-march. Thomas amended the maps, with much advice, some of it contradictory, substituting days and half days of camel marching.

A great deal of information emerged about the Beni Harb, the largest tribal confederacy in the Hijaz, whose clans dominated the main route from Yembo el Nakhl to Medina; and Thomas took careful notes. The Jehaine sheikhs seemed to have as great a gift for gossip as Leith fisherwives. He hoped they were as given to exaggeration. He could scarcely believe that the Beni Harb could put thirty thousand foot fighters armed with matchlocks in the field, even though their horsemen numbered only a few hundred; but one could only assume that the numbers were correct; and with a tightening of the stomach, he noted them down. Fortunately, it seemed that, for one reason and another, they would be most unlikely to have the whole fighting strength of the Beni Harb as well as the Wahabi war host on their hands at the same time. Partly to make sure that he had got that straight, and partly for the benefit of Tussun with his somewhat sketchy Arabic, when the end seemed to have been reached, he recapitulated from his notes the enemy forces which probably *would* contest their advance, and the alternative long-term outcome of those encountered.

"From Badr to Jedaida and the pass northward, we may meet two clans, the Beni Sobh and the Beni Salen, combined forces five thousand matchlocks; first class fighting men. If we can overcome them quickly, probably no more trouble from the Beni Harb until we have dealt with the garrison at Medina. If, however, we are held up for more than a few days by Beni Sobh or Beni Salen, they could well be joined by others of the confederacy, another seven thousand foot, maybe, and several hundred horse . . ."

Dark attentive faces bent forward in agreement.

"Also, if we reach Medina but are then held up by a long siege, Saud ibn Saud may well send a relief force from the Najd, joined by as many as fifteen thousand men of the Beni Harb clans to cut off our retreat—"

"Who talks of retreat?" Tussun said quickly and at half breath, in the French tongue.

"No one. But it is a possibility which in any advance, must needs be considered."

Sheikh Muhammed clearly understood the drift of this though the tongue was unknown to him. He stroked his beard, smiling benignly through his new spectacles. "You have grasped the hilt and the haft of the problem, Ibrahim Agha. On the one hand the Turks" (Thomas was growing used to the fact that among the Tribes the whole Egyptian army, Bedouin, Albanian, Turkish and all else, were known as Turks) "on the one hand the Turks will face annihilation if held back for any length of time at Jedaida or outside the Holy City. On the other hand if you reach and take Medina without delay, the matter will be as different as the desert before and after the autumn rains, for almost all the clans of the Beni Harb will abandon the black standards of Saud ibn Saud and rally to yours, Tussun Pasha."

It had been done so skilfully that it was impossible to say at what point the old sheikh had ceased to address Thomas, the man who knew what he was talking about, and began addressing Tussun, the commander-in-chief.

"Say then, most honourable son of a mighty father, now that we have laid bare the bitter with the sweet, is it still in your head to advance against so great odds?"

Tussun sat for a few moments unanswering, his gaze turned down to his own sword-hand; and as the silence lengthened, Thomas grew afraid that the boy had not fully understood, or could not frame in Arabic the reply that must be given. But there was nothing he could do to help. The question had been shot directly at Tussun, as the commander, and nobody but the commander could answer it.

Then Tussun looked up. He spoke in slow and careful Arabic with the usual strong Albanian accent, and the warrior note in his voice was plain to hear. "When the followers of the Prophet, peace be to Him, first set foot in Egypt, were they not fewer than four thousand against five times that number? We are marching to free the Prophet's beloved city from oppression and desecration. Can we doubt that Allah will look with favour on our cause? And if the All Powerful be with us, shall we fear and can we fail?"

Loud and courteous exclamations of approval greeted his words, and the old sheikh agreed, "Truly we believe that Allah goes with you in your high endeavours, and that in His strength you will succeed."

"And with the help of the Beni Jehaine His loyal and valiant servants," Tussun added. "That is a matter that we have yet to speak of."

The silence which followed was broken by the sound of horses whinnying impatiently near by, and the old sheikh gestured toward the sound with a hand like a withered terebinth root. "That is a true word. Yet it is not wise to press forward over hastily, speaking of too many weighty matters in one day; and Allah the All Merciful sends to remind us in the voice of Rani, his servant, that we are to have – did your Honour not promise it – a display of Western cavalry skills in the cool of the day. Alas, I grow old, and weary, and must rest a while to make ready for such delights. So – we have talked enough for one day of warlike things; now we will rest, and make light our hearts with the beauty of horsemanship, and with feasting afterward; and tomorrow we will return to our council, refreshed as by the autumn rains." And on that note the council broke up until the following morning.

"All that talk!" Tussun exploded under his breath to Thomas, as they went down to the makeshift maidan below the village, to make sure that all was in hand and going forward for the evening's cavalry display. "And not one word yet of the thing we came to talk about! Wasted – all wasted! We might as well have gone hawking!"

"Oh I don't know," Thomas said. "We have cleared a lot of ground ready for tomorrow's talking. I should judge that by Hijazi standards we have made a surprising amount of progress."

Tussun gave an angry splutter of laughter. "How can you be so patient? The Turks are slow enough, but that is generally because they hope that if they drag any matter out long enough, gold, or power, will come into their hands thereby. That is a thing that all can understand. These desert Arabs seem to drag things out simply for the sake of the dragging."

"Oh they do," Thomas agreed. "It is a delicate art. To rush forward with unseemly haste into the making of decisions in the Western way is uncouth. Had you not realised? Time is different for the desert people, too, and decisions often are not of their own making. You come to a well, and if the water lasts you may camp there from one full moon to the next. If the water gives out you load up the camels and move on next morning. No good making any decision in advance, and no knowing what is to be until the water runs out or the moon changes."

Tussun looked at him sideways, as they walked. "You sound as though you were of the Bedouin yourself."

"I had more than cavalry training in my first frontier months," Thomas said. "The Bedouin are my second people. It is simple."

They had reached the place where the horses were being made ready, in what little shade a skein of date palms afforded, for the well-rehearsed display. Thomas's own mare advanced a velvet muzzle with gently working lips, and he pulled out the crust of sugar-bread he always carried for her in the breast of his thobe. "Hai-Mai, greedy one – Heart's delight, lend me your skill this evening."

The shadows were lengthening and the early winter evening growing cool, when Thomas and Abu Salan, he who had commanded the unfortunate second troop at El Hamha, led their squadrons on to the makeshift Maidan, and drew them up facing each other across the dusty open space. And the roofs of the nearest houses, the slightly rising ground to the north, and even the feathery crowns of the date palms were crowded with the men and boys of the village.

Thomas flicked a glance at the two youngsters sitting their fidgeting mares on either side of him. Daud ibn Hussein, his bugler and a junior half-brother of Zeid's, and Jassim Khan his standard bearer and personal orderly. They were so young and much would depend on them in the coming display. "The honour of the Arab cavalry is in your hands," he said to them both, aware of the answering pride flashing out from them like a sword from its sheath; and to Daud, "Sound me the Advance."

The two squadrons, following each its own silken pennant, swept forward at the trot, to meet and wheel in two long lines to face the spot under the few shade-trees where fine rugs had been spread and the sheikhs of the Beni Jehaine sat with Tussun in their midst.

Thomas's hand was on the hilt of his sabre, whipping it up in

187

salute, and to left and right in the same splinter of time two hundred and fifty blades sprang clear, splintering back the evening light; two hundred and fifty voices raised the ritual shout "In the name of Ali ibn Talib, the Sword of Allah!" And "Ali ibn Ali Talib! The blessing of Allah be upon him!" the crowd shouted back. Hearing this response, Thomas was aware for the first time just how dear-held was the memory of the Prophet's warrior son-in-law among the desert tribes. He gave the next signal, the bugle sounded again, and the two squadrons peeled apart and withdrew once more to their own ends of the area. At the third bugle call they broke forward again, straight from a stand into a canter, as they swept towards each other.

One after another they went through the disciplined and complex evolutions of Western-style cavalry manoeuvres, providing a display which could not, Thomas felt with pride, have been greatly bettered by the British cavalry itself. It was what Tussun had asked of him; but despite the long-drawn breaths of approval from the onlookers, he knew that, though they must be suitably impressed, it was not the kind of thing that would really make sense to these wild riders of the desert. Well, the next part of the entertainment might take care of that.

He shouted an order, and the men sheathed sabres and sat loose in their saddles. He called a name and Abu Salan called another, and from each squadron a man drew his sword again and headed at full flying gallop to meet in the dusty centre of the arena and lock instantly into what looked like mortal combat.

This was more within the understanding and experience of the Beni Jehaine. All round the open space the excitement ran like a little wind through standing corn. Thomas felt the rise and sway forward, heard the high-pitched applause. He called out another man, to be matched again by Abu Salan, and so continued until a dozen matched pairs of the regiment's best men were closely engaged, sabres glinting through the dust cloud flung up by the horses' trampling hooves.

He sat quietly alert in his saddle and let the sham fight continue for a few whirlpool minutes, keeping an eye well open for any sign of blood getting overheated, which among the Bedouin horse was always a danger at such times. Then, with the onlookers still gripped by the spectacle, still waving and shouting encouragement to this man or that of the swirling riders, made a signal to his bugler.

Again the bugle sang across the sandy space, and the two dozen fighters broke off, turned towards the group under the shade-trees and raised their sabres in salute, then rode back to their squadrons.

It was time for the final flourish.

Thomas snatched a quick glance to where Tussun's white mare should be waiting, hidden beyond the camel thorn that hedged the nearest of the melon patches. The gleam of a milky flank through the barbed branches told him that she was where she should be. He heeled his own mare lightly forward into a canter, heading for the group under the shade-trees; and reining in at what seemed the last instant before he was among them, achieved an expert levade. Then bringing her flickering hooves down again to the baked ground – he would not have cared to try that so near the brains of the senior sheikhs of the Beni Jehaine and his own sword-brother among them if she had not had a mouth like velvet and a trust in him as complete as his trust in her – he saluted first Sheikh Muhammed, his host, and then Tussun Pasha, his commander.

"Tussun, Brother of Nayli," he issued the challenge in the Bedouin fashion, "Grant to my poor Sword the honour of single combat."

A gasp broke from the tribal sheikhs, their faces kindled with eagerness to see what would happen. He and Tussun had both known the effect such a challenge would have, and catching each other's gaze, shared a flicker of inner laughter. Every Arab knew that Turkish etiquette did not permit such informality between a three-tailed pasha and one of his officers, even though they were known to be friends, and they had not yet learned that Muhammed Ali and his family made their own laws of etiquette to suit themselves and the needs of the occasion, as they went along.

"With all the joy in the world, my brother."

Tussun came to his feet all in one movement. In almost the same instant the white mare was out from behind the camel thorns, dancing at the end of her rein, to which a young groom clung. Tussun stepped out from among the sheikhs and setting his hands on her withers swung into the saddle, drew his sabre with a flourish worthy of Ali ibn Talib himself, and urged her straight at Thomas.

For ten minutes or so, alone in the midst of the open space, the two young men put on a display of mounted sabre fighting combined with horsemanship that Thomas reckoned was different both in kind and quality from anything that had been seen in these parts before. Circling and intently focused, they wove their intricate patterns of bright and savage action, smiling at each other straight-lipped and bright eyed with a kind of cool delight through the dust cloud of their own raising.

"Have I not taught thee well?" Thomas said as their blades locked.

"Indeed thou hast taught me well – but first I taught thee how to fly a hawk," Tussun returned, breaking free of the lock to come in under Thomas's guard, and they swung the horses dancingly apart and came at each other again, pleasuring in their own and each other's skill as they had done in so many practice bouts before, but never with quite this added edge to their delight.

"Enough?" Thomas signalled a few minutes later, after a particularly swift and brilliant flourish of sword strokes.

"Enough," Tussun Pasha signalled back.

They lowered their blades, backed their horses a few paces, and gravely saluted each other. Then as the orderlies came running to the horses' heads, they sheathed their swords and dismounted, and strolled back together towards the group under the shade-trees, while the squadrons turned and rode off.

". . . And by Allah! They breathe scarcely faster than if they were but now risen from sleep!" one of the sheikhs was murmuring to his neighbour as they came.

Sheikh Muhammed's feast for the pasha and his officers took place in a long five-bay tent pitched among the palm trees behind his house. A young camel had been killed and broiled. Thomas appreciated the honour and hospitality, but doubted if he should ever get used to the gelatinous texture of camel foal, even when served with mountains of rice, yellow with saffron and pungent with herbs. He did his best to eat as much as custom and courtesy demanded, while still leaving a little space for the savouries and camel-curd sweetmeats that were pressed upon them from all sides, until to his relief, the food was done and the armed Negro slaves were bearing round the first of the endless cups of coffee.

"Forgive my poor fare. Indeed thou hast scarcely touched the food," moaned their host, following the ritual of good manners.

"Nay, the food was most excellent, and we have eaten as much as would suffice for a whole army," Tussun responded with equal good manners, and, Thomas thought, considerably more of truth.

He leaned back and belched to express his own satisfaction, feeling, though overfull, beautifully at home; and thought again with gratitude of the months up beyond Aswan that had given him more than his cavalry training. And when the story-telling started, he slipped easily into taking part in it; and the crowding darkness became the darkness of El Hamha, and the jackals crying out beyond the oasis were the jackals of the frontier desert, and the dark faces intent in the upward light of the coffee hearth were the faces of Zeid and the rest . . . These were his people as they could never be Tussun's. They would come to admire and respect the young pasha who was so unlike what they had come to believe a pasha of the Turkish world must be; they would follow him, some would come to love him; but they could never be his people, as they were Thomas's people; and he felt oddly protective towards his commander, as though the younger man were a stranger in Thomas's country.

Next morning the council continued, if council it could be called, and after hours spent in political digression, long and detailed by-ways of tribal history, and almost as great a wealth of pious platitudes as on the day before, Sheikh Muhammed, his new gold-rimmed spectacles still on his nose, made a long speech summing up the position of the Beni Jehaine. His voice droned on like a fly on a window pane as he told off point after point on his blue-nailed fingers.

It must be understood that almost the whole tribe were on the side of Tussun Pasha in this campaign to free the Hijaz from Wahabi oppression.

But it must be understood also that while they were prepared at any time to fight ibn Saud and his followers, they had, also, a ten-year truce solemnly sworn on the Koran with the sheikhs of the Beni Harb.

Tussun Pasha would assuredly understand that this could

not be broken; also that they could not fight the Wahabis without also fighting the Beni Harb.

The dark faces bent in agreement.

They would seek by all peaceful means to persuade the Beni Harb to break their alliance with ibn Saud; and they held out good hope that the capture of Medina would bring over most of the Harb tribes anyway, thereby freeing the Jehaines of their oath, to move against any of the tribes under the Wahabi banner.

Again the bowed heads and the murmurs of agreement. "All will be well, Insh' Allah."

They would furnish guides for the Turkish army through the Harb country, as far as the Pass of Jedaida, provided that the guides were not asked to draw sword. Also they would protect Tussun's lines of communication through their own country against all comers, Harb or Wahabi.

Thomas, scribbling notes, took particular care to get that point straight, pressing, through Tussun, for the answers to certain questions, with gentle persistence when the old man sought to brush them aside. One thought in terms of victory, but possible defeat had also to be taken into consideration, and lines of communication were also one's line of retreat.

Finally, the old sheikh wound up. Should ibn Saud send another force against Mecca while the Turks were still busy with Medina, the Beni Jehaine would go to the aid of the Grand Shariff.

And that was all. Of present support, open support, despite the ceremonial abbas of gold-worked poppy-coloured silk, no word at all.

Beside him, Thomas felt his commander, who had held himself on an increasingly tight rein throughout, waiting for more, and then, as he realised that there was no more, about to drop the reins and let fly. And they could not afford to make enemies of the Beni Jehaine. He said quickly and quietly, "Sir, have I your permission, since I have the notes here, to answer on your behalf?"

"You have my permission," Tussun said through shut teeth.

And Thomas went through the various points, referring with care to the notes on his knee, that the sheikhs might be fully aware that they were written down and on record. Of the Beni Jehaine's own position, he spoke with a mixture of understanding and courteously implied reproach. The pasha and his forces had hoped – had been led to hope – for several thousand Beni Jehaine fighting men to march with them upon Medina, but a sacred oath was a sacred oath, and not to be lightly broken.

He wondered whether Montrose, towards the lag end of the Annus Mirabilis had felt much the same as this, when trying to cope with his own Highlanders. If so, Montrose had his, Thomas Keith's sympathy. The sense of belonging, of being among his own people that had come up on him yesterday evening was strained to the utmost; but, torn and exasperated, it held.

"And *still* with those red silk abbas dripping with tinsel like dancing girls on their backs!" Tussun exploded for the second time, later in his own tent while they were making ready for the evening meal.

Before Thomas could answer, a sentry's challenge sounded outside the tent; a shadow moved at the corner of his eye, and looking round, he saw Yusef, Sheikh Muhammed's youngest son, standing in the tent opening.

"Salaam aleikum," he said. "I may enter?"

Tussun returned the greeting, "Enter and be welcome, in Allah's name."

The young man came forward, and wasted no time on the usual flowery preliminaries, "Excellency, I come to ask that when you ride against the Wahabis, I may ride with you."

There was a moment's surprised silence, and then Tussun said, "Does your father, Sheikh Muhammed, know of this?"

The young man smiled, a flash of white teeth in a big-boned olive face. "When you and Ibrahim Agha sheathed your swords yesterday evening, my father said to his sons, 'By Allah! If I were your age, I would ride with those two to the gates of Diriyah and beyond,' and I said to him, 'By Allah, I *will* ride with them, if they will accept my sword.' He pretended not to hear me, but he knows."

"But the Beni Harb?" Thomas said.

"I am the son of a lesser wife, and can be spared from the family honour easily enough. If any question be asked, my father can say that I went without his knowledge – Did I not say that he pretended not to hear me?"

Tussun said gravely, laying his arm about the other's

193

shoulders, "Then Yusef ibn Muhammed, bring your sword and ride with us to the gates of Diriyah and beyond."

Across his shoulder, his eyes and Thomas's met. All the planning and effort and long-drawn diplomacy that had gone into this council meeting at Yembo el Nakhl had not been quite wasted; their own exhibition of swordsmanship had brought them one solitary volunteer.

Chapter 19

Thomas had experienced the Pass of Killiecrankie more than once, on route marches, from Perth to Blair Atholl before the 78th was drafted south, and had thought it a dreich and deadly place enough. But in memory it seemed no more than a rough valley by comparison with the Pass of Jedaida viewed from the edge of the palm groves beyond Jedaida village.

The long wall of the mountains reared up, seeming to menace, as though it were live and hostile, the low country and the straggle of palm-fringed villages beneath. Jagged masses of black rock rising in giant heaps from ridge to ridge till the savage crest slashed the sky. And at the nearest point to the village, the chief reason – save for the wells which in the desert are the first reason for any village – for being there, opened the yawning darkness of the pass; the way through the mountains to Medina, running, so the scouts had told them, for three miles, and in places less than a hundred yards wide. Easy to see why ibn Saud, acting through the Beni Harb, had chosen this place for his centre and main collecting point for the dues exacted by virtual blackmail from the pilgrim caravans.

At dawn when the advance guard had reported the village and palm groves deserted by the Beni Harb, they had entered into possession, and, leaving the business of making and securing the camp going on behind them, Tussun had cantered forward with Thomas and a couple of scouts to reconnoitre the pass. In the clear morning light Thomas could see how on the lower ridges on both sides of the track the Beni Harb had built rough breastworks of rock and small boulders from behind which they could fire on all comers in comparative safety.

Even as he looked, there was a crack like a whiplash, and a puff of white smoke wisped away from one of the nearest of the sangars, and a bullet at extreme range spat up a shower of dust and rock-splinters not much more than a spear's throw ahead.

"Near enough, I think," Thomas said, and the little party reined in, while a scatter of random and at that range useless shots rattled the echoes from rock faces, and dust spurted up from the track ahead.

"The message is received," Tussun replied grimly, but steadying his startled mare with a gentle hand. "We shall have to bring them down into the open. If we try to clear the ridges one by one, and the Harb are the fighters and the marksmen they are reputed to be, we shall lose half the army in a day."

"Best order up the guns," Thomas said as they rode back to the main force.

The six pounder field-pieces had already been unloaded from the artillery camels, and in half an hour were assembled and ready for action, though it was another twenty minutes or so before the gunners, short of experience for all Thomas's efforts in that direction, began to bring reasonably accurate fire on to the lower breastworks. Thomas, sitting his horse at the head of one of the flanking squadrons of cavalry, ready to strike inward if the Beni Harb should try to rush the guns, cursed the lack of Colonel D'Esurier. But once the shots started landing on target, results came quickly. By midday when the heat that ricocheted off the black rocks was almost unbearable, all the lower breastworks at the mouth of the pass and for several hundred yards inside it had been destroyed or evacuated. But the sangars on the higher ridges were still untouched, being beyond the elevation of the small field pieces.

Tussun reluctantly ordered a ceasefire and called a meeting of his senior officers in two hours' time.

Now, men and horses took what rest they could in the shade of the palm groves, with strong vedettes posted in case of any sudden Harb attack; and in the fig garden behind what had been the headman's house, Tussun's meeting was deep in argument. The two infantry commanders were protesting strongly against the plan of an infantry attack up the steep slopes in the face of jezail fire from the breastworks. "Doubtless we shall clear the ridges, though with heavy loss," Salah Agha was saying, "but as we do so, the enemy will fall back with comparatively little loss, to the ridge above. By the end of the day we shall be substantially outnumbered."

Thomas found it difficult to fault the argument, remembering the maxim that, all other factors being equal, a force attacking a prepared defensive position should outnumber the defenders by at least two to one.

"Then what else have you to suggest?" Tussun demanded, looking round him from one to another.

Umar Agha answered him: "That we should rely on denying them the supplies, and especially the water, of Jedaida village, to force them to come down and attack us on the level ground, where our more disciplined troops will have the advantage."

Disciplined! thought Thomas, remembering the Albanian and Turkish infantry as he had known them through nearly four years.

Tussun nodded, "I agree that ideally that would be the more sensible course, but" – he opened the full blaze of his tawny eyes upon them, and his voice rose and hardened – "it is a strategy that could take a week, maybe more, to take effect, and we do not *have* a week. Within half that time ibn Saud could be upon us from the rear. If that happens, trapped and without hope of effective relief, not one of us will come out of Jedaida Pass alive!"

Thomas saw the aghas' faces grow blank. For the moment neither of them could think of a counter argument, and in the pause, Tussun pressed on:

"There is no hope of a decisive action this evening, that I know well. At first light tomorrow we shall attack and capture the lower ridges on both sides of the pass. That should take only one, admittedly costly, assault on either side. We shall check and fall back before the cost becomes too great. And meanwhile we shall make the Beni Harb the gift of an obvious tactical blunder to delight their hearts."

His listeners sat forward alertly. Carefully, no glance passed between the commander and Thomas, who had worked the plan out with him in the first place. "We shall overextend the flanks of the assault into the pass until more than half our infantry is outflanked by the Beni Harb and appears to be in the jaws of a trap. When that happens, the tribesmen will not be able to resist the temptation to spring it. They will attack down from the ridges, while their horse and camel men advance round the bend of the defile."

"And we shall be cut to pieces," said Umar Agha, with the air of one pointing out the obvious to a headstrong child.

"You are forgetting the cavalry," Zeid said softly.

"So – we wait to hear of the cavalry."

Tussun's russet brows were drawn close in concentration. "Ibrahim Agha will have half the cavalry concealed in the main palm grove directly opposite the mouth of the pass, ready to charge at an instant's notice, while the rest is out on the flanks, manoeuvring to give as much as possible the appearance of being the whole body. Once the enemy are out from the breastworks and attacking in the open, our infantry should be able to stand their ground against them, even as you yourself have said, Umar Agha. At that point the whole of our cavalry, save for a small reserve will charge, sweeping them, their horse and camel men away."

Thomas thought, 'The cub grows up. Indeed the cub grows up.' He spoke to the young commander standing bright-eyed and frowning in their midst, but pitched his words of support for the other listeners: "Your plan is a good one, Tussun Pasha, seeing that we have no chance but to fight – and win – a decisive action within the next two or at most three days . . ." Without any will of his own, he felt his face crack into a smile. "Certainly Zeid ibn Hussein and I can promise you that the cavalry will be up the pass within one minute from the order." He turned his attention to the two infantry leaders: "Please warn your troops to leave the floor of the pass clear as soon as the Beni Harb attack begins; we shall need right of way if we are not to charge over our own men."

"So – now to work out details . . ." Tussun made a gesture to gather closer the less senior of his officers who had made a kind of outer circle until now. Matters went quickly and keenly now that the main plan had been accepted. And a short while later the fig garden was empty. And there was beginning to be a quiet and ordered coming and going of young officers such as Medhet between the commanders and the troops among the palm groves and the walls . . .

Later, returning from his cavalry lines to the house of the fig garden, which was now their headquarters, Thomas was greeted with the news that one of Sheik Muhammed's elder sons had come in with an urgent warning that Saud ibn Saud had arrived three days earlier at El Rass, with a thousand horse and twenty thousand foot warriors and camel men, all Wahabis of Nadj.

Sheik Muhammed, his father, sent word, the young man

had said, that if the Turkish army did not break through by tomorrow's end they must withdraw during tomorrow's night or find the Wahabi war host across their line of retreat.

Tussun had thanked him and had him fed.

"Where is he? I must speak with him—" Thomas began.

"Already on his way back," Tussun said. "He asked leave to depart at once. His mother is the senior wife." Then he laughed. "No, that is unkind. It was valiant of him to come himself."

Watching from the low rocky knoll just ahead of the palm groves where his best cavalry squadrons lay concealed, Thomas was afraid at first that the push forward into the pass was going to be too obvious a tactical error; but it seemed to be happening so much in the nature of the fighting that the Beni Harb, with the Arab's typical contempt for "Turkish" generalship might just be taken in by it.

The clash of steel and rattle of musketry and the occasional crack of the field-pieces came back in a wave of sound from the rock faces, the note changing as the fight thrust further and further into the defile. The two flanks of the assault had almost reached the great curve that carried the track out of sight. Any moment now – surely any moment now – Thomas gazed after them with eyes narrowed against the sun-glare, straining to catch the first sign of the expected counter attack.

Beside him a horse moved, tossing up its head with a jingle of accoutrements. He assumed, without looking round, that the rider was Medhet, who as usual was with him to act as a galloper. Then Tussun's voice said, "It looks like the mouth of Gehenna."

"They're almost as far into it as we dare let them go," Thomas said.

"What happens if the Harb have not launched their counter attack by the time our infantry have cleared the last of the lower slopes before the bend?"

"Then I think that you must order a retreat. We cannot afford to lose men needlessly. But it looks as though the Beni Harb will counter attack at any moment now; they seem to be giving up the breastworks too easily . . . It could be that they do indeed think themselves to be leading our men on into a trap –

or it could be that their morale is cracking, but I doubt that's the way of it."

For a few minutes longer they watched the fight through drifting smoke that was beginning to fill the gorge.

Still no sign of the counter attack on which the whole plan depended.

"We could provoke a move by sending one squadron up the pass and round into the next reach, where the Jehaine say it widens out," Tussun said.

Thomas hesitated. For no reason that he could lay hold of, he felt slightly uneasy. But something had to be done, and a cavalry squadron loosed up the pass should certainly act as a trigger, to counter attack or retreat . . .

The Turkish cavalry were already out in the open, on both flanks, keeping up a constant dust-raising manoeuvring that made their numbers seem greater than they were; but they had not the calibre for this particular task. Thomas sent Medhet back with an order to Abu Salan to bring his squadron out from the palm grove; gave him quick and clear orders not to enter the second reach of the pass if there was any sign of the counter attack, in which case he was to withdraw, fighting a rearguard action until reinforcements arrived to loose him from the fight.

For a long time, despite all that came after, when Thomas thought of Jedaida, he saw again that single squadron of Arab horse, thin crimson pennant fluttering at their head, trotting smartly up the pass into the drifting smoke.

They had almost reached the curve of the track, when Tussun leaned over and gripped Thomas's arm, pointing with his other hand: "In Allah's name – look!"

But Thomas was already looking.

The tribesmen were swarming out from the breastworks, though in the first few moments it was impossible to tell whether in flight or counter attack. After those first few moments there was no longer any doubt. Above the musketry Thomas heard the first faint fierce trumpet calls from height beyond height, answered from the depths of the gorge like an echo; and from every ridge and ravine and round the turn of the pass emptied a vast battle-swarm of black-robed Wahabi warriors.

The barest few minutes before, on the ridge below which the defile curved eastward and opened into a narrow valley,

200

Abdullah ibn Saud, eldest son of the Wahabi leader, three days of forced marching behind him, turned to his trumpeter and the Beni Harb sheikhs gathered around him:

"In the name of Allah, it is the time!"

The sheikhs flung up their jezails in signal, and among the rocks on the far side of the gorge the sun glinted on musket barrels as the signal was taken up. In the same instant the trumpeter put his trumpet to his bearded lips and sounded the call which was echoed and flung back from a score of places along the mountain flanks.

Abdullah looked far down to his left, where the single squadron of Bedouin cavalry came up at an ordered canter towards the bend. He looked down to his right, where the valley beyond it was filled with Wahabi horsemen and camels. As he looked, the horsemen broke forward in answer to the trumpets, streaming after their black banners that lifted on the wind of their going. The rock faces were moving with the downward flow of fighting men. The horsemen had reached the bend of the defile . . .

"Now by Allah! The Turks are charging!"

Below him the long patient years of Zeid's and Thomas's training were proving their worth. While all around them the infantry were breaking back and turning to run, the squadron was quickening from a canter to a full flying gallop.

Looking down from above like a falcon before the stoop, Abdullah ibn Saud watched with his companions. "Now by Allah and his Prophet," he said, "these dogs fallen from the true Faith, be brave men, none the less! If any of their footmen escape this day, it will be because these blocked the pass for long enough to buy their lives with their own!" To one of the men beside him, he said, "Away down with thee and remind my brother Feisal who is forgetful in such matters that our horsemen must fan out beyond the village to cut off all escape, also that they must not stop to plunder! There will be time for that when all the enemies of the Prophet are dead."

Below him the last survivors of the Bedouin squadron, fighting still, were being swept away as thousands of yelling Wahabis engulfed the rear of the fleeing infantry.

On the knoll at the edge of the date garden, there was no time for shock or outcry; no time for anything but the instant making of decisions. Thomas swung round on Tussun Pasha and in a voice as harsh as a bird of prey's gave him his orders as though he and not the younger man were the commander.

"Do what you can to rally the infantry along the edge of the palm groves, keep the reserve company at least intact. Bid them open their files to let the fugitives through, then withdraw in line, still firing." And as though Thomas were the commander indeed, Tussun Pasha wheeled his horse and made for the reserve.

Thomas turned to his young bugler beside him. "Sound the Advance and keep on sounding it . . . Medhet, get to the left flank cavalry and bid Colonel al Fusari to keep charging the Wahabi flank to slow them down. When he has to, he can withdraw leap-frogging, troop by troop . . ."

The first of Thomas's own squadrons, the men he had trained and lived with for years, were advancing out of the palm groves and cantering towards him; he shouted to Zeid ibn Hussein at their head: "Brother, take the first troop and follow Tussun – on thy heads be his life!"

And as the Arab colonel flung up his sabre in acknowledgment and shouting to his own troop to follow him, headed after the galloping figure of Tussun Pasha, the Scotsman took his place at the head of the rest, and drawing his own sabre, turned back towards the fighting.

It was only then that he saw what had happened during the minute or so that his attention had been elsewhere.

Between him and the Wahabi war host, the gorge mouth was filling with a backward-streaming mass of panic-stricken infantry. No hope of the cavalry charging through them, however ruthlessly, without becoming clogged and losing both impetus and cohesion. Desperately his gaze raked the struggling scene from wall to wall of the pass, and showed him that to the right, where the rock wall fell back at an angle of some 45°, the churning swarm was less dense than elsewhere. He gestured with his sabre, "Follow me – follow me home!"

He heard the thunder of hooves behind him, but could not look back, could only hope that all the squadron leaders had received the order correctly, could only put his trust in Allah and ride, his young standard bearer beside him and his bugler sounding. "Charge! – Charge! – Charge!"

Up the slope towards the gaping mouth of the pass, they

thrust. Still a compact and disciplined force, the first troop and the better part of the second sheared their way through the Wahabi column a hundred yards behind its outspreading van; but behind them and battling to follow on, the rest of the squadrons were caught up and cut off by the still thickening tide of terrified fugitives. Hacking his way out on the far side, Thomas saw a low spur of rock that thrust out from the mountainside at the bend of the defile and headed for it, to regroup. His memory of the last few minutes was almost blank, but his sword blade was foul as a butcher's cleaver.

On the crest of the spur he reined in his sweating and wild-eyed mare, and sat waving his men up past him. Daud was still at his side. He grinned at the young bugler. "That was a charge well sounded! Now sound me the Rally." But his stomach tightened as he realised that not much more than fifty men were still with him to answer the call.

Meanwhile Tussun had seen the infantry reserve dissolve and become one with the fleeing mob before he could reach it. He had seen Umar Agha on a wounded cavalry horse in full flight, ahead of his fleeing troops. He had seen the Turkish cavalry galloping for open country on the far right flank. Near at hand a group of maybe a hundred of his own Albanians stampeded by; he forced a way towards them, his sword flailing above his head.

"Stand and fight!" he was shouting. "Turn and follow me!"

They poured past him with blind panic-stricken faces; if he had been in their way they would have cut him down.

Ibn Hussein and something less than twenty of his troop reached him at that moment, cutting their way through the flood to his side. And they were close behind him and coming up on either hand as he drove his horse towards another clot of his countrymen, the last of any size left in the mouth of the defile. "You!" he was shouting. "Were we not born of the same mothers? Let us not shame them! – Turn, my brothers – turn and follow me!"

His voice raved on at them; they seemed not even to hear, but simply surged on; and despite all that they could do, half the Arab troopers were caught up and swept away by them as driftwood by a river in spate.

He was weeping, tears of rage and humiliation and the horror of what was happening running down his cheeks. He used his sabre on them. Those who it reached ran on heedless of wounds.

Some way ahead he saw the enemy ranks, black under their raven banners. They had reached the abandoned field guns and the impetus of their rush seemed checked for an instant. He made straight for them, howling at full pitch of his lungs, "I am Tussun Pasha; I am the son of Muhammed Ali! Kill me or die, you dogs and sons of dogs!"

Zeid and three remaining troopers followed him.

From his vantage point, Thomas looked desperately out across the defile. Not much dust rose from the rocky ground, not much smoke, for the firing had almost ceased; most of the fugitives had flung their muskets away and the tribesmen had turned to sword and lance, and the scene lay clear, hideously clear, to the sight. There was no sign of the Turkish horsemen, no sign of the infantry reserve; save for a few pockets of desperate cavalry fighting, the whole expeditionary force was in full flight.

Save for fifty or so with Thomas. Save also for five others!

In that confused splinter of time five horsemen burst out from the mass of fugitives and charged straight for the heart of the enemy advance. And Thomas's belly seemed to knot itself within him as he recognised the desperate foremost rider.

He pointed with his sword, yelling to the men around him. "If the Pasha dies we are dishonoured and accursed in the sight of Allah! With me! Charge!"

And as one man, his fifty followed him, forming a rough wedge as they went down the rock-strewn slope and into the thick of the Wahabi war host. At his right flank his standard bearer carrying proudly aloft the lance with its gold and crimson folds flying; on his left his bugler repeatedly sounding the charge, bugle in one hand, sword in the other, controlling his horse with his knees. He settled low into his saddle, crashing through towards the point, so far as he could judge it, of Tussun's impact.

Exhausted and soaked in sweat, bleeding from superficial wounds, his heart pounding in his ears and the red battle-mist hanging before his eyes, Thomas hacked his way onward through the yelling Wahabi ranks. His sword-hand was slippery with blood and sweat, and once the sabre slipped from his grasp to hang from the leather thong about his wrist, but he recovered his grasp and ploughed on. He sliced through the bamboo shaft of a lance, and then the blade broke on the nut-shaped helmet of one of Prince Feisal's bodyguard. He flung the hilt in the man's face, and reaching over his shoulder, drew from the scabbard across his back, in which he always carried it into action, his beloved broadsword.

Ahead of him above the sea of black-robed fighters, snarling faces and upreared horses' heads, rose a black Wahabi war banner, and guessing that Tussun would have seen and charged it, he crashed on in the same direction, slashing to right and left as he went, his dwindling company storming in the red wake he left behind him, until the last line of the black war host broke before him, the last man going down with head crushed under his mare's trampling hooves as he broke through.

There before him, by the Mercy of Allah, Tussun and two of the Arab troopers were still alive, their horses' rumps backed together so that they faced outwards, fighting off six or seven of the enemy while the rest surged past.

Zeid ibn Hussein was not one of them.

Thomas drove in his heel again and again, urging his spent and stumbling mare towards them. A last flare of strength rose in him at finding Tussun still alive. With a savage back-hand blow he all but beheaded the Wahabi warrior whose spear-thrust would have been in another instant in Tussun's flank. Another lance aimed at himself, he hacked apart together with the hand that held it. He was conscious that his remaining troopers had formed a half circle between him and the Wahabi torrent and were fighting off twice their own numbers. Mercifully the main force of the Wahabis and Beni Harb were flooding past, intent on booty. It made sense, something cool and oddly remote within himself knew that. Why waste time and lives on men still fighting hard when there were dead men and wounded for the plundering?

Tussun saw him coming and let out a great joyful and desperate shout: "Tho'mas! Come, my brother, we have lost all but our honour and our swords, let us take as many as may be of these dogs with us, as we go down!"

Ranging alongside him, Thomas shouted back: "We are not going down! We shall live to gain the victory another day! I tell you it is the Will of Allah that we cut our way out of here, and

defeat the Wahabi dogs in His chosen time! Therefore come!"
The surviving troopers were closing up in wedge formation
once more behind him, as he wrenched his mare round, and
riding knee to knee with his young commander, their blooded
swords still busy, thrust through the Wahabi mass towards the
palm groves beyond the mouth of the gorge.

By good fortune or maybe by the Will of Allah, the enemy
was now increasingly taken up with looting. Only ibn Saud's
picked bodyguard of two hundred horsemen and some of
Prince Feisal's guards, easily recognisable in their ringmail
shirts and nut-shaped helmets, were still hunting the wreckage
of the Egyptian army to the south. The dust sank. The fighting
for the pass was over.

"Who would think to find so hot a courage in a Turkish
Pasha?" Abdullah ibn Saud said later, reporting to his father.
"And the other, his sword-brother, the one who comes from
Scot-land, to take service with the Turks! Would that he had
taken service with us for he is the bravest of all our enemies –
our men would not have disobeyed my orders and left the hunt
to go after booty, had he been with them!"

Chapter 20

On an evening towards the blistering mirage-haunted end of
summer, Thomas and Tussun took their evening ride along the
shore north of Yembo Port, their small escort headed by the
indestructible Medhet, left at some distance behind. They had
been racing their horses through the shallows, finding pleasure
in the speed and the coolness of the flying spray. Now they rode
more steadily, their shadows reaching inland across the sand,
deep in talk on their way back.

It was eight months since the defeat at Jedaida, since the
night they had burned their camp and pulled back, leaving the
war-chest and their four field guns and their dead in the
enemy's hands, but with the battered remains of their troops
who had come in to the rallying bugles sounding through the
dark. Thomas's mind went back to wild-eyed riderless horses
answering the familiar call, and he remembered, as he had
remembered so often since, one of his own troopers coming
in urgent search of him through the turmoil, telling him
something that he did not hear clearly concerning Zeid ibn
Hussein.

"Zeid? He's here? Where is he?" he had demanded in the
beginning of relief.

But the relief had been short-lived.

"Nay. Not Zeid but his mare. She has returned—"

"I come," Thomas had said, already turning back with the
man. It was hard to see what good he could do by coming, but
there was some thought in him, a desperate hope that if he saw
the mare for himself he would find that she was not Zeid's after
all – some mistake. There were many white mares in the
Bedouin cavalry . . .

But when he stood a little removed from the other horses in
the lee of a camel-thorn hedge, the shadowy silver shape,
trembling and distressed, who swung her head towards him as
though in desperate hope for a moment that he was someone
else, was Zeid's mare and no one else's.

"She must have heard the bugles and she came," someone said.

By the light of the burning camp he saw the shallow gash in her flank and the broad track of blood all down her shoulder with no wound to account for it.

"Put her with the reserve," Thomas said. "She's in no state to carry a rider," and his voice cracked with the dryness of his throat. He fondled her for a moment, laid his cheek against hers as Zeid had been used to do, then turned and went his way about the myriad other things that must be seen to before there was time for grieving – if ever there was time for grieving again . . .

At first it had looked as though none of the infantry had escaped, except by changing sides, but eventually, in one way and another, the rags of half the army had straggled back to Yembo, although only the cavalry had brought off their arms and equipment; and here in Yembo they had been pent up ever since.

As soon as word of Jedaida had reached Mecca, the Grand Shariff had openly joined the Wahabis with all his forces, and the war seemed over. But the bulk of the Beni Jehaine had remained loyal to their pledge to Tussun. They had, in fact, mustered all the men they could spare and sent to warn Abdullah ibn Saud and the Beni Harb that they would resist any advance on Yembo.

"And that," Tussun had said, "is what is called being true to one's gold-rimmed spectacles."

It seemed that the warning must have given Abdullah ibn Saud seriously to think. Certainly the Beni Jehaine combined with what yet remained of the Egyptian expeditionary force could prove a dangerous obstacle, while even if he reached Yembo he was unlikely to be able to breach the old Mameluke fortifications since he had no guns except the four light field-pieces captured at Jedaida, and no man trained to handle them.

At all events the swarming Wahabi attacks which they had feared had not come. Tussun had been given the time he desperately needed to pull the troops together again, build up their shattered morale and get them back into some kind of fighting order; while Thomas, with a reconstituted regiment of Bedouin cavalry, had been stationed at Yembo el Nakhl as a forward post to let their friends the Jehaine see that they were not proposing to hide safe behind a living screen of the tribes while playing no part themselves in the defence of Jehaine territory.

As soon as he had received his son's report of the Jedaida disaster, the Viceroy, with his usual competence and speed of action, had started again from the beginning. With an end to the Mameluke troubles, and his elder son's businesslike success as Governor of Upper Egypt, his country's finances were already improving, and soon fresh supplies of gold, arms and ammunition were reaching Yembo Port in a steady flow, to be followed by reinforcements: three infantry regiments, and with them Ahmed Bonaparte to take over the position of second in command.

Thomas, though he was grateful to the Turkish Agha for the loan of a fine horse and even, in an odd unwilling way, for having bought him in the first place, had no liking for the man himself, quite apart from his reputation for cruelty and the unsavoury practices of his private life, and did not relish the prospect of serving under him. But he fully realised that Ahmed was a brilliant soldier of long experience, and one of the few aghas (Umar and Salan had been shipped back to Egypt in something very like disgrace) on whom Muhammed Ali believed he could completely rely in a tricky situation. And he did wish that his friends and supporters would not be so sure that he must be feeling jealous and slighted that the Turkish general and not himself was to be Tussun's chief of staff in the forthcoming campaign, and would not try so hard to offer loyalty and consolation.

"You yourself have made me the khasnadar, the treasurer of this expedition," he said, laughing, in answer to a fresh outburst from Tussun. "I could scarcely play both parts, and, if we were to change places, I do not think that Ahmed Bonaparte would make as good a khasnadar, as I do."

"That is assuredly true, my brother. I have heard it said that Ibrahim Agha is the first incorruptible khasnadar there has been in a score of years."

Thomas smiled ahead between his horse's ears, "Because I have refused a bribe here and there?"

"Maybe because you have contrived not to make enemies in the refusing."

"Why should I? I have nothing against a fair price for a fair service or for those who feel like it. So long as the bargain be fairly kept." At least they were steering away from the subject of the new second in command.

"So long as the bargain is fairly kept . . ." Tussun said thoughtfully. "Thomas, you have talked friendship with the tribes all those long waiting months, winning over even the Beni Harb for the time being, so that we may hope for an open road when we march for Medina with the autumn rains. Do you believe that their bargains will be fairly kept?"

"I think so. But make no mistake, it is gold and nothing but gold and the hope of more that has bought Shariff Ghalid's solemn promise, yet again, to come to our side in the hour that we free Medina." Thomas heeled his mare into a canter. "And the rains cannot be long now. Oh, but it will be good to be on the move again, before the sap dries in us and we grow old and shrivelled, pent here under the guns of Yembo!"

The shadows were blending into one another as pool runs into pool before the rising tide, though on the tawny crests of the mountains eastward the last of the sunlight still lingered. In the first of the melon fields as they came towards it, a little group of men were gathered, staring all one way towards some point in the crystal luminance of sky above the southern horizon. Someone pointed and cried out, high and triumphant: "Praise be to Allah, Canopus is in the sky!"

Canopus, the Messenger of the Rains. Maybe still a month away, but still, the Messenger of the Rains.

On an evening upward of two months later, the watch fires of the Egyptian army were spread like the golden eyes in a peacock's train about the south-western side of the Holy City.

They had met with little resistance on the march; they had passed through Jedaida as though it were a field gateway, save that field gateways are not generally littered with the bones of men and horses picked clean and dragged apart by jackal and vulture. Only at Badr there had been a brush with local tribesmen in which Tussun had come by a sword gash above the left knee, cracking the bone; not deep, and so long as no threads from the cloth of his loose breeks had been carried into the wound, not dangerous, said the army surgeons (but Thomas wished that Donald had been with them instead of left behind in Cairo). But there was no doubt that for the next week or two he could not ride and would be better without even the lurching of a camel litter, so he had been left behind with one of the surgeons and his own personal troops, while Ahmed Bonaparte had taken over the command and Thomas, for the time being, was back in his old position as chief of staff.

From the slightly raised ground at the end of the camel lines, he could look out across the gently undulating plain filmed with sparse green by the past autumn rains, to the city's walls rising among its famous fig gardens and groves of fronded palms, and see rising above the ramparts, to catch the last of the evening light, the slender minarets and great green dome that marked the Prophet's last resting place. Even the Wahabis had not quite dared to pull that down.

He had wondered, through the long waiting months in Yembo, through the slow gruelling march, what he would feel when he drank in his first sight of the Holy City. He felt a kind of stillness deep within himself; otherwise nothing that he would not have felt before any strong town that must be taken, any captive city that must be freed. In the last level sunlight that sent his shadow reaching out before him, he gazed with narrowed eyes at the scars that the day's bombardment, fallen silent now, had left on the walls. Only surface scars. He had not thought that the light Turkish field guns would have much effect on such walls, and he had been right. But heavier pieces, even if the Viceroy had sent them, would have been beyond the power of men and camels to haul or carry along the old pilgrim route.

He turned, the thick dark folds of his scarlet-braided fariva swinging behind him, and began to make his way back, a familiar figure followed by many eyes, through the crowded camp and the acrid reek of brushwood and camel-dung cooking fires, to the commander's great black tent crouching in the midst of it all.

The sentries before the tent opening parted spears to let him through. Inside, the low flames on the coffee hearth fluttered and keeled sideways in the draught. The lanterns had already been lit and hung from the tent poles, and by their light Ahmed Agha, with a bottle of wine at his elbow, was writing on an upturned ammunition box, while an orderly stood by to take the finished despatches. He looked up as Thomas entered, nodded to him to wait, and returned to his writing.

Just within the looped-back entrance, Thomas waited. There was a scent hanging in the air, floating like oil on water above the usual mingling of goat's hair, tobacco smoke and sweat and the raw Greek wine. It reminded him of the various Houses of Delight that he had visited with Tussun from time to time in Yembo. Beyond the heavy folds curtaining off the next bay, which in a Bedouin tent would have been the women's quarters, something moved, the movement ending in a high-pitched squeal. Thomas wondered idly how many perfumed and painted boys the commander had in there. At least two, by the sound of it.

He watched the man writing at the makeshift table, seeing in the lantern light the fleshily handsome face; the cruelty at the corners of the mouth not quite hidden by the curled moustache; the small capable hands that could almost have been a woman's. A flicker of physical revulsion woke in him as it always did when he found himself near to Ahmed Bonaparte. At least, he thought, the man was no more than half drunk, as was fairly usual with him. If the stories about him were true, it was only in victory, or at least when the fighting was over, that he celebrated with the full drunkenness which unleashed the more unpleasant side of his character.

The commander finished his page, scrawled his flamboyant signature across the foot of it, sanded, folded and sealed it with the usual blob of brown beeswax, and the red onyx that hung on a chain round his neck.

"More bull's blood," he said to the orderly. And when the man had brought another bottle and set it in place of the empty one, and finally departed with the despatches, he sat back and turned his full and slightly bloodshot gaze upon Thomas:

"Well?"

"With the guns we can bring to bear, we can keep up the bombardment for months without breaching the walls," Thomas said.

The other nodded, as one receiving the answer that he expects. "And we cannot afford a long siege. Nor, if the scouts have made true report and we outnumber the Wahabi garrison by less than two to one, can we afford to get held up in a long struggle for strongly defended gateways, with consequent heavy losses."

"I should judge that once we *are* inside, many of the Medinans will join forces with us and so bring up our numbers," Thomas said. "Unless of course the scouts' reports are out of date, and ibn Saud had already sent in reinforcements before we got there."

The commander set the tips of his jewelled fingers together and looked at them, focusing with care. "I believe that we may discount that possibility. The Tiger of Arabia is not one to waste men or effort. The walls of Medina City are stronger than light gunfire, and the citadel is virtually impregnable. There is already a garrison of some two and a half thousand of his picked troops. He will, I judge, be confident of Medina's ability to hold out. He will be sure that, after a few of our assaults have been beaten back, the Beni Harb will change sides again, and we shall be hopelessly trapped." He looked up again into Thomas's face. "Ibrahim Agha, have you any experience of mines?"

At four o'clock in the morning, the high call of the muezzin floating down from the minarets of Medina woke the faithful to prayer. In the besieged city and the camp of the besiegers alike, men woke as much of themselves as need be – life-long usage had taught them how much that was – and gathered in the streets or mosques or the spaces between the tents, to make the ritual prostrations and intone the prayers that sanctified the start of the day. And among the sheltering fig gardens on the north of the city and in the long carefully propped tunnel that passed beneath the wall itself, men prayed silently and without movement, hoping that Allah would accept the prayer so, since the silence was for the freeing of His Holy City.

"Praise be to Allah, the Lord of the Worlds, the Merciful, the Master of the Day of Judgment. Guide us into the path of the Blessed . . ."

Three days and nights they had been driving the tunnel: now it was finished, the powder kegs stacked at its inmost end, no longer visible in the faint glint of the hooded lantern, for the false wall of stones and rubble that they had built to contain and concentrate the blast. Through the chink left in the wall, the slow match led in like a small deadly serpent, a whip-snake entering its hole.

The devout wailing of the morning prayer reached the three men crouching in the tunnel. And after the prayer was silent they waited still, Thomas holding his watch close to the gleam of light that made dim tensed masks of their sweating faces.

They should be able to hear when the diversionary attack came on the southern gate, but sound could play odd tricks in such a dog-hole, and it was best to time the thing as well. The long moments dragged by; and then they heard it, a distant surf of sound across the city that was the voice of the attack and the answering voice of the Wahabis hurling themselves to the defence.

Thomas nodded, and returned the hunter to its accustomed fold in his waist-shawl. "Medhet, Yusef, it is time for you to go, my brothers," he said to the two remaining sappers. Then as they hesitated a moment: "Get out!"

They faded backwards into the darkness. Thomas waited, listening to the faint brush of their movements, until he knew that they were clear of the tunnel, then he opened the lantern a crack and kindled a short length of match in the candle flame, and transferred the tiny fleck of fire to the end of the fuse. It hissed for a moment, crackled, and sank, then strengthened and began its slow inexorable creep towards the hole in the retaining wall. His heart was banging short and hard in his throat, the walls and roof of the tunnel pressed against his shoulders and the back of his bent head seeming to contract as though to hold him there . . .

He forced himself to wait, watching the fuse until he was sure that it was not going to fail; then turned and flung himself on all fours after the other two. The tunnel had no end. Everything had gone slow like time in a dream, a nightmare, as he clawed his interminable way towards the entrance. Then the fresh air of dawn was on his face, and the branches of the pepper tree that shielded the entrance were tearing at him as he crawled through. He scrambled to his feet and ran, heading with bursting heart for the far side of the fig garden.

He reached it and flung himself face-down, hands locked over the back of his head, just as, behind him, the night roared up in flame and red ruin. The shock-wave leapt upon him, battering him into the ground, then dragging him back deafened and winded, like a savage undertow. For a splinter of time, everything was quiet beyond the woollen ringing in his head; then sound was reborn and gathered strength; a great shouting from within the city, answered all around him as the assault party leapt in from where they had been hidden among the twisted roots.

Thomas was up, too, and at their head, and they were running, sword in hand, for the broad breach that had opened in the city wall.

Through the blast deafness singing in his ears, he heard their shouts: "Allah, il Allah!" And shouted with them, "Allahu akba!" at full pitch of his lungs. The smell of burned powder and the smoke still hung in the breach as they scrambled up and plunged over the scarce settling rubble to thrust back the first wave of the defenders racing to meet them.

Chapter 21

All morning the fighting had raged through the sandy streets of Medina and across el Barr, the city's broad maidan, as wave after wave of Egyptians, Turks and Albanians came pouring through the breach. The Wahabi garrison, beset from all sides once the Medinans, rising to join their rescuers, had taken and flung open the gates, had fought like tigers, but engulfed and beaten back, their survivors had fallen back on the citadel. By the day's end the whole of the outer city was in Ahmed Agha's hands.

Thomas, leaning on his sword and looking across the sacred precinct, let his hot eyes rest on the huge green dome marking the Prophet's tomb, that rose, remote and calmly uncaring as the moon, above the sandy space dark-littered by the bodies of men lying as yet where they had fallen. Again, he had wondered what he would feel when he looked upon it, when its ground was beneath his feet, this second most sacred spot in all Islam. He felt nothing at all. He was too tired. And he had yet to see to the lodging of his men.

The days passed. The streets were cleared of bodies and the black cloud of vultures that had fought over them departed back to their sky-wide circling. Ahmed Bonaparte ordered the building of a cairn of human heads hacked from Wahabi bodies, where the road entered the Pilgrim Pass on the way from Yembo, for a visible sign to travellers of how the Haj route had been opened to them again. For three weeks they laid siege to the inner city, the citadel, where the surviving garrison still held out against them. They could have starved the defenders out in time. But surely the Lion of Arabia would not leave his loyal garrison to its fate indefinitely, and they could not afford to merely sit on their haunches waiting for time to do their work for them until the Wahabi relief force came.

In the end it was red hot shot heated up over great fires on the maidan, and lobbed over the lowest part of the defences from field guns at their maximum elevation, that ended the siege.

216

Few of the glowing shot cleared the ramparts, and those that did for the most part fell where they caused little harm save the starting of small fires and maybe the deaths of a few men. But at noon on the last day, with the supply running low, one of the missiles landed on the flat roof of a magazine, and ploughed its way through to the explosive and incendiary material within.

The magazine went up in a great cough of flame, the shock-waves rocking the buildings in the outer city, and fire leapt above the ramparts, red against the vast billow of smoke that blotted out the sun. When the use of their ears returned to citizens and attackers, they heard thinly the screaming of men torn to pieces and the thin, high, bird-of-prey sound of desperately shouted orders. Presently the flames sank and the smoke cleared.

At evening a white flag on a spear shaft appeared above the main gatehouse.

Ahmed Agha, standing at a short distance from the gate, said with an air of pleasant satisfaction to Thomas standing beside him, "It seems they have had enough. I thought we should see that before sunset."

"Are you not going to order a ceasefire?" Thomas said.

"Oh, yes, but it would be a pity to waste the firewood," the commander said, and gave the signal to the gun team, whose master gunman, on the point of firing, had checked and was looking towards him. The crack of the field pieces split the waiting silence; and the last red shot went on its way, but failed to clear the parapet.

Thomas let his breath go gently.

Ahmed Agha spoke without hurry to the bugler who stood behind him: "Sound the ceasefire."

The call echoed away in the sunset light, and in a short while a head appeared beside the white flag, and a voice, harsh and croaking, drifted down: "I, Hammud al Rakshi, Captain of Medina, ask speech with Ahmed Agha, Commander-in-Chief of the Turkish Host, concerning terms of surrender."

Ahmed Agha set his hands to either side of his mouth and shouted back, "I, Ahmed Agha, Commander-in-Chief of the Egyptian army stand here, oh Hammud al Rakshi. Therefore do you come forth now, that we may speak together before the gate of the citadel, concerning the terms of surrender."

217

A hand went up in acceptance, and the head and the white flag disappeared together.

"Cover me," the general said to his escort, a few moments later, as the postern of the heavy timber gates creaked open just wide enough to let one man through.

"I come with you," Thomas said, half statement, half question.

"You remain with the escort. There is no danger. The Wahabis are men of honour, and will not shoot under the white flag."

"Yet only a fool takes his second-in-command with him into a possible trap," Thomas thought. "And you are no fool when you are even half sober." And hearing the snick and rattle of the breech bolts as the escort readied their muskets, paid silent tribute to his commander's courage, as Ahmed Agha walked forward alone to meet the Wahabi captain.

He watched the two come together on the open barbican before the gate; the thickset Turkish general, brilliant in gold-laced blue and crimson, arrogant as a fighting cock; the tall man in black Wahabi robes, his headdress laid aside and a bloody clout bound about his head, the white flag on its spear-shaft across his shoulder, unarmed, though the glint of jezail barrels in the evening sunlight here and there at shooting embrasures showed that he was being covered by his own men.

Thomas watched them, trying to guess, from a shift in stance, the movement of a hand, how the thing went, while the long moments crawled by and the light thickened. At last they parted with the ritual gestures of courtesy, the Wahabi captain to melt backwards into the shadows of the gateway where the postern opened for his passage; Ahmed Bonaparte to return with his game-cock strut to his waiting escort.

Even as he did so, the black Wahabi banners above the ramparts came fluttering down.

"So, that is an end to one lair of the black dogs," he said with an almost shocking pleasure to his second-in-command.

"They have surrendered on terms?"

"But of course. They lay down their arms and march out at dawn, with food and water for three days, to rejoin Abdullah ibn Saud at Diriyah."

Thomas looked at him in some surprise. He would not have expected generous terms from Ahmed Bonaparte.

The Turkish general saw the look, and his full lips curved in a smile. "My dear friend, we have enough on our hands without taking prisoners."

It seemed a reasonable enough point, but there was something in the smile that Thomas did not like.

Before dawn next day the crowds were thick on the maidan, and lining the streets from the citadel to the Damascus Gate, to watch the defeated garrison march out. Thomas with the cavalry was stationed beyond the gate, where the road ran down through the palm groves and gardens to lose itself north-eastwards in the desert. The palms were no more than dark feathered shapes as yet, but the smell of the dayspring was in the air, and beyond the jagged rim of the mountains eastward, the sky was lightening to a watery green, taking on a faint creeping wash of pink and cool lemon. The city gates already stood wide, and it seemed to Thomas that something, an uneasiness, seeped out through them like an invisible stain spreading across the sand. He had sensed it earlier, even before the muezzin's call to morning prayer, as he came down through the streets from his quarters in the Governor's Palace, to join his men. The horses seemed uneasy too, ready to take fright at shadows. The green pigeons taking off from the palm trees, circling overhead on clapping wings, all but threw them into a panic.

"Softly, softly, jewel of my heart! Have you never heard pigeons take off in the dawn before?" Thomas soothed with voice and hand his startled and fidgeting mare.

The east was growing brighter; the colour draining from it to leave the whiteness of pure light behind. The first rim of the sun slid up over the mountain line, and dazzled straight into the eyes of the waiting Arab cavalry. From the heart of the city a trumpet call like a spear pricked the bubble of the morning quiet; and in its wake faint sounds arose, a kind of surf of sound but with jagged and ugly overtones. Wrenching round in the saddle to strain his gaze in through the dark mouth of the gatehouse, Thomas thought suddenly of a pack of wild dogs he had once seen pulling down a wounded donkey. A scatter of shots made sparks of sound above the rest, and, from the top of a tall building that showed above the ramparts, a puff of powder smoke wisped away on the morning wind.

219

Medhet, close beside him, was shouting in his ear: "It sounds like a running fight! In the name of Allah, what is happening?"

Thomas was sitting wrenched round in the saddle, his eyes narrowed as he strained to see the answer to that question. There was a flicker of movement in the street, beyond the gate, then in the darkness of the gate arch itself, men running, a smother of shouts and cries. Into the open spilled Wahabi warriors, running for their lives, and after them, yelling with blood-lust the tribesmen of Medina. Weapons caught the morning sun in shards of light. A solitary shot cracked out from the gatehouse roof, and a tall man with a bandaged head pitched in his tracks, another ran a few paces spouting blood from his throat, then fell, others were going down.

"The tribesmen and Medinans have turned on them against the terms! And where in Allah's name are our troops?" Thomas ripped his sabre from its scabbard, "Follow me! – use the flat of your blades!"

He swung his mare round and sent her across the gateway, the rest of the squadron thrusting after him. He was in the midst of a sea of wild faces, yelling, red-eyed. There had been some mischief at work during the night, and from the maddened look of the good citizens of Medina, hashish had played a part in it. He beat up a brandished sword, forcing his way between the last of the black-robed fugitives and the wolf pack that flooded after them. The man with the bandaged head suddenly appeared almost under the mare's forehooves, and as Thomas wrenched her aside, the Wahabi captain came to one elbow and glared up at him. He was aware for a fleeting instant of eyes that burned like hot coals into his, and a gasping of "Treachery! – Allah's curse" that ended in a vomit of blood from the open mouth.

He was facing inward toward the gate, Medhet at his shoulder, the squadron spread in ragged wings on either side, charging the yelling mob, driving them back by sheer horse-weight and the flats of their blades. He heard himself shouting evil words: "Back, sons of misbegotten bitches! Back, breakers of faith, if you would not be damned to all eternity! . . ."

Slowly the frenzy seemed to sink, and the thrust of the mob slackened, while all the while he was aware of the surviving Wahabis – he could not tell how many or how few; he could not turn his gaze for an instant from the snarling surge of men in front of him to look behind – running for the cover of the fig gardens and away into the desert beyond the screen that the Arab cavalry had flung across their rear.

Towards evening of that day, Thomas and Ahmed Agha confronted each other in one of the chambers of the old Governor's Palace which the Turkish general had taken over for his headquarters. They faced each other standing, for it was not the kind of interview for which one sat down.

"And how many of those whose escape you so valiantly covered this morning do you imagine will get through to the camp of ibn Saud?" Ahmed said, playing with the great rough-cut ruby on his forefinger. "Unarmed, without water? My way might have been not only quicker but kinder in the long run."

"Nevertheless," Thomas returned stubbornly, "they surrendered on terms, and the terms were broken. Apart from all else, you must see – with respect, Sir – how desperately important it is that Saud ibn Saud and his Wahabis, aye, and the tribes and the citizens of Medina, should see and believe that we are keepers of our word."

"It is for that very reason that I intend to see justice done on the ringleaders." Ahmed paused an instant, his head cocked towards the window, listening to the angry hornet-hum that was the voice of Medina still seething with unrest. "Considering the display of righteous indignation that you have made about this whole incident, I should have imagined that you would have found it very much to your taste to take charge of hunting down those same ringleaders."

"I have small taste for the hunting down of men. But maybe I would if I thought for one moment that the evil had begun with them."

The arched brows lifted. "And you do not?"

"No," Thomas said, "I do not."

For a long moment they looked at each other, the unspoken accusation hanging in the air between them.

"If you were not the property of Tussun Pasha, purchased from me at, I admit, a very handsome price, if you were not Tussun Pasha's *friend*" (the word became an insult) "which gives you certain advantages and protections, I think, yes I really think, you might come to regret that ever you stood up to

221

me with that look on your face . . . But Tussun Pasha is not yet returned to us – how if I order you to deal with this matter?"

Sickness twisted in Thomas's guts. He wanted to hurl insult for insult into the fatly handsome face. He swallowed the insult along with the desire to vomit, and said gently, "If you remember the contents of yesterday's despatch, Tussun Pasha will be returned to us in a very few days." And then still more gently, through shut teeth, "Don't order, Sir, don't order."

For a long moment the silence was so intense that he heard the tick of the silver hunter tucked into its fold of his waist-shawl, then Ahmed Agha shrugged and turned away to take up his furred mantle from where it lay across the divan. It seemed the interview was at an end.

"Have I leave to return now to my own men?" Thomas asked.

"I think – not," the Agha flung on his cloak. "Ah, I do not *order*, but I would much prefer that you remain in your own quarters here in the Governor's Palace. Perhaps you will give me the pleasure of supping with me this evening."

Clearly Ahmed Bonaparte did not want him marching out to his tent in the cavalry camp outside the walls; anything, for the moment, that might suggest however faintly, a rift between himself and his second-in-command.

Thomas's quarters in the Governor's Palace were not unlike his old lodgment in Cairo, a couple of rooms at the head of a spiral stair, but these rooms were above the arched gateway between the inner and outer of the palace gardens. Chambers which must once have been beautiful before the Wahabis in their puritan zeal had smashed the intricate window frets and defaced the flowered tilework on the walls. Fortunately it seemed that the followers of ibn Saud could allow beauty if it were the work of Allah and owed nothing to the hand of man, and so the gardens below the ruined windows, though they had received no care during the years of Wahabi overlordship, and were a wilderness and in part a desert, still blossomed into beauty here and there, where half-dead bushes still flung abroad white scented trails of jasmine and the many-petalled roses of Damascus, and the tall spears of iris leaves rose through the tangle in odd corners after the winter rains; and the water in the leaking cisterns still reflected back the sky through the matted weeds.

222

Thomas, having excused himself early from an extremely uncongenial supper party with the general, stood by the window and heard the faint trickle of water rising to him out of the starlit darkness of the garden, and, beyond the cool delicate arabesque of sound, the more distant turmoil of the streets, where the hunt for the ringleaders of the morning's massacre was going on.

The hunt was getting out of hand; was being deliberately allowed to get out of hand. That was why it had not been ordered until evening, Thomas judged. Night was the time for such a hunt; torches in a mob had a great power for rabble-rousing; horrors could come about in the dark which the commander would find it harder to disclaim all knowledge of if they happened in the daylight . . . The Turkish and Albanian troops were not used to taking a city without being allowed their spell of rape and looting afterwards; there had been a good deal of grumbling in the past three weeks, and now that the citadel had fallen . . .

Thomas flung away from the window and paced about the room, then returned, and stood leaning his forehead against the splintered remains of the fretted shutter, and listening to the ugly sounds from the streets. There was nothing he could do about what was going on. He could not order out his own troops, turning one part of the Egyptian army against another. That would be unthinkable – as unthinkable as it was to bide here, listening to the sounds from over the wall and letting them go by as though they were just something blowing on the wind.

In two or three days, by the Mercy of Allah, Tussun would be here – if only he could have been here tonight . . .

Somewhere not far off a woman screamed, like a hare with a stoat after it. A hideous sound that went on and on, tearing the night apart, and then was lost in the general tumult. Thomas turned again from the window, and caught up from the sleeping place the old weather-faded burnous he had been using as a bed covering and flung it round his shoulders. Crossing to the outer room he shouted to the orderly who had just brought in fresh water, "I am going out, I may be a while."

And went striding down the stairway and out through the side postern, automatically making sure as he went that his sword sat loose in its scabbard. He did not know what he was going to do; but with the second-in-command of the expeditionary force hidden under the anonomity of a shepherd's burnous he might be able to do *something*, cool one hot head. Save one soft-bellied citizen. "Allah, All Merciful, All Compassionate, let there be something!" he prayed.

Because if there was not, he would carry the voice of Medina's agony, Medina being raped, in his head until his dying day.

Chapter 22

He was out in the street and heading towards the distant turmoil. It seemed to be the northern quarter that they were looting, the living quarter of well-to-do merchants and the like, which in the nature of things would yield the richest harvest; but small bodies of looters had split off from the rest and were busy in all quarters on their own account. Torchlight flared at the ends of streets, shadows were running. Thomas shot out an arm and laid hold of one of them, and had his sabre-point to the man's throat before he knew what was happening. "What means this evil in the streets?"

The man stared wildly in the low moonlight. "No evil! We do but punish those who threw in their lot with the Wahabi dogs!"

The evening's work, it seemed, had come a long way and turned a few corners since the Albanians had been called out to hunt down the ringleaders of that morning's massacre of the Wahabi garrison. Thomas flung the man aside and strode on.

He had not very far to go before he came upon the thing that Allah the All Merciful had for him to do.

At the corner of a narrow street he came upon a knot of Albanians with a flaring torch gathered round something they had penned in a doorway. Their savage glee, their throaty shouts and high laughter, something in their whole aspect made him think of boys tormenting a terrified cat with an old tin dipper tied to its tail, and he pushed into their midst.

Pressed back against the door stood a woman in the usual black street-going abba, or what remained of it, for it had been torn half off, revealing the gleam of tulip-striped silk beneath. They had torn off her veil and yashmak and her hair hung loose and tousled about her face that showed curd-white in the torchlight. Her eyes, widened in terror, found and clung to his face as he came, as though he were someone she had known would come, but who was almost too late. She twisted away from a hand that reached for her breast, screaming to him, "Effendi! Help me!"

Thomas had emerged in the forefront of the throng. He made no show of using even the flat of the naked blade in his hand, but the torchlight played on the bright steel. "Let the woman alone," he ordered.

There was a splurge of laughter, and one of the men returned, "She's only a brothel girl. If you want one, go and find her sister."

"She is no such thing," Thomas spoke with the voice of authority. "I know the Daughters of Delight as well as any of you! Get back."

"It is Ibrahim Agha!" someone said.

"It is. And Ibrahim Agha bids you in the name of Allah to take yourselves back to your quarters before he has time to recognise your faces and remember them afterwards!" He felt the laughter grow less sure and the savage purpose slacken. Getting between them and the girl and careful not to turn his face from theirs, he reached back and gathered her into the curve of his arm, dragging her hard against him. It was no moment for the niceties. "Come," he said, "I will take you home."

"I have no home," the girl said, and he sensed rather than saw her snatch a horrified glance back towards the red glow of a house burning at the far end of the street.

"These men?" Thomas asked.

"No, others. We sought to escape, but they killed my father – the servants ran away . . ."

Thomas was already thrusting their way out of the small group now turned sullen and unsure of themselves. Someone shouted after him that Ibrahim Agha was not above stealing other men's quarry rather than hunt for his own; that the Agha knew a girl worth the taking when he saw one . . . He felt the girl grow rigid in the curve of his arm. "Do not be afraid," he said quickly. "No harm shall come to you – no dishonour." And a moment later, as he realised that it was weakness and not fear of him that was making her stiffen and stumble and grow so heavy, "Are you hurt?"

"Only a little," she said. "But I bleed."

"Hold up. It is not far, but if I have to carry you I shall have no hand free for my sword if we should need it."

He felt her brace herself for a valiant effort, and strode on, half taking her weight, his sword ready in his hand, through the

226

torch-flickering and uneasy ways, with the wild-dog turmoil fading behind them but still menacing in their ears. Keeping to the black sides of the streets where the light of the moon did not yet reach, he brought her back safe to the Governor's Palace. The guards on the small side-gate from the fig garden never kept over-careful watch, and now were off on their own affairs, and they passed through unchallenged into the peace of the ruined garden-court. Thomas slammed his sword home into its sheath and swept up the girl, who by now was almost a dead weight, into his arms. A few moments later he was climbing the turnpike stair, kicking open the door of his quarters, coming to a halt in the lamplit outer chamber, with a sense of having reached a small island of quiet in the midst of storm-tossed seas.

Jassim, who had been sleeping in a corner, stumbled to his feet, blinking. "What have you there, Ibrahim Agha?"

"What does it look like? A girl. The streets are in a turmoil, they have burned down her home . . ."

Thomas crossed the outer chamber and gained his own sleeping quarters, and laid her down on the cushioned divan. "Bring the lamp closer; she's wounded—"

"We should not look at her," Jassim Khan protested. "It is for a woman—"

"Meanwhile she's bleeding," Thomas snapped.

The boy brought the lamp closer, keeping his face averted. He had been well brought up. "Is she a brothel girl? If not, her father—"

"She is not a brothel girl," Thomas said for the second time. "And it seems she has no father to trouble about her life less than her honour. Any brothers we will deal with as best we may when the time comes."

In the pool of light the girl lay very still, her eyes closed, her narrow face grey-white in the tangle of her dark hair that was harsh and vital as a horse's mane. Thomas took one look and then turned his gaze quickly and carefully away. She would not have left her face bare to him had she been conscious, and to look into it, after that first involuntary glance, would have been to outrage the custom of her world, which had been his world for five years now. He turned his attention to finding where she was hurt. It was not hard; her left hand was twisted in a fold of her torn abba, and the black cloth which could not show a stain,

227

showed juicy in the lamplight as though it contained ripe mulberries.

Very carefully, he untangled the sopping folds and laid them back. Jassim drew in his breath with a hiss, as the hand was laid bare. The fourth finger and the top of the percussion were sheered off by a slanting sword-cut, the top joint of the third finger hanging by a strip of skin. She must have flung her hand up instinctively to ward either herself or someone else from the blade.

"Put the lamp down here beside me," Thomas said. "Set water over the fire to warm. Bring towels and clean linen and the flask of arak – oh, and my muslin turban-scarf."

"The one with the gold fringe?" Jassim sounded shocked.

"If that comes first to hand."

"Won't your shirt be enough?"

"For bandage linen, yes, the other is for her to cover her face from us. Quickly now."

And as the orderly rose and crossed to the camel bag in the corner, he pushed back his sleeves and drew the Somali knife from his waist-shawl. The sooner she was rid of that bit of dangling flesh, the better; and Allah knew how little chance there would be of getting a hakim, even one of the army medics, through the streets that night.

It was only a moment's work to cut through the thread of skin, and then he set to cutting away the blood-sodden folds of black cloth and gathering them together with the pathetic remains of what had lately been a living fingertip – the nail was still perfect, beautifully shaped and well cared for, its untouched perfection suddenly twisted at his guts – and dropped them into the bowl that Jassim brought for them, to be carried away and burned. The blood which had almost ceased to flow only increased a little with the severing of that final filament; he staunched it with one of the rough linen towels, and began to bathe and clean up the mutilated hand.

"Tear me some strips for bandages," he said. "But first cover her face lest she awake and find herself unveiled before strangers."

Jassim, who seemed by now to have come to terms with the unorthodox situation, had indeed brought the agha's best turban-scarf, one that Tussun had given him, and squatting down beside him, arranged it with a kind of grudging gentleness to cover her hair with soft folds, drawing the end across her lower face and straightening the gold fringe with meticulous care on the cushion beside her head. Then he turned himself to tearing up Thomas's spare shirt into bandage strips, the sharp sound of tearing linen ripping asunder the quiet of the room that had seemed so withdrawn from the city's turmoil.

Having bathed away the blood which by now was only oozing, Thomas reached for the flask of arak which Jassim had set beside him. He had rigidly obeyed the Prophet's ruling on alcohol since the day that he had become a Muslim; but, remembering Donald MacLeod and his wound-cleansing techniques, he had always carried a flask of the stuff with him in his saddle bags on campaign. Now, having bidden Jassim to pour away the bloodstained water, he splashed a little of the fiery liquid into the bowl and taking the girl's hand dipped the oozing finger stumps into it.

He had expected the knifework would bring her back to consciousness, but it seemed that the confusion of pain in the mangled hand had been too great to take account of the few moments of added pain. But the bite of raw spirit on raw flesh (Thomas remembered his own hour) was another matter. The hand that had been lax and unresisting in his suddenly flinched and fluttered, then returned to stillness, but this time a tense and rigid stillness that came of conscious will.

His eyes flicked to the girl's face, and saw hers wide open above the folds of fine muslin; eyes of the surprisingly light grey that he had seen before, though not often, among the tribes, looking up at him in bewilderment from under slender black brows with a frown-line pencilled deep between.

She gave a small startled cry as the surprise of her own pain struck her, then fumbled up her sound hand and found the careful fold of muslin across her face.

"Lie still," Thomas said. "There is no need for fear."

"The soldiers – my father—"

"I will go back when I have bound your hand, and discover what is to be found out about your father."

"There is nothing more to be found out; the soldiers killed him," she said, her voice dull and the words faintly slurred, as though her tongue were stiff in her mouth. "Ayee! my hand is in the fire—"

"No, but it is hurt. Soon the pain will ease." Thomas set

229

aside the bowl and took the linen strip which Jassim held out to him, and began careful bandaging.

The grey eyes were still on his face, searching, with somewhere at the back of them the look of a wild thing ready to bolt. "What is this place? How came I here?"

"I brought you here. The street is not a good place to be tonight. This is a place where you are safe. Lie still and the Peace of Allah be with you."

He finished his bandaging, knotted off the strip of linen, and got up, holding his own stained hands well away from himself. There was blood on his burnous too, but that would be nothing strange in the streets tonight, and it would serve until he got back. "I leave her in your care, knowing that I can trust you," he said to the boy. "Let her sleep if she can. Give her a drink if she asks; watch her well, and if the blood starts to come through, add more bindings, but do not undo what I have done. We will get a hakim to her in the morning. Also a woman to be with her – as old and ugly as possible. Bar the door after me and let no one in until I return."

He went out, hearing the door bar dropped into place behind him; and down the curling stair and along what remained of the elegant colonnade, checking to rinse the half dried blood from his hands in the water that still trickled grudgingly into an old fountain basin; then plunged back into the crowding city ways, heading for the place where he had come upon the girl.

The tumult in the streets was subsiding; he heard horses' hooves, and at a cross way a small knot of Turkish cavalry swept across the street and on down the chasm of the narrow way opposite, in the direction from which the main uproar still came. He heard shouted orders. Ahmed Agha must have decided that the pillage had gone far enough and it was time to use his undeniable powers of discipline.

He reached the place he was heading for; it was empty now, and at the far end of the street the roof of the burning house had fallen in and the flames were sinking in the chambers nearest to the street. In the entrance, lit by the flames that still streamed upward from the inner part of the house, a man lay in a black pool of blood with his head half hacked from his shoulder, his empty eyes of a startlingly pale grey, staring up at the cold uncaring moon.

When Thomas got back to his quarters, after a pre-dawn visit

230

to his own troops, unsettled and straining at the leash in the camp outside the walls, and a few hurried words with his fellow cavalry colonels as to the night's happenings, the girl was sunk deep in the sleep of shock and exhaustion. He slept what remained of the night in his outer room, with Jassim curled in the corner. And the next time he spoke with her, her hand had been re-dressed by one of the army surgeons, and Jassim had found an old woman of great hideousness among those in the commander's kitchen, who squatted on guard like a vast and benevolent black toad in the corner of the inner chamber.

The girl had drunk some milk – the part empty cup was still beside her – and pulled herself up to sit propped with cushions against the wall. Thomas's turban scarf still covered her hair and was drawn across her face, and above it her eyes, filled with questioning, seemed to be waiting for him as he came in. The stillness of shock was still with her and seemed to fill the room; a strangely impersonal room now that everything of his had been carried out of it.

He came and squatted on his heels before her, palms together, head bowed a moment in formal greeting, "Salaam aleikum, Lady, how is it with you?"

"It is well enough with me," she said; and then: "I have remembered now, how I came to be here. I have remembered the streets."

"Better if you could have been spared that memory," Thomas said.

"I owe you my life, Effendi. More than my life."

Thomas said, "I also; there is a thing that I owe to you. If Allah had not granted it to me to save something out of last night's evil, I should never again have been free of the sights and sounds of last night in the streets." He hesitated. "I went back to your house, to look for your father. The flames had not touched him, but – I am sorry – there was nothing to be done."

"I know," she said, "I saw the blow fall. They cried out that it was because they knew that he had sold goods and horses to the Wahabi, but I think it was because they knew that he had gold."

"Allah's pity upon you," Thomas said. "Have you brothers? Any other kin?"

She shook her head. "My father came out of a far-off tribe to take my mother for his wife. There was blood feud between

231

their tribes, and her people cast her out. She died when I was young, and my father was a strange man and took no second wife, and I am all the sons and all the daughters of my father's house."

She spoke calmly, with a kind of quiet desolation, but also with precision, not asking for pity, but seeking only to explain to him her exact position.

Something in the manner as well as the words jolted him under the heart. "Then do you count me for your brother, for as long as you have need of one," he said.

For a moment she regarded him in stillness, head up, then bent it a little sideways. Something in the angle, something also in her tone when she answered, suggested also that her voice when not dulled by grief and shock might be beautiful. "By what name shall I know my brother?"

"By the name of Ibrahim, commander of cavalry in the army of the Sultan." He returned her gaze steadily. "But I swear to you that neither I nor my troops had any hand in last night's work."

"That I believe, Ibrahim my brother."

"Is it permitted to ask the name of my sister?"

"It is permitted," she said after a pause. "Thy sister is named Anoud."

A sharp explosion of clucks from the black toad in the corner warned him that they had gone as far as Arab custom allowed, maybe further, even in these unusual circumstances, between a man and a woman who were not in fact related. Anyway, the commander of cavalry in the army of the Sultan had other matters waiting to be dealt with that day. It was time he left.

He got to his feet. "Let Anoud, my sister, bide here and rest in safety," he said, and returned to the outer room, where all his belongings were stacked and Jassim Khan stood ready to help him on with his braided fariva and see that his combined bandoleer and sword belt was full and securely buckled on. Behind the closed door of the inner chamber, he could hear the black toad scolding: "Shameless one! To speak so with a man who is *not* thy brother, whatever he may say! To tell him thy name—"

And the girl's answer: "The man saved my life, and it lies in the hollow of his hands, and my name with it. It is his right."

The words lingered in his mind waking odd resonances, as he went down to rejoin his troops.

Chapter 23

About noon of the same day, Tussun Pasha rode into Medina followed by his escort, still a little wound-stiff as he slid from his saddle, and demanding loudly to know the meaning of the pile of heads he had met on the Pilgrim Road.

Later, when he had had time to look about him, when he had been greeted and had received back his command from a hurriedly sobered-up Ahmed Agha, there was a gathering of senior officers in one of the still-standing buildings of the citadel, at which he heard sundry reports, and at which Ahmed Agha found himself being first congratulated on the capture of Medina and then called on to account for his actions over the past thirty-six hours.

Tussun summed up, a Tussun still white from his wound, but whiter still, Thomas judged, with the need to suppress his anger and act like a man with ten years more experience in diplomacy and the handling of awkward situations than he actually possessed.

"The Wahabis yielded on terms, and according to those terms they were to march out with two hundred baggage camels, to rejoin Saud ibn Saud at Diriyah. Only thirty camels were provided, so that they must leave the greater part of their gear and supplies behind. We will not say that you personally arranged for the greater part of them to be slain, all unarmed, as they marched out, by the tribesmen and the citizens of Medina, since there is no proof; but certainly you made no attempt to use your own troops to stop the massacre—"

Ahmed Bonaparte, looking thoroughly sobered and a good deal shaken by the speed with which elaborate congratulations had turned into this calling to account, tried to cut in, but the young hard voice with its strong Albanian accent rose and overrode his attempt:

"At evening, and only at evening, when the ringleaders, if there were any, had had time and to spare in which to escape – or to sink back into the general crowd – you order them to be hunted down and dealt with."

233

"Time had to be allowed for hot blood to cool," Ahmed Bonaparte made himself heard for a moment. "We had no intention to execute any man, but only to capture and hold them until your coming, Excellency."

Tussun seemed not to hear him. "And under the cloak of this hunting, you allowed looting to break out. Houses have been fired, citizens have been killed, women and young sons raped! Have you forgotten how great is our need that the tribes should learn to trust the word and the honour of the Sultan's armies?"

He paused at last, waiting for an answer, his fingers white-knuckled on the hilt of the dagger in his belt.

Ahmed Agha's face changed from its usual olive colour to a dirty greyish yellow. His full dark eyes darted round the room from face to face of the men about him, and found no support anywhere.

"It is also not without importance that the tribes should learn to know the strength of the Sultan's arm," he said after a moment.

"But not in *this* way!"

"Mercy is a great thing, but Your Excellency is still young and impressionable. Take heed that you do not grow soft like the soldiers of the West" (Thomas thought of several things that he had known his own kind to do, and wondered what in the world could have given the Agha that idea) "through listening too closely to your Western friends." The full dark gaze rested for a moment on the Scotsman's face, and there was an uneasy stillness. Thomas looked levelly back. Ahmed Agha went on: "I have something longer experience than yourself, Excellency, of the needs of men. Turkish troops, as well as your own countrymen, are used to being allowed the run of their teeth after a victory."

"Here in the Holy City? And against the express orders of the Viceroy? Against *my* express orders that there should be no pillage?"

"It is easy to give orders far from the scene of the fighting."

Into the silence that followed came the wailing call to evening prayer, floating across the roof tops of Medina.

And the men in the high bleak chamber of the citadel turned themselves towards Mecca and prayed together. And when the praying was over turned back to the matter in hand.

Tussun's voice had regained courtesy, though a cool courtesy

234

with the steel below the silk, when he spoke again to his second-in-command. "Ahmed Agha, it is very clear that you are a sick man; were it not so, were you in full possession of the health and strength necessary for so onerous a position as yours, none of this would have happened."

"Was it the action of a sick man to capture Medina for you?" Ahmed said.

Tussun gave the merest whisper of a shrug, "Perhaps you did not yourself realise the toll of your strength taken from you by this superb and crowning action of your career. Now that you do realise it, I suggest that you wish to resign your position as my second-in-command and return with all honour to your own estates in the Delta."

For a moment Ahmed seemed about to spring to his feet, but he held himself rigidly seated in his place in the circle.

"How if I refuse your most generous suggestion?"

"If you refuse," Tussun said, the steel becoming deadly under the silk, "I greatly fear that your sickness will prove mortal; or that you may suffer an accident as fatal – a loose girth when you ride, a fall on the stairs, a stray shot from some foolish marksman out after gazelle . . . I strongly advise you, in the name of Allah the All Merciful, that you do not refuse."

For a long moment the two men looked at each other, and for that moment Thomas, uncomfortably shaken, saw naked murder in the eyes of both, before the veils were discreetly drawn.

"You shall have my resignation in the morning," Ahmed Agha said in a kind of creaking whisper. "And now – we sick men have early need of our beds; have I Your Excellency's permission to retire to my own quarters?"

"May your sleep be calm and refreshing, in readiness for tomorrow's journey," Tussun said sweetly.

"Do you think that he will still be in his quarters tomorrow morning and not off and away on affairs of his own?" Thomas asked, a short while later, as he and Tussun made their way down from the citadel in the dusk, the sky turning to green crystal behind the flat roof tops and minarets of Medina.

"Surely – unless he can fight his way past the guard that he will find on the doors and windows if he attempts to so much as cast his shadow outside."

"There are times," Thomas said, "when I scarcely recognise

235

you. That was skilfully done; I can feel the chill of it between my shoulder-blades yet."

They walked a few steps in silence, hand in hand according to the usual custom of friendship. Then Tussun said, "Yet there was a time when I ordered your death, my brother."

"That was an ordering of a different kind."

A few more steps, and then Tussun broke the silence again in a changed tone: "Let us go to your quarters, and drown the memory of this evening in coffee and your medicinal arak."

Thomas checked abruptly, remembering what he had scarce had time to remember all day. "That we will do; but first, before you come to my quarters, there is a thing that I should tell you."

They stood in the middle of the narrow street, touched by the dim marigold light that filtered down from the fretted window just overhead. Tussun flung up his head with a shout of laughter. "So it's true! You *have* a girl stowed away there!"

"I have," Thomas said a little stiffly, "but I did not know that it was common knowledge."

"You didn't silence the men you took her from."

"If you know that, then you know the manner of her being stowed in my quarters. The mob had killed her father and burned down her home and wounded her in the hand. She had no kin, nowhere to go. Therefore I gave her shelter – with something fat and female out of the palace kitchens to guard her honour, in a chamber having a door with bars on the inside."

"Tho'mas – Tho'mas my brother – you do not need to speak so to me; I understand that she is not one of the Daughters of Delight. Better for you, maybe, if she had been."

"How so?"

They were walking on again now, in the direction of the Governor's Palace. "Because then she would have had a life to go back to."

Thomas was silent, brought face-to-face with problems that he had not got round to confronting before.

"She has no kin? No father? No brothers? You are sure she spoke the truth?"

"Very sure."

"So. No one to play the man's part, to be responsible for her, to use the family authority on her behalf – to exact blood for her dishonouring . . ."

236

"I have said that I will be her brother as long as she needs me."

"But you are not, are you. In the eyes of the law and the faith you are nothing to her. And we shall not remain long in Medina. What will become of her when we march out?" The young voice was concerned, worried on his friend's account.

And Thomas heard his own voice answering, as though it was something that he had been considering for weeks, "I think that if she agrees, I should marry her. In that way I can leave the cloak of my protection spread over her, even when we march from here."

Tussun gave the matter due consideration as an old married man.

"There is much to be said to that. It is time that you took a wife and got sons to come after you. But if you should wish to be rid of her after a while, it will be difficult for you even though there will be no dowry to return, with no father nor brother to hand the girl back to."

"It will be difficult for you when you wish to be rid of me again, with no father nor brother into whose keeping you can return me," Anoud pointed out three evenings later.

He had left her three days' breathing space; he could not well leave her longer, not knowing how soon he himself might be ordered elsewhere. He had found a kindly disposed imam to visit her and lay the plan before her, since she had no kin to do so. But she, it seemed, had been less afraid of offending against the custom than he was; maybe she felt that what had happened to her, breaking her off from the normal pattern of life in her world, had also freed her somewhat from its restrictions. At all events she had sent him word that she begged leave to speak with him personally on the matter.

So he sat on the evening of the third day, as he had sat on the morning of the first, on his heels before her, as she sat propped on piled cushions against the wall, with Kadija more like an amiable black toad than ever, squatting in the same corner. She was dressed in garments of Kadija's procuring, deeply blue, less fine than the silks she had been wearing on the night he brought her there, but at least free of the taint of blood; but she still wore his gold-fringed turban-scarf by way of veil and yashmak. The room had become more clearly a woman's

237

chamber, the cushions more softly coloured, an embroidered hanging on one wall, a branch of fragile almond blossom in a tall brass vase. But it was still the inner chamber of his own narrow quarters above the garden arch. Presently he would make suitable arrangements for her, when the question of their marriage had been settled.

"It will be difficult for you, when you wish to be rid of me," Anoud said again, gently but firmly pointing out the problem as though she were his sister indeed.

"Among the people I come from, we do not get rid of our wives," Thomas said. "Sometimes we make them unhappy; sometimes we mistreat them, as we would not mistreat our horses. But we do not thrust them back into their father's house." It was very nearly true.

The grey eyes above the soft folds of muslin were steady on his face. "So it would be for life," she said. "Then it is a harder choice than it would be if it were made by *our* custom."

Thomas said "If, when peace comes again to the Hijaz, there should come a time when you wish to be free, I promise that you shall go, according to the custom of your own people."

"Yet if I do *not* wish to go, you will hold yourself bound for life, according to the custom of yours?"

"Yes," Thomas said, simply.

The long lids dropped for a moment, then rose again, and the grey eyes returned to their steady regard. "Then for your promise, I promise also, that when the time comes that you wish to take a second wife—"

Thomas made to interrupt, but she checked him. "Among your people it is not the custom to take a second wife? It must be sweet, sometimes, to be the only one, but hard at other times . . . So, when you wish to take a second wife, you must follow the custom of *my* people, and do so; and I will welcome her and treat her as a younger sister, as the chief wife should do."

"If ever that day comes," Thomas said, half smiling, "I will hold you to that promise." He would have liked to reach out and take her hand, the sound hand with which she held the soft folds of the scarf across her face, and hold it, and rub his thumb friendliwise over the fine-boned back of it where the blue veins branched under the olive pallor of the skin. Suddenly he remembered the feel of her and how she fitted into his arms as he carried her up the stair, but he knew that he must not touch

238

her again until after the wedding ceremony; and the instinct was a very small and fragile one, gone as swiftly as the shadow of a moth on the lamplit wall.

"When can you be ready?" he asked.

"Within a day and a night, if need be – yet grant me a while to mourn my father."

"You shall have as long as may be. How long, I do not know, for I do not know when I shall be ordered from here; and I must be sure you have the safety and support that I can give you, before I go."

"Then give me a day and a night of mourning, and when they are passed, I will be ready for my Lord," said Anoud.

News of the taking of Medina ran like scrub-fire through the Muslim world, and was received with joyful relief by most of it. The Grand Shariff Ghalid at once announced that he was joining the Sultan's forces in their campaign to rid the Holy Land of heretics, and threw Mecca open to the forces of deliverance, also the great port of Jiddah, to serve better than Yembo had ever done as a base for Egyptian supplies and reinforcements.

Mustapha Bey, he that was son-in-law to the Viceroy, entered Mecca in triumph at the head of the Viceroy's Turkish reinforcements; the troops being forbidden their usual butchery on entering a captured town, so that the lives and property of the Meccans were better spared than those of the Medinans had been.

From Mecca, Mustapha Bey attacked Teif, the summer capital of the Grand Shariff, which had been in Wahabi hands since they had captured it with hideous slaughter in the name of the True God, ten years before. The Wahabi garrison fell back into the hills, on the strong fortress of Terraba. And there for the present, they were left to themselves; for Terraba had a reputation to raise the hair on the back of the neck: a strong fortress in bad black country, which since the death of its sheikh some years before had been ruled over by his widow, Ghalia, with a welcome for any man who counted himself an enemy of the Ottoman world. Added to that, Ghalia herself (how else could a woman hold such men and such a place?) was known to be a witch. Altogether a place for not meddling with, so long as one could put off the meddling.

The chief cities of the Hijaz were now in Egyptian hands, but

239

the power of the black-robed zealots from the heartland was still unbroken beyond the mountains; and even in the Hijaz flying Wahabi squadrons menaced the caravan routes and constantly attacked the Egyptian army's supply trains; so that, while Tussun set to work to clear up the situation in Medina and heal the wounds caused by Ahmed Agha's brutalities, Thomas found himself living much the same kind of life, on a larger scale, as he had lived at El Hamha in his first months with the Bedouin cavalry. A policing job intensified now and then into small-scale savage warfare from which the long-distance patrols often returned with riderless horses in their midst.

Well into April, when the fragile colour-wash of desert flowers and grasses was already beginning to dry up, and the hills were turning tawny as a lion's coat, Medina received a new governor, Quera al Din, one of Muhammed Ali's generals, sent out from Egypt for the purpose. And Tussun received orders to return to Jiddah at last, while Thomas with four hundred picked sabres departed for Mecca to keep an eye on the Grand Shariff.

The time for Anoud to mourn her father was over; and the time to make ready for her wedding was come.

Thomas, who had taken up residence in his tent in the cavalry camp, had not seen her again during those weeks, but with Tussun's enthusiastic agreement he had her moved from her cramped lodging in the small rear room of his own quarters to much larger and pleasanter rooms in the harem of the Governor's Palace, opening on to the more shady pleasance of the women's court; and in his little leisure time had scoured the souks and craftsmen's quarters of the city for pretty and comfortable things, embroidered cushions, a finely chased brass lamp, a coffee pot engraved with verses from the Koran, to make it pleasant for her. She had asked, through Kadija, that she might have a loom and he had found one for her; also embroidery material; the women of Medina were noted for their skill. He would have given her a lute, many Arab women could play, but he remembered her hand. Better leave that for the time being. Selling a pair of silver-mounted pistols of his own, he bought her a belt of gold chain-work strung with coral and turquoise; every woman should have gold for her wedding. Her morning gift he possessed already, a piper's silver plaid brooch of the 78th that he had bought long ago in a Cairo souk with an absurd aching in his throat, and carried with him ever since until it became almost a kind of talisman. It was of no great value in terms of Maria Theresa dollars, but it had values of its own which he thought Anoud might appreciate. So the almost unknown girl, her needs and his own obligations towards her, made a shadowy constant background through that time, and he found it oddly pleasant.

His moment of panic came during the actual ceremony, if ceremony it could be called, in the private Majlis of the Governor's Palace. Nobody present but the witnesses (two Medinan sheikhs), a couple of the bridegroom's fellow officers, Tussun, young Medhet with a late rose tucked into his turban scarf as though he and not Thomas were the groom, Thomas himself and the imam, a small man with a face like a little red-eyed Highland bull under the longest turban Thomas had ever seen. A fretted window opening high in the wall made him wonder if Anoud was there. He remembered that sometimes the bride herself or her kinsfolk arranged for her to be close by and hear the ceremony, sometimes not; it was no business of the bridegroom's. But present or not, when the few words before witnesses were spoken, they would be bound together.

The imam was speaking to him now . . . "Ibrahim Agha, is it your wish that you take as your wife, the woman Anoud bin Aziz ibn Rashid?"

A Muslim wedding was not such a great matter after all, he told himself; he could denounce the girl as easily as he could marry her, so long as he paid the proper price and did her no dishonour. He could take other wives – it was a thing that need scarcely change his way of life at all . . . But nevertheless, because Anoud had no male kin to take her back into their home, and because he had been bred among people whose view of marriage was different, he knew that once the words before witnesses were spoken, he would be bound to her as surely as though she had been standing beside him and the words spoken by a minister of the Presbyterian kirk, and their names written down afterwards in the parish register of births, marriages and deaths.

"Until death us do part . . ."

"It is my wish," he said.

The imam turned to Tussun, who had taken it upon himself, as Thomas's commander, to play her father's part.

241

"Tussun Pasha, commander of all the Sultan's forces in Medina, is it your wish that you give the woman Anoud as wife to Ibrahim Agha who stands before you?"

"It is my wish," Tussun said.

"Then be it according to the wishes of both of you."

And that was all.

Thomas wondered if it was only imagination that he heard a faint sigh from behind the window fret, and remembered the torchlit garden-court of the house in the Fatamid quarter on the evening of Tussun's wedding, but he hurriedly brushed the memory aside.

Chapter 24

The heat of the day had faded to a thick coolness like milk, and the scent of the late jasmine and the pale spikes of the henna flowers in the half dead wilderness of the women's garden hung heavy on the air, mingled with the resiny smoke of torches, as Thomas's friends – a larger company than had been present at the ceremony – saw him on his way to the harem on his wedding night.

Most of them had partaken freely of arak, and grown lewd and happy, but Thomas himself, sticking firmly as ever to the injunction of the Prophet, must go to his night of nights stone-cold sober on coffee and rose sherbet, which he had always found abominably sweet. He wished that Colonel D'Esurier could have been there, and Zeid; Zeid above all . . . He was inclined to think that he had made a quixotic fool of himself, and to wish that the whole thing was not happening.

Yet had not the Prophet himself married the widows of his companions who had died of battle, to give them the shelter of his mantle? But those had been marriages in name only . . . Tussun's arm was across his shoulder, and Tussun's voice, laughing and a little thickened with arak, proclaiming in his ear, "This is the night of all the splendours! Go to it, old desert falcon, it is time you were begetting sons!"

They brought him to the door of the women's house and thrust him in with friendly thumps on the back and much good advice. The door shut behind him. He heard their voices and laughter outside, but knew that, though Tussun and Medhet would make the gesture of guarding the door for a while, there would be no attempt to follow him.

He was alone, the empty stair before him lit by a torch in the angle of the wall. Somewhere close by he sensed movement and lighter laughter, but there was no movement to be seen.

He began to climb.

The stairs ended in a wide entrance chamber from which arched doorways led away on three sides to inner chambers and little screened balconies. At the far side, a door stood ajar, letting out a slender shaft of lamplight to mingle with the milky pallor of the rising moon that pooled the empty floor. The sense of life near by, breath caught, eyes watching, was stronger here. Kadija would not be far off, he thought, and with her the other women she would have brought in to help make ready the bride. He crossed to the door and pushed it open, shutting it firmly again behind him, and turned to his left, where a curtain, not quite drawn, let out a stronger lamplight to meet him.

He had chosen the group of rooms with care, largely because they contained this particular one, and was not surprised that Anoud had taken it for her private chamber. The beautiful blue and white hyacinth tiles that lined the wall niches, the delicate star-and-lozenge fret of the window traceries, had both escaped the destructive fervour of the puritanical Wahabis and were almost unbroken; the whole chamber was faded, weather stained, the ceiling blackened with lamp-switch, but it had been a beautiful room and still retained the ghost of its beauty as dried flowers will sometimes retain the ghost of their living scent.

The lamp that he had found for it burned on a low sandalwood table, and by its light he saw Anoud sitting among the piled cushions of the divan, beneath the window whose shutters were set wide to catch the soft night air from the garden. She was waiting for him, pressed stiffly back to the wall behind her with an air of being pinioned against it.

"The blessing of Allah the All Compassionate be upon the night," Thomas said, and crossed the room and sat down on the divan beside her. Her gaze, that had seemed to be waiting for him at the door, tracked him across the room. She moved a little, making room for him. But nothing more. Was it going to be all for him to do?

He had been instructed by Tussun and others, that he must strip off her clothes, and that she would probably resist him; that it was the right, almost the duty of a well-brought-up girl to resist him as strongly as she pleased (he remembered the claw marks down the sides of Tussun's face when he returned to his friends after his own marriage night); but that equally it was his right and his duty to fight down her resistance. She would expect it of him.

Only he could not make himself believe that this remote girl sitting tensed against the wall beside him, was expecting – at least in the sense that Tussun meant it – any such thing. And he could not think how to begin. A kiss with his arm round her would have seemed the obvious way; but he had also been warned by Tussun that the one thing he must not attempt to remove without her consent was her yashmak, that some women, otherwise stripped naked, went through their whole wedding night with their faces still veiled. And she seemed much too withheld and anonymous inside all those loose garments for him to even consider putting his arms round her. Yet instinctively he knew that physical contact, the communication of touch, older than any spoken language, was the thing they both needed at this outset.

Except for her eyes, her hands folded together in her rose-crimson lap were the only part of her that was accessible. He reached out and took them between his, feeling that they were cold. She tried to draw the wounded left one away. He did not let it go.

"No," he said, "don't do that."

"It is ugly."

Thomas turned it to the light of the lamp and examined it quietly. The wounds had healed well and cleanly, save for one place where the little finger should have been, which was puckered and slightly crusted. The scars were still purplish, but eventually they would fade. Holding her hands, he noticed them properly for the first time. They were slim and hard, almost like a boy's. "It is not ugly," he said seriously. "Those are honourable scars, don't hide them as though they were something to be ashamed of."

He looked up and met her gaze, and for the instant a trace of a smile hovered between them. His hands moved a little further, up under her loose sleeves. The palms of her hands were traced with delicate bridal patterns of red-brown henna; the scent of spikenard and lemon-grass came to him from within the gold-worked breast folds of her thobe. When he turned to the business of unfastening her belt – the belt with the gold cords and drops of turquoise and coral – one hand moved for a moment to check him, then fell away to lie palm open on the cushion beside her. Whatever her rights, it seemed that she was not going to exercise them. Had she perhaps been told that coming of an alien people he would not understand them? Or did she

245

feel her life to be already his in some way that stripped those rights from her? Quietly and methodically, with careful concentration, he set about undressing her, while she slipped down further into the cushions and made no attempt to withstand him. The Lady Nayli had not been in the least like this . . . He shied away from the memory that had remained for so long an evil taste in the back of his mind; striving quickly for a happier one to drive it out; but Jenny Cochrane laughing in the sun-warmed grass had not been like this either; nor had the Pleasure Pavilion girls of his acquaintance. Certainly it had been a mistake to have rigidly obeyed the Prophet and come to his wedding night quite so stone-cold sober. Maybe if he had had just one cup of arak it would have been better for Anoud too. He glanced at her apologetically, and found that while he had been concentrating on other matters, she had taken off her yashmak.

She lay completely naked to his gaze now among the bright embroidered cushions, and looked up at him, gravely waiting, while he knelt over her, looking down. It seemed to be the first time that he had seen her face, for the one other time, the first time of all, it had been not so much a living face as a white mask of shock. Now the mask was gone, and he was looking at Anoud herself. She was no beauty, her nose was too long and her jaw too sharply angled for a woman; but her mouth, the colour of watered wine, was wide and mobile with great sweetness in it. He liked her mouth. Her body was too thin for Arab tastes, and he was surprised to see how pale it was in the lamplight, silky pale as a freshly peeled almond save for the faint flush remaining where the hair had been plucked from under the arms and the woman-parts at the base of her belly and between her thighs. He had heard that women suffered that torture before their marriage night, the hair stripped off with plasters of melted sugar and lemon juice by the older women, and his own flesh cringed a little in sheer physical sympathy. Kadija had done her work well, not a hair remained, but the lips of the girl's vulva were still sore.

He pulled off his turban and began to unbind his waist-shawl.

In a little he was as naked as she in the lamplight, his own scars exposed in exchange for hers. He lay down beside her, one arm across her body, and reached to quench the light. For an instant the darkness was opaque and webbed with violet clouds before his eyes, then his sight cleared to receive the cool wash of moonlight through the window fret, a delicate arabesque of light and shadow, stars and lozenges across Anoud's body. He felt her tense without moving, and said, "Do not be afraid. We have all night before us, and I will not do anything until you tell me that I may. I will not do anything all night, if you do not want me to."

"If you do not do anything all night," Anoud said in a small dry voice, "do you know what the women will say when they come to look for the signs and find none? They will say I do not please you; or that I have been wanton, and you found no barrier to your spear where you should have found it."

But Thomas could feel the fear still cold in her, and did not know what to do about it, being unversed in how to deal with that particular situation. Horses were another matter, horses he understood . . . He fell back on the familiar, and instinctively began to calm and reassure her much as he would have calmed and reassured Lulwa his favourite mare, with hand and voice, drawing his hands lightly, caressingly, over shoulders and arms and flanks, talking to her softly; the words did not matter, only the voice, and he scarcely realised that he had drifted into telling about the hills of his boyhood, the Lowland Scots words slipping in and out amongst the Arabic unnoticed. "You would like the hills around Broomrigg. Green, they are, and bonnie in the spring; and the curlews at their mating up on the high moors; and the hawthorn scenting . . ." And never even thought how he had spoken much the same words to the Lady Nayli, because that time they had been for his own sake, and this time they were for the girl's, and therein lay all the difference in the world.

Under his hands and against his body he felt the fear sinking away and a faint warmth waking. He could see her face in the patterned moonlight, turned up to his from among the strong dark mane of hair, the lips parted, a questioning line between her brows. "I do not understand," she said, "but the sound is sweet."

Without knowing that he was going to do it, Thomas bent his head and kissed her, tonguing her lips apart. She made to twist her head aside, brought up her hands as though to thrust him off, then surprisingly, linked them together at the back of his neck, and relaxed, her mouth growing soft under his though she did not yet know how to kiss.

He had all but given up words, and betaken himself to small crooning sounds; his hands had changed their purpose, and were playing with her, their caresses straying nearer and nearer to the secret places, seeking to rouse delight in her to match the faint unexpected shimmering of delight that was waking in his own loins, the sense of urgency between his thighs. "Come, bonnie love, come – come—"

He felt her stir, her breathing quickening as she pressed towards him. He felt the first tentative movement grow and blossom as she parted her thighs to let him in.

Later, much later, with the moon already sinking, he left her, pulling the heavy folds of his burnous over her that she might not grow cold while he was away, and went down the stair and out by the side door into the garden-court.

The water in the half empty pool that was greenish and scummy in the daylight, was bright now under the sharp-edged black shadows of the vine leaves, and shattered into fountaining quicksilver as he plunged in. He ducked his head under, and came up blowing, obedient to the Prophet's law that after lovemaking every part of the body from the crown of the head to the soles of the feet must be cleansed by ritual bathing. The coldness of the water made him catch his breath. He was sharply aware of the night about him; the faint white stars of the jasmine flowers, the swooping and swerving flitter of bats overhead, feeling himself one with them as though he had one less skin than usual between himself and the world, the worlds, outside his own being, aware of the water-like trickles of white fire on his body as he climbed out, the shapes and sounds and scents of the night, the full ripe face of the tide-pulling moon. He had never felt quite like this before, never been so piercingly aware, even in that long-past hour in the desert that had turned him to Islam, of the one-ness of all things in the hand of God.

He wrung the water out of his hair, and went in again through the side door. Back in the chamber with the hyacinth tiles, he felt for and found the rough cotton towel that lay ready, and rubbed himself down. The moon had changed position and no longer came in through the window fret, and the chamber was very dark; only the quiet even breathing told him that Anoud

248

was there and asleep. Soon the voice of the muezzin would float out over Medina in the day's first call to prayer. Soon it would be time to give her the piper's plaid brooch that was his morning gift to her.

But not just yet; there was still a little of the night left. He was still cold from the cistern under the moon. He slipped in under the burnous with a sense of homecoming, and lay down against her to get warm between her breasts. She roused a little without waking, and put her arms round him. It was not that he had forgotten the Lady Nayli, but he was free of her, for she had lost all power to cast ugly shadows in the back of his mind. A lovely contentment welled in him, like the clear-skied quiet after storm. He had received his own morning gift.

Two days later, leaving a strong garrison under Din Agha to hold Medina, Tussun and Thomas left the Holy City, the one for Jiddah, the other, with his picked four hundred, for Mecca; both at the outset following the same way, the ancient Pilgrim Road that linked the two sacred cities of the Prophet.

A mile or so out of Medina where the track entered the hills, at the place where Ahmed Agha had raised his cairn of heads – now taken down and buried – Thomas wheeled his horse aside from the dust-raising column, and climbing a low outcrop of rock, sat for a few moments looking back the way they had come. The morning light was already beginning to quiver, so that the distant walls among the green of palms and fig gardens might almost have been a mirage that would dissolve away as he looked at them. He knew this was the last view he would have of Medina until he came riding back, whenever that might be, and he felt for the first time the tugging ache of the man who no longer rides free, but has given hostages to fortune and must leave part of himself behind him every time he rides away. Would all be well with her until he came again? He had left money, enough to last until presently he could send more. He had put her in the care of the new Governor. She had Kadija with her; but *would all be well?* How if there was a bairn on the way? What harm could come to her, and he not there—

Someone reined in beside him, and Tussun's voice said, "It will still be there when you come riding the other way, and so, I dare say, will she."

The words were lightly spoken, but there was a raw, almost

angry note in the voice that made Thomas turn quickly to look at his friend.

"You think I am a fool?"

"Any man is a fool who gets himself bound up in a woman's hair, as you have done."

Thomas looked into his face a moment. "I was not jealous at *your* wedding."

"You had no need to be."

"And two nights since, you were not jealous at mine. It was you who bade me take a wife and father sons."

"That is a different matter. And two nights since, I had no need to be jealous."

"Tussun, my brother, how are things changed since then?"

They sat their fidgeting horses and looked at each other.

"You know that as well as I do." Tussun's voice was no longer angry but young and tired and a little forlorn.

And Thomas did know. "Listen," he said, "do you really think that the heart has room for only one love at a time? One day, assuredly, there will come a woman for you – aye, I know that the mother of your sons is not she. When she comes, and you hold her under your cloak, will you forget me?"

"No," Tussun said after a moment. "Allah knows it. There is nothing, and no one, in all the world could make me forget my brother."

"You see?" Thomas wheeled his horse, and leaned across to grasp his friend's shoulder. "Come, or we shall lose the column."

He was smiling a little, his eyes narrowed into the heat shimmer, as they rode down from the outcrop. "It is overlong since you and I last rode the desert ways together. Praise be to Allah! Life is good!"

He did not look back again before the first hill shoulder hid Medina from sight.

Chapter 25

In the world outside, Bonaparte had marched on Moscow and failed, and made his terrible retreat, and Wellington had seized his chance to advance into Spain, winning a resounding victory at Salamanca.

And on the roof of the tall and tottering rooming house near the great Pilgrim Gate, where he had his quarters, Thomas who had received the news in a letter from Donald MacLeod many months earlier, wondered what part his old regiment had played in it all as he leaned on the parapet and looked out over Mecca in the fading light, then turned his thoughts to other matters. The autumn rains had come, and in Medina there would be greenness among the fig gardens, and the bitter orange trees in the Governor's garden would be in flower. But in Mecca there was no greenness to be called up by the rains; it remained, as it had been when he first saw it, a dust-coloured city that seemed rooted, like an outcrop, among low dust-coloured hills.

It was hard to believe that there had been a city here before the Prophet was born; a city for him to be born in, and already holy in an older faith; holier, maybe, than it was now. But small and little known. The city had grown great purely on the Haj, the annual pilgrimage by which and for which it lived. Hence the broad processional streets, the many rooming houses, the huge caravanserais that made it also good for a garrison town.

Thomas's mind ambled back over the months since he had ridden in with his four hundred picked sabres behind him, and gone up to the citadel to report to the Grand Shariff. The hot, parching months of the summer, the nights when he had slept up here on the roof for lack of air to breathe within the house; the desert mirage dancing in the noontide heat, while he struggled to keep morale and training from trickling away; to keep his men ready for what might happen, when there was no particular sign of anything happening at all, while the atmosphere of the Holy City ate into discipline and morale.

He had expected something of Mecca, despite the warnings of devout Muslim friends, a spiritual experience. He had found nothing but a run-to-seed city chafed threadbare by its Wahabi garrison, and with no thought in its head, now that it was free again, but what it could make out of the renewed pilgrim trade: cheap-jack souvenirs already beginning to appear in the souks, the prostitutes' quarter humming in anticipation, the jumbled buildings of the Great Mosque freshly daubed with red and green paint to catch the eye. He had never felt as near in sympathy to the puritan Wahabis as he did in the Holy City of Mecca.

He did not even really know what he and his four hundred were supposed to be doing there; providing stiffening for the Shariff Ghalid's troops, of course, in case of a Wahabi attack. But as to keeping any kind of eye on the Grand Shariff himself, they could make fairly sure that he did not actually open the gates and invite the black-robed ones inside; but as to whether or not he was carrying on any kind of correspondence with ibn Saud, or what ideas he harboured inside that narrow handsome head . . .

So the long summer had dragged by. And then two months ago, when the heat and drought had built up to their most intense and men had already begun to watch for Canopus with its distant promise of relief in the night sky, Muhammed Ali had landed at Jiddah with two regiments of infantry, while two thousand cavalry and much needed reinforcements for the camel train had come down by the land route to meet him there. The souk talk was that the Sultan in Istanbul had been flicking him on to finish off the Wahabis for some time, but that he had not been able to risk coming until Ibrahim Pasha, his son, had Upper Egypt firmly enough in hand. The souk talk also was that he was displeased that the campaign had become bogged down and made no further progress since the taking of Teif, and had come to take matters in hand himself.

Had he the remotest idea, Thomas wondered wearily, what campaigning in the hot season with half the wells dried up would actually be like?

In Jiddah, the Viceroy had been officially greeted by Tussun in his capacity as Pasha, and had then come to Mecca to be greeted by Shariff Ghalid in a splendid ceremony at the Great

Mosque, in which both had sworn on the Koran, neither to take any action against the interests of the other. He had then set up his headquarters in the huge long-emptied school buildings alongside the mosque. And for the last six weeks or so the two leaders had been engaged in tortuous negotiations which seemed unlikely ever to be over.

Thomas's guess was that neither of them trusted the other the length of a musket barrel, despite the splendid oath on the Koran; and while Muhammed Ali had more than a thousand troops excluding Thomas's four hundred with him in the city, Ghalid, perched in his citadel on the hill, had half as many again, and twelve light-calibre guns. And so they sat and looked at each other, smiling courteously and stroking their beards. It was a situation, Thomas reckoned, much like an open powder keg, only requiring a spark to go up at any moment.

Aye well, it seemed likely that in one way or another, the thing was coming to its head. Hard otherwise to think why Muhammed Ali should suddenly have summoned his son to join their negotiations (remembering that as Governor of Jiddah, Tussun was technically the chief representative of the Sultan in the Hijaz and therefore not subject to anybody else's orders at all). Thomas's spirits lifted at the thought of Tussun's coming in the next day or so; perhaps by and by they would even get a day's hawking. It would be good to share a day's hawking with Tussun again, if Allah willed it . . . The light was fading fast, clouds banking up along the mountains north-eastward; there would be more rain in the night, and the desert like Paradise in the morning.

On the point of turning away and going down to his evening meal, a fleck of movement on the track from Jiddah caught at his attention, and he checked, watching as three riders took shape, one riding ahead, the other two following a little behind in the manner of servants or an escort. Not really knowing why, he lingered, watching them as they drew nearer, riding hard to reach the gate before it was closed at dusk. And as he watched, it seemed to him even at that distance and in the fading light, that the leader had an odd likeness to Tussun. Maybe something in the way he sat his horse, maybe something in the carriage of his head . . . But the distance was still too great for sight to tell him these things – some intangible recognition of the heart . . .

253

'Ach away! Don't be a fool,' he told himself. He had been thinking of Tussun and his imagination was playing tricks on him. Tussun Pasha, Governor of Jiddah, would scarcely come riding in at day's end, garbed as a desert Arab and with an escort of two men. He shrugged and turned away, and went down to his supper and evening rounds of the great caravanserai just within the gate, where his cavalry were lodged and stabled.

Next morning a little short of noon, he returned from mounted sabre practice to find Medhet waiting for him in his quarters and big with news.

Tussun Pasha had ridden in, very early. He must have camped with his escort on one of the wells, rather than go through the complications of arriving after the gates were closed for the night. He had gone to the apartments made ready for him in his father's headquarters, and within half an hour the Grand Shariff had gone, with eight lancers in golden turbans by way of escort, to visit him. Then something had happened, no one knew what, but something. It was said that the Grand Shariff had appeared at a courtyard window, and ordered his escort, waiting below, to return in peace to the citadel and wait for him there. Yes, assuredly something must have happened; but it could not have been anything dire, for, behold, one of Tussun Pasha's men had been here but now, with word that Ibrahim Agha was to meet him at the Desert Gate after the noon prayer, bringing his best falcon. "He said that there are hubara for the taking, and the desert will smell sweeter than this city, after last night's rain."

Thomas sent for his second mare, and took up his hooded falcon from her perch in the corner of the room; he had only the one, having come to terms with the needful economies of a soldier with a wife to keep, his pay usually in arrears, and an aversion to augmenting it in the common way by accepting the odd bribe here and there. He refused Medhet's plea to ride with him as his falconer, answered the call to prayer in the wide court of the caravanserai along with his groom and those of his men who happened to be there, praying, as he had done often enough before, beside his fidgeting mare and with Bathsheba sitting hooded on his leather hawking cuff, then mounted and clattered out, heading for the Desert Gate.

He found Tussun already there, his falconer with a couple of salukis behind him, and himself in a glowering temper. "You

254

have kept me waiting," he said accusingly, without any greeting.

"It was almost noon when I received your message," Thomas said, unruffled. He had learned with the passing years not to be ruffled by Tussun's moods unless they actually threatened murder, and sensed that the present anger was not in fact aimed at him. "I waited but to get my falcon and my horse, and to pray. Which of those things would you have had me leave undone?" He smiled into the other's darkened and miserable face. "Salaam aleikum, it is good to see you again, my brother."

Tussun seemed to force himself clear of his black mood for a moment to greet his friend. "And you. It is good to see you, Tho'mas."

They embraced quickly, leaning from the saddle, but his arm round Tussun's shoulders, Thomas felt rage and misery still vibrating in the younger man. This was something bad. Well, whatever it was, he would no doubt have heard all about it before they returned from their hawking.

They rode out through the gate together, the falconers following behind, past the wayside graves and the few sparse date palms, and took to the desert.

In the Wadi el Mahrat a few miles ouside the city, the autumn rains had woken a faint green flush, the tiny brief-blooming mauve and yellow sand flowers among the rocks, and the camel thorn and threadbare acacia scrub was in leaf, and breathing up from the ground into their faces rose the incredible, heart-stopping incense of the desert after rain.

The salukis were unleashed, and in a short while put up a hubara from a clump of acacia bushes. Tussun unhooded his falcon and flew her in pursuit. She made her kill cleanly, and was retrieved from where she squatted mantled over her prey and glaring at the falconers as they came up, with a mad marigold eye. Thomas's bird took the next quarry. And after that Tussun's bird missed her kill, though she returned sulkily to the lure.

"Change birds," Thomas thought. "You'll ruin that bird if she misses her next kill."

And as though the urgency of the unspoken message had reached him, Tussun shouted to the falconers for his second bird. "Bulchis is off her game today." But when she was brought, he took her impatiently from her handler, so that she was startled and bated from his fist, to hang for a moment screaming, head down from her jesses. Tussun righted her, but before he could get her properly settled, the saluki put up another bird; and Tussun, in too much haste, unhooded her and flung her free. The falcon, thoroughly startled and quite unprepared, took off, hung for a few moments with heavily beating wings, while she made some kind of attempt to get her bearings, then made for the quarry just too late. The inevitable happened; the hubara plunging into the acacia scrub, scattering twigs and leaves, with a crash as of a high diver breaking the water, while the saker missing her kill, veered aside and up, to sit, ruffled and glaring, on the branch of a terebinth tree.

Now she would be the very devil to get back.

Tussun rounded on the falconer, who was already uncoiling the lure: "Get her back, thou incompetent son of a she-camel!"

Thomas was settling his own saker, trying to keep her isolated from the tensions around her. Tussun's falconers, calling and whistling softly, were advancing on the terebinth tree. The saker waited until they were close beneath her, then stooped from the branch. For an instant it looked as though she were coming to the swinging lure, but in the last moment she swerved up again and was off in a new direction, her jesses streaming behind her. Tussun made a strangled sound in his throat that was almost a sob of fury.

The thing might go on the rest of the daylight hours, until by Allah's mercy they could wear her out and take her sleeping. If they failed in that, she would end somewhere tangled by her jesses, carrion for the kites in her turn.

Tussun was cursing already; he wrenched his horse round and made to go after them.

"No! Leave be!" Thomas bade him. "If you go after her in this mood no one will ever get her back."

Tussun swallowed, and seemed by a great effort to get a grip on himself. He dismounted, Thomas with him, and they turned aside into the sparse shade of the thorn scrub, leading the horses with them. The whistling and calling died into the distance, and only the thin hum of insects hung like gauze on the still air.

"Now," Thomas said. "What's amiss?"

"What should be amiss?"

Thomas's met the other's hot and angry gaze. "I don't know. But I have never known you misfly a falcon since you gave me my first hawking lesson. Nor have I ever known you to insult your servants for something that was your fault and none of theirs."

"You will hear most of it soon enough anyway, and you will think the worse of me."

"So – tell me yourself, and it may be that I shall not think so much the worse of you as I should if I heard it from another."

The drone of insects among the scrub seemed to grow very loud.

"I have broken faith," Tussun said in a rush. "I have broken the laws of hospitality. I am dishonoured among the tribes."

"I think," Thomas said very gently, "that you should tell me the whole story, beginning at the beginning and ending at the end. That way it may be that we shall both understand what it is that you are talking about."

And standing with his arm over his horse's neck, Tussun told:

"My father sent word to me at Jiddah to come to him with a full Governor's escort of a hundred men, for he had need of me. So I came. Two days since, one of the merchant-kind joined us as we made camp for the night, and brought me word from my father that the next night – last night – we should camp on the wells an hour's march short of Mecca: and I, with only two of my men, should ride on in the guise of merchants, entering the city at dusk, only just before the gates were closed. One would meet me at the gate and lead me to my father."

Thomas remembered the three figures on the road.

"So I came to my father," Tussun said. "He told me that he had a firman from the Sultan, empowering him to retain the High Shariff Ghalid, or to depose him, as he thought fit. He showed it to me. He told me that he had decided to depose him. He told me that he could not trust Ghalid; he could not forget how Ghalid did not join me according to his promise, at the outset of the campaign, and the alliance that he made last year with the Wahabis at Badr. He said he could not risk making his own advance into Najd if Ghalid was behind him, liable to change sides again, cutting him off from the Red Sea and the lines of communication and retreat."

"All of which is true," Thomas said, as the younger man broke off again.

"I know. I said to him: 'Oh, my Father, I see the soundness of these reasons. Now, therefore, do with him what it seems to you must be done; it is no concern of mine.' I was glad that it was no concern of mine. But I wondered – a little – why he had sent for me. He said 'You are not bound by the oath between us, sworn on the Koran; and here in the Hijaz, it is you, the Governor of Jiddah, and not I, who are the direct representative of the Sultan. The matter is for you to handle.'"

"And so you made the arrest," Thomas said into the heart of the next silence. And then: "You were *not* bound by your father's oath on the Koran."

"There's more to it than that."

"Tell on."

"Ghalid had to be got down from the citadel and into my father's headquarters with a small enough escort for him to be taken without fighting – Tho'mas, you see that?"

"Yes," Thomas saw that. Once blood was shed in the matter, the whole Hijaz might well go up in flames.

"That also was for me to do. To get him there, helpless, and when he came in good faith, to take him captive under my father's roof."

Thomas nodded. There did not seem to be anything to say that would have much point in the saying.

"At first I refused. But my father talked on and on, and I knew that his arguments were sound, though it was the soundness of military necessity, not of truth. I was with him half the night, and in the end – I took my orders. My father's man who had brought me there, took me out of the city again, over the wall by the roofs of the lesser caravanserai. And I went back to our camp, and this morning rode in with my escort – Abdin Bey in command, with pennons and kettle drums as befits the Governor of Jiddah. Did you hear us?"

"I was out at mounted sabre practice."

"I went – oh very publicly – to my own quarters in my father's house, and within half an hour Shariff Ghalid came down from the citadel with only a token escort, to wait on me. He had been told that I should arrive this morning, and I suppose he had some idea of getting my ear before I had time to speak with my father. I received him in an upstairs chamber, pleading weariness (that was true at all events), and we drank coffee and sherbet and exchanged courtesies for a while. And all the time I felt like the man you once told me of who betrayed the prophet Jesus – Judas Is-cariot? When the courtesies were done and he got up to leave, I told him that the stairs and surrounding chambers were full of my men, and that he was no longer ruler of the Hijaz, and that I had orders to send him to the Sultan in Istanbul. I thought he might try to call up his men, but he only said – he said, 'Allah's will be done. I have spent my whole life in wars with the Sultan's enemies, and cannot therefore be afraid to appear before him.' I wish my father or I came as well out of this as he did at that moment."

"And then you made him appear at a window and bid his escort go back peacefully to the citadel and wait for him there."

"You have heard that?"

"From Medhet, who hears all things."

"He said, 'How if I refuse?', but he said it in such a way – as though he was almost amused, interested to see what we would do . . . I said: 'If you refuse, it may be that the Hijaz will go up in flames, but you will be the first to die.' Abdin Bey had come in and had a pistol pointed at his head at fairly close range, but truly I do not think that it was needful. Afterwards he wrote a letter to the commander of the citadel, bidding him not to fight, but to hand all over in peace to Muhammed Ali, the Sultan's Viceroy in Egypt." A flicker of a smile woke in the young weary voice: "It seemed to me that I had done enough of my father's dirty work, and he could take on from there, and set me free for an afternoon's hawking."

It seemed to Thomas that he could hear, very faintly, the sounds of the falconers returning. "And what will happen to Shariff Ghalid now?"

"No harm. I have my father's word that he shall take his family, his slaves and his treasure into whatever comfortable exile the Sultan decrees; and I know that he will keep his word in the matter because he does not wish to earn the title of faith breaker, more than need be, among the tribes. But he has earned it, and made me earn it also. Ghalid is no longer High Shariff of Mecca and ruler of the Hijaz; and my father does not understand how little the wives and treasure and comfortable exile count for, beside that."

"His Excellency your father has not lived in the desert as we have done; he does not know many things that you and I know."

"And evil will come of this morning's work, for all his efforts to turn it aside."

"Oh yes," Thomas said. "Evil will come of it; but there was nothing else to be done if the campaign is to push on."

Tussun had been staring down at his own hand on his horse's mane. Now he looked up, meeting Thomas's gaze. "So you – you would have done the same, in my place?"

"Oh yes," Thomas told him, "I would have done as you have done; and after, I would have felt just as sick as you feel about it, Tussun my brother."

The chief falconer appeared in the mouth of the scrub-filled hollow, the missing saker sitting angry and bedraggled on his fist. "We have got her back, Excellency – In Allah's name pray you do not fly her again today."

"I have done enough harm for one day," Tussun agreed. And swung himself back into the saddle. "Come, we will return to the city."

Chapter 26

Muhammed Ali kept his word as to the wives and treasure. He appointed a distant cousin of Ghalid's, a man who he knew he could handle, to be Grand Shariff in his stead. He let it be understood that he had received orders from the Sultan to depose Shariff Ghalid, and not merely permission to do as he thought best. But few people believed him, and evil did indeed come of that day's work, despite all the Viceroy's efforts to turn it aside.

The dust had scarcely settled behind the outgoing High Shariff and his escort, when Shariff Rajik, his finest cavalry leader, who until then had been acting as Commander of Irregulars for the expeditionary force, gathered his horsemen and rode out of the Hijaz, while many others of the Grand Shariff's Bedouin allies melted away overnight to join the southern Wahabis.

A month later, Muhammed Ali, launching his new campaign, ordered Tussun with three thousand infantry and a thousand horse under Thomas, against the fortress town of Terraba.

The expedition was a disaster from the start.

They should have covered the distance from Teif into the eastward mountains in eight or nine days' camel march, but the tribes along the way, furious at the Viceroy's treatment of the Grand Shariff, turned it into a running fight; sniped at the column from behind every rock, forced a skirmish for every well and waterhole, so that the march took more than double the expected time, and the Egyptian troops arrived in poor condition for the storming of fortresses, having suffered casualties – not heavy, but enough – and with supplies already running low.

And of all fortresses, they had no heart for the storming of Terraba, with its black reputation and its witch-widow commander, known to be possessed of the evil eye . . .

They made their camp within reach of the last well before the town; one well among four thousand men with their horses and camels, the water so strongly alkaline as to be almost undrinkable; but at least without a dead goat in it. Poisoning the wells was the one thing the tribes could seldom afford to do.

On the first day they tried storming the place, after a long softening up by gunfire from their six light field pieces, but were flung back with heavy losses. They brought off their wounded, those they could, at evening; their dead still lay for the most part sprawled among the almond trees below the dark fortress walls.

A couple of long black tents for the wounded had been pitched in the shelter of a rocky outcrop, and the army surgeons were moving to and fro among the shapes on the ground. Thomas, squatting beside one of the shapes, was aware of the familiar sick-tent smell of blood and ordure, the throat-catching reek of hot pitch and astringent herbs and the acrid smell of pain; aware also of a low ceaseless moaning, somebody cursing as ceaselessly through shut teeth, somebody crying out under the hakim's cautery. Two men lurched by, carrying a third who no longer belonged among the living. The nearest of the lanterns hanging from the tent poles showed him the face of the man, one of his own troopers, beside whom he squatted. Always, after fighting, he would put in whatever time he could spare among the wounded; any wounded, but his own had first claim on him.

He felt the man's hand tighten convulsively in his, and the dazed eyes clung to his face. If he lasted until morning it was as much as he would do. Thomas knew the look, knew the strangely empty feel of the hand, for all the tense strength of its hold. "You will not leave us to *them*," the man said, his blanched lips scarcely moving.

"There is no question of leaving, Musa," Thomas said. "We are here to take Terraba, not to retreat from it."

"That is as Allah wills. But however Allah wills, you will not leave us to *them*?"

"No." Thomas said, "Have no fear of that."

The man's eyes half closed as the reassurance reached him, the clinging hand grew slack. Thomas's own grip tightened for an instant; then he withdrew his hand and got up. "Sleep now, my brother."

He ducked out through the looped-back opening, and made

his way up towards the dark crouching shape of the headquarters tent. There was an odd restlessness in the camp, a constant coming and going among the cooking fires and between them and the horse and camel lines; a mood that was not like the normal mood of a war camp at the day's end; not even like the mood following an unsuccessful attack, which in Thomas's experience was most often a kind of bloody-minded apathy. This was something different, an uneasiness that made him think of thunder in the air or bees about to swarm. A mood which had little outward sign save for that constant drifting movement and the way men gathered into knots and glanced behind them for no cause, but which was all the more disquieting for that.

Just short of the commander's tent he glanced without any special intention at the fortress rising above its thickets of apricot and almond trees at the head of the wadi. The sunset light was fading from its walls, twilight spreading up over them like a bruise, though the last glow was still the colour of ripe apricots on the mountain crests beyond. Only at the highest point of the fortress, a light pricked out as though from a tower window. Ghalia's window, maybe, and the witch looking out of it, down the Wadi to the camp below. For the moment something in Thomas's normal state of consciousness seemed to slip sideways, and the superstitious Highland blood in him took over and showed him the prick of light as an eye; the golden eye of something watching like a great cat. He was aware of others in the camp beside himself looking the same way, or carefully turning their gaze away as though avoiding the golden stare; as though to meet it would be to let something in . . .

He shook his shoulders, and turned his own gaze firmly back to the dimly firelit entrance of the commander's tent.

Beyond the heavy back-thrust entrance folds, Tussun and Abdin Bey and the other senior officers were gathered. Thomas joined them. The evening pile of rice and goat flesh on its brass tray was in their midst, and they were talking as they ate. He leaned forward and balled up a neat mouthful of it with the fingertips of his right hand, concentrating on the meticulous performing of the small action, as though it were a barrier against that odd unchancy moment outside.

"If we had bigger guns — " one of the men said.

"If-if-if. How would we get heavy guns up here?"

263

"Then, Allah knows it, we might as well have none at all, and be spared the company of those accursed artillery camels, for all the use that these light fieldpieces are against strong-built walls such as Terraba."

"And we cannot sit here on our haunches and starve them out, with our own supply lines gnawed ragged behind us. We shall starve ourselves before they do."

Tussun said, "I was not there, but was the problem not much the same at Medina?" And turned to look at Thomas, several of the others following suit.

"The walls of Medina are set in earth above volcanic tufa," Thomas said. "Seemingly Terraba springs from solid rock."

"More difficult to mine," Abdin Bey agreed, "but impossible?"

Thomas spread his hands "Who can say?"

"I am thinking that maybe Ibrahim Agha could say," Tussun told him, and Thomas saw something not far from desperation in his friend's face. "This I know, that whatever is done must be done swiftly, before the Thing that is abroad in the camp has time to breed."

There was a silence in which Thomas heard far off the jackals crying behind the uneasy sounds of the camp. The men about him stirred, or grew for a moment unnaturally still. He saw Abdin Bey making the sign against the evil eye with a hand only half concealed by his sleeve. "Allah have mercy on us!" he thought. "We all feel it, the leaders as well as the led. It only needs one more thing – even quite a small thing . . ."

"With your permission," he said formally, "I will take two to cover me, and reconnoitre the walls before dawn."

But the reconnaissance was never made, no mine ever driven under the walls of Terraba.

Not much above two hours later, scarcely past the time of evening prayer, Tussun stood with Thomas at his shoulder, again confronting Abdin Bey and the senior Albanian officers. Tussun Pasha was in a blazing rage. Thomas was not, but only because he had learned over the years that rage, when nothing could be changed by it, was a waste of time and energy and served only to cloud the judgment.

"They say they will not attack Terraba again," Abdin Bey was repeating stubbornly. "It is abroad in the camp that Rajik and his horsemen are close by in the hills – sent by ibn Saud from Diriyah."

"There has been no report of them from the scouts," Tussun said.

"The scouts have already played us false as to the strength of the garrison here at Terraba. Many of them have melted back into the hills. Your Honour, they are no longer to be trusted since — "

"Since?"

"Since His Excellency the Viceroy – let Your Honour forgive me – found it needful to treat the Grand Shariff in – a certain way."

"His Excellency the Viceroy, my father," Tussun began, and broke off, aware even in his rage that an undignified shouting match was not the answer.

Abdin Bey went on, staring straight in front of him: "The men say, furthermore, that it is well known the Sheikha Ghalia is a witch, able to throw a cloak of invisibility over those she chooses to befriend, and this camp may be surrounded even now by her Wahabi garrison and by Shariff Rajik's cavalry."

"Are they children to be frightened by children's tales of djinnis and afrits?" Tussun demanded.

"No. Yet they are but mortal men . . . It is said that she can turn herself into a great cat, and tear out the hearts of men."

"As much is said of any village crone."

"And who shall say there is not truth in the saying?"

Tussun said, "You too? You too, Abdin Bey? You are no better than the rest of them!"

Abdin Bey did not answer, but stood his ground, giving his commander back look for furious look.

The junior infantry colonel spoke up for the first time: "Excellency, we speak for our men. If the thing that is in their hearts finds a place also in ours, shall we be blamed? It is well known that the Sheikha Ghalia is indeed possessed of the evil eye. The men – all of us – feel it upon us, and we are afraid. Do you not feel it? Ibrahim Agha, do not you? If we attack Terraba again, terrible things will happen; we shall all be destroyed — "

"Are you not soldiers? Is it not for this that you take your pay?"

"It is not only for our bodies that we fear, but for our very souls."

"Your souls are safe in the hands of Allah," Thomas put in quickly, also speaking for the first time.

But the memory of those strange few moments on the way up from the hospital tent was with him still; his sense of being watched, held powerless in the sight-line of a great golden cat's eye. He understood what was within these men, as Tussun, often described as being brave as a lion, but who in actual fact was merely one of those born incomplete, with no normal sense of fear, could not possibly do.

He tried, all the same, loyally backing the pasha's furious attempt to make the officers change their minds, to talk fresh heart into the rank and file, until the moment came for accepting the ugly truth.

Afterward, alone with him in the torchlit tent, he put the thing straight to his friend and commander: "There is no way that you are going to take Terraba with these men, if you try forcing them they will fall apart into a disorganised rabble; they will melt into the hills and probably throw in their lot with the Wahabis."

"So we are to march back to Mecca and say to my father that we failed to attempt Terraba for fear of witchcraft? I do not think he will be made happy."

"We have already attempted Terraba, and have heavy losses to show for it," Thomas said. "We had already lost men enough before we got here, having, as Abdin Bey pointed out, lost the loyalty of the tribes for a certain reason, and received false information as to the strength of the Wahabi garrison. I suggest that we pull out before dawn, while we still have the cover of darkness, and retreat to Teif – some of us should make it – and say *that* to your father the Viceroy."

"That also will not make him happy," Tussun said after a long silence. "But Allah's curse upon it, I see, I do see Thomas, that we have no choice."

"None," Thomas said bleakly.

The officers were recalled and given their orders. And the desperate and all too short night began. Thomas sent up a prayer of thankfulness that there was no moon. There was too much light for comfort even so, for the watchfires must be kept up as for any other night, while in what there was of darkness between them, men came and went about the business of striking camp. They buried their dead shallowly on the fringe

266

of the camp with rocks piled over. There would be nothing for an enemy scout to think strange in that; no war camp left its dead over from one day to the next. What little food remained was divided up and issued, two days' rations to each man; water bottles were filled. The small-arms ammunition boxes were stacked ready for last-minute loading on to the artillery camels. To dismantle and load the guns would be sure to catch watching eyes and betray their purpose; the guns must be spiked at the last moment and abandoned. The three long tents must also be left standing, but all that they contained was brought out of them, including those of the wounded who could walk or ride or lie across a camel. For those too sore hurt to be moved, there was another kind of mercy: shadows beginning to disappear into the emptying hospital tents, and come out again stooping to cleanse the blade of knife or dagger in the rough grass between the rocks.

Thomas, eating his morning issue of dates and hard goats-milk cheese on his way down to the horse-lines, was aware of that shadowy coming and going through every fibre of his being, remembering Musa's plea of last evening – "You will not leave us to *them*?" He had given the needful order; but he was thankful that the mercy-stroke was given by friend for friend, kinsman for kinsman, and he had no need to play any further part in the matter.

At which point the thought of Musa brought him up with a jerk. In all likelihood he was safely dead by now, but you could never be sure with stomach wounds, and if he was not? The man had always been something of a lone wolf, what if there was no one who counted themselves his friend to perform the last act of friendship for him, and he was left to the impersonal mercy of the army surgeon? Thomas spoke a quick word to the officer who was with him, and went swiftly back through the disintegrating camp in the direction of the hospital tents.

In the furthest of the two, a shielded lantern still hung from one of the tent poles, casting a dim pool of light over the centre bay, while the end bays were lost in shadows; a few still figures lay there under their cloaks, and a couple of men were moving among them. "Musa ibn Aziz?" he said to one of them. The man pointed to a figure lying beside the tent pole.

"Dead?" Thomas asked.

"No, Sir, but he knows nothing. We left him until the last, in case one came," the man said simply. "But now it is the time."

"And I have come," Thomas said, and knelt down beside his dying trooper.

The medic was wrong. Musa ibn Aziz was past speech, and the stink of death came up from the wound under his cloak; but his eyes were open and a still living man looked out of them to meet Thomas's gaze as though he had been waiting for him to come.

"You have borne the pain long enough," Thomas said. "Now it is time for rest."

He saw the faintest flicker in the sunken eyes, heard the faintest check in the tortured breathing, and knew that Musa understood.

"Shut your eyes."

But the eyes remained open and holding to his. A look of tranquillity came into them, as though the man behind them was already slipping free . . .

Not for an instant taking his own gaze away, Thomas drew the Somali knife from his waist-shawl. "Go in peace," he said. "May Allah the All Merciful receive you into his Paradise," and slipped the point home under the angle of the jaw.

The blood came in a bright jet, the trooper's body bucked for an instant and then lay still as his head rolled sideways.

Thomas got up and walked out, stooping outside the tent to clean his blade by driving it into the threadbare grass between the rocks.

The surgeon had gone already, back to oversee the loading up of the wounded, and behind him in the hospital tent, nothing moved.

None of the wounded would fall alive into the hands of the Wahabis.

Chapter 27

Thomas had just reached the horse-lines, and on the far side of the camp the last minute task of spiking the guns was all but completed, when the attack came, and came with no cry from the outposts, no moment of forewarning. A sudden surge of sound, a clashing of steel on steel, a howling as of fiends out of Eblis that broke like a wave all along the piled thornwork on the Wadi side of the camp. "Oh God!" he thought. "The infantry pickets! They must have been asleep – or fallen back on the main body without waiting for orders!"

Someone close by was shouting that the witch-woman had indeed spread her cloak of darkness over her followers. "I warned you! I warned you!"

Running for the place where his own horse was tethered, Thomas's ears caught from far away to his right, across the growing tumult, the nearing thunder of hooves bearing down upon the camp from the further side. This time there was warning in plenty, from the cavalry pickets, as the enemy horse rolled into them: into and through and over, and came sweeping on; and above the scream of stricken horses a name yelled as for a war cry: "Ghalid! Ghalid!"

Muhammed Ali's treatment of the Grand Shariff was indeed bearing bitter fruit.

The horse lines were a swirling chaos in darkness shot through with ragged light from the torches that still burned at the end of each picket line. But there was something of order in the turmoil, for Thomas's troopers, already on standby for the march, were swinging into the saddle and wheeling their horses to face the oncoming menace. Thomas's own mare was ready for him and as he sprang into the saddle, and the trooper at her head slashed her free, suddenly like two faithful shadows Daud and Jassim Khan were ranging up on either side of him. "Sound, Form Troop!" Thomas shouted to the young bugler, and the call sang out, fierce and bright as cock-crow above the tumult.

The men formed up roughly, still forming, half in their stirrups as they swept forward to meet the in-flooding wave of Wahabi cavalry.

They came together with the shock and roar of a breaking wave where tide and current meet. In the dark there could be no form or pattern to the fighting. To Thomas the attackers were a black whirlpool-mass from which the tattered torchlight struck out the animal glint of wild eyes and bared teeth and deadly flicker of steel. Shadow-riders were plucking brands from the watchfires and galloping with them through the camp. One of the hospital tents was afire and going up in a great sheet of flame, and by its light the swirling shapes of men and horses gained for the moment form and substance. In the midst of all, Thomas was shouting to his troopers, ordering, encouraging. He could hear the bugle calls from the far side of the camp, where Tussun was struggling to rally his men. But the infantry were beyond rallying. With the fear not only of death, but of damnation upon them, they were flinging down their weapons and streaming away, abandoning transport animals and equipment, trampling their own dead and wounded as they ran.

No orders could reach Thomas through that chaos and in the dark, but guessing clearly enough from the unmistakable note of terror and dismay, what must be happening elsewhere in the camp, he knew that it was for him to thrust his own men for a shield between the Wahabis and the fleeing infantry and hold back the pursuit as best he could. "Sound the charge," he shouted to the shadow riding on his left, and again the bugle crowed sharply imperative through the surging dark; and again the Bedouin cavalry drove forward, yelling, against the Wahabi host.

"Allahu akba! Allahu akba!"

The first promise of day was beginning to glimmer in the eastern sky; and from the dark mass of the fortress at the head of the Wadi, the one light still shone, like the unwinking golden eye of a great cat watching the Egyptian camp empty of life save for the abandoned pack camels in the baggage lines, and black shapes that flapped about it vulture-like in search of loot; and silent and smoking, while the dark rivulets of men streamed westward from it as blood streams from a crushed body, leaving only death behind.

Full daylight found them among the outriders of the hills

through which their line of retreat wound back towards distant Teif, the desperate infantry still straggling ahead, the Bedouin cavalry still grimly playing their part as flank and rearguard. At least the retreat was no longer quite a rout; with the faint sense of shelter of the hills about them the infantry had steadied somewhat, and Tussun and his officers had been able to win back some kind of control over them.

From the slight lift in the ground, where he had drawn his horse aside for a few moments, Thomas sat looking down and taking stock of the situation. Away ahead the infantry was raggedly on the move, but even at that distance with a sullen and disheartened look to them that was grievous to see; and few enough of them, compared with the force that had come that way three days before. The cavalry was in better case. Its second regiment had been virtually swept away in the fore-dawn attack, but during the first hours of the day the survivors had returned in ones and twos and small tattered groups; now they were joined with what remained of his own regiment, in the rearguard.

Earlier that morning they had been fighting a stiff rearguard action, each half in turn covering the other half's retreat; but now the enemy pressure on their rear had slackened, seeming to fall back on itself for the moment. There was still spasmodic sniping from among the rocks, but nothing more; it was almost as though the hunters did not wish to push the hunted along too fast; as though they knew something that the hunted did not, and were in no hurry.

Uneasiness prickled in Thomas's tired nerve ends. 'I am not liking it,' he thought. 'I am not liking it at all.'

His gaze returned from the cavalry to the weary straggle of the infantry up ahead. Men and horses alike were in sore need of rest, but there could be no rest for any of them till they were through the pass – the Pass of the Meeting Place, where two tribal territories came together – and down to the wells on the far side. Thinking of the wells, Thomas ran his tongue over his dry lips. There was water in the leather bottle at his saddle bow; most of the men would have full water bottles since they had been ready for the march when the attack came, but there would be no more till the first ridge of the high hills was behind them and they came down to the wells, however long that took them. They should make it by nightfall with luck; but how

271

much luck could they count on between now and then? His mind went to the narrowness of the pass ahead of them; the black and jagged defile that could so easily be the jaws of a trap.

Once through that and across the tribal boundary the country opened up somewhat, and they might stand a chance. Always supposing, of course, that the wells were not too strongly held against them. If they were, and they could not break through to the water, then they were finished. The thing was as simple as that, so there was no point in sitting here agonising about it. He took the water bottle from his saddle bow and allowed himself one mouthful of warm foul-tasting water, holding it in his mouth for a long moment before he swallowed, then pushed the wooden stopper back into the bottle, slamming it home with the flat of his hand, and rode down to rejoin his men.

Through what remained of the morning hours they pushed on and upward into the mountains, while the occasional report of a jezail, the puff of smoke from a seemingly empty hillside, the singing bullet into their midst, bringing down horse or man, kept them from any false ideas about having lost contact with the enemy. They returned fire when they could see anything to fire at, which was seldom; when they came near to the pass it would be time to send covering parties ahead; to do that too soon would only mean needless losses . . .

It was well past noon and the defile not far ahead when Thomas saw one of the scouts haring back along the line of the ragged column. He pulled his horse clear of the rearguard and rode forward to meet him, and a few moments later was looking down into the man's grey sweat-streaked face staring up at him past the arch of the mare's neck.

The man was fighting for breath. "The guns – They are bringing up – one of the guns — "

Something kicked below Thomas's breast bone. "The guns were spiked."

"Maybe in the swiftness of the attack, one – was missed or – the spiking was not finished – They can bring it up – camels – on to the spur that overhangs the defile just – beyond the highest point – "

"But how in Allah's name could they have got ahead of us with such a burden?"

The man shook his head like a worried dog. "There will be

272

other ways . . . shortcuts not known to us who are not native to these hills, but familiar enough to the scouts who — "

"Who betrayed us," Thomas said harshly. "It is not needful that you remind me." He saw inside his head the narrow defile choked with retreating infantry, and the gun crouched above them on its spur . . . "Tussun Pasha knows this?" he asked.

"I am from Tussun Pasha now. He sent me to bring you the warning."

"Is there any way known to you by which we may get round them avoiding the pass?" Thomas demanded.

"None from here that will not lose us the wells."

"And without the wells, we die."

"It is certain."

"Then we must pass through the defile."

"But Ibrahim Agha – the gun – "

"How many are with the gun?"

The man rubbed his forehead with the back of his hand. "Maybe three score, maybe more."

"On foot or on horseback?"

"On foot, with the three camels, manhandling all the rest that the gun needs."

"How armed?"

"Jezails and captured carbines."

"There is a way to come at them? You can guide us?"

The man nodded. "There's a goat track. Have to leave the horses before the last stretch."

"Then by Allah's will, we will take care of the gun, if — " he checked an instant, looking down into the dark sun-narrowed eyes that looked levelly back into his.

"If I am to be trusted? If this is not a trap to lead the flower of the Bedouin cavalry to their deaths? No trap, Ibrahim Agha."

Thomas said, "I trust you." He grinned suddenly. "I believe that I might trust you even if I had a choice in the matter."

The spur that thrust out above the angle of the defile was swarming with men. The gun camels had been unloaded and led aside and hastily tethered behind some rocks; and on the furthest point, positioned to sweep the narrows below, the gun had been assembled and was being made ready for action. Clearly among the enemy, probably among Shariff Rashid's followers, there were some who knew one end of a field gun from the other.

Their confidence, it seemed, had caused them to neglect posting scouts, and the surprise was complete as Thomas and his band of dismounted cavalry came down upon them out of the sun, firing as they came. Men scattered and fell. Some of the Wahabis swung round their jezails and returned ragged fire, while others whirled about to meet the onslaught sword in hand. "Ya Allah! il Allah," the war shouts burst up and beat to and fro among the jagged slopes. Thomas discharged his pistol into a howling face, then thrust it back into his waist-shawl and betook himself to his broadsword. It was hot and ugly work and for a while the thing could have gone either way. He lifted up his voice again and again, "Allahu akba! God is great!" and made for a black-robed warrior with a sword in one hand and a long curved dagger in the other, who seemed to be the leader . . .

At the end, the few remaining of the Wahabis fought like tigers, backed about their captured gun, and died where they fought. With the suddenness of a dissolving dream the struggle was over; and the silence of the high hills came back. A silence that sang in the ears beyond the low bubbling wail of a wounded man and the harsh call of a vulture circling high overhead. Bodies lay grotesquely sprawled among the rocks. No time just now for separating friend from foe.

Thomas spoke to Daud, beside him still: "Sound the signal. One long, followed by three short."

The notes of the bugle sounded thin and clear through the waiting quiet and as they listened, from beyond the head of the pass came one long note in answer.

"They will pass in safety now," one of the troopers said. "But the hunt will not be far behind."

"It would be a sad thing to waste a gun set up and ready to our hands," Thomas said. "Maybe we can do something to discourage the hunt . . ." He issued quick orders, posting scouts on the higher slopes against surprise. A hurried investigation among the rocks, where the gun camels were tethered, showed that the Wahabis had taken thought to bring up not only powder and ball but also the implements of gunnery. Only one thing was lacking; water for the sponging down after each discharge. Well, there was a way that problem could be got over; and in any case they would not need the sponge until after the first round had been fired; and another investigation showed that the first round, together with its flannel-cased charge of black powder, was already in position, with a headcloth rammed in after the ball to prevent it from trundling out of the muzzle when the gun was depressed for firing down into the defile.

Thomas took out his tinder box and kindled the slow-match which was already in the linstock, then gave it to the steadiest of his troopers, and calling up three more, stationed them two on either side of the gun – less chance of confusion in the long run if they mounted a full gun's crew, each with their own quite simple task to perform.

Even as they heaved on the wheels, manhandling the gun round to fire along the line of the defile, the forefront of the retreat came into view, a weary draggle-tail of men lurching blindly along, herded and kept moving by the mounted flank guards like sheep herded by their dogs.

Thomas, kneeling to squint one-eyed along the barrel, took careful aim through the sparse branches of the wild almond trees on the slope of the spur, sighting on his own people against the time when they should be past and the men filling the defile were the enemy; for the Wahabi would be quick to realise, if they had not already done so, that something had gone amiss with their plan, and return again to their hunting.

While the retreating infantry passed below, Thomas gave a hurried gunnery lesson to his motley crew as they crouched waiting, shielded from below by the almond branches. A rattle of musket fire from the rear told them that the pursuit had indeed closed in again; and the rear of the ragged column had taken on a driven and harried look, though there must still be a screen of cavalry between them and what followed after. For a few moments the defile below was almost empty, and then the hard pressed rearguard spilled into view; the foremost knot of cavalry checking almost below the spur and wheeling round to cover the retreat of the squadron that followed after, close-hounded by the black swarm of the Wahabis.

Thomas spoke to the man who held the pole sponge. "We shall need that wet, before we load the second round, and the one thing that the Black Brotherhood forgot was a water skin."

"The water bottles — " the man began.

"Forget about the water bottles, the water is for drinking."

The others looked at him with dawning understanding. "It is not decent, Ibrahim Agha."

"Better indecent than dead because the gun blows up for lack of sponging out," Thomas said simply.

"Me, Sir?"

"As sponger, the thing is undoubtedly for you to do; the first time, anyway. If your supply dries up, others must take their turn."

Grim laughter took the gun team, and the sponger, with outraged face, went aside and squatted, then turned back to his place, the sponge on its pole satisfactorily dripping.

"Nobly done, my brother," Thomas said, watching the defile. The last of the cavalry had gone through, to form cover for the men below the spur to withdraw in their turn. The first thrust of the Wahabis must be allowed through, to be dealt with by the rest of the cavalry as best they could, if the gunfire was not to take as much toll of his own men as it did of the enemy; but after that . . .

"Pricker," Thomas said, and the man holding the long slim spike thrust it down the vent to pierce the flannel cartridge.

Thomas chose his moment with precision, rose and stepped aside: "Fire."

The man with the linstock leaned forward and applied it to the vent. There was a burst of flame and a crack and roar that seemed as though it must split the rocky hillsides. Hideous sounds came up from the defile; sounds that might have come from the mouth of Eblis; and as the smoke cleared a little Thomas saw through the wild almond branches, starry with their first fragile blossom, the bloody carnage in the narrows: men screaming and falling, men cut horribly in two. It never ceased to surprise and appal him, the damage that one seemingly slow-moving roundshot, even from a mere three-pounder, could cause in a close-packed mass of men.

They ran the gun forward again from its recoil, and resighted it. "Sponge," Thomas ordered.

The sponger, still with an almost comical look of outrage, thrust it down the bore to quench any smouldering fragments.

"Cartridge."

The loader thrust another cartridge into the muzzle and the sponge-man reversed his staff and rammed it home.

"Ball, load." Somebody else's headcloth, tightly rolled, went in to hold the round in place.

"Fire!"

And again the gout of flame and the hill-shaking crack; and the sounds from the defile as from the mouth of Eblis.

But by now the Wahabis had realised what was happening, and the long-barrelled jezails were returning fire, aiming for the gun flashes on the spur. And though the almond trees gave them a certain amount of cover, the air was full of the unforgettable whine of musket balls in flight as the bullets came round their ears.

"Keep down as much as you can!" Thomas shouted to his crew; and to the men standing guard, "Keep your carbines ready and watch the high ground: they may try to get round and come down on us from above."

Presently the crack of a carbine and a satisfied grunt from behind told him that the precaution had not been needless.

But it was not only from behind and above that the danger came. With the reckless courage of desperation, men were swarming up the steep sides of the spur through the rocks and the wild almond trees, and in a dozen places along both sides of the spur hand-to-hand fighting was breaking out.

Amidst it all, working purposefully and steadily, Thomas and his crew continued to fight the gun; though ammunition was beginning to run low. The sponge man went down to a musket ball, and the firer, misjudging his position, was caught by the recoil and fell back clutching a broken arm; but each time another man stepped forward into his place, and the three pounder did not cease to fire. There were sharp-shooters now among the rocks up the far side of the ravine; notably one, higher than all the rest, unseen save for the fleeting glint of the sun on a jezail barrel and the repeated puff of smoke wisping away on the light hill wind, and for three men on the spur lying dead.

Thomas shouted to the best marksman among his troopers: "Harmid Zultan, shoot me that man."

"Aywa, Sidi." The man grinned with a flash of teeth, taking aim. But in the instant before he pulled the trigger, the whiplash crack and the puff of smoke came again, and he spun round and fell, drilled through the head.

"Hold fire!" Thomas ordered his crew. He crossed to where

277

the trooper lay still twitching, with the back blown out of his head, and took up the fallen carbine, which by chance or the mercy of Allah had not discharged. He dropped to one knee and took careful aim, longing for the stock of his Baker rifle against his cheek. He drew a deep breath and held it, waiting. Again the sun glinted on a gun barrel, and for a splinter of time half a head appeared, made visible only by its own betraying shadow on the sun-scorched rock behind it. In that instant Thomas pulled the trigger. He felt the familiar kick of the carbine against his shoulder, and the shadow was gone from the sunlit rock, and in its place was a ragged blot of darkness that held even at that distance the vital throb of crimson.

He laid the carbine down beside his dead trooper and turned back to the waiting gun crew. "Sponge – "

As though that shot had been some kind of signal, the defenders of the spur gathered themselves for one final and supreme effort. When it was over, and the swarming attack, flung back for the last time, fell away in defeat, and the last of the black powder smoke drifted away, the defile was like a butcher's yard.

A jagged silence settled over the hills, broken only by the harsh cry of the wheeling vultures. On the spur among their own and the enemy dead, Thomas and his men stood to get their breath back.

The Egyptian troops would be well clear by now, and with the narrows past and the country opening up to them, the hunt would probably not come again in force, but content themselves with raids on the retreating column.

"Insh' Allah, they will reach the wells before night," one of the men said.

"Insh' Allah, so shall we," Thomas returned, looking round at them as a man may look at his brothers.

"What do we with the gun?"

"Nothing," Thomas said regretfully. "Save make sure that it is not used again for a while. Slit up the cartridges and scatter the powder. There is little enough left; it is well the thing ended when it did."

They scattered the black powder to the hill winds, and heaved the gun over the edge, watching it somersault down over the rocks, gun and carriage parting as they fell, to join the red and reeking mess below. They laid their own dead in a neat row, taking their arms and water bottles, and left them to the vultures along with the Wahabi slain. They bound up one another's wounds as best they could with strips torn from their own clothing.

"Time we were on our way, my brothers," Thomas said. They took a mouthful of water each, no more; they had a way to go yet, and maybe more fighting ahead of them before they reached the wells. They turned the gun camels loose, and headed like weary old men for the sheltered place where the scout and a couple of their comrades waited for them with the horses.

By the mercy of Allah, being across the tribal boundary and with the usual uncertainty in such matters, the wells were not held against them; and at evening, with what remained of the Terraba force bivouacked about the water behind hastily flung up defences of camel thorn, and the spent horses grazing under guard on the thin grass round about, Thomas and his commander stood together, looking back towards the hills that stood up dark against the eastern afterglow.

Tussun said with a glint of bitter laughter in his voice, "This is getting to be a habit with you."

"What is?"

"How do you say it? – pulling my fat out of the fire. One day you will do it once too often."

"I'd not be too sure I've done it this time – not yet," Thomas told him. "We have a long march ahead of us before we see the roses of Teif again. And I doubt the Black Brotherhood will just sit back and watch – unless for the pleasure of seeing us starve. We are going to have to live off the country; and Allah knows it, this is an ill country for living off."

"If we are driven to it we shall eat horseflesh," Tussun said. "We shall get back to Teif . . . But the rearguard work will fall to you and your squadrons, and we must keep some of the horses for that."

The laughter died out of his voice, and his hand on Thomas's shoulder was shaking. "Not that getting back to Teif seems especially worth while. Nothing seems very much worth while, tonight."

"That's because you are tired," Thomas said with masterly understatement.

279

"And you are not? Oh my Tho'mas, we are all tired – or dead. Well, let us admit it, we have had a tiring day."

They moved off together to visit the weary pickets, making a careful way among dark bodies that slept where they had fallen, in the few hours respite that sleep could give them, before they took up again the long desperate struggle back to Teif.

Chapter 28

In the open desert westward, the hills would be already beginning to parch in the growing heat of springtime, but up here in the high country around Teif there was still a silken sheen of green along the Wadis, and the myrrh and the tamarisk scrub and even the occasional grove of almond trees still gave shade among the rocks where the winter freshets had run. And Thomas, following the narrow hill track that would come down presently by a short-cut, to meet the pilgrim route from Medina, his small escort of three troopers behind him, felt the sense of quickening in the blood that came with the springtime among the hills of his boyhood, but which in the desert seemed to belong rather to the time after the autumn rains.

But as always when he rode that way, his mind went back to the ragged remains of an army retreating along it from Terraba, close on three months before. They had struggled back to Teif, those of them who finally made it, little more than a third of the infantry that had set out, about half the cavalry. Odd that, when you thought of it, since the cavalry had borne the brunt of the rearguard fighting, the whole way back. What a waste of lives, and Terraba still to be taken. And His Excellency Muhammed Ali had not been pleased. Slightly mollified, yes, by the increased reputation for valour which his son and his son's cavalry commander had brought back with them from that hideous retreat, but pleased, no. Tussun had found this unjust and unreasonable, especially when one considered that the disaster stemmed from the Viceroy's own breach of faith with the High Shariff. But Thomas could sympathise with him. For himself, he found that the knowledge that one had kindled a blaze of reputation, even among the enemy, was not much consolation for having lost more than half one's men in doing it.

He blinked, and shook his head, as though to shake out from it the image of weary and blood-stained ghosts lurching along the way.

One thing about the Viceroy, he was as resilient as a catapult thong. He had set about bringing up reinforcements and fresh water supplies, and gone on consolidating his position in the Hijaz. Having failed to drive the Wahabis from Terraba he had turned to a naval attack on Quinfunduh further down the coast, which, although now isolated in Ottoman-held territory, was still in Wahabi hands; and which, if taken, could provide a land base for a further drive into the southern interior. Also, Thomas guessed, a possible gateway to the Yemen with its highly profitable coffee trade. Well, it would make a change from tobacco.

Tussun had hoped to be put in command of the all-Albanian force; but the Viceroy had given that to one Zam Aglou, renowned for his blood-lust and skill in piracy. Zam, so said the report, had captured two small ships supplying the garrison with arms and ammunition, and turned their guns on the mud brick fort, which had fallen after a desperate resistance, during which Zam Aglou had offered a bounty of two hundred piastres per Wahabi head or pair of ears.

Thomas remembered his own and Tussun's dealing with Ahmed Bonaparte after the taking of Medina, and wondered if they had been over nice, but rather thought not. The thought of those heads and ears stuck in his gorge though he had not heard of any displeasure on the Viceroy's part.

Meanwhile, Tussun was back in his pashalik of Jiddah, and making sure that it remained in the right hands to act as his father's supply base, and he, Thomas, was here kicking his heels between Teif and Mecca in command of Muhammed Ali's elite cavalry corps, with no prospect of being sent anywhere else in the near future.

Not much more than a year ago, that would have irked him intolerably, but there had been changes in his world since then . . . When it became clear that the present pattern of things was likely to continue for a while, he had asked permission of Muhammed Ali, taken three rooms over a goldsmith's shop behind the Mecca Gate caravanserai and sent Medhet off to fetch Anoud and Kadija.

That morning advance riders had announced the nearing of the spring trade caravan from Medina, and he had handed over for the day to his second-in-command, and ridden out to meet it.

The track rounded a sheer buttress of the hillside, and there below him, winding its way between the great rocks of the defile, was the caravan route. Nothing to be seen of the caravan as yet, but away beyond the hill spur that hid its further reaches from sight, a cloud of dust was rising.

She might not be with this caravan at all, he had only been able to give her very short notice, Thomas warned himself. On the other hand, she might. He touched his heel lightly to his mare's flank, urging her forward, and was off and away down the boulder-strewn slope, the troopers behind him. A swallow-tail butterfly fanning its enamelled wings on a rock beside the way, roused as the horses' shadows swept over it, and fluttered up and across his path like a moment of joy given outward seeming. Thomas went weaving his mare down between the rocks at a speed which made his troopers shrug and glance aside at one another, grinning, then turn their attention to the task of keeping up with him without breaking either their own or their horses' necks. The head of the caravan was coming into sight as Thomas reached the level ground and reined in. He could hear the beat of the camel bells, a bronze sound, a brown sound with a kind of bloom on it. Keeping to the side of the broad, scarcely defined track, he rode on to meet it.

As it came into closer view, the long ragged string of men and beasts seemed to spool out from the fold of the hills as though it would go on for ever. The tall disdainful camels, ridden or carrying their great loads of bales and boxes, swaying forward, the merchants and traders mounted or trudging on foot, the dark robed fierce-eyed horsemen of the caravan guard. Save for the bells and the occasional shout, there was a surprising lack of sound. Thomas was always surprised at how silently a caravan moved, save for the twice-daily chaos of getting under way or falling out for the night. The first camels were level with him now, rocking by, the great bulbous feet coming down and spreading, velvet-silent with a little puff of dust at each step, snakelike necks swaying against the sky. Thomas turned in beside the leading rider. "Salaam aleikum. Are you captain of the caravan?"

The man looked down at him from his swaying perch, out of bright dark eyes that seemed full of desert distances behind the folds of his headcloth which he had pulled across his face, the authority of each man recognising the authority of the other.

"Effendi, I am the captain of the caravan."

"Have you women with you?"

"It depends who asks, and for what purpose."

"I am Ibrahim Agha of Muhammed Ali's cavalry force in Teif. The woman I seek is mine."

"How should I know who and what and the ownership of the curtain-hidden ones in my caravan?" The man jerked his head backwards. "There are women gathered together in the mid-part of the line. Go you and ask among them."

Thomas flung up his hand in acceptance and salute, wheeled his mare, and, while his troopers fell back a little, began to ride down the caravan, his eyes narrowed into the honey-coloured haze of sunlit dust through which beasts and human figures loomed towards him. Some way down the line, he came upon the women's litters all together, box shaped or gondola shaped and set crosswise, so that taking camel and litter as one entity, the gondolas in particular made him suddenly think of enormous and rather ramshackle dragonflies. Idiotically, he hoped that Anoud would be in a dragonfly and not in a box. And for the moment he was cold-afraid that she might not be in any of them. He knew that all had been well with her a short while ago; every official messenger between Mecca and Medina had carried letters written, or to be read by, the professional in the souk. But something could have happened since the last letter. Again, he knew, as he had known it years before when Tussun went off campaigning in the Sudan while he was left in Cairo, the fear of loss that is one of the prices of love . . .

And then he saw Medhet riding beside one of the dragonfly litters; Medhet waving like a palm tree in a high wind, and making his horse dance and rear.

A few moments later they had come together. "I have brought her!" Medhet said. "Am I not the best, the very prince of all messengers and couriers?"

"You are indeed!" Thomas told him. "Ride on now and tell the captain of the caravan that I am taking the lady and her maid back to Teif. There is no need that she should go first to Mecca and then have the long ride on."

And as his young aide-de-camp disappeared in a triumphant cloud of dust, he found himself riding alongside an elderly she-camel with an expression of weary distaste for the world and all its doings, led by an old man who looked as though he had been created out of the same stuff as the desert itself. He was looking up, seeing for the moment only a camel litter framed of the usual pomegranate wood and covered with coloured shawls like all the rest, but with a sheen of enchantment about it because it sheltered Anoud.

He was suddenly and unexpectedly shy. They had had so little time to come to know each other, and even that little had been almost a year ago. And he scarcely liked to call out to her before the camel men. She must have heard his voice and know that he was there. But the litter might have been empty for all the sound or sign there was of any movement within. Maybe she was shy too.

He raised himself in his stirrups to come as near as might be to the litter swaying to and fro above him, and said very softly, "Anoud, I am here."

The nearest of the curtaining shawls stirred a little, then was lifted back, and he was looking up into the interior of the litter glowing with sunlight filtered through the coloured stuffs; looking up at the shapeless black figure sitting among the stowed bundles of her worldly goods, who might have been anybody, or nobody at all. Only the light grey eyes looking down at him from over her yashmak were Anoud's, and nobody else's in the world, and the hand she reached to him, leaning forward and down, a right hand, narrow but strong, that might have been a boy's, was Anoud's too.

"Tho'mas," she said, "I am here."

Later in the day, having despatched Medhet to see about the return of the camels, Thomas brought his wife, followed by Kadija and a caravanserai porter with the bundles, to the three rooms above the goldsmith's shop.

The rooms were by themselves on the rooftops, and reached by an outside stair from the small courtyard garden behind the house. Roses were coming into bud in tall jars in the courtyard; the heavy scented, many-petalled crimson roses of Damascus. And at sight of them, Anoud let out a small soft cry of delight.

"Oh how beautiful! How beautiful! I did not know that there could be so many roses!"

"Teif is famous for its roses," Thomas said.

She had stopped to smell one of the half-open flowers, lifting back her veil, and cupping her mutilated hand under the heavy velvet head. She let it swing back and looked up at him. "Does my Lord think – it is not our garden, I know – but does my Lord think that I may take one? Just one bud? There are so many coming — "

Thomas, with a sudden boyish sense of pride in his own forethought, said, "I have already spoken on the matter with the goldsmith Ali Karim, and by his leave you may pick one rose every day for as long as the roses last," and forbore to mention how much this arrangement had added to the rent.

He picked a carefully chosen flower, darkest of the dark, and as yet only half unfurled, and gave it into her hand. He had a sudden foolish desire to kiss it first, but Kadija and the impatient porter were both watching. If they had not been, he could have kissed Anoud herself.

Not long now . . . He smiled at her, a smile of content with the present moment, and happy anticipation of moments to come, and turned and went up the rickety outside stair, warmly aware of her footsteps behind him.

The coffee pot and the fretted lamp were unpacked, the familiar cushions and coverlets spread on the divan, and as the days went by the three rooms over the goldsmith's shop began to take on a look of home, the rose of the day in its blue and white vase in a wall niche, Thomas's beloved broadsword propped in a corner.

Thomas himself was to and fro between Teif and Mecca in the wake of the Viceroy; and Anoud had moved, without his really noticing it, into a different place in his life. When he left her at Medina, two days after their marriage, he had not forgotten her, never for an instant forgotten her, but she had stepped back a little, become something beautiful and remote. In Teif she was growing into him, becoming a part of him that did not need to be remembered any more than one needs to remember about breathing.

He had returned from a three-day patrol and was sitting with her one evening in the outer chamber, with the stairhead door open, for the spring was turning towards summer and even up here in the hills the heat of the day was beginning to linger fiercely into the evening.

He was trying to teach her to sing, not very successfully, though with much laughter. The girl's speaking voice was soft, almost throaty, but in singing it took on the high nasal tone of her breed that went ill with the old Scots air, while the

Western scale of seven notes was strange to her and made the tune hard to capture.

> Mount and go,
> Mount and make you ready
> O mount and go,
> And be the Captain's Lady.

"No," Thomas said, "bring it down. Not from the back of your nose, from down here, as you speak. Think of a rock-dove. Your voice is so soft when you speak, Anoud, now listen – "

She laughed and willing as a child eager to please tried again, following him as he sang, her gaze on his face, the little frown line between her brows deepening in concentration. "Tell me again, the meaning of the words," she said, when they arrived more or less together at the end.

But before he could do so, a new sound caught at Thomas's ear: someone whistling in the courtyard below:

> Oh I would ride the wide world over
> A thousand leagues an' three —

There could be only one man to whistle that tune in that place.

Thomas sprang up and crossed to the door. The sky was yellow as a lantern behind the roofs of Teif, the garden full of crowding shadows among which the Pasha of Jiddah lounged at the foot of the stair, tucking a rose into the rakish folds of his turban.

"Tussun!" Thomas went three at a time down the steps and they embraced at the bottom.

"You have picked tomorrow's rose!" Thomas accused him. "We are only allowed one a day and there are not many left."

"Count it as part of your hospitality to a guest."

Thomas held him off at arms' length to look at him. "Oh, it is good to see you, Allah knows it, even with a stolen rose in your bonnet! What brings you up this way?"

"I had to talk over certain plans with my father, and being here, I come to visit my brother. Is it granted that I come up?"

"Give me but a moment to warn Anoud," Thomas said, turning back to the stair.

"I did not know that you had her here with you until the goldsmith told me."

"When it seemed likely that I should be here a while, I sent for her. And she packed the coffee pot and came, like a good soldier's wife."

The outer chamber was empty, all signs of a woman having been there hastily snatched up and carried away to leave it a man's majlis.

He called down to Tussun, who came bounding up the stair to join him. In the doorway he checked, looking about him, then back to Thomas: "Where is Anoud? I thought I heard the two of you up here."

"Which is why you gave warning of your approach."

"One must be on the safe side," Tussun said. "Does she keep closely to the old ways, then?"

"The women of Arabia are not the women of Albania or the Viceroy's family."

"No, I know that. But will she not come back? – I will not seek to tear off her yashmak."

Thomas laughed. "I will do what I may. Sit, and be welcome meanwhile." And he went into the inner room, closing the door behind him.

Anoud, with Kadija's help, was setting out the ceremonial array of pots and little brass cups, all the cherished impedimenta of coffee making. She looked up, smiling. "Your brother is come, and Kadija shall bring you coffee."

"Anoud," Thomas said, "Will you not come yourself, and sit with us a while?"

There was a long silence, then she looked up from the gazelle-skin coffee bag in her hand. "The women of your people, they are not hidden? Not veiled, you tell me?"

"They are not veiled, and they sit down to eat and talk with men. But they are not Muslim," Thomas said, putting the thing fairly.

She was silent again. "And Tussun Pasha?" she said at last. "How is it with the women of his kin, who are of the Faith?"

"They go veiled in the street and on formal occasions, but I have eaten with his mother, and his sister, unveiled."

"It is difficult, this matter of two worlds," said Anoud; and then: "I am of the Faith, but I am your woman and your world is mine. What would you have me do?"

He put his hands on her shoulders, feeling them tense a little under his touch. "I would have you come back into the majlis and sit with me and with Tussun, my brother, because you are the two people in the world whom I love."

"My Lord's brother is my brother also," said Anoud. "I will come."

She did not even replace her yashmak, but merely drew the folds of her veil loosely across the lower part of her face, giving the suggestion rather than the fact of concealment, and, bidding Kadija to bring in the brass tray, followed him back into the outer room.

Tussun, seated crosslegged on the divan, bowed to her over his joined hands, careful not to look too straightly into her face: "Salaam aleikum, may your day be white, Lady."

"May your day be as milk, oh Brother of my Lord," she returned the greeting, and sank down into the shadowed corner of the room.

Kadija like a moving black mountain set the tray with its coffee-making clutter down beside the hearth, breathing, as always, soft and heavy as a cow.

"Bring the lamp," Anoud bade her. "The light begins to fade."

She departed, and after a short time came scuffing back with the lamp, which she placed in one of the wall niches. Then she finally withdrew, disapproval in every line of her surging black rump.

Meanwhile, Thomas was arranging the coffee pots in the customary row beside the hearth, shaking fresh roasted coffee beans into the bowl, beginning to crush them with the brass pestle. In the cities most men of the rank and position that he had attained to had the coffee brought ready-made; but Thomas stuck to the old way, the desert way, and as the host and tent-master himself carried out the whole process for his guest.

Neither Tussun nor Anoud spoke while he wielded the pestle. To do so would have been as ill-mannered as to speak while someone was playing the lute, and Thomas, taking something of the pleasure in his performance that a musician might have done, wove the quick bright arabesque of sound with its cross-rhythms and grace-notes, as Zeid ibn Hussein had taught him in those first months of his desert training. He never crushed the coffee beans without thinking of Zeid. But this evening the memory came for the first time without grief. "He was a good friend to have had. Allah's Peace be with him . . ." He bent all his skill to ringing the pestle and mortar as Zeid would have approved: to make something perfect for the passing moment. And as he did so his own moment of clear joy awoke in him, and the thought – he did much of his thinking in Arabic these days – "Surely by the Grace and Mercy of Allah, I am the richest of men! I have Tussun to ride out with, and Anoud to come home to; Tussun's shoulder to brace against mine in time of battle, and Anoud's arms to cradle me in the night."

A sense of wholeness opened like a flower within him and spread out to include in its unity the quiet chamber and the three of them together in the dappled lamplight. It is seldom given to mortal man to be happy and to know he is happy, not in some regretted past or hoped for future, but now. And when it is, he must walk softly, lest the Gods grow jealous . . .

The small shining moment passed as swiftly as it had come, and he saw that the water in the pot was rising to the boil, and the coffee beans were sufficiently crushed. He tipped them carefully into the water and added the cardamom seeds from their small embroidered bag, and their aromatic scent filled the chamber.

With the fragrance of the bubbling coffee wafting about them, it was once again the time for talk.

Tussun said abruptly, "Have you heard the news?"

"I am but now returned from three days' patrol. What news would that be?"

"Saud ibn Saud is dead."

It took a moment for the words to penetrate. The Tiger of Arabia seemed always to have been there, and it had seemed as though he would be there as long as the desert sandstorms blew. "He was killed? How did it come about?" Thomas said.

"No, he died in his sleeping rug like a mere mortal man. Of the fever that comes with the springtime."

"How are the mighty fallen," Thomas said. "Who will take the leadership after him? Abdullah, I suppose." He thought of the smoke-spitting rocks of Jedaida, and the black-robed Wahabi flood. "Will that be to our advantage do you think?"

"Only time can make that clear," Tussun said, soberly. "He has all the old Tiger's courage and daring. I wonder if he has the other qualities he needs. They say Saud's last words to him were to bid him give battle always in the mountains, never to come down against us into open country."

"Which sounds – if it be true – as though his father also had his doubts . . ."

Anoud, who had been listening with silent attention, entered the conversation for the first time. "My father used to say that neither of Saud's sons had his strength or his judgment, or his" – she hesitated a moment over the word – "his political skill. My father said that if the old Tiger died before he had made all things secure, the day would surely come, by Allah's mercy, when the Najd as well as the Hijaz would be free of the Black Brotherhood."

Both men looked at her in surprise, and she seemed to become suddenly aware of herself. She drew the folds of her veil more closely over her face, and said in a hurried whisper, "Let my Lord forgive me. My father sometimes talked to me as though I were a son."

"We will hope that your father was right," Thomas said, smiling at her.

And Tussun looked at her directly for the first time. "Your father was fortunate in his daughter," he said, speaking as easily as though she had indeed been a son.

The coffee was ready for the long-drawn process of pouring it from pot to pot until it reached the little brass cups that stood waiting. There were only two. Thomas glanced at Anoud, a question in his eyes. She gave an infinitesimal shake of the head, and drew her veil closer over the lower part of her face; and he did not press the matter. It was enough that she had come to sit with them while they drank coffee and ate the dates stuffed with almonds in the blue and white bowl; enough that she had spoken in front of Tussun, and as composedly, almost, as the Vicereine could have done; that for love of him she was coming, by little and little, out of her enclosed world into his. Presently there would be more talk between him and Tussun, more speculation as to the outcome of the Tiger's death. For the moment it was enough that they should drink coffee in Anoud's quiet presence, and be together, all three of them together.

291

Tussun leaned forward to take one of the little brass cups and hold it for filling. And as he did so, three glowing petals dropped from tomorrow's rose in his turban – he must have picked one that was already overblown – and fell with a faint rustle to the floor.

Chapter 29

News of the Wahabi leader's death did something to raise the morale of the Egyptian army, which at the time was uncomfortably low, partly owing to their pay being even more than usually in arrears. But the next piece of news brought it crashing down again.

The Quinfunduh expedition had ended in disaster. The Albanians had wasted the water supply within the walls, and though they had manned the wells that existed some miles outside the town, they had not fortified them. So a month after their capture from the Wahabis, several thousand of the Black Brotherhood came down upon them, routing the well-guards, recapturing what was now the only water supply. In the fortress, Zam Aglou had exploded the magazine and taken to the ships, abandoning many of his own men, some four hundred horses and as many camels and all the captured guns.

The ships had reached Jiddah, but they were unwatered and unprovisioned and many more were dead before they made landfall. Zam Aglou's own vessel did not reach Jiddah at all; but he had not, it was thought, suffered shipwreck but merely decided that it might be healthier to return to his old trade of freelance piracy.

The hot summer months crawled by, filled for the most part, for Thomas, by long desert patrols to keep the reopened trade routes safe for the passing caravans, while Tussun, stuck sweltering in Jiddah and Yembo, held the ports secure for the steady inflow of troops and supplies, guns and cavalry-horses from Lower Egypt.

For Muhammed Ali was once again making good his losses and building up his forces for the new campaign that all men knew would start as soon as the Haj was over.

"But first the Haj. This year we shall celebrate the Haj as befits the most sacred occasion in the Muslim year," said Muhammed Ali walking one evening in the palace garden refreshed by the first autumn rains, "To the Glory of Allah the All Merciful, and for the raising of morale among the army and throughout the Hijaz."

He was in the habit of commanding the company of one or other of his senior officers or officials on these evening strolls, and tonight it was Thomas's turn.

"After so many years under Wahabi oppression, all men must be shown how great a thing it is that the Hijaz is free again to receive pilgrims to the Holy Places."

Thomas was silent, wondering whether the Viceroy had forgotten that the Haj had arrived and been celebrated, though admittedly in somewhat lean fashion, last year.

Muhammed Ali glanced round at him as they walked, brushing a clove carnation against his full bearded lips; and laughed, seeming to read the unspoken thought in the disconcerting way that he sometimes had. "Last year's Haj was but a beginning, a poor timid thing – a few pilgrims, two meagre caravans scarce worthy of the name."

"But maybe it was all the more valiant and beautiful in the sight of Allah for that very reason," Thomas said.

The Viceroy nodded. "Maybe, maybe. But Allah knows also (and Muhammed His Prophet) the hearts and the needs of fighting men . . ." His gaze travelled reflectively up the slender dark streak of a cypress against the translucence of the evening sky. "And of the desert people, and of the merchants with gold in their saddle bags. This year the Haj will return to its old splendour. For the first time in ten years the Damascus caravan is on its way. And pilgrims from Istanbul and Asia Minor are already arrived at Port Suez. This year the Haj will bring the trade that it was used to bring to the Holy Cities."

Thomas had known His Excellency the Ottoman Viceroy of Egypt long enough not to be in the least surprised at this view of the revived Haj not so much in terms of spiritual regeneration, as of trade and propaganda. There was a good deal of sense in it, he supposed, for a man in the Viceroy's position.

"This year, also, there is no doubt that many will go on from Mecca to visit Medina and pray at the Prophet's tomb according to the old custom." The Viceroy looked round at him again. "You will take as many of the Arab cavalry as you deem necessary and act as escort for this further pilgrimage."

Thomas's mind went to Anoud and the arrangements to be

made; the usual complications of life for a soldier with family ties. "And afterwards? I return to Teif or Mecca?"

"You will not return to Teif or Mecca for a considerable time." Muhammed came to a halt, and the two stood facing each other. "You will, I make no doubt, have heard that Quera al Din, the Governor of Medina, is lately dead?"

"I have heard something," Thomas said guardedly. He had heard, among other things, that the Governor – the Amir – of Medina had died by poison.

"That is small cause for grief, the harshness of his rule and his mishandling of the tribes made it certain that he must shortly have been removed in one way or another. The fact remains that his place is now empty and must be filled with all reasonable speed."

Thomas waited.

Muhammed Ali said conversationally: "I therefore intend – Tussun, who is of course the direct representative of the Sultan in the Hijaz, is with me in this – to appoint you as his successor, to clean up the trouble he has left behind."

For a moment Thomas was not quite sure that he had heard correctly, or, if he had heard, that he had understood. "Excellency, I am not worthy," he said at last. It was the correct response, but he felt the truth in it as well. "The Governor of Medina must surely be of the Prophet's world – have you forgotten that I am a Scot?"

"There is nothing in the Koran to say of what race the Governor of Medina shall be." The Viceroy moved on again, speaking more as man to man than ever he had spoken to Thomas before. "Are you afraid that this comes only because you are my son's friend? There is no need. I assure you that I do not bestow such honours, such extremely *demanding* honours, for such reasons . . . You are known to be well liked and well trusted by the Medinans and by the Beni Harb. The reputation you have gathered to yourself through Jedaida, the capture of Medina and the retreat from Tarraba leaves no doubt as to your courage and skills as a soldier and a leader of men. You are one of the very few among my senior officers who I know that I can absolutely trust. These be good enough reasons?"

Thomas, still feeling slightly winded, said, "These be good enough reasons." And then: "For my part, I swear on the name

295

of Allah the All Compassionate that, while I live, I will not betray that trust."

"I know it." The Viceroy had returned to his more viceregal manner. "I shall not invest you until the last day of the Haj celebrations, but I give you this forewarning that you may have a short time to grow accustomed to your advancement, and to make any domestic arrangements that may be necessary. But I need hardly tell you the matter is not to be made public until the day of the investiture."

Thomas went back to the three rooms above the goldsmith's shop, and did not make the matter public, even to Anoud. It was not that he did not trust her to keep silence. But it had always seemed to him that the Viceroy's word, once given, was binding until and unless something happened that made it advisable that he should take it back. If something happened before the last day of the Haj that made it seem advisable that he should change his mind . . . Thomas wanted the governorship of Medina. He was not overwhelmingly ambitious, not more than any career soldier who knows his own worth; but now that his climb from the ranks of the 78th Highlanders had brought him within sight of such a shining goal (and he knew that it was one that he could handle; that he had it in him to make a good Governor of Medina) he wanted it desperately, and had the feeling that if he spoke of it in advance, even to Anoud, it would disappear like the faery gold that changes overnight to withered leaves.

The days passed, Mecca throbbing like a drum with its preparation. The souks were spilling over with wares, from gold and fine silks to the meanest tourist trash to catch the eye and loose the purse strings of the pilgrims; dealers in horses and camels converged from all quarters of the Hijaz to encamp under the walls alongside the tents and horse-lines of the garrison, which had for the most part been withdrawn from inside the city to make room for the influx. The holy places broke out in fresh coats of garish paintwork.

Thomas, on duty with the cavalry still within the walls, saw the great pilgrim caravans come in, filling the wide streets with surging rivers of men, women and beasts, the shouts and cries of the camel drivers, the dry-throated and weary ecstasies of the pilgrims, the great caravan masters leading the way in the luxury of litters slung between swaying soft-footed camels decked with tassels and ostrich plumes and the slow clonking bells; rich men on fine riding camels, hidden women in shawl-hung litters; the poor or especially holy on bare feet, some gazing about them in awed realisation that their life's longing was upon them and they were in the Holy City at last, some too numb with weariness to gaze anywhere but straight ahead, as they stumbled by towards their appointed caravanserai or camping space. Over two or three days they came from Damascus, from Istanbul and the Gulf cities, from Cairo bearing in their midst the Holy Carpet; and with them tumblers and fire-eaters, musicians and performing beasts.

On the days that followed, they performed the established rituals. In the forecourt of the Great Mosque they circled the Ka'aba seven times like swarms of soldier ants, thrusting and jostling to get near enough to kiss the Black Stone set into its wall. They visited the Place of Abraham and drank from the sacred well of Zam-Zam. They ran between the twin hills of Safa and Martha. They went shopping for a riding camel or a bolt of silk, a silver bracelet or a crude pottery model of the Ka'aba.

On the eighth day of the festival, the crowds swarmed off to camp at the Oasis of Mina six miles away, and on the day after, pushed on to Mount Arafat where the Prophet Abraham had shown himself willing to sacrifice Ishmael his elder son at the command of Allah. There they listened to a sermon delivered from the slope of the mountainside, before returning to Mecca next day to throw stones at the Devil, and finally take part in the great Feast of Sacrifice, the Id-al-Adha, to celebrate Abraham's willingness and Allah's Mercy in the last instant providing a ram to take the young man's place.

Muhammed Ali played a leading part in all this, entertaining the great ones of the caravans, walking himself bare headed and bare footed in the processions to the Holy Places, providing two camels and six sheep for sacrifice at the Id-al-Adha, a sign of piety and charity (since the sacrifices, save for the sacred portions, were eaten by the poor) that bordered on the ostentatious. Some of the Medinans, some of the garrison also, joined in the rituals, though, as they had not had to make the journey, this did not count as making the Haj, but only as a meritorious act. Thomas did not; he had prayed in the Great

Mosque often enough, kissed the Black Stone, drunk from the Holy Well when he first came to Mecca, and had found less of God in these things than he had found in the empty desert. He wished that he could have made the show of piety, even so. How was it different from his rigid abstinence from alcohol, his regular praying five times a day, his ritual washing every time he lay in the way of love with Anoud? He was not sure, but the difference was there, and he held aloof from the great public demonstration of the Faith.

On the last day of the Haj ceremonies he was formally summoned to the citadel.

He went, followed by Medhet in a state of game-cock pride, and clad in his best abba of honey-brown camelhair with the gold edging on the shoulders, his fringed turban-scarf swathed with more than usual care, his sword hilt and cartridge belt polished by Jassim Khan until they glinted in the sun. And in the State majlis of the Governor's quarters in the citadel the Viceroy received him, surrounded by officials and senior officers. An unhooded saker on its stand in the corner of the room watched the scene with an intense golden stare as Thomas, with a court official on either side of him, crossed the rug-strewn floor to kneel with due formality before the cushioned divan on which the Viceroy sat.

"Salaam aleikum. God's greeting to you, Ibrahim Agha," said the Viceroy, as Thomas bowed his head an instant over his joined hands.

"Salaam aleikum. You sent for me, Excellency."

"I have sent for you, for the purposes you know of," said the Viceroy.

Thomas waited, his eyes quiet on the other's face.

"Taking cognisance of your worth and qualities, it is my will and the will of Tussun my son that you should become Amir of Medina."

"What can I say, save that I am honoured," Thomas said.

Muhammed Ali held out a hand to an official beside him, who placed in it a parchment scroll tied with threads of golden silk.

"Swear that you will faithfully uphold the Sultan and his Empire, that you will carry out the duties of Governor with all the strength and skill that in you lies, that you will have no false dealings . . ."

The list lengthened.

298

"All these things I swear," Thomas said when it ended. "In the name of Allah the All Merciful, the Lord of the Ages, and of Muhammed his Prophet."

The repetition of the words, the solemn oath-taking, threw up most unsuitably into his mind the other ceremony of a like kind in which he had played the central part. And for the moment the wide airy majlis above the rooftops and minarets and the swarming crowds of Mecca in the throes of the Haj dissolved away; in its place was the small dark room over the armourer's shop, with the wheels and footsteps of the Edinburgh streets outside, and his father and Mr Sempill and himself standing round the table on which lay his indentures. He saw again the close-written sheet catching the grey light of the rainy afternoon beyond the window; heard Mr Sempill intoning from it as though he was in kirk, and his own sixteen-year-old voice repeating after him the long string of promises – to be sober and honest and responsible for his own laundry . . . Ten years ago; nearly eleven. It seemed a whole lifetime away; and yet in that moment it did not seem to have taken long in the by-going.

The narrow office room faded and he was back in the Viceroy's majlis with the voice of rejoicing Mecca washing in through the windows.

"In the name of myself, Muhammed Ali, and of Tussun Pasha of Jiddah and representative of the Supreme Sultan here in the Hijaz, I appoint you Amir of Medina," Muhammed Ali was saying.

He held out the scroll with its dangling gold threads. Thomas took it with a deep obeisance and raised it to his forehead.

Muhammed Ali made a summoning gesture to another man who stood by with a garment that was creamy and rich with goldwork folded across his forearms. The man stepped forward and shook out the folds of a magnificent burnous of milk-white camelhair laced with more gold then seemed to Thomas quite seemly.

"Ibrahim Agha, Amir of Medina, you are already a man with three swords, which is enough for any man to serve Allah," the Viceroy said. "Therefore receive instead this cloak of honour from our hands."

The hand of Medhet appeared from somewhere beside him, to take the scroll and leave his own hands free. Muhammed Ali leaned forward and spread the burnous over his shoulder. He slipped his arms into the long loose sleeves, over the abba he already wore. He made obeisance again with joined palms. "Excellency, I thank you for the honour that you do me."

There was a ring too, a big rough-cut ruby. "Receive lastly the signet of the governorship." It hung heavy on his forefinger, the colour of fire, of pride, of blood . . .

The Viceroy had risen; he raised Thomas and kissed him on the beard. "You will ride for Medina on the sixth day from now, in command of the escort, with those who continue their pilgrimage from Mecca, and take up your appointment on arrival."

"As you command, Excellency." The straight creamy folds falling about him, Thomas stood taller than any other man in the room, and aware of it. Then he added, a little hurriedly lest he should be dismissed with the thing not yet asked, "Is it permitted that I take two days leave?"

"Immediately?" asked the Viceroy, with a trace of amusement.

"As soon as I have arranged matters as to the escort, and handed over to my second-in-command here."

"For what purpose?"

"That I may ride to Teif, and make certain arrangements of my own."

"Two days and one night, then." The Viceroy's lips twitched under the splendour of his moustache. "See that she does not keep you longer."

Thomas, followed by four troopers, rode to Teif wearing his Cloak of Honour. After this, it would be put away in a camphorwood chest and only brought out for the greatest and most formal occasions. But now he was riding to Anoud in his new glory, no matter how travel-stained it got in the process, with a boy's triumph and a man's joy in doing honour to the woman he loved. It was a foolish gesture, he knew, but somehow necessary.

It was evening when he entered Teif, gritty from head to foot with hard riding, left his horse in charge of the troopers and headed for the three rooms above the goldsmith's shop.

In the garden behind the house the roses were over. Next year there would be dark damask roses again to scent the narrow court, but he would not see them, and Anoud would not pick the permitted one a day for her tall blue and white vase. For a moment regret touched him, for something that had been lovely and was now past, but the shadow was gone as quickly as the shadow of a bird in flight.

At the foot of the outside stair he passed a woman with a bundle coming down, too tall and narrow to be Kadija, anonymous as usual in the black street-going robe. Nothing remarkable in that, there was a good deal of coming and going among the women at all times, and he did not wonder who she might be, as he stood aside to let her by, then took the steps himself two at a time.

As he entered the stairhead door, calling her name, Anoud came through from the inner room to meet him.

He held his arms wide as he always did, and she came into them, slim pale arms rising from the loose sleeves of her abba to clasp him round the neck, her body, thin as ever – he had never managed to get any flesh on to her – pressed against his, her face in the hollow of his neck, the scent of iris and sandalwood whispering out of her hair. They always greeted each other in silence in the first moment of coming together.

In a little, she leaned back in his arms, her hands still loose-linked at the back of his neck, her eyes gravely questioning. "Oh my love, what brings you to me so fast and so dusty in this fine new mantle that I have never seen before?"

He laughed ruefully, glancing down at himself. "I did not know that I was so dusty, and now I have made you dusty, too. But I have a thing to tell you that will not wait."

"Tell me, then," she said.

"I am this morning appointed Governor of Medina."

"So-o. Then Medina has a worthy Governor," Anoud said, and came in close to him again. "My heart is joyful for the city, and for you, and for me because I am your woman and your joy is mine." And then after a few moments: "We shall be leaving this place soon?"

"On the sixth day from now. We travel with the Haj caravan. I must be away from here tomorrow morning, for I command the escort. But I will send Medhet for you. Can you and Kadija be ready so soon?"

"We were ready in fewer days than that, before. But Tho'mas, I also have a thing to tell you that will not wait."

301

"Tell me then," he echoed her words.

"I am with child."

Quite why it should have seemed so astonishing, Thomas never knew. Women did have children, often enough. But this was different; this was Anoud. An almost painful shaft of joy lanced through him. He wanted to hug her fiercely close, and at the same time he was almost afraid to hold her at all, lest he harm her or the child in her belly.

"Anoud – a child? – my child?"

He did not realise that it sounded like a question until she laughed.

"Who else's?"

"Fool that I am! But are you sure there is a child?"

"Quite sure. I have missed two moons; and also – that was the hakimi you must have passed at the foot of the stair."

Thomas usually spoke love to Anoud in the Arabic terms of endearment that would sound familiar to her ears, but in this moment he reverted to the tongue and the homely ways of his youth, his arms around her, rocking her from side to side, his face buried in her hair.

"My Bonnie Love," he said, "my Bonnie Dearie . . ."

Chapter 30

At the gates of Medina Thomas ordered the escort to fall back, that the caravan might enter well ahead of them. The arrival of the Haj, and the new Governor's entry into his city were two separate things, and he felt, with a Scottish sense of the fitness of things, that the separateness should be carefully maintained. When the religious procession was lost to sight and sound, and not until then, he ordered the escort to advance once more, and made his own entry to the bright song of bugles at the gate and the liquid throb of kettle drums, in the way that his own men, and maybe the Medinans also, would consider fitting. Anoud, far into the city in her shawl-draped dragonfly litter, would be listening for the skirl of his coming, too.

Next day he presented himself to the senior sheikhs, took over from Nayli's husband, Mustapha Bey, who as lately made commander of the garrison had been acting as deputy, and took up residence in the Governor's Palace, with Anoud once more safely lodged in the women's quarters.

Less than a fortnight later, Tussun rode in from Jiddah by way of Mecca bringing with him news, somewhat stale, from the outside world that Napoleon Bonaparte had capitulated in the spring and been exiled to an island called Elba. Bringing with him also, eight hundred foot and five hundred cavalry at his heels, and a fair-sized camel train swaying and bubbling in the rear. And an hour or so later, when he had had time to wash off the dust of the long march and have something to eat, he and Thomas were standing together in the eastern bastion of the citadel, well out of hearing of the sentries who moved to and fro along the rampart walk of the square keep above them.

Leaning on the breastwork, Thomas looked out over Medina, thinking, not for the first time, that the layout of the city was like a plaid brooch, with the citadel for the central boss, and the broad courts of the outer city raying out round it as the spokes of a wheel, and beyond, the winter greenness of date and fig

303

gardens against the lighter green of melonfields, and away
beyond, tawny in the evening sunlight and streaked with the
crocus-purple shadows of the defiles, the mountains rising
range beyond range in the Kassim and the Najd. Tussun, he
realised, glancing aside at his companion, was gazing in the
same direction, and not merely as a man looks at a distant
view, but with speculation and a very definite purpose in his
gaze.

"Well?" Thomas said as the silence lengthened.

"Well – my father having celebrated the days of the Haj with
due splendour for all men to see, is now about to launch his
campaign into the Najd." Tussun pulled his gaze back from the
eastward mountains and turned, resting one arm along the
breastwork: "How many men can you give me, Tho'mas, to
add to those I have brought from the coast?"

"For what purpose does he need them?" Thomas asked with
caution. "And for how long? I cannot strip Medina of its
garrison indefinitely."

"My father would have me advance to Henakiah with as
large a force as may be, loudly giving it out, in the manner of
the big-mouthed Turks, that I intend to capture El Rass and
Aneiz."

"A feint, I take it?"

"Surely. A diversion to draw off as many of the Wahabis as
may be, while my father with the rest of our forces advances on
Kulukh. We are not to get drawn into any action, if it can be
avoided, but hold them in play in the mountains for as long as
there is need. No more than a month, maybe much less."

Thomas did a quick reckoning-up in his head, reviewing,
unit by unit, the troops at his command. "One regiment
Albanian cavalry," he said after a few moments, "two hundred
of my own irregulars, seven hundred in all – seven hundred and
one, counting myself." He grinned.

So within three days Mustapha Bey was once again deputy
governor of Medina; and Thomas and Tussun with their little
army were heading into the mountains. And if, in her chamber
with the hyacinth tiles in its wall-niches, Anoud wept her heart
out, she did not do it until they were well away, and so Thomas
did not see her tears.

On a night upward of three weeks later, in the mountains a
day's march north of El Rass, he was thinking of her and the

304

bairn who was still part of her, as he came down the wild goat track from visiting the last vedette on his late night rounds. It was generally in his few moments of solitude, and at the day's end that his deep and almost unconscious awareness of her surfaced into conscious thought, in the cold cloak-wrapped moments before sleep that he turned to her as a traveller turning home . . . Away below him, a score of camp fires and the torches at the ends of the horse- and camel-lines spangled the broad plateau, where they had bivouacked to wait for word from the scouts. The diversion had done its work well. Weeks of the deadly game of hare and hounds with Abdullah ibn Saud, a kind of marsh-light mountain warfare in which they contrived to avoid being once brought to action. Abdullah, for once badly served by his scouts, had been led to believe that their thrust was the real thing and their force much larger than it was, and had come north into the Kassim by forced marches, with ten thousand men (around a third of his army), leaving his brother Feisal with the rest to confront Muhammed Ali in the south. The colossal cheek of the enterprise was enough to take the breath away.

But two days ago they had lost contact. The Wahabi leader had appeared simply to melt into the mountains, and it was for word of him that they waited now.

It was extremely worrying, and Thomas worried accordingly. Could it mean that Ibn Saud had awoken to the true situation, and simply dropped them like a dead mouse and returned south to rejoin his brother? Could it mean that he was lying up somewhere in ambush . . ? There was not much to be done until the scouts returned, and certainly little purpose to be served by racking one's brains until they lost their thinking edge and went stale. Thomas, hunching his sheepskin-lined fariva more closely round him against the thin wind that harped along the ridges, allowed his mind to go wandering back to Anoud.

The track levelled for a few paces, rounded a jagged rock buttress and then fell away more steeply towards the plateau. And below him, darkly blotted against the camp fires, a figure was climbing up towards him silently, as one learns to move in the mountains. Thomas's hand went to the pistol in his waist-shawl. But in the same instant a pebble turned under the climber's foot and went rattling into the abyss beside the track, and the figure cursed in Tussun's voice. Thomas's hand fell away from his pistol.

"You should not whistle in the dark in enemy country," Tussun said, breathless and reproving, when they came together a few moments later. "It helped me to find you, but it could have helped a sniper too."

"Was I whistling?" Thomas said. "I did not know. What brings you seeking me? Has a scout come in? Is there news?"

"No scout, no news, but you have been over long, and it was – it is – drawing on to the time for prayers. Too dark to tell a black thread from a white one. It is right for a man to pray in company with other men, not alone with the rocks and the empty spaces."

And almost in the same instant, as though his words had been timed, from the camp below them, infinitely small and clear in the vastness of the mountains, rose the call to prayer.

Side by side on the goat track, their faces turned as near as they could judge towards Mecca, the two young men prayed together, kneeling, standing, bending to the ground, making the familiar ritual movements, speaking quietly the familiar words:

"Glory be to thee, Oh Allah, Blessed is Thy name. Exalted is Thy Majesty. Praise be to the Lord of the Worlds, the merciful, the compassionate . . ." The final exchanged greeting. "Peace be with you, and the Mercy of Allah."

The silence of the high hills came back.

They did not continue at once on their way back to the camp but, as though by common consent, the thing unspoken between them, lingered, half sitting half leaning, in the little bay where the rocks fell back a few feet and made a shelter against the thin chill wind. Below them the comfortable man-made freckling of camp fires, and, beyond, the world dropping away into a black intensity of nothingness out of which the peaks of the next range rose into sight. There was no moon yet, but the sky was full of stars, and the wheeling winter constellations were enough to touch their crests with a bloom, a kind of dew of light. Enough also to call a faint spark here and there from the hoar frost on the rocks against which the two men leaned. Thomas touched the rock surface at his side, and sensed with exquisite clarity the faint electric prickling of the frost melting under his fingers. He seemed to have one less skin than usual, tonight, as he felt sometimes with Anoud; as few skins as a bairn to come between him and the living universe to dull the touch of its splendours and griefs. He put out his other hand and met Tussun's warm clasp.

"What was the tune you were whistling?" Tussun asked in a little while.

"I told you – I did not know that I was whistling."

"It was the tune you were trying to teach Anoud the day in Teif when you said I had picked tomorrow's rose. A sad tune."

Thomas's mind went back to the three rooms over the goldsmith's shop, and showed him Anoud's intent face as she tried to follow the unfamiliar notes. He smiled in the darkness, and made another melted fingerprint on the rock beside him. "It will have been 'The Captain's Lady'. Yes, a sad tune, not a sad song, though."

"Are you sad, Tho'mas?"

"No, I was thinking of Anoud, and I suppose the song came into my mind."

"Do you think of her very often?"

"Sometimes," Thomas said. "I don't need to think of her. She is part of me as you are part of me."

"I used to be jealous of her," Tussun said thoughtfully, after a few moments.

"Not now?"

"No. Not now . . . Was Anoud ever jealous of me?"

"I don't know," Thomas said. "If she was, she hid it better than you did. But certainly she had as much cause to be – and as little."

"Sometimes I think it must be hard to be a woman. There is so much that they cannot know, so much that they cannot share." There was a deep content in Tussun's tone.

'What an extraordinary *naked* conversation this is,' Thomas thought. 'As naked as the mountains themselves. Couldn't hold it in any other place, at any other time . . .'

Aloud he said only, "They have been good, these weeks in the high hills."

Tussun shifted into a more comfortable position. "When I – if I live to be old and grey-bearded and sitting in the shade while my son's sons ride out to war, I shall remember them, taste them again on my tongue, and the taste will be good."

"For me also," Thomas said.

They sat in silence a short while, unwilling to let the present moment slip into the past, all the same.

"You told me once something out of your sacred book before you came to the Koran," Tussun said at last. "Of a prince and a shepherd – Daud and Jon'a'than?"

"Yes."

"What became of them?"

"Daud, the shepherd, became a King."

"And Jon'a'than?"

"He was killed in battle, and his enemies hung his body on the walls of their stronghold." Beyond the mountains the sky was beginning to take on a faint snail-shine of light, where presently the moon would rise. "And when Daud learned of it, he went through the ranks of the enemy, none able to stop him, and cut down Jonathan's body and brought it away," Thomas said, not even aware that he was adapting the story to suit his own needs.

Tussun, who rode his feelings more loosely than the Scot, said, "I would do that for you, Tho'mas, my Brother," and then: "Would you do that for me?"

"Yes," Thomas said, and was startled by what he heard in his own voice.

He pushed off from the rock wall. "It's time we were getting back to camp. Added to which it's cursed cold up here, and I have no wish to be found frozen solid as one of those rocks in the morning."

They went on down the steep track. The fires drew nearer, soon they could catch the waft of burning thorn scrub and camel dung on the mountain air, and the sounds of the camp came up to meet them.

A messenger had come in, brought by one of the scouts, while they were away. The man sat waiting for them beside the commander's fire, his face in the flame-light grey with the exhaustion of hard riding. He delved into his pouch when they came towards him and produced a packet sealed with the Viceroy's seal.

He touched it to his forehead. "From His Excellency your father Muhammed Ali."

Tussun took it, broke the seal and unfolded the crackling sheet, from which the Viceroy's own black slashing handwriting sprang up in the firelight.

Leaning to catch the leaping light, Tussun read in silence. And Thomas, watching him, thought that the callant had learned to shutter his face as he could never have done in the early days of their friendship. He saw the tawny eyes widen a little, then narrow again in concentration, and that was all. When he came to the end, Tussun refolded the paper and thrust it into the folds of his waist-shawl. "My father writes that he has taken Kulukh, and is now moving on Terraba – May Allah protect him against witchcraft."

He ordered food to be brought and, sitting down cross-legged, turned to the messenger. "While you eat, you shall tell me the details of the action, which are lacking from my father's letter."

The remains of goat's meat stew was brought, and rice and arak, and the man told, between ravenous mouthfuls of food and drink.

Feisal with his twenty thousand Wahabis had begun well, it seemed, taking up a strong defensive position along the range of hills strung between Kulukh and the village of Bissel. He could not easily be attacked there, yet Muhammed Ali could not by-pass him and advance into Najd without sacrificing his lines of communication.

"But truly, I think this suited your honourable father well, for he will surely have had no mind to move forward into the Najd without first breaking the power of the Brother-hood."

At great length and in great detail, for weary though he was the Arab passion for long-winded detail had not deserted him, the messenger recounted for them the names and strength of units involved, from the Hijaz irregular cavalry to the two batteries of light field guns. He told of the time-honoured ruse by which, on the second day, the Viceroy had lured Feisal from the hills into open country against what all men knew to be the death-bed orders of the Old Tiger – a ruse of pretended flight which made Thomas, listening intently, think suddenly of history lessons at Leith Academy, and King Harold's house-carls lured into breaking ranks at Hastings. It was one of the few bits of English history he had learned there.

Even then, said the messenger, it had been a close-fought thing, the Wahabis fighting bravely and stubbornly until, in the end, under repeated charges of the heavy cavalry and the artillery on the flanks, the main part of Feisal's army broke; and after that, thanks be to Allah, the end was sure.

"When your father saw the Wahabis in full retreat," said the man, reaching the triumphant climax of his story, "he offered a bounty of six dollars a head. There was a pile of – ah, more than five thousand before his tent, when I rode away."

A short while later, Tussun having summoned his senior officers, he and Thomas faced each other in the light of the lantern in the commander's tent in the brief interval before their arrival.

"Well, and what are our orders?" Thomas asked.

"I am to take my troopers and rejoin my father as swiftly as may be," Tussun said. "You are to take yours and return to Medina."

The weeks in the Kassim were over.

Chapter 31

By the time the next news reached Medina, Terraba had fallen, Ghalia's magic having presumably failed her, and the Turks had looted the town; another force had been ordered off to Quinfunduh to finish the rout of the southern Wahabis, and Muhammed Ali was free to advance into the Najd – when his army should be in fit condition to do so. The losses at Kulukh and before Terraba had been crushingly heavy. Despite which, the Viceroy sent news of his victory triumphantly back to Cairo and to the Sultan. Then he awarded himself a kind of Roman Triumph, in the course of which twelve of the three hundred Wahabis who had yielded to him under promise of quarter were impaled before the gates of Mecca. An error of judgment, which lost him the support of many of his remaining allies among the tribes.

Thomas, hearing in Medina, could only hope with a friend's anxiety for the honour of friend that Tussun who had not of course been able to rejoin his father and the remnant of the main army before their return to Mecca, had been clear of that Holy City again and away back to Jiddah before it happened.

The months passed, taken up for Thomas with the day-to-day business of the government of Medina, while Muhammed Ali in Mecca reorganised his forces yet again, and Tussun yet again kept Jiddah open and functioning as a supply base for his father.

It was a kind of uneasy threshold-time before the reopening of the campaign.

In early May, with the shadows growing short and the mirage already beginning to shimmer across the open country, news reached Medina from beyond the borders of the Muslim world. Napoleon Bonaparte had escaped from Elba, and landed to an enthusiastic welcome in France. The Bourbon garrisons had rallied to him as one man. France and Britain were at war again.

"Does your heart tell you that it is your war?" Anoud asked

311

her husband, sitting under the fig trees in the Governor's garden.

"No. But I think it might become my war. Almost anything might happen. If the British reoccupy Sicily – if the Russians find a pretext for attacking the Turks – "

Suddenly the future that seemed to belong to Arabia and the struggle against the Wahabis, but to Arabia most of all, lost substance in his mind and began to melt and form and re-form like the rolling mirage.

Meanwhile Medina must still be governed . . .

Only a few days later Thomas was conscientiously sitting in on a law case. It was a very complicated case between the Beni Harb and the Beni Sobh involving the return of a dowry after a divorce, the disputed ownership of a small herd of camels, and echoes of a blood feud of the previous century. The arguments grew more and more tortuous, the heat in the forecourt of the mosque was intolerable, and Thomas had a headache thudding dully behind his eyes. But the cadi, the judge, had invited his help in unravelling it, and so he sat on and on and on, striving to keep track of the arguments and think of some solution which would bring justice without further bloodshed.

But he was not fated to hear the case out to its conclusion. In the midst of a seemingly endless stream of irrelevant reminiscences from the oldest and most prosy of the Sobh sheikhs, a faint ruffle of movement drew his attention to the street entrance, and he saw one of his own officers standing there deep in urgent speech with one of the Guard. Even as he looked, the guard stepped back, and the captain came quickly towards him through the crowded court and stooped to speak in his ear.

"I beg you forgive me for interrupting the hearing, Sir. Tussun Pasha has just ridden in, and demands to speak with you instantly."

"I come." Thomas spoke his excuses as quietly into the cadi's ear, and without interrupting the aged sheikh in his flow, got up, bowed to the court, and followed the messenger out into the street.

"What's amiss, Hassan?" he asked.

The captain shook his head. "I do not know; but he arrived riding like a madman, with less than a score of his bodyguard with him. There are more troops following on behind, I gather;

but whatever it is, it is something that will not await the normal rate of march."

Tussun was in the Governor's private majlis, flinging to and fro from door to window and back again like something in a cage too small for it. He swung round at the sound of Thomas's step on the threshold, revealing a face white with dust – but he was caked white with journey dust from head to foot – haggard and angry eyed.

"Where were you?" he demanded.

"Hearing a case in court," Thomas said "I came as soon as Hassan brought me word that you were here. Have they not fed you? Is anyone bringing warm water?"

Tussun made an impatient gesture. "That can wait."

They met in the middle of the room, their arms round each other in a harsh embrace that all but drove the air out of both of them. "What is it that cannot wait?" Thomas demanded after a moment, holding him off at arm's length.

"My father has returned to Egypt. He left Mecca four days ago for Yembo. He'll have sailed by now."

"But in the name of Allah the All Merciful, why? What has happened?"

"Napoleon has escaped from Elba — "

"That I know," Thomas said. "But your father will scarcely be off back to Cairo in such haste for that cause alone."

Tussun shook his head with impatient vehemence. "There's more – the Capitan Pasha has sailed from Istanbul with almost the whole Ottoman fleet and many thousands of troops, and is believed to be making for Alexandria. It can only mean that those curs of the Sultan's Divan have planned to seize Egypt back from him – from my father – while he and most of his army are in Arabia, campaigning on the Sultan's behalf! This is our thanks for freeing the Holy Cities — "

"Tussun," Thomas said, still gripping his shoulders. "Is there proof of all this?"

"The Fleet is under way, and heading for Alexandria. What else could be their purpose?"

Thomas could not think of any, and felt no particular surprise, having gained in the past few years some experience of Turkish intrigue and record for treachery.

"So — " Tussun was almost sobbing with fury against the Divan, and almost more, it seemed, against Muhammed Ali.

313

"My father has abandoned his advance into the Najd, given orders to the High Shariff that half the Jiddah revenues are to be paid to him in Cairo for the use of his war-chest, instead of to me for the use of mine; and merely sent me a despatch informing me of his immediate return to Egypt and his reasons for it. He has given command of the Mecca, Teif and Terraba garrisons to Mustapha Bey without making it clear that he is subordinate to me, and has made no arrangements that I can hear of for me to receive any further money or supplies!"

It made surprising and almost sickening hearing; Thomas could not help feeling that there was a mistake, a misunder-standing, a failure of communications somewhere along the line. The Viceroy was a highly competent administrator, who would surely appreciate the dangers of leaving rival comman-ders in the Hijaz. Also, though he no doubt realised that Tussun did not have his elder brother's abilities, there was no question but that Muhammed Ali loved his younger son best of all his children. Not likely, then, that he would depart for home, however great the need for haste, leaving the boy behind without supplies, gold for the war-chest, or even orders.

"You did not see him before he left?"

"No. Did I not tell you? Only the despatch to tell me of his going!"

"Easy now. Easy, my Brother."

"I am not one of your horses!"

"Indeed I had noticed. None the less, calm down and listen to me – No. *Listen!*" His hands tightened on the other's shoulders. "The threat of the Ottoman fleet attacking Alexan-dria gives him no alternative but to make all speed back, not even waiting to speak with you, or to make arrangements and give orders for the campaign. But he will attend to all that as and when he may. Probably there is a long despatch arrived at Jiddah before now, or already on its way on to Medina after you as fast as the courier can ride."

Tussun had quietened, listening with his tawny gaze on Thomas's face. He drew a long steady breath, and said quite quietly, "If the despatch does not come within the next few days it will not find me at Medina, nor anywhere in the Hijaz."

"Why not?" Thomas demanded, his stomach tightening with the need to cope with whatever was coming next.

"Since I have been left to carry on the campaign as best I may, and since with no pay nor supplies coming in, I cannot afford to wait, I shall take the action I wanted to take immediately after Kulukh. I shall march into the Kassim and carry the war to ibn Saud's threshold."

Outside, the muezzin was calling to afternoon prayer.

Later, when Tussun had washed off the dust of his hard riding, after an evening meal eaten in constrained silence, because it had to be eaten in company with army officers and senior members of the Governor's entourage, they betook themselves to the eastward-facing ramparts where they had talked before a few months earlier, one of the few places in Medina it was possible to talk safe from all possibility of listening ears, and there continued the discussion as though it had never been interrupted.

What horrified Thomas was that Tussun had it all coolly and carefully worked out. It was no mere impulse in the heat of the moment. Despite the speed and fury of his arrival from Jiddah, he had clearly given his plans detailed thought and come to a decision from which it would probably be impossible to shift him.

"I have a thousand Albanian infantry, three hundred Turkish cavalry and two hundred Jehaida irregular horse," he was saying, counting them off on his fingers. "They should be here tomorrow. I have ordered up eight hundred infantry – about – from Yembo el Nakhl and Barr; they should be here in three days. This time I ask you to lend me only three hundred of your cavalry: a strongly held Medina is vital to the safety of the Hijaz. When they are all assembled I shall give them three days' rest. Then I shall march on Aneiz and El Rass."

"So," Thomas said, when the level voice checked for a moment. "We are to advance with some two-and-half thousand men. We are to march across two hundred or more miles of mountain and desert, against a prince who brought ten times that number against us at Jedaida. Are you mad?"

"It is not so mad as it sounds." Tussun's eyes were beginning to brighten dangerously. "Can you not imagine the effect that our victory at Kulukh must have had on the northern tribes who have been held down under the rule of the Brotherhood all these years? The whole Kassim is ready to rise! With their help,

315

and if Allah wills it as surely He must, we will strike at ibn Saud in his very heartland of the Najd, and we shall prevail!"

"It is still madness," Thomas said.

"No, and no, and no! If we wait we shall lose all that we have gained in the hearts of the tribes through Kulukh. I told my father that, months ago, before he lost some of it by that butcher's business before the gates of Mecca. There's still enough support for us in the Kassim if we move fast; if we delay it will all drain away and we shall be too late."

And Thomas recognised the truth of that. "Madness still. But I suppose if Alexander conquered an empire with three hundred . . . At least we shall be in familiar country."

"Tho'mas, my Brother," Tussun said steadily, "I said 'I', not 'We'."

"Oh no," Thomas heard himself say. "If you go, I go, as before."

"But it is not as it was before, with my father returned to Egypt . . . You must know that after Jedaida and Terraba, after those weeks in the Kassim, after the nearly eight years that we have been sword-brothers, there is no man in the world that I want to have riding with me as I want to have you. But you know also that you are the only man I can completely trust to hold Medina in the face of all odds." He was frowning in concentration on what he had to say. "This city is the vital hinge by which hangs the safety of my force marching north-east, and the safety of the whole Hijaz to the south . . . You know as well as I do that my father might well have failed at Kulukh if *we* had not drawn off ibn Saud himself and a good third of his men to counter our advance from here. If Medina falls, I shall be cut off and destroyed, the Beni Harb will change sides again and all the Hijaz will be overrun. Tho'mas, we have freed the Holy Cities once, we cannot risk losing them again."

Thomas had dropped his hands lightly from the other's shoulders. He was silent a few moments, gazing out across the city to the hills north-eastwards, as he had gazed that evening in the winter that was past. Once again he was thinking how Tussun had changed. Hard sometimes even to glimpse the golden boy who had given him his first hawking lesson in exchange for a thrust in tierce. Hard also to recognise the spoiled brat who had ordered his murder in a fit of drunken rage. 'We have come a long way in nearly eight years,' he thought. 'I wonder if I seem as changed to him.' This proposed march into the Kassim was as much a gamble as Napoleon's landing from Elba. The tribes of the Kassim might still join him against the Wahabis. And if they did not? Tussun and his little army would be lost. But his arguments about Medina were unanswerable. Mustapha and his Albanians could not be relied on to hold out. If a large force from the Najd came westward, Mustapha would probably pull out, back to Mecca or even Jiddah, leaving Medina to be attacked without hope of relief. Ibn Saud would understand as clearly as Tussun that Medina was the key to the whole Hijaz. Thomas knew that none of the other commanders was as competent as he was to hold the second Holy City, with all that that entailed.

He turned slowly from the breastwork, and the high hills of the Kassim.

During the next seven days Thomas worked as Tussun's supply officer throughout all the hours that Allah sent, and at each of the five times a day he prayed for some word from the Viceroy to halt his son's wild plan. But no word came; and on the seventh day, Tussun's expeditionary force was ready to march.

Thomas had ridden out with Tussun to the head of the column drawn up beyond the East Gate of the city, and now they sat their horses together, drawn a little aside into the tiger-striped shade of the date palms, in the last moments before the march. It was early morning, but already the heat danced like a midge cloud ahead of them, and every movement of the horses' feet raised a small puff of dust. In the rear the camels grumbled and snarled, somewhere a horse flung up its head and whinnied along the line. The good people of Medina who had come out to see them off called blessings and farewells and obscene jests; somewhere down the line a child got among the horses' hooves and was removed screaming. And over all the scene shimmered and churred the voices of the cicadas.

Thomas had been reminding his friend, for maybe the dozenth time, there being nothing else of all the things that needed saying that it was possible to say, of the necessity for keeping effective flank and rear guards.

Tussun smiled at him with none of the impatience he would normally have shown. "I will remember all that I have learned from you, my brother; even, if need be, that lunge in tierce."

317

An officer rode up to report the column ready to move off. The time had come.

"I will hold Medina for you while the breath is in me," Thomas said quickly. "But if the time comes when your need is more urgent than the city's, then in Allah's name send for me, and Medina must fend for itself. I'll come."

"A thousand leagues an' three." Tussun's face cracked into a grin that was still a boy's, after all.

"A thousand leagues an' three." Thomas echoed the words and the grin.

They embraced, hard and fierce and quick, leaning from the saddle, then wheeled their horses apart.

Thomas reined back his dancing mount, while the other took his place at the column head under the black and golden wing of his personal standard.

The bugler put the bugle to his lips and sounded for the march, and the liquid throb of the kettle drums was added to the sound of hooves and the jingle of accoutrements as the head of the column rolled forward on the track that ran north-eastward into the mountains.

Thomas flung up his hand in a last salute: "Allahu akba!"

From the head of the column a young triumphant voice with a strong Albanian accent shouted back to him. Almost at once the figure at the head of the advance guard was lost, hidden by the ranks of cavalry trotting after, and by the dust-cloud that began almost at once to rise. But for a while the black and gold standard rose clear above the dust, and he watched it into the distance and the heat shimmer.

The infantry followed, the main guard, and the camel train with the guns, the rearguard after a gap. He sat there watching as they passed, the bobbing heads of the horses, the high-held turbaned heads of the men.

The look of high hope was on them, a bloom like the dew on grass before the blistering sun sucks it up. The last of the rearguard passed, and the rolling dust cloud swallowed them from view. Then, with a word to his small escort, Thomas touched heel to his horse's flank, and headed back towards the city gates.

Suddenly he realised that for the past half hour he had forgotten Anoud. Anoud with the cool grey eyes and the small head set on the long slender neck like a flower on its stem, and

318

the belly swollen like a watermelon with the bairn which should be born within the month. It was not merely that he had not thought of her. As he had told Tussun, he did not need to think of her, she was a part of him. But for that half hour or so, she had ceased to exist in his world at all. Now his love for her twinged to the quick within him, mixed with a kind of compassion. Tussun was right, it must be hard to be a woman.

Chapter 32

The first news came surprisingly soon, only thirteen days after the little army had marched out, when a Beni Sobh horseman arrived back at Medina with a despatch – more of a racy private letter, in actual fact – and Thomas, reading it, seemed to catch the tones of Tussun's voice behind the hastily written words in the commander's own hand.

On reaching Henakiah, more than a quarter of the way to El Rass, he had been joined by upward of four hundred horsemen of the Mitair tribe and a hundred of the Beni Ali, bringing their numbers up to almost three thousand; and had not Tussun *said* that the whole of the Kassim would rise to join him?

Thomas frowned, and uneasiness stirred within him, the Mitair and the Beni Ali of the north-east were not the whole of the Kassim. Furthermore they had never given allegiance to the Wahabi, but being completely nomadic, moving between western Kassim and northern Hijaz had contrived always to avoid subjugation by the black-robed Brotherhood.

The next few lines were more encouraging:

We had the good fortune to meet a party of the Beni Ali just come south from Ghat, and learned from them that a caravan of more than a thousand camels – Syrians, and stronger than the Arabian breed, and destined for ibn Saud – would be reaching El Rass two days later, and would pasture there, a couple of miles beyond the city, for one night on their way through to Diriyah. So I left our Beni Ali guides and the Turkish cavalry to form a screen for the infantry and the camel train, and pushed on with the Egyptian cavalry and two hundred of your Jehaine allies, two forced marches; you couldn't see us for our dust-cloud! We reached the oasis, and attacked an hour before morning prayer, just as the caravan was being marshalled. The Wahabi escort was taken utterly by surprise, and we killed or captured every man! By the time the folk of El Rass sent out a party to investigate, the rest of

320

our cavalry was coming up. So here we are, the masters of more than a thousand splendid camels, for which ibn Saud has already paid! I will get the spare beasts back to you as and when I can.

For the past six days we have been surrounding El Rass.

'What with?' Thomas almost groaned. 'About four hundred horsemen by my reckoning. Oh God!'

It was a bluff, of course, but now the infantry and the camel train have come up, and we are as strong as the defenders, if not stronger; and I send this off to you, knowing that you will be clucking like a mother hen if you do not soon hear from me. I have great hopes that the El Rass sheikhs will join me in the next few days, now that they see how strong we are and what sure hope we have of victory . . .

The exhausted messenger, questioned by Thomas after he had eaten, but before he rested, took a somewhat different view of the situation. "If the sheikhs do not join forces with us, I do not see what the next move can be. Also it would have been well if we had actually seen El Rass during our thrust into the hills last winter; the walls are twenty feet high and the scouts have it that they are sixteen feet thick in places, and I do not think our six pounders will make much impression on them."

Thomas lay on his back and looked up at the stars of high summer through the broad-fingered vine leaves. Mid-June. In Scotland it would be hardly dark at all. Here the dark was long and heavy; too hot to sleep within doors. So he had had a tent-curtain slung across two sides of the vine arbour on the roof of the women's quarters, making it into a small makeshift pavilion for Anoud, now breathing deeply and quietly beside him.

The faint waft of air that had no coolness in it, stirred the leaves and died away again into the distant voice and hoofbeat and dog-bark stir of the city waking to a new day. Soon the stars would be paling. It was past the hour of morning prayer. Generally he did not come back to bed after morning prayer, but today there was nothing that needed his attention for an hour or so yet, and the night had been a disturbed one. The bairn was due, maybe even overdue by a day or so. He knew that it was so sometimes with a first child; and Anoud was too tired and heavy and uncomfortable for easy sleeping. She had begun to have evil dreams, too; earlier in the night she had woken crying his name, and lain, shivering in his arms and unable or unwilling to tell him what she had dreamed, for a long time before she had drifted off to sleep again. She had not roused at the call to prayer, and he had left her sleeping, sure that Allah would make allowances for a woman who was about the exhausting business of bringing new life into the world. And after praying in the courtyard with the men of the household, he had returned to lie quiet beside her for a little while.

But now he was not able to capture the quiet of the hour before prayer, and his thoughts, worn ragged with anxiety, had gone back to Tussun before the strong walls of El Rass. How was it with him? What was happening? Surely soon there must be news? It was a fortnight since that last word had come. He had written a hurried reply full of military advice. Other things as well; he could not remember now what they had been, those other things, and the messenger, fed and rested and mounted on a fresh horse, had departed once more, trailing his own dust-cloud behind him.

Since then – nothing. Only the daily business of governing and holding Medina. But surely any time now, word must come . . .

As though the intensity of his own anxiety had called it up, there came to Thomas suddenly a faint impression of distant hoof beats; so distant as to be like the sounds inside one's own head that one heard sometimes in the dead silence of the desert at night. Imagination of course, it had played him this kind of trick before. It was gone now, anyway, as though swallowed by some fold in the ground.

He turned his awareness back to Anoud lying beside him. The darkness was becoming thinner, watered with the first grey forewarning of the dawn, and he could see her, shapeless among her loosened clothes, her head tipped back a little on the cushion. He wanted to be able to make love to Anoud again, lie completely close to her again, his mouth on hers, all the length of his body along hers, like two halves of something joined together into a whole, a water-reed above its own reflection that makes perfection. Soon now, he thought, he would be able to do that again, not having to arch himself around that vast pumpkin belly. He raised on his elbow to look down at her. He could see the faint pallor of her face among the dark outflung masses of her hair, and realised that her eyes were open and waiting for his.

"May your day be white," he whispered.

And she returned the morning greeting of acquaintances in the street, with a thread of laughter, "May yours be as milk."

He bent his head and kissed her. He tried to put his arm round her, but even as he drew close, the bairn woke and kicked him in the belly.

They drew apart, laughing.

"Peace, small one, it is thy father," Anoud said.

"It is jealous."

"*He* is jealous."

"Are you so sure? Always so sure that he is a boy?"

"Only a boy could be so strong within me. Besides the hakima says that he is a boy." Her voice had a soft crooning note in the dark. "A son for my Lord, to carry his sword after him."

Thomas remembered something he had meant to say to her last night; it had been so late when he came to the little pavilion. "Now that the time is so near, we must be thinking about a house for you."

"I am well enough in the harem court of your house, the women's quarter of your tent," she said quickly.

"But it is your right, according to the law of the Prophet," Thomas spoke into her hair. "As the mother of my child, it is your right that I provide for you a house of your own, to be yours even if, maybe, you seldom bide under its roof – I saw such a house yesterday in the spicers' ward, a small house with a small courtyard – just room enough for a rosebush in a jar."

"Not yet," she broke in, her whisper hurried, almost frightened; she put up her hands and held on to him round the neck. "Not till the babe is safely born!"

"Is it unlucky?" Thomas asked. "In my country – my birth country – many women will not have a cradle in the house-place before the bairn is born." He was dropping small random kisses on her upturned face. "So – we will talk again when the bairn is born and all is well. But then we *will* talk, because I am a selfish man and I shall be the happier for knowing that you have the added security of a house of your own – because it will refuge

323

you as my love would refuge you; you and the bairn — " He broke off. He was making it sound as though he would not be there, and a little shiver ran through his body. "And sometimes, when the times of peace come, and maybe I can take a breathing space from the governorship, you must go there and make ready for me, and I shall come to your house — " he whispered, trying to retrieve the situation, "Insh' Allah."

"Insh' Allah," Anoud echoed. "God willing."

From somewhere below there came the sounds of a small disturbance; a hurried arrival, maybe, and a few moments later the sound of hurried feet on the steep outside stair, and the voice of one of the harem eunuchs in breathless urgency. "Ibrahim, Ibrahim Agha – "

Thomas was already half up. "What is it?"

"Come at once – A messenger – "

In Thomas's mind any messenger meant word from Tussun. He stooped and kissed Anoud once more, hard and hurried, and pulled away her hands which were still clinging about his neck, and getting up, went out between the tent curtains, straightening his thobe as he did so.

"What message? Where is he?" he demanded.

"How should I know the message, Effendi? One of your officers is waiting at the gate of the women's court." The eunuch stood aside at the stairhead for his master to take the lead, and Thomas plunged down at breakneck speed and headed at his long stride across the court.

Just beyond the gateway in the light of the flambeau that always burned there, one of his own officers waited for him.

"One of the patrols has brought in an officer sent by Tussun Pasha," the man said. "They found him lying unconscious beside his dead horse on the Henakiah track. He has been carried to the caravanserai within the Eastern Gate. I have saddle horses waiting."

"And his despatch?" Thomas held out his hand.

"There is none. Maybe he fell among thieves, or maybe there was no time to write, and he carries it in his head."

"And he's unconscious."

"He was beginning to come to himself when I left. He said there were six of them when they set out; and that he has a desperately urgent message from Tussun Pasha for the Governor. The surgeon is with him and says he cannot last long."

"Oh God!" Thomas thought. "Oh God – oh God – oh God!" They were in the outer court by now, he was swinging into the saddle of one of the waiting horses, clattering out with one stirrup flying, past the guards at the main gate, and away down the street, scattering chickens and goats, beggars and pye-dogs and all the first swarming of Medina waking to the new day.

In the wide central court of the caravanserai, filled with the morning activity of horse and man, he dropped from the horse's back, flinging the reins to his companion, and turned to the trooper standing before one of the arched chamber entrances that surrounded the place. "Where is he?"

The man stood aside, and Thomas strode in. Paling lamp-light met him, from a lamp held high by one of Abd el Rahman's henchmen, and in the heart of the light the army surgeon knelt, supporting the head of the man who lay there on a spread camel rug. For a moment Thomas thought that the man was already dead, then he realised that Abd el Rahman was trickling water drip by drip between the swollen and blackened lips. He knelt down at the man's other side. Seeing the grey and ravaged face, the crusted and gaping sword-cut that laid cheek and temple open and bit into the neck under the jawbone, he recognised Jusef ibn Muhammed, that son of a lesser wife, who would never now follow them to the gates of Diriyah. The man's eyes were shut. If not dead, had he sunk into uncon-sciousness? But nobody trickled water down the throat of an unconscious man. He looked up, and met the surgeon's warning look, and signalled a message: "Am I too late?"

Abd el Rahman shook his head very slightly. "His will to deliver his message to you has kept him in this world – just – until your coming. But do not expect more than a few words. The effort to speak again will kill him."

Thomas leaned forward and took the other's hand in a strong grip "Jusef, my friend, what word do you bring from Tussun?"

A spasm crossed the grey features. The dying man opened his eyes, seeking for Thomas's face, trying to focus on it. |

Thomas leaned closer, holding the gaze that fastened and clung to his. "What word?" he said again. It seemed a cruel thing to drag the man back from wherever he was already half gone, and demand that final agony of effort from him. "Tell me what word you bring."

325

Jusef ibn Muhammed snatched a shuddering breath. "Rass too strong – ibn Saud marching – from Diriyah . . ." The words came in a broken whisper; Thomas had his ear close to the dying mouth, to catch them. "Tussun Pasha – come with all speed – Mines . . ."

"Yes," Thomas, said. "What more? Jusef, try to tell me more."

But the other's eyes were already slipping past him to some far horizon. He pulled them back by a supreme effort. The breath was rattling in his gashed throat, but his last words came more clearly than those that had gone before, and came moreover in a fair imitation of the Scots tongue, the phrase clearly learned by heart and so often repeated in his mind that now it came more easily than the words of his message which he had to search for among the mists of fading consciousness.

"A thousand leagues an' three," said Jusef ibn Muhammed, a long shuddering breath racked his body and his head rolled sideways.

Thomas knelt beside him a moment longer, holding the suddenly empty hand. Then he laid it down, and getting to his feet, turned to the waiting officers he had not noticed before. He had to steady his voice with care before he could trust it. "Council of war in the citadel in half an hour. All senior officers to attend. See to it, Malik. Sulman – " he turned back to the surgeon, "see to all things here for me. He was a brave man, and my friend."

Grief rose in his throat for yet another dead friend. He did not look again at the body, but strode from the chamber with a set face. An orderly stood in the gate arch, holding his horse. He took the reins and mounted without a word.

The words of the old song were singing themselves in his head in Tussun's voice, with the Scots brogue that was imitated from his own, as he rode up through the narrow streets to the citadel:

> Wild callants were we baith
> Chasing the red deer herd . . .

And the winter breath from the high hills of Kassim was in his face.

Full daylight, and the first shimmer of heat hung beyond the

326

high windows of the majlis in the citadel, where Thomas sat confronting his senior officers gathered round the coffee hearth; but the coffee hearth was cold.

"I am taking two hundred and fifty picked men. Each colonel of cavalry will provide a half squadron of his best troopers, all fit for a forced march to El Rass. My own bodyguard will bring the detachment up to strength. Each man will have a good spare mount, so I must ask you to let me have our five hundred best horses. Better say five hundred and fifty; that will give us fifty reserve mounts who can act as pack animals on the way up."

He heard his voice going on, level-sounding, in charge of the situation; not quite his. The morning sun through the high window was painting a sword-blade of gold on the dusty air. "Every trooper will carry flour, dates and butter for five days, water for only three – we can fill up from the wells at Henakiah. Each man will carry powder and ball for two major engagements." He singled out Medhet's eager face. "Medhet have materials for four large mines – of the power we used here – included with the supplies on the spare remounts. It seems that what Tussun Pasha took with him may not have been sufficient for the work of breaching the walls."

He paused a moment. The young Egyptian clerk looked up from his scribbling. Mustapha Bey spoke urgently into the moment's silence: "Ibrahim, this is madness! To take a mere two hundred and fifty cavalry across three hundred miles of desert which by now is infested with enemy tribesmen! Take at least a full regiment with the best horses, and let the other two follow after you as fast as they may."

Hassan ibn Khalid, the Egyptian colonel, added his own plea: "Mustapha is right. So small a column will simply be swallowed up if you meet a Wahabi war host. How can you hope to reach Tussun Pasha, still less relieve him, with not much over two squadrons at your heels?"

Thomas looked from one to the other, and spoke slowly, weighing his words as he went along. "My Brothers, I have given careful thought to all this – hurried, I admit, but a man does not necessarily think the worse for having to think fast. And in the first place, Tussun did not send for a relief force, if the few words his messenger was able to speak have any meaning, he sent for *me*. I am simply taking a large enough escort to ensure, in the light of the information we possess, that

327

I and the mining materials which it seems he stands in need of, together with a useful addition to his cavalry, reach him before ibn Saud and his war host do so."

He was not at all sure that his decision was the right one. Tussun *might* have intended him to bring all the troops he had, save just enough infantry to hold Medina until help could come. But he dared not risk losing the city and control of the Jedaida road, because of what Tussun *might* have intended. As to the messenger's last words, so obviously learned parrot-fashion, they were just the call of friend for friend. The mines, surely, were the thing, and speed. Speed that called for the lightest possible force.

"In the second place, I cannot endanger Medina. I dare not take even one whole regiment, while ibn Saud can bide his time until we are well away reinforcing Tussun, then outflank us to the south, cut Hijaz in half and isolate the city." He was repeating Tussun's own arguments, "Medina is the vital hinge by which hangs the safety of Hijaz and the safety of Tussun himself and his expeditionary force. Mustapha my friend, as commander of the garrisons here it is for you again to act as deputy governor of Medina and the northern Hijaz while I am away. Hassan ibn Khalid, for the same space of time you will act as overall cavalry commander, while you, Togra Aziz, take overall command of the infantry. Medhet — "

He had intended leaving Medhet also, to ensure that the largely Albanian infantry gave no trouble, but while he hesitated, wondering quite how to put that without insulting the Albanians, the young man said with complete certainty, "I go where you go, Tho'mas. Am I not your oldest friend in the world? Was I not your friend even before Tussun Pasha?"

And meeting the bright steady gaze, Thomas thought, 'After all, why not? Togra is not brilliant but he's a good officer.' "You go where I go," he agreed, and saw the look on the faces of the men, all friends and comrades-in-arms, who he had ordered to remain in Medina. "It's an unfair world, my brothers" he agreed.

The council brought to a close and orders issued for the march at the fourth hour after noon, Thomas, with Mustapha, who as deputy governor must of course know of his planned movements, spent the next half hour or so with his senior guides, all camel men and experienced caravan escorts, poring over rough

328

sketch maps of the north-eastern Hijaz and western Kassim. Last winter's thrust had not been by any direct route, being meant to consume time and draw off troops from the main Wahabi army for as long as possible; beside which it had never actually brought them within sight of El Rass. Now the route had to be worked out, with speed as its main aim. El Rass was upward of three hundred miles away, the direct route lying partly through "good desert", partly over mountain country. Riding hard from 2 a.m. to 7 a.m. and from 4 p.m. to 9 p.m. with changes of horses every two hours, it seemed possible that they might reach Tussun in three days and nights, at the worst in four . . .

Studying the maps, which were not properly to scale, and therefore of extremely doubtful value, Thomas cursed inwardly the fact that none of the Beni Ali were there to act as guides. The entire tribe had vanished into the northern fastnesses of the Kassim, and he suspected that they were positioning for a massive raid on their hereditary foes the Aneiz as soon as they heard of the fall of El Rass. Jusef ibn Muhammed of course had made the ride both ways, and would have been invaluable, but Jusef was dead . . .

Well, if he and his little band were to fall in with a Wahabi war host, that too must be the Will of Allah.

With less than an hour left before marching time, Thomas, having seen to all those things which it was for the commander of the expedition to see to in person, was able to snatch a little time to return to the Governor's Palace to gather up his own gear and bid goodbye to Anoud.

He went first to his own quarters, and shouted to Jassim Khan for his burnous – he was still in his white thobe, and unarmed save for his Somali knife thrust into his hurriedly tied waist-shawl. The boy was already waiting. So were his sabre and pistols, his bandoleers with the cartridges burnished like gold. "I was not so fine as this when I went to be made Governor!" he said laughing. "Surely you send me into battle shining like the sun!"

"Send? I come with you!" the boy said quickly. He was already armed to the teeth.

"Surely you come with me. Are you not my standard-bearer? Have my saddlebags sent to the mustering point."

Thomas flung away to the harem court.

329

Anoud stood waiting for him in her private chamber with the blue hyacinth tiles in the wall niches; very straight, very still in the centre of the room, his great broadsword which he kept in her quarters, lying in her arms.

"You will be wanting this?" she said.

"You know, then."

"All Medina knows." She held the sword out to him. The hilt and silver scabbard-mountings were freshly burnished like the rest of his equipment, and he realised that she herself was clad in her best, proud with gold, all the gold he had ever given her.

He took the sword, feeling the familiar balance of it and, slipping the baldric over his head, settled it across his shoulder. Some women would have cried and let their hair fall loose, making the parting harder for him than it was already. Anoud kept her usual quiet, only it seemed to him that her eyes were larger than he had ever seen them.

"You have to go now? At once?" she said.

"In only a few minutes, but those that are left are yours. Heart of my heart." He put his arms round her, and she leaned into the curve of his shoulder with a sigh.

But after a moment she looked up, laughing, but not so far from tears after all. "All these hard-edged things, man things, belts and weapons, these killing things! It is as hard to come close to you as it is for you to come close to me!"

"When I come back. I will lay aside the hard-edged things, and the babe will have come to birth, and we shall be able to come as close to each other as ever we did, as close as two can come in this world."

She caught her breath. "I wish you had not to go just when the babe is due."

"I also." He bent over the curved prow of her belly with awkward tenderness, and kissed her, slipping his tongue between her lips, tasting the sweet soft water of her mouth. "May Allah spread the cloak of his protection over you, and may the birth be easy, my most dear."

"I do not care that it should be easy," she said, "so that it brings your child safe into the world."

"It seems to me a great and wonderful thing that I shall have a child of your bearing. But, remember, you matter more with me than ever a child could do." A few moments later, as he loosed his arms, she stood back from him, panting a little.

"Go now," she said.

"Anoud, do you know how much I love you?"

"I know," she said, "Oh my Lord I know – greet Tussun for me when you meet."

He caught her into his arms again for one more awkward kiss, then almost thrust her away, and turned to the door.

Below in the courtyard his mare stood waiting in charge of a groom. He mounted and gathered up the rein.

At the last instant, in the outer gateway, something made him turn in the saddle and look back.

A woman had come out to the head of the steps that led from the harem court. Anoud had flung on her dish-dasha and pulled her veil across her face, and so was as anonymous as any other Arab woman outside the protective privacy of the women's quarters. But the same knowledge-of-the-heart that had once shown him Tussun beyond the gates of Mecca in the dusk, told him that Anoud had covered herself, and come running, as a girl of his own people might have done. It was the first time she had ever done such a thing; the love within him twisted in his belly, and sharply, piercingly, as he had not allowed himself to do while he held her in his arms, he wondered when – if – he should hold her again.

He flung up his hand to her in a wide, sweeping gesture of farewell, then turned his mare and heeled her from a stand into a canter, out through the gate and away towards the citadel and his waiting squadrons.

Chapter 33

Sitting in the mouth of his small and sparsely equipped tent, his morning coffee untasted on the rug beside him, Tussun watched the sky brighten in the east beyond the palm trees, watched the activity of the camp growing out of the fading darkness: half his infantry taking up their positions behind the shallow breastwork, while the other half, morning prayer being over, set about their own morning meal; horses being watered, ammunition issued. He smelled the familiar acrid smoke of dung fires, heard the usual bubbling snarl from the camel-lines, and tried to force his thoughts out of the aching confusion in his head into some kind of order.

He was still convinced that the sheikhs of the Kassim would have risen to him if there had been time, but that lightning march of ibn Saud's had altered their minds for them. The sons of bitches had refused to join him, and thereby left him trapped between the strong and well-manned walls of El Rass and an approaching Wahabi war host.

Could he have pulled out, then? No; the lesson of Tarraba had taught him that. It would be suicidal madness to start a retreat across three hundred miles of mountain and desert in the face of a vastly superior enemy force. There had been nothing he could do but hold on where he was, and send an urgent call to Thomas for reinforcements.

As long as the Ottoman troops were the besiegers, they could use all the oases to pasture their own camels and the thousand captured beasts, but the arrival of ibn Saud three days since had turned them from besiegers to besieged, outnumbered by more than four to one, and he had been forced to pull in his outlying posts and concentrate his troops and animals in two oases to the south-west of the town and on the ridge that linked them. It was a reasonably good position against most things but famine – which the Wahabis, sitting on their haunches like waiting vultures across miles of surrounding desert, knew perfectly well. The wells in both oases were good and he had food for his men and horses for some days yet; but he would have known himself even if his camel men had not told it to him, that in two days he was going to have to choose between losing most of the camels and trying to cut his way out. There was always of course the possibility that he might be able to exchange a thousand of the camels for extra supplies for the rest under the flag of truce. Abdullah must badly want the camels (he had only one camel between every two musketeers at the moment, if the scouts spoke truth) and would not wish to see them dying by hundreds in his enemy's camp. It was just possible.

It all depended on Thomas really, as so much generally seemed to depend on Thomas, on how soon he could arrive with the relief force – always supposing that Jusef or at any rate one of his escort, had got through. It could not be for another twenty-four hours yet, at the most wildly optimistic, even if he was making a forced march with the cavalry regiments and no infantry . . .

The orderly who had come out from the tent to take the wasted coffee was pointing and shouting. The rim of the sun had broken clear of the great dunes eastwards, and light and colour was spilling down the curved slopes; away to the right two horsemen were coming at full gallop down the scarp, their sand cloud trailing behind them. Beni Ali scouts of the all-night patrol. The camp was not completely surrounded by the Wahabis, and they were still able to send out the night patrols, though there was always a strong risk of running into the enemy cavalry screens. Tussun got up and strode to meet them, followed by the two young officers whose duty was to be always at his heels.

The men brought their horses to a plunging halt, already shouting as they dropped from the saddle. "It is the Wahabis. Something afoot, oh Tussun Pasha: nearly half of Ibn Saud's war host has ridden out before dawn!"

Tussun swung round on his young attendants, bidding one to summon the senior officers, the other to fetch his horse. Then he turned his attention to the scouts and their report.

It came breathlessly, but clear enough. About an hour before dawn and some six miles to the north-west, the two had dismounted to lead their horses down a ridge too steep to be negotiated on horseback without a dangerous amount of noise, when they had become aware of the sounds of a considerable body of cavalry advancing up the stony bed of the Wadi just below them. "We hid behind a boulder, quieting the horses as best we could and waited. They were so close below us that even in the starlight we could see their black cloaks, and from time to time when one spoke, we could make out the accent of the Najd."

The column of horsemen had seemed unending, "as many as the stars in the Milky Way", but it was followed by an even longer column of camel-mounted infantry; and, afraid that dawn would find them still pinned down on the slope, they had taken advantage of the sounds of the camels passing to get back to the top of the ridge and secure their horses on the far side. Then they had lain up in some thorn scrub that broke the skyline and watched until the last of the Wahabi force had passed, just at dawn.

"And this force? How many in horse and foot?" ("As many as the stars in the Milky Way" seemed a rather loose estimate.)

"More than a thousand cavalry, somewhere between two and three thousand camel men," said the scout who had been doing most of the talking.

Tussun thanked them – with irregular troops one must always remember the courtesies – and dismissed them to food and rest. The officers he had sent for had come up by now, mounted, and one of them leading his horse. He swung into the saddle and rode up to the crest of the ridge, giving them a condensed version of the scouts' report as they rode. From the high ground he could see the walls of El Rass crowded with men, so also the fringes of the Saudi encampment, while on the level ground below the walls, cavalry were manoeuvring in full view. "Does it seem to you," he said to the men around him, "that yonder are a few men trying to look like as many as were there last night?"

But he was speaking his thoughts aloud, to himself as much as to them . . . "It must be Tho'mas – the Amir Ibrahim. Their scouts have brought word of his coming, and Abdullah is away to intercept him. But when and where? They must be at least a full day and night's march away. Well, he shall fight us as well."

He spoke to the senior infantry officer beside him, but the words were for all those listening. "Barak, concentrate all but one company of foot on the northern oasis, and strengthen the breastworks – but not too obviously. Make sure the companies remaining in the southern oasis understand that they are not being sacrificed; if their position is attacked in strength they are to abandon the camels and retire to join the rest." He hesitated, thankful that at least his brain seemed to be working again. "The northern oasis you will defend to the last." He turned to another officer: "Jacoba, concentrate all the cavalry save for a hundred Turkish troopers under Jemal, among the trees at the north-west corner down there. They are to carry food and water for two days, maximum powder and ball for those with carbines. The second Turkish squadron will remain on the ridge to give support to infantry." With the Beni Jehaine commander he remembered the courtesies again: "Ibn Salam, may I ask you to join forces with Jacoba, your men to form our right flank when we break out to follow the Wahabi column."

"I am your servant and your brother, I hear and obey."

Tussun turned again to the cavalry commander: "Jacoba, place my personal squadron in the van, the Egyptian cavalry on the left, the Jehaine on the right and the Turks in the centre rear; the whole force in a loose wedge shape." He touched the other's shoulder. "Go now and give the orders."

Doubt suddenly struck at him again. A few moments ago he had felt in clear-headed command of the situation; but now he was wondering – Had he been over impetuous and issued his orders hours too early? He turned to Banda, the leader of the Beni Ali: "At what time should we march out in order to overtake the rear of the Wahabi column by say two hours past midnight?"

But instead of answering, the tribesman asked a question in return, gentling his fidgeting mare as he did so. "Are you so sure that the Wahabis will meet the Amir Ibrahim at two hours past midnight and not at today's sunset?"

"But – " Tussun felt as though he had taken a blow beneath the ribs. "Even if they march through the heat of the day, could they be as near to us as that, by sunset?"

"It is possible," the man said. "Just possible. But only if he has ridden ahead with a small body of picked horsemen and enough spare mounts."

Tussun looked at him in consternation, taking in the implication of this. Horrible doubts crowded in on him. If he advanced too soon, and came up with the Wahabis with Thomas still far way, the Black Brotherhood would destroy

335

him, then turn back to Thomas at their leisure; if he advanced too late, they would destroy Thomas and his small force before he, Tussun, could come up with them . . .

"Banda — " he began. But in the event, the decision never had to be made; for at that instant one of the Beni Ali turned, cocking his head to the north wind.

"What is it?"

"*Quiet* – Keep that mare still!"

For a long moment the listening stillness took them. Fortunately they were well above and slightly upwind of the ordered stir from the camps.

It seemed to Tussun that the silence was thick in his ears like wool, as he strained to hear through it, his eyes fixed on the tribesman's face.

Then the man let go his breath, gently, through widened nostrils. "Bugles," he said, "a cavalry call."

A few moments later it seemed to Tussun that he caught something himself. Something on the edge of sound . . .

"They're sounding the charge," the Jehaine officer said.

"There it is again – And again – "

"That is from the Wadi el Aas," Banda said. "With the wind in this quarter."

"In Allah's name where is that?" Tussun asked with a dry throat.

"Only two miles beyond where the Wahabis were sighted two hours ago."

Tussun gathered his reins. "Banda, leave two of your men with the Turkish cavalry. They are slower, and may lose touch without guides. Ride with me as *my* guide." He turned to his bugler, who had come up with the officers: "Sound 'Saddle up' then 'Assembly' for one minute, then sound 'Mount horses', and keep on sounding it."

He drove his heel into his mare's flank, and plunged away down the slope followed by the others like a skein of wild geese, the bugles sounding for the assembly as he rode.

The cavalry had been drawing ammunition, but hearing the bugle and seeing their commander racing back down the ridge, they made for their horses.

Tussun, on his way to take his place with his personal squadron at the head of the rough arrowhead that was soon forming, reined in for a panting moment beside the Turkish commander. "Follow me with all the speed you can make for the Wadi el Aas – take the Beni Ali guides with you. We shall not wait for you; if we are already engaged when you come up with us try to form on our left flank and provide a rearguard."

He wrenched his mare's head round and made for the head of the formation. There was no time to speak to the groups who were being left to hold the camp, but no need either; word that a relief force was on the way would be racing around the oases like quick-fire, to put heart into all who heard it and did not know how desperately small it almost certainly was.

He brought the mare dancing and fidgeting into her appointed place. Behind him, as he looked back over his shoulder, the cavalry had a rough-disciplined and formidable look, their morale suddenly high at the prospect of action after the long, dull, heart-draining days. He lifted up his voice to them: "We go to meet our brothers who follow the Amir Ibrahim and to crush the heretics between us" – as though he cared about all the heretics in the world. We go to save Tho'mas! There was no time for more. "Sound the 'Advance'," he ordered the bugler beside him. The call crowed through the morning air.

The head of the column swung forward, rank after rank behind him. The black and gold of his personal standard lifted and spread on the wind of their going. They broke from a trot to a canter, then as the bugle sounded again, into full gallop.

The speed of their movements had taken the screen of Wahabi horsemen by surprise. Some knots fell aside from their path, others tried to bar their way to the hills, and were ridden over or hurled back. Tussun's bugles were still sounding the charge. "Tho'mas! Tho'mas I am coming. Hear me! I come!"

But the wind blew the calls back towards the south.

Chapter 34

The sun was not yet over the skyline, but the eastern sky was brightening behind the dark etching of thorn scrub that clothed the dunes, and in the morning twilight colour was already seeping back into the world. Thomas and his two squadrons had left the high hills behind them, and since the stop for morning prayer they had been pushing on through low sandhills. It was strange territory, for the winter thrust northward had never brought them so near to El Rass, which according to the scouts was less than an hour's ride away. So near, and yet . . .

Thomas, riding at the head of his little column, flanked by his bugler and his standard bearer, was remembering the far-off outline of a horseman pricked against the sinking moon, that they had glimpsed from last night's camp. Maybe it was no more than a wandering Bedouin. Maybe it was not even that; the scouts had found nothing; maybe they had simply begun to see things, catching the vision from each other, as one could do sometimes after hard riding in the desert. And certainly the past days and nights had been hard enough . . . They had taken on an odd dreamlike quality now in Thomas's mind, and a fevered dream at that, of struggling desperately for speed through precipitous mountain ways and over loose slipping sand, of heat and flies and exhaustion; but they had made it, and in reasonable fighting trim. And to Thomas the sudden silver spray of birdsong from among the oleanders of the dried-up wadi bed to their left seemed to answer to something spent but triumphant within himself. "Hold, Tussun my brother. Hold fast, I come, I come."

But the scouts and the small advanced guard were falling back in a hurry over the low sand-ridge ahead.

He shouted the order to halt, his voice jarring on the morning silence of the desert, and rode forward, followed by Daud and Jassim Khan.

At the foot of the slope he came together with Nassyr el Badr.

The tribesman reined his horse back on its haunches, hooves driving deep into the sand. "Many hundred of Wahabi horsemen at the far end of the plain yonder! Less than a mile ahead – many more horse and camel men coming down from the higher ground on three sides – "

The scouts had come up; one of them nodded, "At least a thousand cavalry and as many camel men, more coming up."

"No chance to fall back," another put in. "They have scouts on the ridges."

No mere wandering Bedouin, then. For a moment the breath tightened in Thomas's throat. He let it go again, carefully. "Is there any other route that we can take to get by them unseen?"

The rim of the sun was blipping up over the rim of the eastern dunes, and already the shadows of men and horses lay long over the sloping sand.

"No," Nassyr was quite certain. "The only other possible track is three times longer, through the foothills, and they could block it long before we made El Rass."

"The plain ahead, then, is it wider than this? How is the surface for horses at speed?"

"Much wider, and firmer ground."

"So, then, the first thing would seem to be to gain it."

Thomas sent off his orders to call in the flank and rearguards and form them up in their own troops, then turned to his bugler. "Sound the 'Advance', Daud, and keep on sounding it. The wind is from the north-west, and if Allah wills it, the sound may reach Tussun Pasha."

They burst over the low ridge and down into the plain beyond. Praise be to Allah, it ran south and they would not have to fight with the rising sun in their eyes. Nor would the enemy. There, less than a mile ahead, in a wide horseshoe arc, the Wahabi force was already advancing. Well over a thousand horsemen by now, and behind them twice as many camel-mounted infantry, and even as Thomas looked, narrowing his gaze into the growing light, hundreds more camel men were swarming in over the slopes to east and west, lengthening the arms of the horseshoe.

This must be the greater part of ibn Saud's cavalry, Thomas thought, with a kind of bitter pride as they swept towards each other. The young Tiger might easily have raised his full strength of camel men again since Kulukh, but it was unlikely that he could have done the same with his horsemen. If he and his two squadrons must die this morning, and it seemed extremely likely that they must – even an attempt to retreat before they had crossed the ridge would only have resulted in their being hunted down like beasts, and a foul death instead of a clean one – what a blow to Wahabi power they could strike, taking, if Allah willed it, twice their own number with them! Also it would almost certainly save Tussun, whatever the hole he had got himself into.

There was an odd sense of ritual upon him; and it seemed upon the Wahabis also; for, half a mile apart, both commanders as by common consent, gave the order to halt. Across the level ground, as the sun cleared the skyline and light spilled down the eastern slopes, Wahabi and orthodox Muslim confronted each other, the last faint wind of the morning stirring their standards sideways before it died into the growing heat.

Thomas felt as though he were two men, one numbed by the suddenness of disaster, one standing beside him, calmly weighing up the possibilities, giving orders in a voice which did not seem to be quite his, for the four troops to join up in close column, and for weary mounts to be changed for fresh ones. Then calling up his officers. There was one chance yet . . .

"If it may be done, I will gain us half an hour or so of breathing space," he said to the handful about him, who were also friends. "Partly to give ourselves and our horses time to gather our strength before we charge." He saw the small east wind smile on their faces. "Partly because it may be that Tussun Pasha is even now coming up on the Wahabis' rear." The smile deepened at the thought of taking the ranks of the Brotherhood front and rear. "Wait here while I try for a parley, but do not let the men dismount or break ranks until – unless – you see me wave my arm. Now, Daud, Jassim, with me." And without another word, the other two following, he wheeled his horse and rode towards the enemy line.

There was a stirring in the centre of the Wahabi battle-mass, and out from under the black banner rode a tall man with two companions following after him, making his horse dance and caracole, wincing from bit and spur as he came.

"Salaam aleikum," Thomas called the customary greeting as they drew near.

They reined in no more than a lance length apart. "I am Ibrahim Agha, Amir of Medina. By what name do they call you?"

The other's eyes held a kind of smouldering delight, "Men call me Abdullah ibn Saud, Lord of the Najd, among other things. It matters little what they call you, Oh heretic dog from another land, for in a little while you will be dead, and your followers with you, and we shall appoint a true believer as Amir of Medina in your place."

Thomas, never having come face-to-face with his old enemy of Jedaida, studied the dark, reckless hawk features with a detached interest, noting the small fleck of spittle at the corner of the mouth. What a thing was religious fervour. "Abdullah ibn Saud, we are here it seems by the will of Allah, to fight His battle, but to fight as brave men fight, not to insult each other. Now, in the belief that you are a man of honour, I lay before you this challenge; that you send two hundred and fifty of your best horsemen against us to fight man to man for the Glory of Allah – and then your next two hundred and fifty – and your next! Abdullah ibn Saud, do you dare to do that?"

For a moment he thought Abdullah was actually going to accept the challenge, despite the muttered protests of his two companions. Then he shook his head. "We are not here to play games of chivalry, but to obey Allah's word as to the cleansing of Islam from the infidel and the heretic."

It had been worth trying, but Thomas was not really surprised. "Then in the name of Allah the All Compassionate grant us the half of an hour that we may make the Last Meal in His name and pray before the fighting joins between us." He saw his enemy hesitate, and pressed on. "Do you dare to deny us that which the Prophet himself instituted when he received the Divine Injunction before the raid of Dhat al Riga?" Another moment's pause. "Do you fear that we shall run? Or that the hearts of your own men will grow small with half an hour of waiting?"

"I fear neither of these things. Receive your half hour's delay," said Abdullah ibn Saud.

341

Playing for every instant of time that might bring Tussun and his force up with them, Thomas pulled out his Edinburgh watch from the folds of his waist-shawl. The time was two minutes past seven. He showed it to the enemy leader. "Your watch agrees with mine?"

"Well enough, I make no doubt."

"I go now to join my men. We shall follow the instructions of the Prophet, peace be to Him. At two minutes past the half hour, stand ready to receive our charge."

"We will stand ready, Ibrahim Agha, one-time Amir of Medina." For an instant something that was almost a smile lit behind the dark face. An odd thing is liking between men. Thomas answered it, then wheeled his mare and flinging up a hand, cantered back to his men.

By the time he reached them, they had dismounted, but were standing still in their troop formation, each man holding his horse. They looked at him, each face carrying an unspoken question. "I have gained us something under half an hour, to eat, rest and pray," he said.

A few moments later, standing on a couple of ammunition boxes, where every man of his squadrons could see him and hear his words, he spoke to them for the last time:

"My comrades-in-arms, you who are my friends and my brothers, in less than half an hour we shall charge the Wahabi war host, and unless it should come to pass by some miracle that Tussun Pasha is close behind them, we shall charge them alone, and in so doing, pass by the shortest, but also the surest way to Paradise." Was he so sure? He who often felt as though he were fallen between two faiths? But whatever his own doubts, they were not for passing on to the men now listening to him, the men he must lead to death with all the belief in their cause, all the heightening of the heart that he could put into them. "We fight in the name of the Prophet, against those who have trampled down his people and desecrated his tomb; therefore let each of us set our hearts to sending four, even five of these heretics to Eblis, before we ourselves come to the gates of Paradise. We can do this thing, for are we not the very flower of fighting men? Our names will go down in song wherever men sing of past splendours; for today, few as we are, we shall save the Holy Land."

He came down to practicalities: "Now we make the Prayer

342

before Action, as the Prophet ordered it. No. 1 squadron will pray and then rest for ten minutes, while No. 2 squadron eat their morning dates standing, sword in hand. Then No. 2 will pray while No. 1 eats and stands guard." There was little time for more, for he must not erode the last few precious moments, but one thing more had to be said. "As for myself, who came among you as a stranger from a strange land, no man has ever been happier in his friends, no man has ever been prouder of the troops he led. I am honoured that I make this last charge in your company. The mercy of Allah the All Compassionate be with us all! Now pray."

They tossed up their weapons, saluting him with a shout so great that it startled the distant Wahabis and the high-cruising vultures in the sky.

Thomas sprang down from his makeshift platform and went a little aside with his officers. He took out his dates and began to eat, joined by the rest of them. One could give and receive the final orders just as well with one's mouth full, and so save time. "My friends, as I have already said, it is for us to account for as many of the Wahabi cavalry as may be, before we ourselves go down. Therefore ignore the camel men and concentrate on the horse. This is clearly part of the host that has cut Tussun off, but he must surely be alive, or they would have boasted of his death. If we can cripple a good proportion of their cavalry, he should be able to cut his way free." He spat out the date stones into the sand. "I shall lead the centre, in wedge formation, straight for Abdullah's standard. You, Hassan and you, Anwar, will follow close for two hundred yards, as though we are charging together as one double squadron. But when the bugle changes from the canter to the charge, you will peel off your troops respectively left and right and charge their cavalry wings.

"Remind your men that we must strike the enemy as three tightly clenched fists, as we have trained to do, over the years. If we hold formation, knee to knee, we shall drive deep into them and kill far more than if we hit them loose and flying like a banner."

Around them the men who had been praying were standing up and drawing their swords, while the rest made their ritual ablutions in the sand and set themselves in order for prayer.

343

"There is one thing more," Thomas said. "We must send word of what has happened back to Medina, that Mustapha may know and bring up a force to Tussun's relief, or to meet and cover him if he succeeds in fighting his way through. One of you must ride back, and ride alone! If I send an escort, the Wahabis will think it worth pursuing, whereas one man, even if they see him, they may not trouble about." Suddenly, unexpectedly even to himself, he grinned: "If a group gallop off, the Wahabis will tell all Arabia that half of us fled in terror before the action."

There was a dry laugh in appreciation of this.

He looked round him from face to face, seeing flat refusal on them all, until he came to one on which the refusal sat like open mutiny. "Medhet, will you ride for me to Medina?"

"No," Medhet said.

"If I order you?"

"How will you make me obey? Whatever your orders, once the charge is begun, who shall stop me from riding with it?"

There was a murmur of agreement from the other officers.

"No one," Thomas said. "That is why I do not order, but ask you as a friend." He gathered in the rest with a quick glance. They had to share in this; they had to hear, and Medhet had to know that they heard. "I ask a greater courage than I ask of myself or the rest of us. It is easy for us to charge swiftly and gloriously to death among dear comrades; you may have to die slowly and horribly – and alone."

Treating the matter as settled, he embraced the others, quickly and warmly, one by one; and then as they turned away to join their troops on guard or at prayer, turned back to the one of whom he was asking the harder thing. "Don't look at me like that, Medhet."

"That was not fair," Medhet said. "I could have disobeyed your order."

"I know," Thomas said. "Which as you know, is why I asked. There is another thing that I have to ask of you; that if you get through, you will do what you may for Anoud and the babe that will most like have been born by now. There is money laid by, and Mustapha has my instructions concerning her, and Tussun, if he ever wins back to Medina will befriend her; but it is you, my oldest friend, who I am depending on."

344

"What I can do, that I will – if I also win back to Medina."
His voice was dried out and husky with emotion.

"So. Then take my Lulwa, she has not been ridden this
morning, and whichever is the more rested of your own horses.
Take food and a goatskin of water, a second carbine — " He
pulled the Governor's ring from his finger and pushed it on to
Medhet's hand. "This must not fall to the Wahabis."

"All these things I will take," Medhet said; and then: "They
have been good, these eight years since El Hamed."

"I would not change them for all the years of a long life."
Thomas kissed him, held him close a moment, noses touching,
eye smiling into eye. "Tell Anoud that I sent all my love,
Tussun also, if you see him again. You know that it is yours
for all time. Now go, and the blessing of Allah go with
you."

He turned away, pulling out the heavy silver watch. He had
just five minutes left for his own prayer. He made the ritual
ablutions in the sand and took his place between Daud and
Jassim Khan.

He did not even notice the odd jumble of his praying, for it
seemed as it had done that other time in the desert beyond El
Hamha, that he had reached the place where all things and all
faiths were one in the hollowed hand of God. "Praise be to
Allah, the Lord of the Worlds, the Merciful, the Compassionate, the Master of the Day of Judgment. Guide us into the path
of thy Blessed – Oh God, I thank Thee, I have loved and been
loved, I have served with and commanded *men*. Receive my
soul O Lord."

On the sand before him he had set the silver watch. The
hands showed less than two minutes left. Tussun and his troops
had not arrived, and it was time to be moving. Allah would
forgive him for being brief.

He got to his feet, and mounted his horse, which Daud
brought for him along with his own, and took his place at the
head of the V-formation, bugler and standard-bearer swinging
into the saddle on either side. At a little distance the spare
horses were picketed, to be taken by the victors afterward.
"Jassim, your father will be a proud man when he hears of this
day's work," he said to the young standard bearer; and to
Daud ibn Hussein: "Your brother waits to greet you. Use
sword and bugle as you did at Jedaida, you are a man now and

345

may kill twice as many as you did then! Now sound the 'Advance'!"

He reached over his shoulder and drew the great broadsword that had been his beloved companion through so many fights. "Follow me!"

The clear bugle notes tore into the morning; the squadrons broke forward from a stand to a trot, then into a canter. Thomas raised the blade above his head and brought it down, catching the sun in its dazzling arc: "Oh my brothers, charge! For Ali ibn Talib!"

"Ali ibn Talib!" Two hundred and fifty voices roared behind him.

"Allahu akba!"

"Allahu akba!"

Beside him Daud was sounding the Charge – Charge – Charge –

As they broke into a headlong gallop the Wahabi battlefront under streaming banners came plunging forward to meet them.

Thomas was aware of the green banner of Medina streaming back on the wind of their going. Above the yelling of the Wahabis as the space between them narrowed, he was shouting, unaware that what he shouted above the wild cries of his Arab cavalry, out of some ancient darkness that beat within his own blood, was the battle cry of the 78th Highlanders: "Cuidich 'n Righ! Cuidich 'n Righ!"

He was away like an arrow for the place where the black banners of the Wahabis marked their centre. The two side troops, following his orders, had peeled off right and left a long time ago – it seemed a long time ago, but time meant nothing any more.

"Cuidich 'n Righ!"

There was less than a hundred yards now between the flying arrowhead of cavalry and the huge disorderly mass of the Wahabi battle front that swole darkly on his sight. He singled out the first of the enemy for his sword.

The Egyptian squadrons, yelling like fiends, were travelling at twice the speed of the enemy when they struck the Wahabi ranks.

"Cuidich 'n Righ! Allahu Akba! To the Gates of Paradise, oh Muslims! Follow me, follow me home!"

Medhet had got clear under cover of the dust-cloud, and was riding like a man possessed on the first stage of his solitary way back to Medina. Three hundred miles. Presently he would ease his pace, use sense and judgment in the husbanding of his horse's strength and his own; since if he died on the journey, Thomas would have denied him the last charge in vain. But for the moment he rode as if Shaitan himself were after him. And the one thing, as it seemed, that kept his heart from breaking within him, was not that he must get through to summon help for Tussun, but that Tho'mas had set Anoud in his care, had called him his oldest friend and said that he was relying on him. He slowed to a less mad pace, and turned his horses' heads into the hills, making sure that his pistol was in his waist-shawl, the extra carbine across his saddle.

But three hundred miles away in the Governor's Palace in Medina a little group of servants had come running, and were gathered wailing at the foot of the outside stairway that led up to the roof of the women's quarters.

And in their midst Anoud lay crumpled among the twisted folds of her sleeping shift, that slender neck of hers bent sideways at an unnatural angle, her grey eyes wide and sightless, staring up past them into the morning sky and the pigeons wheeling overhead.

Closest beside her, Kadija squatted, swaying to and fro on her vast haunches. "Aiee! Aiee! If I had not let her sleep on! But she slept so badly, and what sleep she had broken by ill dreams, these past moons – and with the babe overdue . . . She was asleep and I let her be; and then it must have been that another of her dreams came upon her, and she sprang up and ran out of the pavilion crying out his name as though she heard him calling, 'Tho'mas! Tho'mas' – I tried to catch her but she was too quick for me, and she missed her footing at the head of the stair, with the weight of the child – Aiee Aiee! Allah's pity upon women."

One of the harem eunuchs, squatting beside her, burst into frightened tears. "The Amir will have our heads when he comes back — "

347

Kadija rounded on him: "Quiet, fool! What matter for thy worthless head? Or mine? But he will not come back. She knew. They will sing songs about him, they will call him The Bravest of the Brave. He will have all the things men care about. But he will not come back."

She bent across Anoud's body as though to shield her from something. Again she said, "Allah's pity upon all women."

The fighting was over, and on the fringe of the spent battlefield Abdullah ibn Saud stood looking about him, while the surgeon knotted the bandage-strip about his upper arm to stop the bleeding from a deep sword-cut.

"Another victory like that, and we shall lose Najd," he said to his second-in-command leaning wearily on his sword close by.

"The Egyptian force is dead to a man," said the other, between triumph and regret.

"So are more than three times as many of our own horsemen."

One of the Brotherhood came running, his hand and the hem of his burnous juicy as though with ripe mulberries. "We have found Ibrahim Agha lying over yonder. Do we take his head?"

"No," ibn Saud told him. "No heads this day. Show me where he lies."

He followed the man, picking his way through and over dead and dying men and horses, slipping once in still warm offal. Overhead the vultures were gathering, their harsh cries added to the ugly sounds of the battlefield. One of the Wahabis was gathering up the green and golden rags of the banner of Medina. Close by, Thomas lay half under his dead horse among a twisted clot of bodies, his own men who had died about him, and the Wahabis they had pulled down with them in that last inmost core of the fighting. He was pierced by a score of spears, hacked and gashed almost past recognition, but no man had attempted to rob his body, at least not yet; and his great broadsword was still in his hand, the faded rose-wine velvet of the hilt-lining stained to a deeper crimson, for the hand that held it was hacked half through at the wrist.

"So die all infidel dogs," said the Wahabi.

"He had our own banner down once," said ibn Saud, "I saw it go. It is pity that he was a heretic and therefore damned . . .

348

Truly if he had been with us and not against, we should have been the more fortunate; for as I said it at Jedaida I say it again, he was the bravest of all our enemies."

From far to the south-west, in the direction of El Rass, Tussun's bugles were sounding across the hills.

Afterword

There was now, as Tussun must have known, no one in the northern Hijaz capable of raising and leading a relief force strong enough to overcome the Wahabi war-host. On the other hand, Abdullah ibn Saud must have felt himself no longer strong enough to be sure of destroying Tussun's troops and any relief force that did come. And even if by unlikely chance the Wahabis should gain the victory, it would not mean the end of the war, but only another wave of Muhammed Ali's seemingly inexhaustible resources of men and supplies into the Najd.

Agreement between the two commanders was reached after three days. Tussun did not in fact possess the power to agree a peace treaty without the Sultan's approval, but was too exhausted and too heartbroken to realise the fact.

At all events the peace treaty was made, ibn Saud renouncing all claim to the Holy Cities, declaring himself a dutiful subject of the Sultan of Istanbul, and swearing to allow peaceful passage to all caravans through his territories; Tussun agreeing to release all the towns of the Kassim still in his hands, and recognise Abdullah's control over all tribes pasturing in the north.

In the autumn of the same year, 1815, Muhammed Ali denounced his son's peace treaty and continued the war, this time with Ibrahim Pasha, his elder son, in command of the new expeditionary force. It seems likely that whatever ibn Saud had intended, the Wahabi tribal leaders had intended all along to continue the war so soon as they were in a position to do so.

But all that ceased to be any concern of Tussun's. He returned to Egypt in the same autumn, and in disgrace with his father was exiled to the Delta in command of a garrison stationed there to resist any Turkish invasion. And there in the following September, he died of plague, aged twenty-four.

The threat of the Capitan Pasha and the Ottoman fleet never

materialised, though it must have seemed real enough at the time. But what possessed Muhammed Ali in his hurried withdrawal to meet it, to leave his favourite son without war supplies or orders, remains (so far as the writer can discover) a mystery to this day.